All But the Fall

by

Kim Turner

Sun River Ranchers, Book 1

All But the Fall

Cover Art by *Debbie Taylor*

The Wild Rose Press, Inc.
PO Box 708
Adams Basin, NY 14410-0708
Visit us at www.thewildrosepress.com

Publishing History
First Yellow Rose Edition, 2018
Print ISBN 978-1-5092-2257-5
Digital ISBN 978-1-5092-2258-2

Sun River Ranchers, Book 1
Published in the United States of America

It had been a long time since a woman had caught his attention to this extent. Nope, he'd never had anyone, even Pamela come this close. Something about the chemistry between them was stronger than he'd ever known could exist. She was consuming him fast, and he damn well liked it.

Last night after checking on the horses, Jenna had driven them to a local diner for supper. The meal had been fine, but he'd caught himself watching her every move as if he could etch a bit of her into his mind and heart. Yep, he had it bad. And watching her drive away opposite his direction for home had left him all but empty.

The good thing was she hadn't run again from his touch, but it was hard to judge where the boundaries were with her. What he really wanted was no limits— holy damn, she was beautiful inside and out, and he had a few ideas about how much he'd like to discover even more. And while she'd told him of her past, which was pretty trusting, he had to wonder if there was indeed more. Someone somewhere had broken this beautiful creature, and if he had his way, he'd bring her back and hang on tightly for the rest of his life—if she'd have him.

Dedication

For Kimmy…because you believed in this story long before I did.
And for Wendi, because contemporary cowboys bathe regularly. Love ya, sis!

Acknowledgements

Thanks to SherrieLea Morgan for "throwing me under the bus" and pushing me to pull this story back out. And as always the following people dove right in to read and offer suggestions at the drop of a hat and often times more than once—Marcia Scott, Connie Bartley White, Dianna Shuford, Maggie Worth, Dennie Garrett, Clare Roden, Carol Opalinski. You guys rock!

Thanks to Christie Metternich and Lisa Janey for time spent reading carefully through this story!

Chapter One

The meeting room was more crowded than expected for the first day on the set. Aaron Decker leaned hard against the folding metal chair, scanning the oversized canvas tent with a cautious eye. It was typical for a western television series, with a number of extras already clad in their eighteen-eighty's old west style clothing. Adding to the entourage was one of his horses tied near the front, for dramatic effect. The kick-off for the first day of filming would begin after a brief press conference, which was a waste of time and usually all for show.

The press held steady to one corner, popping off flashes as actors, actresses and extras made their way inside, mingling in party fashion. He locked gazes with his brother, Gabe, who appeared less than amused as he stood with their gelded quarter horse, Charger. He chuckled to himself when his brother's gaze strayed following several women who made their way to one corner of the tent. Some things never changed, like the fact Jeremiah still hadn't shown, though it wasn't often his youngest brother was on time for anything.

The director of the series, Horace Leland of *Leland Films,* entered the tent followed by a number of others, all taking seats behind the tables at the front. *The Bounty Hunter* logo tablecloths covered the tables inside, sporting crossed western pistols and a silhouette of a cowboy jumping a horse. The lead players in making the television series and some of the top actors found their places. Among them the famous Drake Masters, who would play *The Bounty Hunter* hero, *Shane Walker*. The pretty boy from New York grinned, his pearly whites saluting the crowd of cheering women. Typical. He and his brothers had worked a number of television series over the years, providing horses and riding as stuntmen and as extras. He'd been around enough to know how it worked. The actors played their parts, the women swooned and he jumped horses for a paycheck.

The Bounty Hunter was predicted to do well and word had it. That it would be picked up by the networks for several seasons. That meant consistent income and a chance to put a down payment on the one hundred acres that backed his family's ranch in Sun River. With any luck he'd start the working ranch he'd dreamed of operating for teenage boys trapped in the foster care system. Boys much like he and his brothers before Sarah and Amos had adopted them. He shook his head, recalling them taking in three misfit unrelated boys who gave them nothing but trouble from the start. He ran a hand through his hair. It might be his far-fetched dream was right in his grasp. With what he'd make on this series, which was close to home, he'd be able to start building on the first forty acres by next spring.

"Welcome to the first season of *The Bounty Hunter*." Suit-dressed Leland smiled as spectators and actors erupted in cheers. "And we are fortunate to have cast Mr. Drake Masters as our lead, *Shane Walker*. Ladies and gentlemen, I give you *The Bounty Hunter*."

Drake tipped his hat toward the crowd. It was

apparent the dime store cowboy had purchased his hat at Helena Regional Airport on his way to the set. Aaron smoothed his beard as women around the tent chattered amongst themselves, some fanning as if faint from seeing the Hollywood legend in person. *A wanna-be cowboy. Perfect.*

"Bro." Jeremiah shuffled into the chair beside him, resting his elbows on his knees, still wearing his fire department uniform.

He eyed his brother with speculation, lifting a brow and glancing at his watch.

"Late call." Jeremiah stifled a yawn.

He'd figured as much. As a paramedic, Jeremiah pulled the regular twenty-four on, forty-eight off at the fire department, working search and rescue all over the northwest.

Horace continued at the podium. "We've got a number of items to cover. Filming will begin today if we have all the players. Production and film crews? Lights? Props? Wardrobe and make-up? Grounds?" The director glanced around, getting a raised hand out of the lead for each group.

"And some of you are already dressed for the occasion. I need to remind everyone that we are all about to time warp back into the eighteen-eighties and we're going to make everything seem as real as possible, including the animals." The flashy director pointed over his shoulder to Charger, who nibbled along the grass at tent's edge.

Jeremiah stretched his legs out in front of him, tucking his hands behind his head, his sandy blond hair curling out from under his fire department baseball cap. "Charger looks less than enchanted."

"But Gabe's in his element." Aaron nodded where across the tent, the camera man before him was focusing in as Gabe chatted with the pretty blond reporter holding a microphone.

His youngest brother chuckled. "That'll tickle Lily pink."

Aaron couldn't resist a smile. Lily, his five-year-old daughter, loved when any of their animals appeared on television. And while cartoons were her favorite, she stayed transfixed when her own pet horses were the star of the show.

He'd brought her to the set a few days ago. They'd walked around the little ghost town so he could get a sense of what filming might encompass. The ground had been littered with nails and metal shards from tossing up an old west town overnight. He'd made a game of it with Lily, seeing who could hurry to find items to put in a bucket, clearing the grounds around the barn. She was thrilled at the *game*, and he'd hid his annoyance, though after a brief discussion with the men from props, the set had been cleaner on his morning walk through.

His contract provided for a small barn, but the structure hadn't been reinforced well enough should real weather hit. Given the set was located north of Helena, there wasn't any doubt harsh weather would come again before spring. Gabe's truck held two heaters that would need to be unloaded later. The horses didn't need much in the way of warmth, but the gas-powered units would knock the chill off the barn, even in a blizzard.

"A lot of stunts are planned, and we are still in the process of adding to the set. Our little western town will continue to grow as we film this series. The catering tent will be open every day we film. I think a lot of you know the wonderful Sally Wang out of Denver." Horace introduced the petite Asian chef who smiled amidst claps, cheers, and whoops. "You can let her know of any of your special dietary needs."

Aaron shot a quick glance at his brother. He didn't know what had happened to the hint of romance between Jeremiah and Sally on a set a few years ago, other than distance. His brother sat stoic, not giving him any hint he was bothered. But if he knew his brother, he was bothered. Probably hot and bothered.

Leland nodded in Sally's direction once more. "We have a medical tent that will be staffed by a registered nurse. Jenna Wilder will also serve as a nurse consultant for filming medical scenes, since she has a vast knowledge of the medical history of the old West."

The nurse blushed, giving a nervous wave to the noisy crowd. He sat forward, unable to take his eyes from her as Horace went on with his introductions. Her long dark hair was pulled back in a pony tail, and she had the most captivating amber eyes. She leaned closer to Sally, both ladies whispering, all smiles.

"A splinter should do it," Jeremiah hinted, pulling him from his thoughts.

"Huh?" He narrowed his gaze on his younger brother.

"A splinter might get you into the medical tent." His brother was quick to dodge the elbow Aaron sent his direction as he made his escape outside.

Aaron turned back in search of the nurse who had disappeared along with Sally. He glanced at his thumb where he'd dug out a nice size splinter earlier. Maybe he should've waited, but he wasn't here to chase women. He was here to make a living and besides, he had Lily to think about and no time to for a relationship that might get him burned—again.

He slipped outside, catching up with Gabe who was leading Charger back toward the corral. "Want to get those heaters inside the barn?"

"Let me put him out." His brother glanced at him. "Filming starts in another hour. Who you gonna use for the opener?"

Aaron shoved his hands in the pockets of his denim jacket. The production lead had requested a calm horse for the bounty hunter to ride during the shooting of title takes. They had brought two of their Morgans, Maxus and Thor, both excellent jumpers and similar enough in their brown coloring to pass for the same horse on film.

"Thor's in a better mood. Maxus is acting up as usual. Had a tough time getting him into the corral." He glanced at the horse that perked his ears on their arrival.

"He hates being away from home." Gabe turned Charger out into the corral with the other horses and closed the gate, tossing the bridle over his shoulder.

Aaron trotted to the back of the truck and let the tailgate down. He grabbed the first wooden pallet, carrying it inside the barn. Returning for the second, he carried it to lie beside the first.

Gabe waited at the truck, scrolling his cell phone. "Jeremiah got the camper hooked up."

"We got it good here. Water and electricity, even in the barn." He growled as they lifted the first heater. They traveled with the fifth-wheel camper so they had a place to stay in between filming and to keep an eye on the horses. Twenty minutes from home, meant he could spend most nights home with Lily, which wasn't always the case when he worked a set.

"I'll call it good if they have Wi-Fi." His brother eased his end of the heater to the palate.

"Wi-Fi's coming." Aaron moved the heater to a better position with a heavy groan.

"All right then, I'm in." Gabe adjusted his baseball cap on his short dark hair.

"Of course you are, *Mr. Media*." He lifted a brow, teasing his brother.

"I know you care little for the press, it's expected that I, as the most handsome of the brothers, be the one on camera." Gabe roared in laughter.

He rolled his eyes. "You're so full of shit. It wasn't the interview; it was the blonde with the mic."

"Got her number, too." His brother gave him a wink as they lifted the second unit.

"Keep the women to one at a time on this set. I need the pay off from this job." He warned with a slight grin as they jostled the second heater inside the barn.

"I've gotta meet the production boys. They're talking about a ramp for a jump. Episode five." His brother grunted with the effort of setting down his side of the heater.

"I read that scene, more like a bridge jump." Aaron stood again. He was the one that trained their horses for stunts, jumps being part of it, but sometimes what was called for on a script didn't plan for the safety of his animals, and that came first.

"One side of the bank to the other, as if from a bridge, but over the deeper part of the river. You're on at two." Gabe headed outside the barn, as he followed.

He glanced into the sky, the afternoon sun giving a

hint. "What time is it?"

"One-thirty." His brother trotted toward the set.

He turned back for Thor. He hadn't had a chance to read the script he'd been handed earlier and pulled it from his back pocket. The first take would be for title captions with the cowboy hero doing a variety of runs and gallops. Shoving the script back into his pocket, he grabbed Thor's bridle and walked into the corral meeting Maxus.

"Nope, you're too ornery for this take." He rubbed the horse and moved across the corral to Thor, who was more interested in the fresh pile of hay he'd put out for the animals earlier. He placed the bridle and bit and then led the horse outside the corral, adding the old west blanket and saddle to the animal. Thor was the best choice, given he had no idea how much riding experience Drake Masters had under his belt, and Maxus was hard to handle.

He grabbed the brush and began running it across the horse to free him of dust. Thor gave him an appreciative nudge.

"All right, wise guy." He brushed harder to appease the animal.

"So you're part of the stunt team? The 'fall guy' I believe they call it."

He turned to the female voice behind him, finding himself face to face with the nurse. *Well, I'll be damned.*

She smiled and after a moment of hesitation moved closer.

He grabbed Thor by the reins, his mouth going dry. "Yep."

"Jenna Wilder, nurse consultant. Let me guess,

rodeo cowboy, probably bull riding?" Those amber eyes sparkled along with her grin.

"Aaron Decker. Stunts yes. Ranching yes. Rodeos, not so much." He held out a hand, taking hers. She was spectacular up close and he had to remind himself he wasn't in the market for the most part and he needed this job.

She pulled her coat tighter as she admired Thor. "Scared of falling?"

He shook his head. "Nope. Scared of the landing."

She glanced at him and laughed with a nervous edge. "I'd have to agree."

"You got a nice sized medical tent." He'd seen it earlier in the week when he and Lily had explored the set. It seemed once again that Leland had spared little expense on making sure everything on the set was done well.

She looked that direction and back. "I was surprised. I've got all the modern equipment, medications, a cart, and even an A.E.D."

"Automatic external defibrillator." He added his knowledge of the equipment Jeremiah often talked about.

"Medical experience?" she asked as she patted Thor's neck.

"My brother Jeremiah's a paramedic. You'll see him and Gabe, the one with the horse in the tent around here a good bit." He studied her as she traced a hand along Thor's side. She was some kind of beautiful, and he had to remind himself to take a breath.

"He's a beautiful animal. A Morgan, right?" Her amber eyes grazed across him again.

"Yep. You ride?"

"When I was younger." She shivered as the wind picked up.

"I've gotta get him to the set, but there's a lot of down time in between takes. These guys get restless and need the exercise, if you'd like to ride sometime." He should know better than where his thoughts were going.

She nodded after a brief hesitation. "I don't know, maybe some time, though it's been quite a long time."

"You don't forget." He had to admit the idea of teaching her meant he'd have his hands on her, and that made things a little more than interesting, though it had seemed her tone sounded abrupt. Final. Ah, he knew better, and getting tangled in a relationship on the set would only complicate his work.

"I won't keep you." A hint of a blush touched her cheeks. "Is this where I am supposed to say 'break a leg'?"

He shook his head. "Not with horses."

"In that case, how about happy filming?" She began walking back toward the medical tent, turning to smile his direction once more.

"Better." He tugged Thor behind him toward the little western town. She was very easy on the eyes if nothing else, but his life wasn't in a place where he needed to add a woman to it. He shook his head. Here he was, on the set of a television series with Hollywood babes walking all over the place, and the one woman who'd managed to capture his attention was the behind the scenes nurse consultant. There had to be something wrong with this picture, or things on this set had gotten a bit more than interesting.

Chapter Two

"Jenna, you're needed in trauma-two." Shay McKenzie grabbed a pile of charts at the nurse's station, whipping her blonde ponytail off her shoulder in a frenzy of sorting reports from the lab.

"Is that before or after they commit us all?" Jenna kidded with a smile, letting it fade as she signed onto the computer, searching the electronic medical record. It had been a hectic shift but glancing at the clock, it was almost time for report.

Brianna Carlton, registered nurse and Jenna's best friend, leaned against the counter. "I'll join you both. We can commit ourselves as a trio to the mental health unit. Think they'll take us?"

Jenna lifted her brows. "I'm sure they'd take you."

"They wouldn't know how good they had it if I showed up." Her best friend challenged with a swing of her hips as she sashayed away to her work, letting out a huge laugh.

"On second thought, they couldn't handle you at all." Jenna opened the next chart, taking a look, giggling to herself. Trauma-two could wait. The man with a broken leg had already been splinted and was sleeping off his booze, waiting on his ride.

The three-year-old boy with a fever in room four was waiting on discharge papers. She headed that way and re-assured the nervous parents that his fever was coming down and he would be released soon.

She smiled to herself thinking of Mason, her twelve-month-old son and the light of her life. After this shift was done, she would begin her new job, which would give her more time home with her son. She dropped by room five where the man with the broken leg was still sleeping. She entered his vitals into the Electronic Medical Record and passed by the desk again.

"Shay, has five's ride shown up yet?" she asked, taking a sip from her water bottle.

The unit clerk glanced at the board above her. "The sister called, said she'll get him when she gets off work later tonight."

Brianna met her gaze as she returned to the counter, laying down her clipboard with hint of excitement. "Ready to hit the Hollywood limelight?"

"It's not the limelight, it's a consultant job." She smiled, a blitz of anxious nerves flowing through her. Taking the job with *Leland Films* as set nurse and medical consultant was her first venture away from patient care.

"Oh, you are going Hollywood, and I couldn't be more proud." Brianna began tapping on the keyboard of one of the computers. "The chest pain in six is a good case of indigestion. He's going home. I think he'll avoid the pasta bar from now on."

The edges of Shay's lips dropped. "We won't get to see you near as often. Bummer, but we're all proud. And you start right away?"

"Yep, I'm due on the set Monday. And I'll be here to work a shift now and then." She touched Shay's shoulder.

"Our Jenna's gonna get that script of hers in the right hands yet." Brianna glanced up with pride. "How was the pre-meeting on the set?"

"Great. I have a medical tent with all you could ever want, a radio and cart and every piece of equipment I listed." She shrugged as it seemed no expense had been spared.

"Did you get to see Drake Masters? I would pass out cold if I saw him." Shay pretended to swoon, placing the back of her hand against her forehead.

Brianna patted her heart, her long dark weaves falling across her shoulder. "That's one fine specimen of a man."

"I saw him when the cast was introduced." Jenna answered though her thoughts went back to Aaron, where they had been for several days now. She'd only gone to the corral to take a look at the horses, but his deep green eyes and tender voice had been enough to captivate her. She pushed thoughts of him away wanting to shake her head. A relationship wasn't something she could fathom at this point in her life—or likely ever.

"And how about other men on the set? I might need to spend time being the second nurse in command." Brianna batted the eyelids to her chocolate eyes.

Jenna shook her head. "Oh, you can come along any time you like. There are actors and crew all over the place for those of you who are desperate."

"I'm not desperate, but I am always on the lookout for the one and only Mr. Carlton." Bri defended cocking her head to the side.

"Look no further." Dr. Gates handed Shay a stack

of clip boards.

Brianna eyed him with skepticism. "You have a wife and six children. Haven't you learned what causes that yet?"

"Yes, but I can't keep my hands off the woman." The physician laughed and glanced at Jenna. "So, how is working as a nurse consultant going?"

"It's been interesting. I helped the make-up ladies dress a few gunshot wounds, making them look realistic for practice. It was a lot of fun." She'd also enjoyed talking with Sally at the catering tent, and of course, she could add Aaron Decker to that list, though as much as she'd been thinking of him, it was best she put a stop to it right away.

"Well, congrats on the new job, but don't forget about us low lifes here in the E.R." The doctor glanced at Shay. "We're all done here, huh?"

Shay looked up from the computer. "Shhh, don't jinx us, but all are treated and streeted."

"I'll see you all in a few weeks." Jenna hugged the clerk, and the doctor and turned toward the locker room with Brianna following.

"I'd tell you I am going to miss you except you live right next door and tonight is ice cream and movie night with my best guy." Brianna jerked her locker open, sifting inside.

"I'll be on the weekend shift in no time and what's tonight, Mexican or Chinese?" She had to smile. The new job would change things little for them, best friends since college back in Virginia.

"Thai. So how about your script, have you learned what you thought you would?" Her friend tugged on her jacket and tossed her purse over her shoulder, then closed her locker.

"Not yet, but I'll learn the ropes." Jenna's pulse raced thinking about it. She'd dabbled at novel and script writing for years. And when she'd heard a television series was being filmed nearby and it had to do with the old west, she'd opted to apply on a whim, surprised she'd gotten the job.

"How you do it, nurse, nurse consulting, writing, and mommy. But are you taking care of you?" Bri leaned back against the lockers, eyeing her closely.

"I'm fine." She turned her attention back to her locker, avoiding her friend's gaze.

"Hey, it's me, remember?" Brianna was quick to remind her in challenge.

"Yes. I am sleeping well, writing, and now I will have more time with Mason. I'm fine. Really, I am." She answered with the surest smile she could manage, though there were times she wished she could convince herself.

Brianna adjusted her purse, opening the door to the staff lounge. "Bring my sweet date to me in pajamas and a clean diaper, and you can rest tonight."

"You got it." She led them down the hall and out the back door of the emergency room and into the parking lot where they parted ways at her SUV. She climbed inside and turned the engine, looking on as Bri took her corvette toward town where she'd pick up dinner before returning home. Friday night date nights were common for them and meant takeout and playing with Mason until long after bedtime.

She supposed she couldn't blame Brianna for worrying about her. She wasn't sure if she'd ever quit looking over her shoulder and there were still times she woke with nightmares, but the past was now behind her. She shook her thoughts and smiled instead, anticipating picking up Mason from Mrs. Lucy. The elderly Cheyenne woman adored her son and made it easy for her to do the work she needed to do. She did have her life back, and while it had taken some time, she was ready to face the new job and the changes it would bring, such as a better schedule with her son.

****

Aaron urged Maxus along the ridge west of base camp. Dressed as an eighteen-eighties cowboy, complete with hat and bandana, he needed the horse to make a ramble down the hill and jump the narrow portion of the river at the bottom. Cameras were rolling on both sides of the river, with crew holding reflectors and lights to enhance filming. While he resembled Drake Masters from a distance, the film guys would edit the footage to make it seem like Masters was the one who'd made the jump.

Horace Leland looked into the camera and then up. "And...action!"

Aaron took Maxus to a gallop, ignoring the cameras and letting the horse take the lead. Maxus could do this jump with ease and picked up more speed nearing the river. He urged the horse, leaning back to counter his weight as the animal found his footing, kicking up dirt behind him as they got closer to the water.

He clucked his tongue lifting the reins. "Up."

The horse leaped on command and landed with ease on the other side, stirring up dust as he hit ground again. Behind them, cheers erupted, but Maxus kept going as the script called for the bounty hunter to ride until he faded from the camera's view.

"That's a cut." Horace's voice echoed across the river.

Aaron turned Maxus, satisfied with the smooth jump. He returned over the small wooden bridge used by the camera crew, Maxus' hooves clanking across the wooden boards. Arriving closer to the cameras, he glanced at the director, who was reviewing the instant footage on one of the monitors.

"No, the lighting's all wrong in the foreground. Run it again." Horace pranced away with his usual smirk.

This is how things were done. Maxus' jump had been smooth, but the director expected perfection. They could make the jump again, but more than twice would fatigue the animal, putting them both at risk.

"Sorry, Aaron." Jack Henderson, lighting crew lead, spoke as he rode back by.

He gave a nod urging the horse ahead about the time that Horace lifted from the monitor again and yelled. "Places."

Aaron galloped Maxus back toward the ridge, catching a glimpse of Jeremiah talking to Gabe—and Jenna. Both of his brothers with the nurse made him pause, though he'd sworn off women for a while now. He'd been busy on the set and hadn't had a chance to speak to her again, but it appeared his brothers were doing a fine job of things. *Get your head in the game, Aaron.*

"Is the horse ready?" Horace, again.

He raised his hand signaling Maxus was good, though he wasn't so sure about himself.

"And action!"

Once again he took Maxus along the same path down the steep ridge, nothing much different from before. They reached the bottom, and he pulled the reins to keep Maxus on target. He urged the horse with the same command, but Maxus stopped dead in his tracks at the river's edge. Somewhere while flying through the air toward the frigid water, Aaron cursed. The cold water was going to hurt.

And then he hit, breaking through and sinking deep, his breath knocked from his body with the impact. Fumbling for control, he hit the rocky bottom with his back. Growling under the dark frigid water he kicked for the surface, gulping for air as he found it. *Son of a bitch!*

Swimming in the numbing water, the frenzy of commotion on the bank was almost comical. His old west clothing was soaked through and heavy as he inched ahead. In the shallow water, he stood to walk, his boots sinking in the muddy soil. Gabe had Maxus by the reins and stood at the edge of the river near Jeremiah.

"You hurt?" Jeremiah grabbed his elbow, pulling him up the grassy bank.

He shook his head, teeth chattering. "Just…frozen."

"Damn Maxus, can't ever predict that horse's mood." Jeremiah steadied him, handing him his soaked cowboy hat.

Gabe met them with the horse. "You all right?"

"Yea." He shivered, water sloshing from his boots as he shook the water from his ears. It was evident he was going to work hard for his paycheck today, right along with the animal who'd just dumped him.

Horace raced over as if concerned, still holding the radio in his hand. "Get the nurse in here. Can you shoot again?"

Aaron nodded as Jenna trotted from her cart toward him, carrying a small bag, her stethoscope in hand.

"I'm fine." He grabbed Maxus' reins from his brother. She was doing her job, but besides the dull ache in his back, he was good. He walked past them all, disgusted at another take. The first take had been good but getting Maxus to cooperate for a third time was questionable given the ornery horse.

"He gets like that when he's focused." Gabe must've said that to Jenna. He didn't turn back, this being a matter of pride. He'd just had his ass dumped in the river by a horse who thought he was in charge and right in front of the woman he hadn't been able to keep out of his head since meeting her. He shook with the cold, and he knew darn better than the thoughts he'd let play along about her the last few days.

"Get him to wardrobe. Twenty minutes folks," Horace's yelled from his chair.

Aaron stopped at the wardrobe trailer, shivering as he tied off Maxus. He patted the horse, groaning against the sting of his back. "If you'd follow the rules, things would be easier on me and you."

"Oh my Lord, Aaron, you're frozen. Are you sure you aren't hurt, honey?" Sheila, who managed wardrobe with her husband, Brian, helped him out of his jacket and vest. His body shuddered in spite of his efforts to ignore the cold gloss of water on his skin.

"I'm good. Sorry about the hat." He handed the sopping piece to her in exchange for the large towel.

"We have more hats, but we don't have more

Aarons. My lands, Horace can't go with one take of anything." She fussed over him turning to shout toward the back. "Brian, honey, could you turn up the heat?"

Aaron turned, struggling out of his wet undershirt, spotting Jenna inside the door. He hadn't known she was there as he was stripping, not that it mattered much on a set.

"Kick out of your boots." Brian entered drawing him away, the elderly balding man a foot shorter and always in a hurry. "You got some scrapes on your back, use the towel."

He stepped out of his water-soaked boots and shucked his trousers, bending to pull his wet socks off. Brian scurried away with the wet clothing, leaving him to contemplate standing in his boxers alone with Jenna. He glanced at her again.

"Your brothers sent me." She ambled closer, though she dropped her gaze.

"I'm fine." He stepped behind the short dressing screen, removing his boxers and drying himself, well aware she still moved closer. Had he not felt like a land bound iceberg, his body might have stirred with the fact she was watching. He stepped into another pair of boxers and from behind the screen, tugging the towel across his shoulders, still disgusted at the spill.

"You're bleeding." She grabbed his shoulder to turn him and used the towel to dry the blood, surprising him.

"Can't feel much in the cold." He'd feel it by morning without a doubt, but her fingers along his skin was enough to make him suck in a fast breath that wasn't due to the cold.

"Sit." She motioned to a chair, lifting her brows.

He sat with a soft grumble to himself, deciding she wasn't taking "no" for an answer.

"I don't think your horse wanted to make that jump a second time." She ran her warm fingers along his spine and ribs causing him to shudder and contemplate the thoughts he shouldn't be having where she was concerned. Thoughts that abruptly reminded him of the reasons there wasn't a woman in his life.

He grimaced when she hit a tender spot. "He throws his weight around."

"Leave this open to air. Ice and Ibuprofen. You aren't broken." She pressed the towel to his back again, "but you're probably hypothermic."

"Goes with the territory." He glanced at her. Damn, she was beautiful, but he'd known that the first time he laid eyes on her when filming had opened.

"And here I thought it was rodeos that were so dangerous." She brushed a strand of hair behind her ears, blushing at his continued gaze.

He stared at her, powerless not to do so. Her amber eyes were one thing, but her full pink lips were entirely something different. Yeah, he'd like to get a taste of those lips… Damn, he had it bad, but that wasn't going to happen. At least not now. His life was too busy, and he was on the edge of what he'd been waiting on for a long time.

"Well, be sure to hang on this time. I, on the other hand, am not watching." She shook her head, stepping away and breaking the intensity of his thoughts.

"Scared of falling?" He shot her a raised brow, thinking he might need another dunk in the river after all.

She studied him for a moment and smiled. "Scared

of the landing."

He called after her. "You watch. He'll do it this time."

"Ibuprofen and ice, Cowboy." And just like that she was gone.

Brian returned with dry boots "Here ya go, Aaron. Horace is already wondering where you are."

He snagged another glimpse out the door. He hadn't had a thought without Jenna since he'd met her and for that matter, he'd found himself awake at night thinking of her. Nope. He had no room in his life for a woman right now—so why couldn't he rid his mind of her?

Sheila handed him his shirt, vest, and trousers. "She's not married from what I hear."

He pulled the shirt on, one arm at a time, turning back to her, hoping he hadn't been too obvious.

"Cat got your tongue?" Sheila, known for her southern cooking, southern accent and southern matchmaking abilities began with the buttons of his shirt as he snagged on the dark trousers.

"Focusing on the jump." He winked, but she'd pegged him.

She smudged make-up on his cheeks and forehead next. "There ya go, another smudge of dirt and you're an outlaw again. Here's your hat."

"Thank ya, ma'am." He slapped the hat on his head, tucking his wet ponytail under it, answering in his best western brogue.

He stepped back outside before Maxus. "This time, I go in the river, you go in. Got it?" He gave the horse a pat and mounted up, galloping to the top of the ridge. Below, his brothers and Jenna were behind the camera crew at the river's edge once more. So she *was* watching. He fought to clear his mind.

"And action!" Horace heralded.

Aaron forced Jenna from his mind and urged Maxus forward, but the horse balked, bucking. He cursed having to turn the animal and start again. It wasn't the horse, it was him. *Get it together, Aaron.*

He kicked and Maxus cooperated, racing down the ridge at a faster pace than before. He gripped hard at the bottom and hung on, keeping his eyes on the far bank. The horse lifted and did what he was supposed to do, clearing the river and landing on the other side with ease.

After riding Maxus through, he dismounted. The landing had hurt. Shit, he'd be sore tomorrow. He pulled the horse along behind him crossing the wooden bridge on foot.

"That's a take. Bring in the real cowboy." Horace spouted the director's voice echoing across the set.

Gabe ambled up taking Maxus by the reins. "What a jackass."

"Yep." Aaron gave the horse a pat as his brother tugged him toward the corral. Horace Leland showed his ass from time to time, but that was no surprise, given the man's success.

Aaron walked to his motorcycle and straddled it for a moment, catching his breath, his job done for today. And there she was again, Jenna Wilder, stopping her medical cart beside him.

"So you watched." He pulled the band from his hair, shaking the wet mass free.

"The director called it a *beautiful take*. Very graceful." She smiled.

"The horse?" He shot her a raised brow.

She laughed but gave him a curious gaze, stopping the engine. "No, not the horse. But you looked stiff on the landing."

That was observant. Hoping he wasn't overstepping some boundary, like the one he'd set where dating on the set was off limits he asked anyway. "You wouldn't want to go riding tomorrow morning?" Damn, he'd done it now. Couldn't even listen to himself when it came down to it.

She glanced at the machine beneath him. "On the bike?"

"Horses." He chuckled. "Five a.m. I've gotta be back here to film around noon, though."

Her eyes widened and she dropped her gaze only to lift it again. "Five? I'm sure my son's sitter wouldn't mind, but it's been a long time and…"

He studied her for a moment, surprised she had a child. "If that's not convenient…"

"No, it should be fine. Mason's a year old and loves his sitter." Her voice held a hint of hesitation. "But…I don't know…"

"You won't be disappointed." He wouldn't be, but he was well aware of the guilt that rode along with leaving a child longer than planned.

"Does five in the morning come with coffee?" Her dark brows lifted, surprising him.

"Yep." Hell, he'd have a four-course breakfast waiting if that was what she wanted.

"Five, then." She sat back in her cart, a nervous edge to her voice. "Meet you here on the set?"

He nodded. So she had a child—well, he had one of those too. She backed the cart up, whipping it around leaving him with a quick smile before she disappeared.

He cranked the motorcycle, revving the engine. Moments later, he was inside the camper letting the hot water of the camper shower soothe his back. It had been a long time since he'd spent time alone with a woman, and the last one had nearly done him in for good. Exiting the shower, he dried and rummaged through the tiny closet, tugging on a pair of sweatpants.

"Just checking on you before me and Gabe head out." Jeremiah entered the camper, slamming the door hard and lifting his bag from the chair. "That's some kind of bruising, brother."

"It's fine." He looked over his shoulder, glancing in the mirror across the room. He was already purple from his shoulder blade down to his mid-back. He headed into the living area of the fifth-wheel camper.

His brother turned toward the door. "See ya."

"Tell Lily I'll call her in a bit." He stepped into his sneakers and then outside the camper, the set now quiet.

"Gotcha. I got Maxus brushed down and fed." Gabe was at his truck. "He did good all except that part where he dumped your ass in the river."

"I'm glad I could take a good dunking for your amusement." He folded his arms. "And don't worry Amos or Sarah with this."

"You know they'll ask." Gabe hopped in his truck and slammed the door, hanging an elbow out the window.

"Then tell them the jump went fine," he urged. There was no sense in having his parents worry over nothing.

Gabe nodded and checked his rear view for Jeremiah who honked from his Jeep.

He sat on the picnic table as his brothers drove from the set. It was his night to stay with the horses, even though the set wasn't far from home. Without Sarah caring for Lily, he wouldn't be able to do the work he did, but between them all, it was rare he ever needed to pay a sitter. He headed back to the camper and shook off the cold once inside. Things would be pretty frigid by tomorrow morning, and he wondered if the temperature would cause Jenna to change her mind. She'd seemed a bit reluctant but had finally agreed. He couldn't believe he'd even asked her knowing damn well he had no business in doing so. He slammed the camper door behind and stopped at the sink.

"Holy shit." He mumbled to himself and lifted the bottle of Ibuprofen from the windowsill. He popped the tablets, reaching for a light beer and chugging them down. Putting his thumb over the mouth of the bottle, he rolled it against his naked back groaning.

Grabbing his cell phone, he plopped down in the recliner, tossing one leg over the arm pushing Jenna from his thoughts.

"Hey, Daddy," Lily answered. "Grandma and I are reading a story about a puppy."

He smiled. "Well, we love puppies. Are you ready for bed?"

"I'm not even tired." She yawned through the phone, smacking her lips.

He closed his eyes picturing her with her long brown curls and eyes much like his own. "Go to bed, and I'll be home tomorrow evening, just in time for supper."

"Promise?"

"Yep."

"Goodnight, Daddy." A big smack of a kiss sounded on the phone. "Did you feel that?"

"Yep, that was kind of sloppy and wet." He grinned as Lily's laughter filled the other end of the phone.

"I love you, baby, let me talk to Grandma." He waited, guilt at not being there flowing through him as it always did.

"Aaron, are you hurt?" Sarah whispered in a high octave into the phone.

He threw his head back in a silent curse. "I'm fine."

"Gabe said you hurt your back." Sarah's tone told him she wasn't letting up on the conversation.

"Maxus didn't cooperate, but I'm good." Damn it, Gabe could never keep his mouth shut. He changed the subject. "How's Amos?"

"He had another good day. He did a bit much though, so he turned in early. You be careful out there." She scolded.

"I promise."

"I love you, son."

"Love you, Sarah. Good night." He hung up the phone, grabbing the remote and turning on the television. Scanning channels, he stopped on the evening news, thinking of Jenna once more. He'd often taken groups of actors and crew riding before or after hours on various sets. It was part of the benefits of someone working on the set when it came down to it, but taking Jenna riding wasn't the same—and he'd damn well known that before asking.

Chapter Three

Jenna drove along the highway headed toward the set, glancing in the mirror to catch her own gaze. What on earth was she doing? It was before five in the morning and way too cold to be out riding horses. The temperature inside her SUV with the heater running full blast and she'd slept little with the excitement and anxiety of spending the morning with Aaron—alone. She didn't know why she'd approached the corral on the set when she had except for her long-ago interest in horses, but Aaron had been there and now this. It had been a long time, and her nerves were proof enough that she wasn't sure she was ready for anything more than a simple ride.

She adjusted her gloved hands on the steering wheel thinking of Mason. A moment of guilt took her, but then, Mrs. Lucy had been fine with keeping Mason a little longer than planned for the day. He adored her, too, and that made things a bit easier.

She shook her head at the conversation she'd shared with Brianna late last evening. Her best friend's jaw had all but hit the floor when she'd told her about Aaron inviting her for a horseback ride. And, of course, Brianna had been full of questions Jenna couldn't yet answer. Yes, he was handsome, and yes, he was safe, not an ax murderer. And she'd had to describe in detail her brief care of him when the horse had thrown him.

Brianna had sat mesmerized at every single word she'd spoken, though there really wasn't much to tell.

"This is just a horseback ride with a nice man and nothing more than that." She scolded, still surprised that Aaron hadn't cringed or run from her mention of a son. Sally, from the food tent, had filled her in on the Decker brothers. Aaron was a rancher, the one who'd signed on for the film jobs, though both his brothers helped where they could. Gabe ran a construction company with a friend they called Tuck, and the youngest of the brothers, Jeremiah, was a paramedic with the local fire department. She'd seen him a number of times at the hospital.

His brothers were both handsome, but it was Aaron who'd caught her attention with his long dark hair and deep green eyes. He had a smile that warmed her, and he was tender spoken even when carrying on a conversation. "A cowboy, biker, stunt guy…" Who knew? She smiled to herself almost as giddy as the teenage girl she'd once been.

Brianna had encouraged her to date. Was that what this was? A date? It had been nearly two years, and though her thoughts were still scrambled at times, things had been going well in her life. And there was something about Aaron that was comfortable and—safe.

She hadn't taken the job with hopes of meeting anyone, yet while all the other ladies on the set were going crazy over Drake Masters, she was happy to sit on the sidelines watching Aaron do what he did. He was beautiful on the horses and in his boxers. She shook her head. "Now what *am* I thinking? I just need to calm down and have a nice time, nothing more."

Good Lord, she was as bad as Brianna, but she couldn't lose the mental image of him nearly naked. He'd been shivering, and when she'd touched the muscles across his back, it had left her wanting more of the same. She'd admired his six pack abs as he'd undressed and dressed again. And even if she was a nurse, her breath had all but stopped at the physical beauty of him.

"Now I know I am crazy." She turned off the highway toward the set, thinking she should've stayed home within the warm covers, snuggling with her son. And while Aaron seemed nice enough, she really hadn't thought she would ever let herself even hint at the possibility of a real relationship again.

She stopped at the gate, showing her badge to the security guard. "Morning."

"Morning Ms. Wilder, you're in early today." Security manager, Doug Forrester, scanned her badge with his laser, glancing inside her SUV.

"Headed for a morning horseback ride." She took the badge back from him.

He leaned on the window. "Awful cold for a morning ride. You're being escorted by one of those Decker boys then?"

"Yes, Aaron." She tucked her badge away, inside her jacket.

"Well, I'm sure you're in good hands." He waved her through with a smirk she wasn't sure she understood. She'd noticed him watching her on the set, and he seemed to hang around her tent more than others but he was security. *He is doing his job and you are overreacting. Aaron is fine too, so stop all the nonsense and get on the horse and ride.*

She pulled to the parking area of the deserted set, where a few crew members were scurrying around with props. Cutting the engine, she tugged her heavy coat around her, glad she'd worn layers and brought along her fur lined leather gloves and a toboggan. Tossing her bag over her shoulder, she headed through the make-shift town on foot, darkness enveloping her.

Outside the barn, she took a deep breath before entering, her breath blowing white against the darkness before her.

Aaron turned from where he was saddling a horse, a smile crossing his bearded face. "You made it."

"Well, you said I wouldn't be disappointed." She moseyed closer, her nerves calming with his voice.

He turned back to the horse, tugging the saddle tighter. "It's pretty frigid, saddled these guys in here instead of the corral. Thought with the cold you might have opted out."

She leaned against the stall beside him. "I'm not sure what I am most afraid of, the cold or riding." *Or falling for you.*

"You'll be fine." He handed her the reins to the large painted horse. "I'll be riding Maxus, but this is Scout. He's as tame as they come. My five-year-old daughter rides him all by herself."

She smiled, leading the horse outside the barn as he followed with the other. Sally had mentioned he had a young daughter, but that her mother had '*never been in the picture*.' She wondered what might have happened but didn't ask. Some things were best left alone, and she was well aware of that given her own past.

He glanced back at her, holding her with his deep green eyes. "Scout's a gentleman."

She hoped he was right. She'd grown up in Virginia riding horses through her teens, but it had been a long time since those days.

"Here ya go." He grabbed her bag and tied it to Scout's saddle. "And, at your request." He stepped away to the picnic table and lifted a thermos, returning to tuck it in her bag.

"Coffee." She smiled. "My favorite part of the morning."

"It's leaded, and I added cream and sugar, so I hope you aren't one of those ladies that counts every calorie." He grabbed Maxus' reins again.

"Are you kidding? I'm a nurse, and you don't do a twelve-hour shift without leaded and loaded." She smiled, taking another full glance at the large animal before her.

"Good, you don't need to anyway." He fidgeted with Maxus' saddle.

"What?" She spit the word out before she could stop herself. Had he really said that?

"You don't need to count calories, not by the looks of you." He continued to work on the bridle.

"Thank you, I think." She was still plagued at the fifteen pounds she hadn't lost since having Mason, but it seemed she was the only one that ever noticed that.

He chuckled. "Ready?"

"I think so." She stepped to Scout's side acting brave, though her heart raced. She still couldn't believe that she'd given in to the idea of going riding with him. She'd spent so much of the last two years doing all she could to avoid advances by any man, yet his tender voice and gentle manner made her think this decision the right one for now.

"Lesson one, grab the reins like this." He covered her gloved hands with his own, nerves batting through her. It had been a long time since she'd felt a man's touch and his hand on hers was almost overwhelming.

Even with the barrier of both gloves, warmth enveloped her. She sucked in a breath. *Concentrate on the horse, not his hands. Focus, Jen. He's a nice man and that's all.*

He shifted her closer to the horse. "Reach up and grab a handful of mane, along with the reins. Step into the stirrup all in one motion and pull up on the saddle horn, kicking your right leg behind you."

She did as he said and pulled up, struggling to balance but finding it easier than she'd thought. She settled in the saddle taking a deep breath. He was right, she did remember all so easily. "This is a big horse."

"Yep. Lean forward up hills and back down hills. How're the stirrups?" He pushed her boot further into the stirrup, by holding one hand to her knee and checking her placement.

Her breath caught at his touch once more. "Good."

He looked up at her again. Those green eyes. "Now, let's hope Maxus wants a ride."

"He's the one who tossed you in the river?" She'd thought so.

"Yep, but he's the best jumper I've got." He climbed into the saddle and led the way, both horses falling into an easy canter. "He's a bit high strung, but that's what makes a good animal."

"Aren't you cold?" she asked, the chill working through her even with her heavy coat. He only wore a heavy flannel shirt over several layers but no coat, though he had gloves.

"I'm good. Loosen up on the reins a bit. He'll follow." He slowed Maxus allowing her to catch up on Scout.

"So where are we headed?" She glanced around as the darkened forest opened to them.

He glanced at her and smiled not answering. Here she was at three below zero, riding a horse into the wild unknown with a longhaired biker guy, stunt man, rancher. What was she thinking?

"It's not far." He stared at her for a long time as if thinking of the right words. "So…is there a big kick my ass kind of a boyfriend out there I should be worried about?"

After an initial shock, Jenna burst into laughter. *So he was interested. Oh, God, she could feel her pulse racing at even allowing this much time with him.* "Any particular reason you would ask?"

"No reason." He shrugged hiding his smile by turning his head to the trail.

"So how did you get into films and television?" She changed the subject, the intensity of this possibly being a date was enough to make her thoughts ramble unsteady across the last two years.

He glanced at her with a nod. "I bid for jobs, but some of the larger ranches can underbid what it would cost me to travel and stay on location. This is a nice stint being it's close to home and Lily."

"Your daughter?"

"Yea. She's great. Smart. Beautiful. Guess I'm kind of addicted to her." He beamed. "And your son?"

Jenna's heart melted that he would ask. "He's a year old, about to walk any day now."

He laughed but then asked. "And his father?"

All the blood in Jenna's veins, if not already frozen, chilled further. How was she to answer? "Divorced before Mason was born." She shook her head, but the need to explain further hung in the air. "He changed over time, not who I thought he was."

"That how you ended up here, in Montana?" He glanced at her again and slowed his horse.

Well, that was an easier question. "My best friend, Brianna, and I went to nursing school together in Virginia. We started looking at places to move and when we couldn't decide, we discovered a large sign-on bonus in Great Falls for experienced emergency room nurses. Decision made, though she does have an aunt near Helena or she would have never moved this far."

It was a moment before he spoke again glancing ahead of them. "We have a lot in common. Lily's mother checked out of our lives right after she was born. Motherhood…wasn't her thing. I think we liked the idea of each other but adding a baby to the mix…she was an aspiring actress and we just weighed her down."

"Life doesn't always drop a bowl of cherries, but Mason and I do all right." She was uncertain what else to say but unnerved at the depth of the conversation and what she had shared. That was a first other than Brianna.

He clucked his tongue and led her and Scout around a sharp turn of boulders. "Lily's well adjusted. I learned a long time ago, some things in life have no real explanations."

"She's still an actress then?" She was curious but her nerves seem to frazzle any time she talked of her ex-husband.

He looked at her for a moment and then answered, his tone dropping in sarcasm. "Pamela Beach ring a bell?"

Jenna's mouth dropped open. Pamela Beach was a household name with multiple motion pictures and her own line of make-up and clothing. "I didn't mean to pry."

He shook his head again. "We never were married. She had no interest in Lily and gave me full custody without any fuss. My mother looks after Lily on the ranch. We all live there, my brothers and I, to help out," he answered. "Watch this incline, lean forward, and hang on." He headed Maxus up, looking back at her as Scout followed.

"This is steep. Can they see well enough?" She held on tightly and leaned forward in the saddle tempted to close her eyes.

"Scout's got it. Hang on and relax. Horses see pretty well." His voice was soft against the quiet dark morning. "Right here is a little tricky, lean forward and press your feet into the stirrups. Scout's got it, just don't panic." He slowed Maxus and showed her how to maneuver a twist of rocks and tree roots, Scout following with ease.

The angle was almost straight up and across rocks that were probably slick. "I'm scared he'll fall or I will."

"Go with it…that's it. It's not the fall, remember?" He backed Maxus up to watch, smiling at her.

Scout jumped to make the climb and Jenna yelped in fright but hung on as the horse made it to flat terrain.

Aaron rode closer and leaned to whisper. "You can breathe now."

She exhaled. "I suppose we have to go back that way."

"Yep. Come on, we're almost there." He pulled ahead, and Scout followed with ease. "And what about Mason's father, what happened?"

She'd thought the climb to change the subject but apparently not. "Uh, he was a politician, not who I thought he was and it just ended." There was no point in saying anymore.

The sky was beginning to lighten in the distance and as they topped a small hill, rushing water sounded. Searching hard through the denseness of trees, the river unfolded before her, so magnificent she forgot she was still on the horse. The crystal blue water was as beautiful as she'd ever seen.

"This is beautiful." She held on tightly as they continued to climb higher. It was all right that she had come, wasn't it and that she had spoken what she did? The ride was nice, but her nerves still rode the edge of her thoughts at having discussed her past.

"Yep." He stopped Maxus and dismounted, walking to Scout and holding his bridle.

"Loosen your left foot from the stirrup so it doesn't get stuck and kick over and down with your right." He made it sound easy as she fumbled her way to follow directions. She remembered the feel but Scout was a big horse, bigger than the one he rode by comparison.

"Okay." She dropped to the ground, losing her footing and falling back into him.

"Whoa." He steadied her, his hands on her hips.

"The drop was further then I thought." She pulled free of his grasp instinctively, though his gentleness made her suck in a staggered breath.

"We're on foot from here." He grabbed the blanket roll off the back of Maxus, tying both horses. "Grab your bag."

She untied her bag and tossed it over her shoulder. The chill near the river was degrees colder, her breath hanging in the dark air. He took her gloved hand in his own to lead her. She glanced down having not expected the warmth that wove its way through her once more. She followed him along the trail, on the edge of the rocks wishing now she hadn't opted for gloves. It was incredible, the water falls spraying down layers of brown and gray rock all the way to a canyon hundreds of feet below them. "I didn't realize this was here."

"Come on." He climbed up the steep rocks next to them, assisting her to maneuver the higher ones.

At the top of the flat rocks there was an overhang of earth and vines, covering the area they'd stepped to. It was still dark but getting lighter and the ring of rocks for a fire sat ready. *So he had planned this and she wasn't sure how she felt about that.*

He bent and used a striker to light the wood, which took right away, glowing orange and yellow across the rocks.

"You must come here a lot." She smiled a bit nervous as she moved closer, hoping the fire would make things warmer.

"It's a nice break from the set. They may film a bit here coming up. I fish in the canyon pool. You like trout?" He pushed the logs of wood around, glancing up at her.

"I love trout, but I thought you'd rub sticks together for a flame." She set her bag by the blanket he'd dropped to the rocks.

"I can do that if you like, but this is faster, more modern." His grin was contagious as he held up the striker and flicked it. "Just think, if I would have had this in the day of cavemen, I would have been king."

She couldn't help but laugh. "If you were a cave man, the dinosaurs would have eaten you or you would have frozen to death."

His laughter echoed through the canyon, and he leaned to spread the blanket, sitting and patting the spot beside him.

She sat, looking into the fire as it continued to come to life. So he had planned on her and this fire. She removed her gloves, setting them aside, holding her hands up to warm them, the heat warming her instantly.

"How does a nurse end up on the set of a western television series?" He grabbed the thermos from her bag and poured the tin lid full. *God he's so handsome up close.*

"Well." She took the cup from him. "I've worked the emergency room for a number of years and saw the series was being filmed locally and submitted my resume. I was hoping with it being Monday through Friday, I would have more time at home with Mason, regular eight-hour days. I miss so much working twelve hours, it's his whole day."

"And?" He waited.

How did he know there was more? "Promise you won't laugh?"

"Promise." He crossed his heart with his fingers and shifted closer to her.

"I've written western historical stories and scripts, novel-like stories for a while. I thought being a nurse consultant could teach me more about the business, allow me to make connections." She shrugged. It wasn't a far-fetched dream with what she was already learning on the set.

He sat forward and stoked the fire with a long thin stick. "Sounds like a plan."

"You really think so?"

"Sure. This business is all about who you know." He continued with the fire, glancing at her.

"Well, my friend Brianna loves my stories but fusses because I write so much." She shook her head. It was true.

"Gotta have dreams." He sat back again, close enough that his body rested against her, the heat of him warming her further.

Good Lord…he was so intoxicating she wanted to touch him, but fear plagued her. This was so hard. "And what do you dream about?"

He was quiet for a long moment, then took a deep breath and tossed the stick into the fire. "Our ranch is small for the most part, forty-six acres. We've about eighteen horses and board a good number more. I've been thinking of purchasing the land that's attached, across the river. One-hundred acres. Promise you won't laugh?" He raised his eyebrows, waiting, but his smile was teasing her.

She crossed her own heart in mimic. "I promise."

"I want to build a ranch for foster boys, the older kids that might never get families." He continued looking out across the ridge, lost in thought for the moment.

"Really?" How admirable what that? Was this guy way too much or what?

"My brothers and I are adopted." He glanced at her

40

again. "Amos and Sarah took us when Gabe and I were twelve and Jeremiah eight."

"So you aren't biological brothers?" she asked, having wondered of Gabe's silky dark hair and eyes and Jeremiah's total lighter features of light brown hair and blue eyes.

"Nope. We were in a group home together. I was a little rough around the edges, rebellious, and when the group home closed, we were separated. I got a nasty set of drug-using foster parents. The man accused me of taking money, and I got the beating of my life, ended up in the hospital for weeks." He shook his head and continued. "Clarice, the social worker, pulled me from there, and I stayed with her until she brought me to meet Amos and Sarah. I acted tough like I needed no one, and when Amos talked to me about living at the ranch, I informed him I wasn't coming without my brothers. I thought if he knew I had brothers, even though at the time we weren't tagged with each other, he wouldn't want me. The plan backfired." He laughed the glow from the fire sparkling across his eyes. "The very next week Clarice took me back kicking and screaming, and when we got there, Gabe and Jeremiah were waiting. Apparently, Amos asked who they were, and Clarice had the answers. Took some doing but she got it all done."

"That's an incredible story." In spite of her fear, she placed her hand in his. He was so easy to talk with, and it had come naturally, though her nerves still played havoc inside her. She thought to pull her hand back, but he held on tightly.

He looked down and gripped her hand even tighter. "If I could manage to get the money together, I can do right by some of the kids out there. I'll have what I need for a down payment on the first forty acres shortly."

Jenna sat amazed. "That's really special, Aaron." Oh God, she shouldn't have taken his hand, touched him. She shouldn't let him think she was ready for any kind of relationship because she wasn't and likely never would be.

He pointed. "Look ahead at the top of the cliffs in the distance."

She tracked her gaze that direction. The sky began to lighten from a dark gray to a crystal light blue. He tugged the blanket around them and chills ran the length of her body, but it wasn't from the cold. The warmth of him radiated down her side and the only sound was the rush of water as the sky began to brighten.

The edge of the cliffs turned orange as the sun began to rise. Little by little the graying brown of the forest was highlighted, giving the corpses of sleeping trees life. Finally, the full round sun freed itself from the cliffs and hung bold in the cold blue sky. Blinking, she glanced at him, and before she knew what was happening, he leaned closer. He was going to kiss her. No, he couldn't, not yet. She wasn't ready. But she wanted the kiss, didn't she? Oh God, his breath was warm, and his lips tender as they softly met her own. She closed her eyes forcing away the dormant fears that tried to return and let his warmth spread through her, wanting what she'd done so long without.

Chapter Four

Aaron pulled from the kiss, touching Jenna's face with one hand, gazing into her amber eyes. He really hadn't planned to kiss her, but the moment had caught him off guard. It had been a long time since he'd been so consumed by a woman he couldn't breathe. Her lips had been tender and the sweetness of her breath intoxicating.

"That was breathtaking," he whispered.

"The…sunrise was…beautiful?" Her voice wavered so slightly.

"I'm not talking about the sun." He gave her the hint of a smile, brushing back a strand of her hair and placing his lips to hers once more, tender and soft, losing himself in the feel of her as he wrapped his arms around her to pull her against him.

Suddenly, she pushed him away and struggled from the blanket taking off on a run away from him and the fire, leaving him at a loss. *What the hell?*

He jumped up to follow, calling to her. "Jenna? Jenna…wait."

But as fast as she'd run, she stopped, uncertain of her direction. He caught her and touched her arm, as out of breath as her. "Jenna?"

"I'm sorry, Aaron…it's not you. I can't." She leaned her shoulder against a large tree, but she didn't look at him as she sniffled.

"Jenna?" he whispered, easing his grip but not letting go.

She didn't say anything, but the rushing of the falls covered the sound of her tears, which made his gut clench. What the hell was wrong?

"Look, if I've overstepped some boundary…" He stepped closer, close enough to smell the strawberry scent of her dark hair. In spite of thinking she might turn around and sock him one, he tugged her gently to him. She resisted at first, but he held tightly, not releasing her.

"Shhh," he whispered trying to soothe her. She was shaking, but he now understood that it wasn't from the cold. After a moment, she collapsed into him, and he sat them both to the ground, cradling her between his knees and against his chest.

She wiped her eyes and spoke through gasps of catching her breath. "It's not…you, really. You didn't, overstep…anything." She glanced at the river. "I'm not ready. I mean I thought I was, but—"

"It was just a kiss, Jenna. I had no other intentions." Though that kiss had been a hell of a lot more than that for him, maybe he'd rushed the moment. It dawned on him then that if her son was only a year old; she'd not been long from any relationship. Maybe things weren't over for her yet.

She looked up at him, her eyes red and smeared with mascara. "But my first since…" She turned back to face the river and it was some time before she spoke. "It's just too soon."

He sat stunned for the most part. Her words were sincere, but while the kiss was a surprise for him too, he hadn't meant to upset her. He'd been right in guessing it was fear he'd seen in her eyes and it now made sense.

"You must think I'm a case." She shook her head. "We should head back. You didn't deserve this."

He took a deep breath. Kissing her had been powerful for him. She was gorgeous, smart, and everything he hadn't been looking for and he wasn't going to let her off the hook that easy. "No, I don't think that, but don't shut me out, Jenna."

She pulled from him, standing up as he rose behind her. "It's probably best, Aaron, I'm not going to be any good at this. I mean Brianna has encouraged me to meet someone again, but I'm not even sure how to do that anymore."

He turned her to face him. "Look, I don't have any expectations here, other than to share time and get to know you. I didn't even plan to kiss you, but you were just so damn beautiful watching the sunrise."

Jenna gave him the hint of a smile, wiping her eyes again. "You are so sweet, Aaron, and I do want to try, but I'm so…afraid."

He touched a finger to her lips. "It's okay to be afraid, but not of me. You are worth it. Of that I have no doubt."

Her sad amber eyes searched his face. "I want to be worth it."

He took her by the hand. "Come on, you need to warm up by the fire. You're shivering."

She followed, holding onto his hand so tightly he glanced down where her knuckles were turning white. She sat and tugged her gloves back on one by one. He led her back to the fire, pouring her more coffee and handing her the cup.

She sipped, her hands trembling. "It's been nearly

two years but it's still very raw. I didn't expect to react the way I did…"

"Maybe you need those feelings to come to the surface to deal with them." He offered, still perplexed at what she had divulged, but sure he didn't understand it fully.

"I thought I had been." She shook her head, the strawberries surrounding him again.

"I'm glad it wasn't my kiss that brought you tears." He touched her cheek and leaned down to make her look at him.

A bit of a smile edged her lips. "The kiss was fine…"

He snapped his fingers and shook his head with a slight grin of his own. "I was kind of hoping for spectacular."

She laughed then. "How about extraordinary? Sorry, I ruined the moment."

"Naaahhh." He gave her a wink, wishing he could take away the sadness that still lingered in her eyes, anger welling in him at the idea of what she might have been put through. He pulled the blanket around her, hoping he had an inkling of a chance, a bit frightened himself at the aspect. Maybe he shouldn't have kissed her so soon, but he'd been too caught up in the moment. A woman like her should never know what it was to be broken, and so he'd wait and let her take the lead, but he wasn't about to let her slip from his grasp.

****

The ride back to base camp was quiet, leaving Aaron confused. Jenna had hidden her fears behind a few smiles and had made small talk but it had seemed forced. He guided Maxus, leading her on Scout to the backside of the little western town where filming was in progress. They needed to stay out of view so they took the longer turn on the outside of the parking area back to the barn.

"Guess there's a shoot-out at the O.K. Corral today." He glanced back toward the saloon where a film crew sat on the outside holding lights and cameras. Blanks shots snapped and echoed around town, and the minimized voices of the actors could be heard as they rolled through their lines.

"Did you know the real fight at the O.K. Corral was in a very small area, like six to ten feet? The whole fight lasted less than thirty seconds." She lifted her gaze, with the first real smile.

He was well aware of the details but she was talking and that was a good thing. "Really?"

"And Wyatt Earp was the only one who didn't take a bullet," she added.

"You read up for your writing of the time period, then?" he asked, and she nodded as he dismounted outside the barn. She did the same this time on her own. He tied both horses and turned to look at her, wanting to hold her so bad he could taste it. "Are you all right?"

She took a deep breath and met his gaze. "I will be, Aaron. I kind of feel it was foolish now."

He walked a little closer. "No need for that. You are worth it, Jenna."

"Thank you." It was the slightest whisper as she dropped her gaze.

"Aaron?"

He and Jenna both turned to Drake Masters walking their way. Dressed as an eighteen-eighties cowboy in dark pants, boots and vest, sporting replica revolvers in the holster low around his narrow hips, he smiled and offered a hand. "Hey, I wanted to talk with you before the ride this afternoon."

Aaron leaned in and took his grip, wanting to curse the bad timing. He still wasn't certain where he stood with Jenna, and he didn't want to leave things off balance.

Drake glanced at Jenna taking her hand next. "You're the set nurse. I remember you from the opening day events."

"Jenna Wilder. I'll just be going so you two can work." She glanced at Aaron and then turned, leaving him with the actor.

"Aaron, I was wondering if we could discuss the stunt for this afternoon. I've ridden horses for years but falling from one on purpose. I'm afraid I might need a lesson or two." Drake smiled, starch white teeth gleaming.

"This is the fall with Thor dragging you, but I've got that part. Your job is to fall away on the pillow matting." He had already rigged up the saddle that he needed, and Thor would handle it fine with him taking the real fall while Drake hit the pillows.

"Yea, but I've gotta fall off that horse like I know what I'm doing." The actor added with concern, but chuckled. "I'm thankful you're the one getting drug through town though."

"I was about to saddle up Thor." Aaron glanced behind Drake but Jenna was long gone, leaving a crevice through his center. He'd hoped to end the moment with at least the touch of his hand, something personal.

"Sorry, I didn't mean to interrupt." Drake glancing

behind him and back.

He shook his head. "It's fine."

"I suppose I should thank you for the spill you took in the river the other day, making my job look easy." The actor followed him into the barn. "Not sure how you took that cold splash."

"Goes with the territory." Aaron shrugged. He'd been dumped in worse places over the years and cold water was a bit better than hard dirt when it came down to it.

"That's why I thought you might be better at teaching me to be a 'fall guy'." Masters' laughed, running a hand through his dark wavy hair, hat in hand.

"There's a right way to fall." he acknowledged and then next hour was spent showing the actor ideas of how to let go of Thor and fall free of the horse, rolling onto the blow-up mat. The important task was timing and falling on cue. The tabloids played Masters as a Hollywood player, a different woman on his arm at every event, but he seemed down to earth. That he'd asked for help was huge. Some actors wanted to do their own stunts, and others opted out. Footage of the real Drake falling was needed, but it would be Aaron who hit the ground being dragged along behind Thor eating dust.

After he'd gotten Drake secured with the fall, he took Thor to the set to wait on their turn to ride. He needed to suit up and ride Thor on a gallop through the middle of town, pretend to get shot, fall from the horse, and be dragged by the animal to the end of town.

Concentration was difficult as he'd not been able to push Jenna from his mind. He hadn't meant for their time together to go as it had, but then maybe it was best given he wasn't sure he was ready for something more himself.

He tied Thor off and walked to the wardrobe trailer.

"Aaron, got you all set buddy." Brian nodded toward the pile of clothing on the bench near the door. "I'll help you get suited up. I found a bicycle chest protector and back plate, so you won't get skinned up. It'll fit well enough under your clothes."

"That'll work." He shucked his jeans and T-shirt, donning protective knee and elbow padding along with the chest and back guard, with a dark long sleeve shirt underneath for added padding.

"Let me tape you up so it won't slide when you hit the ground." Brian pulled out duct tape and began stripping it along the chest and back protector. "You got Maxus or Thor on this one?"

"Maxus might like a chance to drag me around, but Thor will be nicer about it." He chuckled at the truth of his favorite ornery horse. Maxus was his best for jumps but the horse had a mind of his own, smart as hell too when it came down to it.

"Well, that spill gave you a hell of a bruise." Brian tore the tape away securing the last edges of the back plate.

"Yep, I feel it." He pulled on his cowboy trousers and stepped into the boots. His back still ached and the upcoming fall wouldn't help, but he could ice down later.

Sheila came from the back, carrying a brush and a handful of black pony tail bands. "Hi Aaron, the script says you aren't so dirty today, but you need your hair banded and up."

"She loves your hair, probably because I have none." Brian rubbed his bald scalp.

Aaron sat down as Sheila started on his hair, lingering as she pulled the brush through. "I saw you ride back in town with the nurse a while ago."

"Help." He glanced at Brian for pity.

"Not a thing I can do about her, Buddy, she's a hopeless romantic." He handed Aaron a holster and guns.

"I am not, but she is very pretty and such a sweetheart." She teased, pulling his hair in a band and tucking it under the hat she placed on his head.

He stood and winked at her, making it sound simple. "The nurse and I are friends."

"You are on in five." Shelia went back to her work. "You be careful this time."

"Yes, ma'am." He gave her a cowboy nod, dipping his hat, grateful to chat no more where Jenna was concerned.

Ten minutes later he sat on Thor, waiting for Horace Leland's cue. If Thor cooperated this would be one take, but then again working with the famous show runner/director assured nothing was done until he announced it a *take*.

"Places." Leland spat. "Someone get the can of cola off the railing at the saloon, we are in the eighteen-hundreds folks."

One of the crew scurried to grab the can and disappeared behind the fake town.

Aaron waited, noticing Jenna on her cart at the side lines, but then it was her job to be present for the stunts. *Focus. Now would be a good time to do so.*

"Places and action!" Leland's voice quieted the set.

Aaron headed Thor to a gallop. As he passed the barbershop, he pulled his revolver and popped three caps toward the saloon as the script called for. Sometimes playing cowboy was fun. Jolting in the saddle, as if shot, he tossed himself from Thor, still hanging onto the reins and another rope tied to the saddle horn. Hitting the ground, he never slowed as Thor pulled him along the sandy street, dust stirring in his wake. So far so good, except for his back and the breath he'd yet to catch. He held tightly until Thor reached the end of town and with a whistle, he stopped the horse.

He rolled over sitting up and spitting dirt to the ground. His back hadn't needed that, and he growled as he gained his feet again, waiting on word from Leland. It went flawless, but the man never seemed satisfied and the fact that he'd lost his cowboy hat might play a problem. He gave Thor a pat and waited, getting a thumbs up from the camera crew. Well, that would be a damn first. He brushed the dust from his clothing and stretched his back; the ache would be no fun later.

Drake met him as he returned with Thor. "My turn, but I've got it easy."

"Loosen your foot, drop the reins and fall away." He handed Drake the reins and turned to search for Jenna. She'd been waiting nearby, sitting on her medical cart, and he didn't hesitate at all making his way right to her.

Meeting her gaze, he sat in the passenger seat of her cart glancing back where Masters was mounting up.

"I don't know how you do it. That one hurt?" She brushed dirt from his shirt, her face less anxious than before.

"Years of practice and good padding. Ice and heat." He grinned and beat his chest where the protector was still taped in place. His back ached but that would pass, more important right now was making sure she was all right.

Her smile faded. "Aaron, I won't tell you I didn't think about that kiss happening. I even wanted it to, but I suppose I wasn't ready for the emotions that went with it."

"So, I'm not banished to the curb?" He grinned, enjoying the pink flush of her cheeks.

"No." She whispered so softly he wished he could scoop her into his arms again.

"Good, I would hate to break it to Scout that the beautiful lady riding him has dropped us like a hot cake." He waited as her smile erupted.

She nudged him, teasing, as Leland called for action.

"Here goes Masters." He focused on the set.

Thor took off, repeating what he'd done moments ago. Drake was hanging on and at the post office popped his gun three times.

"Slow the horse…" Aaron shook his head, squinting for a better view. Drake let go at the snap of the last gun blast and flipped himself off Thor, his foot snagging the stirrup. The horse pulled him a ways before he dropped to the ground with a cloud of dust.

"Damn it!" Aaron jumped up and whistled stopping Thor, but Drake Masters lay on the ground unmoving. "He hit the ground. Go!" He jumped back on the cart, and Jenna turned the key, pushing the gas and steering onto the set.

"Let the nurse through." Leland spat orders over

the megaphone.

Jenna jumped from the cart and knelt and assessed Drake who was rolling on the ground in pain, grabbing his side.

"Take deep breaths. That's it." She held his head to look in his eyes as he sat up. "Did you hit your head?"

"No. I…guess…I…missed the…mark." He held his ribs, his breath short.

Jenna tugged at his old west shirt, freeing it of his trousers and having to take the time with the buttons. "Let's get your shirt off, you've got some bleeding. Where do you hurt?"

"My side…" Drake worked out of his shirtsleeves, one of the crew assisting him.

Jenna ran her hands along his side, eliciting a yelp. "You could have broken ribs or other injuries that are hard to see. What about your arm?" She reached into her bag for the medicated wipes and began cleaning the deep scrapes on his forearm and elbow.

He cringed, sucking in air through clenched teeth.

"Sorry." Jenna continued. "You need an x-ray of your ribs and arm to make sure. Look at me; did you hit your head?"

"Nope, I don't think so. Was it a take?" Drake glanced up at Leland.

"Excellent, incredibly realistic." Leland rolled his eyes and folded his arms. "All we need now is you injured."

"I'll be fine." Drake stood with help from two crew members.

Jenna stood as well. "Get your footing. Do you feel dizzy?"

He held steady. "Nah, I think this thick skull of

mine is good."

"I still think X-Rays are in order," she offered, with a glance at Horace Leland.

"Take him into Great Falls in the limo." Leland nodded to his assistant. "Ms. Wilder, could I request that you travel with him? He'll need a private room and no leaks of information."

Jenna nodded and lifted her cell phone as Aaron stood in the distance behind all the commotion. She worked with skill and efficiency, and he caught himself just watching her.

Drake glanced his way. "Should've listened closer about keeping my boot free."

"Timing's everything." He backed up with the arrival of the limo, taking Thor's reins from one of the crew.

In a matter of moments, Jenna was shoved into the limo and whisked off to the hospital with the *real cowboy*. It was her job, but he couldn't help but feel a bit of jealousy when it came down to it. He pulled Thor by the reins, heading back to the barn, the ache in his back emerging once more. No matter, he needed to get home to spend time with Lily and if he were being honest with himself, take the cold shower he'd needed since kissing Jenna Wilder.

Chapter Five

Jenna sat in the limo across from Drake Masters, who was kicked back in the long seat, holding an ice pack to his side. She'd been ushered inside the limo so fast; it wasn't until the quiet of the speedy ride that she remembered the last time she'd been in such a vehicle. It had been the evening she'd confronted Vince about large amounts of funds coming into his campaign. Her now ex-husband had blind-sided her with a fist to her cheek, leaving her dumfounded and gasping as he cursed her because it was 'none of her business.'

"Aaron taught me well enough, just happened so fast." Drake pulled her from her thoughts, and the shiver she'd yet to allow.

She glanced at her cell phone where Shay had responded to her text. "The ER's all set with a private room, and security has been notified."

He looked at her with a nod. "Thanks. So…how did you end up as the nurse on location?"

She thought for a minute before answering. He was really a handsome man with his deep blue eyes and shoulder length dark hair. "I was looking for something where I could be home more with my son."

"Well, that sounds like a real good reason." He grimaced. "If this isn't broken ribs."

She shook her head. "Broken or not, I think your stunts are over for a while."

"No problem there." He closed his eyes again, his features still pale.

She glanced out the window as the hospital came into view and thought of Aaron. She'd planned for the horseback ride earlier and maybe somewhere deep inside she had even planned for the kiss, but she hadn't planned to react the way she did. But having been close to no one since Vince… She wanted to cringe as she did feel silly about it now. Aaron was such a nice man, and now he probably thought she was crazy.

As the limo pulled into the emergency room circle drive, she leaned toward the door. "Let me get a wheel chair, and I'll be right back."

"No need for that." Drake moved slow trying to follow her.

"No, wait here." She trotted inside finding Shay at the desk.

"I got five all set up myself. Bri's on the way to take him. I won't be able to function trying to get him to sign his papers for treatment." Shay fanned herself.

"He's really nice. Who's on?" she asked as she pulled a wheelchair closer.

"Doc Gates and I've notified security. They were supposed to be on their way." The unit clerk dialed the phone checking again.

"I knew you would have it together." Jenna pushed the wheelchair outside, next to the limo. Drake got out and sat, pulling his hat low. He was still dressed as an old west cowboy, though his shirt was open and if that didn't make him stand out, she needed to hurry him past the waiting room. Shay buzzed them through to the back and wheeling Drake into room five, Jenna found Brianna waiting.

"Hi Mr. Masters, I'm Brianna Carlton. Let's get you to sit on the stretcher. X-ray is on the way so we can get you checked out." She was heavy into nurse mode which actually meant she might just behave. "Good thing you had Jenna right there to help on the set."

He settled back on the stretcher letting her place electrodes on his chest and then sticking his arms through the sleeves of the gown. "Nice to meet you and yes, Jenna's great."

"Dr. Gates is on the way to see you, but I can get you something for the pain right now with your permission for an I.V. catheter. Are you allergic to anything?" Brianna asked.

He closed his eyes. "Something for pain would be good. I.V's fine. Nope on the allergies."

"Radiology is here so Jenna and I will step out while they get the pictures, and I'll be right back with something for the pain." Brianna grabbed her by the arm and led her from the room. "Girl, am I dreaming or is that some kind of cowboy lust you just rolled in?" Her friend's entire body rippled in a shudder.

"Shay's on the verge of passing out, and I don't need you doing the same." Jenna picked up an I.V. start kit waiting as Bri signed out the medication from the dispensing unit. "Now go medicate him, and I'll be right behind you." She handed off the I.V. start kit and sent her back down the hall as Shay excited room five, bouncing along.

"Look, he signed my clip board." Shay beamed as she returned.

"You didn't ask for an autograph?" Jenna wanted to cringe.

"No, he signed all the paperwork, gave me his insurance and credit card and leaned to sign my clip board. I suppose he knew I was awestruck. He used this pen, too." She touched the pen to her cheek.

Jenna shook her head. "Take a deep breath. We'll be treating you next. I've gotta get his arm treated and dressed."

"You nurses are so lucky." The unit clerk sulked as she made her way back down the hall toward the desk.

Jenna knocked and entered Drake's room once more, after stopping by the dressing cart to grab what she might need for his skinned arm. Dr. Gates was already looking at his arm and ribs. Radiology had gone and Brianna was hard at work on getting an I.V. started.

"I suspect you've got two broken ribs." The doctor turned. "The nurses will get you medicated and bandaged up. I'll take at look at the pictures and let ya know."

"Thanks, Doc." Drake closed his eyes.

Brianna glanced up from where she'd inserted the I.V. catheter. "All done, you did very well Mr. Drake and if there is anything else you need, you just ask. The pain medication might make you dizzy so no getting up alone. I'll get more ice for your ribs." She made her quick escape with the doctor giving Jenna a wink.

Jenna stepped forward. Brianna could have won the academy award with that performance, fluttering eyelashes and all.

Drake took a long look at her as she applied ointment treating the scrapes to his elbow and arm. "Thank you."

"You're welcome." She angled her head, folding her arms.

He nodded. "I didn't think to ask about the horse."

"He's fine; at least Aaron had him by the reins." The mention of Aaron brought back a bit of her worry, but before she could say anything more, Dr. Gates popped through the door.

"Mr. Masters, looks like two fractured ribs. I'll get you some prescriptions for pain, and you'll need to take it easy for four to six weeks. No horses. You can follow up with an orthopedic doc in a few days." The doctor glanced at the written report.

"Thanks, Doc." Drake tried for a smile as he glanced back at her as the doctor disappeared again. "You called it right, broken. Hey, and you'll need a ride home."

Jenna shook her head, surprised at his concern. "It's fine, I can ride home with Brianna and get my vehicle later. She lives next to me."

He nodded tilting his head as he gazed at her. "Say, you wouldn't let me make it up to you with dinner sometime?"

She was flattered, but—

He caught on quick, his smile fading. "I think that must be the '*I have a boyfriend*' look. Aaron, right?"

"Maybe." It was the best answer she had for now. With her reaction to his kiss she thought maybe she'd all but blown her chances with Aaron. Even if he was still willing to spend time with her, she didn't know but that the trust might be lost between them.

"He could go to dinner too?" Drake grinned, making her smile.

"Perhaps later on, when you're better."

"But I have one more question." He studied her again. "If it wasn't for Aaron, you think I might've had a chance?"

Jenna had to smile, though heat rose in her cheeks. "Of course."

He chuckled but held his side and closed his eyes again. Glad for the medications taking hold, she checked his I.V., and the dressing on his arm, and documented his vital signs. She was flattered, but even if he was Drake Masters the gorgeous Hollywood actor, her thoughts were filled with Aaron and the hope she hadn't hurt him or her chance to make things right if nothing more.

****

"Jenna! Girl, *have* you gone insane?" Brianna sat on the love seat handing Mason toys from his basket and shaking her head. "I'm not saying marry the man, but you could have at least let him take you out to dinner."

"Maybe and he was so very nice, but…" Jenna glanced back at the television, where they'd been watching the evening news to see if Drake Masters fall would be shown. They'd done a good job at the hospital of keeping the media at bay but when Drake was being taken to his limo, the paparazzi had snapped away with cameras and flashes, in spite of security's efforts.

"Well, I am just saying I'd never have walked away from that man." Bri rocked her head. "He was adorably cute even though he was hurt."

"Here it is." Jenna turned up the sound with the remote glad to avoid the impending conversation about the Hollywood hero. Mason crawled over to her climbing into her lap and leaning back with his sippy cup as he did each night when he decided he was tired. She smoothed a hand over his baby fine locks looking back to the television as the story began.

'The Mountain News team was on the scene at St. Anthony's Hospital today when Hollywood actor Drake Masters was released after apparent injuries from a fall on the set of The Bounty Hunter, which is being filmed near Sun Prairie. The injured actor apparently suffered broken ribs and an arm injury when he was riding one of the horses on the set for a stunt. We've obtained exclusive footage from a cell phone of the incident and the horse involved as well as Drake Master' release from the hospital.'

"Aaron…" His name left Jenna's lips in a whisper as Thor made the screen for a brief glimpse, Aaron tugging him along. It looked to have been taken after she and Drake had entered the limo for the trip to the hospital, so someone on the set had leaked that footage she supposed. She flipped channels as the sister station was beginning to cover the same story.

"Wait a minute…I know that look. That's him isn't it? The one walking the horse. That's the stuntman." Brianna sat forward and glanced at her.

Yes, that was—him. She said nothing but kept watching the television.

"No wonder you aren't worried about Drake Masters." Brianna waited, tapping her fingers on the coffee table. "Talk to me, girl."

Jenna shook her head, Mason curling into her arms, his eyes closing making her surprised he didn't fight sleep. "There's nothing to tell, or at least I don't think there is."

"I think that ride you planned must have proved to be more interesting than not. Spill it." Brianna moved to sit by her on the sofa giving her no choice but to explain what she wasn't even sure she understood herself. She rocked with Mason; sorry the news had moved past the story. The glimpse of him had all but stopped her heart. Why had she been so afraid? But then she knew all too well her reasons and so did her best friend.

"Jenna?" Brianna lowered her voice an octave.

She took a deep breath. "I don't know. I've listened to you push me to get back out there, date, meet someone. I drove to the set this morning, with good intentions. Oh, God, I did, but I blew it."

"How did you blow it?" Bri's concern was sincere as her smile faded.

"I don't know. He said he hadn't planned it, but then he kissed me and I ran. He was so nice, and I blew it. I know I did. I just ran." She was rambling, and now it all seemed so silly once more.

"Girl, slow down." Her friend's brows narrowed. "Start over?"

"We went riding to where there were waterfalls, and he had coffee for me. He started a fire, and we sat and watched the sunrise, wrapped in a blanket together. It was so nice. I was doing well, but then he kissed me and it all came rushing back—all of it. And I just ran…" She shrugged fighting tears. She so wanted this chance with Aaron, or at least she thought she did.

"He was too much then, pushed too fast?" Brianna hugged an arm around her.

"No, it was so beautiful; his kiss was like nothing I've ever felt before. He must think I am a nut case for running off…" She shook her head, continuing to rock Mason. "Maybe I am."

"Jenna, it's been nearly two years. It is okay for

you to find love again." Brianna tried. "You were done wrong, but it isn't a life sentence unless you let it be."

"I went there thinking I had it all together, but—I wanted that kiss." And she had.

"Then you take it slow but give that man a chance." Brianna lifted her dark brows. "And for God's sake please run your hands through that luscious dark hair for me if nothing else."

Jenna laughed and dabbed at her eyes, nudging her friend. "You're impossible."

Bri held her smile too, brushing back a strand of dark curls behind Mason's ear. "No, I am not, but I am on for babysitting my favorite little dude any time if you need a night off to spend time with this guy."

"He did come to my cart and sit down when we were back on the set but then Drake fell." Jenna took a deep breath. Aaron had acted as if nothing at all had happened at the time, but it had. "I don't know. Sometimes I think I will never quit looking over my shoulder."

Brianna held her gaze. "Vince is too busy with his career, that new wife and her kids for you to worry about him anymore. He has no further reason to bother you."

"We hope." Jenna shivered as picturing Vince in her mind was almost overwhelming. She'd seen him in the tabloids at times, things related to his career and his new marriage, but she still lived in caution most of the time. "Sometimes I worry about what he would do if he found out about Mason. Other times I think he had a right to know."

Brianna shook her head. "He beat you while you were pregnant, Jenna. You almost died."

"I know but I still worry his father will tell him about Mason." She shook her head. "He was there as soon as I arrived at the hospital, and I think he sat with me all night, until he knew I was all right."

"He was with you when I got there; you were so out of it," Brianna added. "I've never understood his love for his son, given what Vince did to you but I don't doubt he will keep that a secret because he cared for you."

Jenna nodded the memories a bit of a blur still. "I believe he thought if Vince got his spot in the senate, his life would finally change, but he'll never change and I won't ever risk Mason... I should've never told his father." She glanced at her sleeping son. Vince's father, Gordon, had sat with her and when he'd asked that she not press charges for the beating, she'd let him know she was pregnant. She'd not known that fact herself until the physician caring for her had let her know that the baby's heart beat was strong in spite of the beating she'd taken. She'd been as shocked as her father-in-law, but Gordon Hanson had simply nodded and she would never forget his words.

'I only want the best for you, Jenna, and this child. Vince is...lost to the madness of this whole thing. I'm sorry he hurt you, but I will make sure you get your personal things and the money you brought into this marriage. You go and never look back as you didn't deserve this. I will handle my son.'

"He won't tell his son about Mason. I think he cared for you too much, and he came through on his promise to send your stuff, even the furniture and the money your father left you." Brianna touched Mason's socked foot.

Jenna nodded.

"So did you tell Aaron about what happened?" Brianna leaned back, folding her arms.

"Not in detail just that we were divorced before Mason was born." Jenna had thought that was enough, if not too much.

"So then what?"

"He said we'd go slow, and that I was worth it." Tears rimmed her eyes but she forced them away, holding her son's face in view. Aaron had been so understanding and wrapped in the blanket with him had brought more warmth to her than she'd known in the last several years.

"You are worth it." Brianna sat forward holding her gaze. "Now you wait right here while I get the chocolate ice cream and two spoons, and you and I are going to discuss letting Aaron inside that heart of yours."

Jenna had to smile, wiping her eyes and watching as Brianna headed to the kitchen. It was time and he was somehow what she'd never expected. When he'd come after her and held her, there was a comfort of which she hadn't felt except while living in her father's home. Some part of her heart wanted to let him inside. And that was what she would do if Aaron would give her the chance once more.

Chapter Six

Jenna made it back to the desk after getting one patient off to radiology and another to critical care for a severe asthma attack. The day hadn't been easy, but it had gone fast considering she'd bid for an eight instead of a full twelve-hour shift. The work on the set was full time but she needed to keep her skills up for returning once filming was over for the season.

She stopped at the desk and caught the knowing glances of Shay and Brianna. "What are you two up to?"

Bri nodded toward the counter where two large bouquets of flowers sat, both of them full of various blooms of exotic flowers.

Shay continued to hold her silly grin. "Don't keep us waiting, open the cards!"

Her first thought was Aaron as she ambled closer and picked up the first card and opened the envelope, thinking she hadn't received flowers in a very long time. But they wouldn't be from him given what had happened would they?

"Well." Brianna leaned over her shoulder, trying to catch a glimpse.

"Do tell," the clerk urged.

"Nosey." Jenna hid the card against her chest for a moment and then read it out loud.

'Thank all of you for the T.L.C.- Drake Masters'

She handed the card to Shay who squealed when she read it. "It's from Drake Masters. Can I keep one individual flower, please?"

"I can only suspect who the others are from." Her best friend angled a lifted brow of knowing.

Jenna's heart pounded against her chest hard enough for her to hear it as she pulled the envelope free and took out the card.

'Beautiful flowers for a beautiful lady.'

It wasn't signed, but typed, which seemed odd. She smiled.

"You must be worth it," Bri whispered and hustled away down the hallway back to work.

"Another secret admirer?" Shay asked.

"Maybe, but, you take these." She pushed the flowers from Drake toward her.

Shay's mouth dropped open. "Oh, I couldn't."

"Yes, you can." Jenna nodded that direction. "I'll get to see him on the set a lot."

Shay picked up the large vase of flowers. "I will save ever last one of these forever. Oh, your guy in radiology is done."

"I'll get him. I think he's going to be released once Dr. Gates reads the report." Jenna grabbed the chart, turning.

"I've got pizzas for the E.R." A teenage boy in a *Pizza Barn* shirt waited at the desk with a large stack of pizza boxes.

"Did any of you order pizza?" Shay glanced at her and the two techs behind her who shook their heads.

"This is the first few, but there are ten pizzas ordered by a Mr. Drake Masters." The young man looked at the ticket and back up. "Where do you want them?"

"Well, uh, right over here." Shay showed him the way to the break room as she spoke to Jenna. "I'll let everyone know, and of course I am writing the thank you note for all of this so you can deliver it to the man himself."

Jenna laughed and headed to radiology for her patient. Walking the hallways of the facility let her catch her breath for a minute. So Aaron had sent flowers and didn't think she was a lunatic after all. It seemed strange that both had come, the ones from him and from Drake Masters.

"Caught you daydreaming." Brianna walked up behind her. "And I know just who about."

She smiled. "Where're you headed?"

"I've got to go to MRI and medicate that demon child you've been hearing scream for the last two hours. Those parents need to get a wrap on this one." Bri wiped her brow.

"He's probably scared," she tried.

"Nope, he's twelve years old and fully possessed." Her friend hissed like a cat, holding her fingers up like claws.

Jenna's spectra link phone chirped, and she lifted it from her pocket. "This is Jenna."

"Uh, you have a visitor, and it's not Drake Masters," Shay whispered from the other end. "I think it might be your secret admirer."

"Who?" She stopped in her tracks.

"Says his name is Aaron Decker." Her voice went up an octave. "How men like this flock to you. Get down here, STAT!"

"On the way." She shoved the phone back in her

pocket, struggling to take a deep breath. So he hadn't walked away from near hysteria with his kiss.

"What?" Brianna questioned. "You just went pale."

"He's here." Her heart pounded so hard against her chest it was hard to speak.

"Who's here?" Bri glanced at her watch, but then looked back up holding her gaze. "Wait a minute. Him? *Him*, him? Aaron him? *The* Aaron? *Aaron*, Aaron?"

"Yes!"

"Girl, come with me. We'll get my little devil medicated, and I'll help you get your guy back in a hurry. I want to meet this man myself." Her friend all but pulled her down the hallway toward MRI, reminding her of all the trouble they use to get into in the college dorms sneaking around.

Moments later, she and Brianna arrived back to the ER, settling the radiology patient back in his room to wait on Dr. Gates.

"Go girl, I'll be there in a minute for an introduction, and I do mean to meet this man." Bri warned with a knowing glare of her chocolate eyes.

Jenna took a deep breath and looked in the mirror behind her groaning. "All right, but you act civilized." She opened the door and walked on her Jell-o ridden legs back to the desk, where she found Shay nibbling on pizza, entering orders.

"This has to be the best pizza I've ever eaten." The clerk nodded toward the waiting room giving her a tentative smile.

She glanced past the desk. Aaron stood, staring out the windows of the large waiting area, which was for the most part empty, all but some of the staff taking a breather.

"Hi." She stepped closer, thankful they were paid little attention.

"Hey, yourself." He stepped forward and hesitated but kissed her cheek. That was her fault wasn't it?

Heat flushed her cheeks. "This is a surprise."

He shrugged. "I thought I could take you to pick up your SUV since you'll be off shift in a bit. Gabe said your truck was still on the set and you were just working eight today, right?" He waited, his deep green eyes breathtaking and his long hair flowing across his shoulders. Good Lord, he was so handsome. Who hadn't grabbed this man and held onto him forever? Why shouldn't she do the same, though the thought was still overwhelming?

She shook herself back to reality. "Brianna was going to take me, but…I'm off in a few. Mason's sitter knew we needed to get my truck."

"I've gotta check on the horses anyway, but there's a catch." He held her gaze, and those deep green eyes melted something inside her. "If the sitter wouldn't mind."

"Catch?"

"The ride to get your truck comes with dinner." He gave her a hesitant lift of the eyebrows.

"I'm sure that would be fine, but I want you to meet my friends." She took him by the hand, her heart pounding and her hopes higher than ever that they could at least spend time and become friends if nothing else.

"I think you've already met Shay. This is Aaron." She made the introduction.

"Yep, we've met. Told you it was no trouble to find her." The unit clerk grinned but the phone at the desk rang and she turned with a roll of her eyes. "Thanks." He smiled, waiting as Brianna walked toward them.

Jenna sent a knowing glare her way. Brianna was a handful and predicting her behavior wasn't possible.

"Aaron this is Bri, my college roomie and best friend." Jenna held her breath as her best, friend who couldn't be trusted, stopped before them.

"It's a pleasure." He spoke first, leaning to reach Brianna's hand, his dark hair falling forward around his face.

"Uh hum. This girl has been holding out on me by the looks of you." Brianna walked all the way around him making a big deal out of the display.

He chuckled and lifted a brow waiting on an explanation, seemingly uncomfortable.

"Oh, will you behave." Jenna wanted to run, but he did seem amused. "She's really not my friend but an escapee from the mental health ward, who's due for her medication or a leash. Aaron's going to take me to get my truck so you are off the hook, but if you could get Mason after your shift."

Bri cocked a brow with a knowing smile. "That sweet boy has no problem with his auntie Brianna. Aaron, it really is a pleasure, and you know you'd best take good care of our girl."

"Got it." He gave her a wink. "I think I'll just step back over here." He turned to walk back to the window

"Oh my God, you didn't just behave like a maniac." Jenna scolded as she took Bri by the arm and entered the break room where her purse remained in her locker.

"He knows I'm harmless, but he's got the eyes for

you. I'll get Mason; you just take your time and call me in the morning." Bri fanned herself.

"You're impossible, but thank you." Jenna opened her locker grabbing her coat and pulling it on and tossing her bag over her shoulder.

Bri stopped her, grabbing her by both shoulders. "Take a deep breath and go out there and give that boy a chance like I told you."

"We're just getting my truck and then some dinner. I will be back later." She gave Brianna a quick hug and opened the door, finding Aaron where she'd left him.

He smiled with those dimples she adored, the ones that peeked through the edge of his beard and a part of her wanted to pinch herself to make sure what was happening was true.

"Ready?" He leaned up from the wall.

She nodded, following him outside the emergency room door to the parking area. "You surprised me."

He waited on her to catch up. "I worried I might upset you, but I do have to check on the horses and I wanted see if you were all right." He stopped at his motorcycle, leaving her perplexed as she hadn't ridden one of those ever before.

"I'm fine, and again I'm sorry for what happened. Stage fright I guess." She shrugged, likening it to their acting world. "But I am glad you came, really."

He shook his head. "No need for that. I wanted to come."

Jenna caught the view of Shay and Brianna at the window gawking with no mercy. "Could they not be more juvenile?"

Aaron glanced at them and turned back to her. "Fan club?"

"Sorry, those two are lethal together. This is so embarrassing." She laughed in spite of it. "Frankly, I expected no less."

"There's only one thing you can do about it." He said it as if it were nothing, a mischievous grin crossing his face.

"What's that?" she asked.

He shrugged, stepping closer and lifting her chin whispering. "Give them something to talk about, if it won't make you run away again."

She smiled, a blush heating her cheeks. "I won't run again, Aaron."

Before she could say anything more he placed both his hands on her face and open-mouth kissed her slow and searing. Her body flooded with heat as he tangled his hands in her hair and danced his tongue against hers. This time she didn't run, but instead placed her hands into his hair, never mind her intrusive friends.

He pulled from the kiss and handed her a helmet. "How was that?"

"Fine. I mean—good, I mean…Oh my God, incredible." It was all she could pull from the depths of her voice. She fitted the helmet over her head, the face plate covering her mouth and muffling her words. "How do I look?"

"Extraordinary!" He tightened the fit, lacing through the strap under her chin and pulling it tight. He grabbed his own helmet and straddled the bike, kicking the stand back and cranking the loud engine. He strapped on the helmet and nodded for her to climb on behind him.

She held onto his shoulders as she kicked her leg over to ride behind him. *Well, this is certainly going to*

74

be up close and personal.

"You good?" he questioned, pulling her hands off his shoulders and around his middle.

She nodded as her breath caught at the intimacy, her gawking friends forgotten. She leaned in close, her chest along his back, the warmth rising between them. As he turned the motorcycle in the direction of the exit, she glanced toward the emergency room window once more where Brianna and Shay were holding their thumbs up. She wanted to cringe when Aaron's chuckle vibrated through her at her friends' antics. She shook her head and held on tighter as he merged into traffic away from the hospital.

Her heart raced as he took the motorcycle to a faster speed once they reached the end of town. She'd never ridden before, and when he leaned into curves, he placed his hand on her clasped hands that were around his middle. She began to look forward to the twists and turns because it brought his touch and gave her a hint of his muscled belly. It was a short ride to the set and she found herself wishing it were longer so she could keep her arms around him, but it was probably best this was all between them for now.

He pulled to a stop on the set after nodding to the security guard, Doug. Odd, the cop hadn't been around her since she'd mentioned her connection with Aaron. Maybe he'd gotten the idea. Aaron cut the engine, waiting for her to climb off the motorcycle. He kicked out the stand and removed his helmet, helping her with hers.

"Did you like the ride?" he asked, setting both helmets on the seat of the heavy motorcycle.

She smiled. "It was fun."

He nodded toward the barn, urging her to follow. "Come on, I need to let the horses out in the corral for a while. Jeremiah came by and cleaned up the barn early this morning on his way home from the station."

"What did you do with Lily today?" She followed.

He opened the barn's double doors, swinging them wide and leading the way inside. "I got stood up. It's apparently more fun to go to the mall in Helena with Grandma than with me to the set."

"Shopping is always a woman's prerogative." She eyed Scout and ambled toward the large horse who hung his head over the stall in welcome. She scratched his jaw and face. "Hi, boy."

"Sarah's taking her shopping for some spring and summer clothes. Of course, I nearly emptied my wallet for the adventure." He chuckled. "It gives Sarah a break from taking care of Amos. Gabe's home with him today."

As he talked, he cut the thin ropes on a bale of hay and grabbed an armful, walking to toss it over for Charger, idle to himself in the first stall. He did the same for each of the animals.

"He's ill, your father?" she asked, walking to pet Maxus who snorted at her, only interested if she had a treat if she were guessing right. The horse turned away and pranced across the stall, more concerned with Aaron.

"Emphysema. He smoked like a chimney most of his life. He does pretty well, but Sarah needs a break sometimes. He's a good bit older than her and can be demanding when fatigued. I saw you on the news taking Drake to his limo. How is he?" He grunted as he tossed in hay for Thor.

"Two cracked ribs and abrasions on his arm. He shouldn't ride horses for a while, but honestly, he was very sincere. He asked about Thor." She glanced his way, wondering if his quick change in subject away from his father was on purpose.

"He had Thor going too fast. So, why don't you pick up anything you need from the medical tent and I'll finish up here, gotta set them out to the corral. Then you can drive me to dinner." He pulled the hose over to Maxus' stall, placing it to fill the trough and going back to turn it on.

"I'll see you in a bit." She trotted outside the barn and made her way to the medical tent, still surprised he had come for her. But somehow, she had managed to relax and just enjoy being with him.

She flipped open the flap of her medical tent, letting it fall behind her as she walked inside surveying the mess that had been left. There were dressings, tape, and splints all over the ground and tables. Figuring someone had tried to grab them for Drake's injuries; she filled her arms and went toward the cabinet she'd organized the week before. It wouldn't take long to put it all away. Gathering a handful of the packaged dressings from the ground she twisted the handle, letting the double door fall open and froze.

Inside the cabinet was another vase of flowers, similar to the ones at the hospital. She touched the small glass vase. Aaron? Maybe that was why he'd rushed her off to the medical tent, though there was no card.

She took the flowers out of the cabinet and set them on the table and replaced the piles of dressings back inside. Busying herself with the chore at hand, she couldn't help but smile.

She turned as Aaron entered the tent, his green eyes holding a smile and one arm hidden behind his back.

"You look sneaky." She leaned trying to see behind him but he twisted and kept her at bay.

He moseyed closer and held out a tiny bouquet of small purple wildflowers.

"They're so tiny." She took the bundle of petite flowers. "I thought I was spoiled by the flowers at work and here." She nodded to the bouquet behind her on the table.

He glanced at them, a puzzled expression crossing his face. "Sorry, but someone else will have to take credit for those."

She didn't understand, turning to view the flowers again. "Drake Masters sent flowers and pizza to the hospital, perhaps he sent these as well."

He shook his head, picking up a few more of the scattered rolls of tape. "Guess I've been outdone."

"Not at all, he was thanking us for his care. Odd he would send them here too." She shook her concern and turned back to face him.

He shoved the handful of items in a bin in the cabinet and turned wrapping his arms around her. "Just so you know, I only deliver handpicked flowers in person because you are worth it and because of this if I may?"

Jenna closed her eyes at the impact of his tender consuming kiss. She hung on tighter, as he pressed, parting her lips. How on earth was this man real? Where had he been a few years ago when he might have changed the course of her life long before now?

Her breath was short, her pulse raced and her body warmed clear to her center at the caress of his hand across her hips and under her breast. She shivered hard.

He broke the kiss and placed his forehead against hers. "I'm going too fast. I hate it when that happens; I've never been good at following the rules."

"Then don't follow them and kiss me again." She wasn't upset with his kiss or his touch, but the flowers had unnerved her a bit. *You're being paranoid. Get it together, Jenna.*

"You'll have to tell me when I'm too much, and it's all right to do that." He took her hands in his. "I love kissing you, and I kinda thought if I did it a lot you'd get use to me faster but I wonder how I'm doing here."

"You're doing fine," she whispered.

He tugged her into her arms hanging on for a long moment. She let herself melt into him, taking in the male fragrance of him once more. She'd waited for this, something real for long enough, though she suspected the waves of fear that rode through wouldn't fade fully for a long time. Her heart raced and her head was spinning, but in his arms, she felt something she hadn't felt in a very long time—safe.

Chapter Seven

Aaron leaned across the corral at the ranch, gazing out across the landscape of cottonwoods and rise of graying rocks in the distance. The wind was brisk and the temperature cold but being outside let him think. He'd spent the evening playing with Lily until she'd fallen asleep in his lap as they'd watched another rendition of some princess mermaid something. He'd put her to bed, unable to count how many hours he'd done that during her life. He didn't want to do wrong by her in reaching for his dreams and—Jenna.

He took a deep breath, sipping his cold coffee from a plastic handled mug. Kissing Jenna had pretty much heated his body right up, that and the feel of her hands on his belly as she'd ridden on the back of his bike had been about as much as he could take. He wanted her and in every way he could have her, though putting his heart out there as he had, there was always the chance he'd crash and burn.

It had been a long time since a woman had caught his attention to this extent. Nope, he'd never had anyone, even Pamela, Lily's mother, come this close. Something about the chemistry between them was stronger than he'd ever known could exist. He shook his head.

She was consuming him and fast, and he damn well liked it, though rushing into a relationship wouldn't do either one of them any good. Last night after checking on the horses, Jenna had driven them to a local diner for supper. The meal had been fine, but he'd caught himself watching her every move as if he could etch a bit of her into his mind and heart to keep her there. Yep, he had it bad. And watching her drive away opposite his direction for home had left him all but empty and wanting.

The good thing was she hadn't run again from his touch, but it was hard to judge where the limits were with her. What he really wanted was no limits—holy damn she was beautiful inside and out, and he had a few ideas about how much he'd like to discover that for himself. And while she'd come around, open to his touch after all, she was still holding back and he wasn't sure of her reasons. Likely the same as his own, the fear of getting burned once more. He could understand that one well enough. Someone somewhere had broken this beautiful woman, and he didn't like it, and no matter how things went between them, he wouldn't hurt her.

He'd never brought a woman home to meet the family or Lily but that was about to change. He wasn't even sure how his daughter might react with his attention on Jenna, but he had thought allowing her to meet his family might quench the worries she held about him and he could see just how Lily might react.

"You're up early?" Jeremiah walked over, dressed in his fire department uniform, sporting a tin mug of hot brew.

He turned from the corral, leaning on the fence. "You headed in?"

"Extra shift, time and a half." His brother zipped his heavy fire department coat, pulling his keys from the pocket.

"Maybe it'll be quiet." He turned up the rest of his own coffee.

"Busy is better. What're you doing out here anyway?" Jeremiah walked closer, giving him a lift of eyebrows.

He played it off. "Just thinking."

"Got your mind on some nurse if I had my guess." Jeremiah grinned, his light hair blowing across his brow with a whip of frigid wind.

He shook his head. When he was with Jenna he couldn't breathe, and when he wasn't with her, he couldn't focus on anything. It hadn't taken Jeremiah or Gabe long at all to know there was an interest between them. "Can't get her out of my head."

"Why would you want to? The guys at station seven say she won't give any of them the time of day, never has. You must have something special going on there, bro." His younger brother laughed. "Lucky for you I never asked her out."

"Lucky for me? Get outta here." Aaron laughed, sending a teasing swat toward his brother.

Jeremiah bent to tie the laces on his boots, setting the coffee mug on the ground. "Been telling you to get out there, brother."

He took a deep breath, his mind whirling. "It's complicated."

"Complicated? She's hot and smart. Sally says while all the other ladies are checking out Masters, she's watching you." Jeremiah shook his head. "What's holding you back?"

"She's five and thinks she run things." It wasn't about him anymore, he had to think of Lily's well-being.

"Lily? Hell, she'll fall for Jenna in a heartbeat. Kids are resilient, she'll be fine. I'm telling you, you don't need to let this one get away, Aaron." Jeremiah stood back up, grabbed his coffee, and turned for his jeep. He climbed in cranking it and driving closer, "I'll be on the set tomorrow afternoon to help out."

He gave his brother a nod and turned back toward the house. Lily would be up soon enough wanting breakfast and Sunday mornings he did the cooking for everyone. The clouds threatened rain if not snow by late afternoon, and while he wondered what Jenna was up to, he'd spend this day inside with Lily playing games and catching up on the wash and chores.

Entering the front door, giggles let him know Sarah and Lily were in the kitchen already. He made his way there and grabbed Lily, tossing her over his shoulder and swirling her around. "I heard a munchkin chattering in the kitchen."

Lily squealed in delight, laughing so hard she lost her breath, her bouncing brown curls bobbing around her face. "Daddddddddyyyyyyyy."

"Aaron be careful, the ceiling fan is an inch above her," Sarah warned, reaching into the refrigerator for a package of bacon, giggling along with them.

He sat Lily back down on one of the bar stools and leaned to kiss Sarah on the cheek. "I got breakfast, you go get that book you've been reading and take a break."

"I know you cook on Sundays, but I can help. What's got you in such a happy mood?" She let him have the package of bacon and moved so he could get into the refrigerator for the eggs.

"Just home with my best girls and today the

munchkin and I are going to wash the sheets and make all the beds in the house." He tried to make the chores a fun thing for Lily. Somehow, she didn't care as long as he was there to play in between the work.

"Jeremiah says Daddy is happy cause he likes the nurse at the movies. Who is the she Daddy?" Lily blurted the words in a flurry, jumping around the kitchen as if her question was nothing at all.

Aaron choked on his own saliva. *What the hell?*

Lily's green-eyed-gaze landed on him as she grinned, and it didn't go past him that Sarah had cocked a brow in waiting.

"Well, Jeremiah has a big mouth if you ask me." He set the bowl of eggs on the counter and grabbed the loaf of bread. "The nurse is my friend, and you'll be the first to know if that changes."

Sarah dropped her gaze but smiled, leaving him a bit unnerved at the whole conversation.

He grabbed Lily and pushed a chair to the stove, standing her in it. "You help me cook the eggs and don't ask so many questions."

"Daddy, are you hot? Is that why you need a nurse?" Lily climbed up and sat on the counter, stretching in her pink pajamas and fluffy kitten bedroom shoes.

"What?" He shook his head, narrowing his gaze on her.

"Jeremiah said Sally thinks you're hot, and the nurse would like to check you out." Lily waited in earnest for an answer and scooted further back on the counter. "Is the nurse going to check if you have a fever?"

It was Sarah who stifled her laughter as she

continued with her chores. His mother was well aware that where Lily was concerned, anything and everything was subject to being repeated.

"I think we need to filter what your uncles talk about in front of you. No, I don't have a fever, and the nurse is a friend. End of subject?"

"Okay, Daddy." Lily smiled, glancing in the direction of Sarah's stifled chuckles.

Aaron's pulse raced. How in the heck his five year old knew this much was beyond him. He continued breaking eggs in the skillet and handing Lily the shells to drop in the garbage, both used to the routine.

"Coffee." Gabe entered the kitchen, going straight for the pot that stayed hot most all day. He opened the cabinet and grabbed a mug, pouring it full and taking a long sip, hot and black.

"Morning." Aaron tossed his brother a glance, while he continued laying strips of bacon in another skillet.

Gabe groaned.

"That bad huh?" He chuckled as it had been after two in the morning before his brother had returned from Helena.

"Just hanging out with the boys. Morning, Ma." Gabe plunked down at the table and glanced at Lily. "Morning cutie?"

"I get to stir the eggs." Lily held up her wooden spoon in the air and then skirted it around the pan of eggs.

"Morning, Gabriel," Sarah answered, putting the broom away and grabbing a rag.

"Amos up?" Gabe scratched his shaggy dark hair and took another sip of coffee.

"He's showering, says he feels good today." Sarah reached for her coffee mug, sipping as she ran the rag along the counter.

Aaron's gut clenched, worrying of his father becoming more of a daily chore. He exchanged glances with his brother. They all worried as Amos' health had declined the last year. He now required oxygen most all the time.

"You put the bread in the toaster. Two for me and Gabe and one for you, Sarah, and Amos. How many is that?" He waited as Lily counted on her fingers.

"Seven." His daughter went about the task with a giant smile.

"Good girl." Aaron remained thankful the conversation had changed from the nurse.

"You going to the set today?" Gabe asked, rubbing his face.

"I checked on the horses yesterday evening. Lily and I can ride out later today," Aaron answered, adding more bacon to the pan, the sizzle making him take a step over to shield Lily.

Gabe nodded. "Uh-huh."

He eyed his brother catching his tone.

"I was out on fifteen yesterday, and I saw some nurse babe on the back of your bike, hanging on tightly." His brother folded his arms and gave him a knowing smirk.

Aaron glared at him. Hell, the fun in having brothers! "And what business of it would be yours?"

Gabe held his hands up. "It's all good."

He enlightened his nosy brother anyway. "She had to ride in with Masters when he took that spill and her SUV was still on the set, remember?"

"Yep." Gabe picked up the paper and began reading.

Aaron turned back to the bacon and eggs. Actually, Jenna had been hanging on tightly and without a doubt he'd liked that part and kissing her had damn near done him in he wanted her so bad. But more than that, he wanted to know her mind, her thoughts, and her dreams. All of it.

"Amos." Sarah turned as Amos made it to the bottom of the stairs.

"I'm fine, Sarah. In fact, I am feeling good this morning." He entered the kitchen with his oxygen tank over his shoulder and the cannula filling his nostrils.

"Well, you shouldn't try the stairs alone. Let one of the boys help you." She rushed behind him to pull out his chair at the table.

"Hi, Papa, I'm cooking the toast and eggs." Lily smiled, working hard on her task as the toastmaster.

"Morning…princess. Morning boys. I am fine to wander the dwelling without a bunch of panic." Amos smiled, talking between breaths.

"Morning, Pop." Gabe glanced up from his paper.

"Breakfast is just about done, Pop." Aaron turned back to the bacon.

"Aaron, you planning on being here today?" his father asked as he adjusted his seat.

"Yep, gotta go to the set later." He glanced over his shoulder.

Amos nodded. "There's a stretch of barbed wire falling away from the fence near the road, thought you might get that today. Don't want the cattle pushing through if they've a mind to it."

Aaron lifted Lily to the floor. "I'll take a look at it

after we eat, looks like rain later in the day." He handed Lily the first plate, filled with scrambled eggs, bacon, and buttered toast. "Take this one to Papa."

"Here ya go, Papa." Lily set the plate on the table, grinning wide and hugging Amos.

"Thank you, Princess." Amos smiled as she walked back for the second plate.

"This one is for Grandma." Lily turned again handing Sarah her breakfast as she sat.

Sarah smiled. "Thank you, ma'am."

Aaron picked up the remaining plates, setting one down before Gabe and then his own next to Lily's. "Come on munchkin, eat up and you can help me mend the fence."

"Wait, blessing." Lily reminded them all as she sat in her booster seat.

"You say it," Sarah encouraged her.

"Bow your head, Uncle Gabe." She inspected everyone at the table for participation.

"Oh." Gabe rolled the paper and leaned forward bowing his head as did Aaron.

"God bless the horses since they aren't home right now and they are on the TV show with the cowboy. Bless Daddy and Gabe and Jeremiah and me and Granny and please bless Papa's breathing. Oh, and bless the nurse. What's her name, Daddy?" She looked up from her prayer, keeping her hands folded.

Aaron wanted to crawl under the table. It didn't help that Gabe pulled the paper back over his face to stifle his laughter and Sarah's lips turned white with her suppression of laugher. *Holy shit, this has turned into a fiasco.*

"Jenna." He spoke her name and didn't look back

up.

"God bless Jenna the nurse and Kittyboy. Amen." Lily smiled as if some great task had been completed and grabbed her fork digging into her eggs. "Kittyboy slept on my bed last night. He knows I'm his mother."

"You do a good job keeping him fed," Sarah praised her. "Such a big girl taking care of him on your own."

Aaron looked at his plate, not that he had an appetite now, but Amos picked up the conversation changing the subject. He was used to Lily praying for all the animals especially the old cat, but that his daughter had done the same for Jenna caught him off guard.

"Gabe, I read there were…some jobs to bid on for contractors near Sun Prairie." Amos studied his middle son.

"Yea, Tucker's headed out there tomorrow. I've gotta be on the set with my brother and his…nurse friend." Gabe bit his bottom lip to stifle his laughter, and Aaron gave him a swift kick to the shin under the table.

"Tucker bids too low…have him boost it a bit this time," Amos warned and scooped his eggs.

"Tuck does all right." Gabe rubbed his shin, still grinning.

Aaron went back to his food. Tucker was co-owner of Sun River Construction along with Gabe, the two men military buddies. The business was nearing five years old and had become quite successful.

"So a nurse," Amos said sipping his coffee with shaky hands, glancing Aaron's way.

Aaron looked at his father, dropping his fork in

defeat. *Really?*

"That's a respectable job. You boys all need to find a good woman and settle down. Aaron, you should…bring her out here to meet us. I could fill her in on my medical history." Amos gave the hint of a smile.

"You could bring her out here on your bike." Gabe let go of a belting round of laughter but stopped with a heated look from Sarah.

"Enough is enough. We're friends, and if it goes any further, I won't need to keep you all updated as it seems my brothers are on the gossip chain, though I was thinking of bringing her here to meet everyone." Aaron got up heading out to the porch. It wasn't that he couldn't share the idea of Jenna, but right now he was already missing her so bad he could taste it and he knew better—he was falling hard. Hell, he'd already fallen.

"I'm kidding," Gabe yelled after him.

Out on the porch he took a deep breath and sat. He might have expected all the teasing, but he hadn't expected Lily's innocent part in it right at the breakfast table. This relationship thing was going to be more difficult than he thought but he still wasn't sure of anything at this point.

"This must be some woman to have caught your attention." Sarah came out to the porch and sat down in the porch swing, pulling her robe tighter.

He looked at her and nodded. He should have known to escape to the barn. "Yep."

"Aaron, everyone is happy for you. Gabe is just being Gabe, but I think Amos would like nothing more than to see you find someone. Me too." She rocked the swing as she talked.

"He is worse every day, isn't he?" He changed the subject, maybe it was his father's condition.

"You know like I do he has good and bad days." She took a deep breath and turned the conversation back. "So her name is Jenna?"

He nodded but talking about his love life with his mother wasn't on his list of priorities.

"You know it's all right to let her in, Aaron. Get to know her. Have fun." Sarah always had an uncanny way of making things seem like they would be fine.

"I've got Lily to think about." He leaned back in the chair, running his hand through his dark hair.

"I can understand you needing to be careful about Lily, but one day Lily will be grown, Aaron." Sarah continued. "You haven't dated more than a few times since Pamela left. You deserve to be happy."

He finally nodded. "It's not Pamela."

Sarah took a deep breath. "It's not Lily either is it? It's Aaron. I was so much younger than your father when we married. My sisters warned me one day I would still be a young woman when he was an old man. I suppose I could have listened and not had the wonderful life I've had with your father. We did everything we wanted to do, including making you boys our family. I don't sit and wait on Amos to leave us. If I did, I would miss out on today. You and this nurse have now as well…and life is short, Aaron, and this is the first woman I've heard you mention in a long time. She must really be something special."

He nodded. "She's uhmm, pretty incredible."

Sarah smiled as she got up. "Then I suggest you ignore your brothers and get on with it."

He glanced out across the ranch, thinking Sarah

always had a way of finding the right things to say to keep him in perspective. She got up to go inside and as she passed by, he grabbed her hand and squeezed. "Thanks, Mom."

Chapter Eight

Aaron pulled his motorcycle to a stop near the camper. Gabe's truck was parked outside the barn and a light burned inside. He'd read the upcoming script. The crew would be building a scaffolding to hold a long ramp that would allow Maxus to jump from one side of the river to the other in spite of the differences in height of the banks. It seemed *The Bounty Hunter* was to escape outlaws by jumping his horse from an old west bridge and land at the water on the opposite shore.

The ramp sketching and measurements looked about right, and he'd spent the last half hour walking along the far side of the river, while Lily played by the shore. Maxus could make the distance, but he'd have to have time to get used to this specific ramp. He'd jumped from ramps before but Maxus could be temperamental and it would take a few weeks of training to get the ornery horse used to the idea. Still the angle and rise of the ramp wasn't that much except for the drop off prior to the water's edge. Landing in the water was one thing, but hitting the ground was a huge problem if a jump like this didn't go well.

He got off his bike and turned to Lily who still sat in her booster seat on the back. She was all bundled in her winter suit to the point she couldn't move, but her rosy cheeked smile gave him his own. She loved to ride and had been doing so since she was a few weeks old, bundled in a chest carrier when she was tiny and never seemingly bothered by the roar of the engine.

"Can I see Charger and Scout? They miss me." She pushed the light brown curls from her face, as he helped remove her child-sized helmet.

"Yep, Gabe's in the barn. I'll be there in a minute." He kissed her icy forehead and sent her on her way, grabbing her backpack full of dolls and who knew what else, intending to toss it in the camper.

"I love your horsey back pack." Jenna moseyed closer, tugging her coat tighter.

He set the helmets and backpack inside the camper and turned back to her. "Well, if you're a good little girl you might get to play with my dolls."

He walked closer, hesitated, waiting on her nod, and then kissed her softly, touching her hair. God, he loved her hair, the soft thickness of the bouncing curls. Out of scrubs she was breathtaking, in spite of the heavy coat. She had curves in all the right places, and it didn't take him long to feel all too physical about that each time he saw her.

"Does Lily come with you a lot?" she asked, glancing toward the barn.

"She was missing the horses. Scout and Charger are her best friends I'm afraid. She's inside, come on." He nodded toward the barn, taking her by the hand. No sense in waiting until she could visit the ranch to meet his daughter with Lily right here and besides, Jenna's presence in his life was no longer any big secret it seemed.

Inside they found Lily on Scout's back in the stall and Gabe watering all the horses, who were moving out of their stalls to head outside to the corral.

"Good morning." Gabe's brows lifted with his nod to Jenna.

"Morning, brother," he answered, hoping Gabe would keep his mouth shut and for that matter, Lily too.

"Hello," Jenna answered.

He turned toward Lily, pulling Jenna along with him and ignoring his brother's knowing gaze.

"Daddy, Scout missed me." Lily spoke to him but held Jenna in her sights.

"I'm sure he did miss you. Lily, this is Jenna." He waited, unsure of her reaction.

"Do you like horses?" Lily leaned across Scout protectively, eyeing Jenna as she walked closer.

"I like them very much. They are lucky to have you taking such good care of them." Jenna traced a hand across Scout's large neck.

"You can ride with us one day." Lily studied her then for a long moment. "Are you a nurse?"

Aaron sucked in a breath. This kid was smart, and there was no telling what might come out of her mouth next.

"I'd enjoy riding with you. Yep, I'm a nurse." Jenna played along.

Gabe broke the awkward silence, tugging Lily from Scout and handing her over the stall to Aaron. "Time for you to get down, I gotta get Scout out to the corral."

Gabe urged the horse toward the opening. "They've been working on the ramp since early morning. It looks like the plans you drew up, footage and all."

Aaron nodded. "They said they would have it done by this afternoon. We can check later this morning."

"I took a look at the landing area; it's about ten feet, so that jump will be fine if Maxus can get over being up so high." His brother's concern was evident as his own.

"I'll see about having the crew help with putting down dirt and clear the area of rocks. He'll do it with some practice, but I won't be able to rush him, though filming that scene's a ways off," he added.

"I don't think I need to remind you Maxus is unpredictable," Gabe warned.

"He can do it." And he could. Maxus was smart. It didn't take him much to learn, and he'd made further jumps.

"I keep hearing about the jump, for episode five?" Jenna walked over to them, following Lily who scampered around the barn.

He nodded. "The episode calls for the bounty hunter to jump off the side of a bridge over the river with the horse and keep riding. We'll do it on the scaffolding to mimic the bridge, jumping Maxus across about ten feet to level ground. He just needs to get used to the ramp."

Jenna's face held a bit of concern. "Do horses do that?"

"Maxus does tricks and plays on T.V." Lily hugged herself to Aaron's side, glancing up at Jenna.

He let Lily finish then answered. "Maxus jumps like a champ, even from a ramp, but this really isn't far at ten feet across or so."

"So there isn't really another way?" Jenna questioned.

"We got this." He gave her a smile and changed the subject. "I'm taking the munchkin here for some breakfast in the mess tent, you hungry?"

Jenna nodded with a smile.

"You can sit by me." Lilly grabbed Jenna's hand leading the way.

Jenna smiled. "Of course, I bet they have pancakes this morning. I could smell them when I got here earlier."

"Me and Daddy love pancakes," Lily added, loud with excitement.

Aaron walked behind them, as they both chatted, instant friends. Something about that felt good, very good and the bit of nerves he'd had with the introduction faded.

As they entered the catering tent, the smell of pancakes and sausage scored through the air, mingling with the musty odor of wet earth, the latest rains having left things around them damp.

"So pancakes for all of us?" He grabbed a tray and got in line behind Lily and Jenna.

"With lots of syrup," Lily added, standing on her toes to see the food in tin containers all down the buffet line.

"Lots of syrup on mine, too." Jenna smiled as he handed her a tray.

"I'm onto that sweet tooth of yours," he whispered. "And, of course, coffee with all the goods."

"Well, it *is* pancakes," she defended, setting her tray on the line and picking up a plate of cakes and helping Lily with hers.

"Seems I remember someone didn't eat until dessert arrived the other night." He reminded her of the night they'd shared dinner. She'd pushed her food around on her plate until the chocolate cheesecake arrived. Then she'd pretty much devoured that, all but the one bite he'd taken of it.

"Well, that was dark chocolate drizzled chocolate cheesecake and women need chocolate," she added, her amber eyes sparkling.

"A proven medical fact huh?" He grabbed a platter of pancakes teasing her.

Jenna smiled. "Everyone knows that dark chocolate is heart healthy."

"Uh-huh." Aaron gave her a wry look, thinking of a few places he might drizzle a bit of dark chocolate. He shook his head. That would take a bit of time he supposed.

"Good morning, Lily pie." Sally came from around the counter scooping up Lily for a hug. "Oh my, you are getting so big."

"Daddy says I better stop growing up so fast." She smiled as Sally set her back to the ground where she grabbed the tongs struggling to add sausage to her plate.

"I think he's right." Sally assisted.

"Good morning." Jenna greeted Sally with a smile.

"Morning and how was your shift yesterday?" Sally asked.

"Fine, just busy," Jenna answered as she turned to head to one of the folding tables under the large tent.

Aaron met gazes with Sally who lifted a single brow in knowing. Why couldn't women let things go? It wasn't enough he'd endured the narrow escape from the barn.

"I see they are working on the ramp thing. Jeremiah says Maxus will be fine with it, but it looks so high." Sally made small talk though he wondered of the fact she and his brother were talking or at least must have been at some point.

"Ahh, Maxus can do it." He shrugged off her concern as he had Gabe's and Jenna's inside the barn. It seemed to him everyone worried for no reason. Maxus had done further and higher jumps but each jump was new. He'd raised both Maxus and Thor since yearlings, and they were both good at following commands.

"Oh, you stunt men never worry, but it scares the heck out of me. Is Jeremiah coming in today?" Sally asked as she began cutting up Lily's sausage.

"Working at the station." He eyed her with interest. "Why would you ask?"

"Oh, well. No reason, gotta get back to work." She escaped, and he let out a chuckle.

"So Sally and Jeremiah?" Jenna titled her head in question.

He shrugged. "They have this on again, off again kind of thing, not sure."

"Then you weren't being nice." Jenna gave him a grin and a soft elbow to the ribs.

"Sally flusters so easily. It's fun." He smiled at the fact she'd noticed.

"Jeremiah gives her kisses when no one is looking. Gabe says he likes Asian babes." Lily took a bite of her pancakes, dancing in her chair as she chewed. "Are you gonna kiss Jenna, Daddy?"

He set his plate on the table. It was bound to happen sooner or later. This kid had a handful of surprises with a big mouth for a five-year-old. He wanted to cringe but looked at Jenna. "Yep, probably. Eat. I think your uncles are educating you a bit too fast these days." When he met glances with Jenna again, her cheeks were pink but she held his gaze. Those amber eyes were worth every bit of his discomfort and hers.

"Hey, Aaron, we got the ramp up, needs some reinforcements, wanted you to come and take a look to make sure on the angle before we sturdy things up." Trey Simmons from production walked up, pushing back his baseball cap.

"I thought you guys might not be finished until the afternoon." Aaron stood and shook the man's hand.

Trey nodded, "I've had the men on it for several days now so we could build it the way you and Gabe suggested. Your brother's already there, taking a look, but he's in a shoot-out in a minute."

He needed to see the ramp and tossed his napkin down, glancing at his uneaten plate of breakfast.

"Lily and I can go to the medical tent for a little while and put band-aids on all her dollies, does that sound like fun?" Jenna offered, getting a squeal out of Lily whose mouth was full of pancakes.

"Are you sure?" he questioned.

"It's fine, come find us when you are done. We'll finish eating, grab our *Horsie* backpack and head that way." Jenna glanced from him to Lily, who remained all smiles.

Aaron forced himself to look at Lily. "Mind your manners and you stay with Jenna until I come to get you." He kissed the top of her head.

"Okay, Daddy." Lily dipped her sausage in the remaining syrup on her plate and stuffed it into her mouth.

"Thanks." He touched Jenna's shoulder and grabbed a pancake, rolling it around a sausage and left the tent on a trot.

Moments later, he was eyeing the ramp with Trey.

"If this meets your standards, we'll have it moved out on the set by the river, near the bridge for your horse to get used to it."

"You used the wood I suggested and the steel bolts and screws? Did you reinforce the base?" He wanted to make sure no corners were cut. He shook various parts of the ramp's lower stands, finding them sturdy.

"The best wood we could find and real steel. If anything needs to be changed, we have permission to do it. Leland wants to keep you guys happy." Trey offered, shoving his hands into his jeans pockets.

Aaron glanced at Gabe who stood beside them dressed as an Indian, wearing braids and feathers in his hair. "What ya think, Tonto?"

His brother smirked, folding his arms and slinging the braids from off his shoulders as if they were irritating. "It's solid, put in those extra flat boards at the base and there won't be much give. This long hair stuff is overrated."

"There's strength in hair like Samson." Aaron bent to his knees looking at the base of the ramp and running his hand along the edges. Smooth and sanded, crafted well.

"Samson, my ass." Gabe studied the fittings, beside him.

He chuckled. Neither of his brothers had ever worn their hair as long as he had. His own long hair had started out as rebellion when Amos took him and his brothers for a haircut years ago. He'd refused, trying to get a rise out of his new father, who let the issue ride, much to his annoyance. He'd worn it longer through school and college, cutting it when he'd gotten his first job, the one he'd left several years later preferring to run the ranch and work odd jobs instead, especially with his father's ailing health. It mattered little except where steady income was concerned. He'd never missed wearing a tie and clocking in and out for someone else.

"How about adding supports here." He pointed to areas along the base.

"Like I told you, solid. I've walked it a few times, trying to check every bolt myself. We'll take care of it." Trey waited.

"It's sturdy." Aaron moved up the ramp followed by Gabe, both looking at every fitting, tracing hands along the wood, pulling and pushing and shaking the ramp, but it gave little even with their combined weights and harsh efforts.

"Did you double the supports at the top?" Gabe leaned back over the railing yelling down to Trey.

"Yep, and we added more support beams to each end and the middle. It matches the bridge close enough to keep Leland from blowing a gasket." Trey kicked at the dirt and glanced back up at them.

Gabe laughed. "Wouldn't bank on that."

Aaron gave his brother a sarcastic smirk. Those who fell for a television show or movie often watched it enough to find mishaps people behind the lens and directing hadn't seen. Regardless, Gabe was right. Horace would find the differences as simple as a glance through the camera and playbacks. The ramp had to look exactly like the bridge or Leland wouldn't complete the shoot.

"It looks good. You guys can get it down to the river in place. I've got heavy cross ties outside the barn you can move down to add weight to the base." Aaron climbed back down the ramp and jumped to the ground before hitting the end.

"We'll get 'em and put it all together so you can practice the horse by the afternoon," Trey offered.

"That'll work." Aaron nodded, as Trey headed out talking on his radio.

"What'd you do with Lily?" Gabe jumped to the ground beside him, the fringe on his shirt and pants snapping back in place.

"She's with Jenna." He said, avoiding his brother's gaze.

Gabe grinned. "Uh-huh."

"What's that mean?" He growled.

"It means you must be hot." Gabe burst out laughing and grabbed Charger's reins and headed off to the set.

"You'd be wise to pipe it down Tonto, you and Jer are teaching Lily a little too much these days," Aaron yelled after him. Who was he kidding? Even if he hadn't admitted it to himself, his brothers and everyone else were onto his interest in Jenna. He followed the small trail behind the old west town to the medical tent, shaking his head.

Entering, he found Jenna sifting through a small box of supplies and Lily playing with her dolls on the small cot in the corner. All of them were covered in various sizes of band-aids and wraps.

"This must be the new hospital in town." He smiled walking closer to where his daughter played.

"Daddy, Jenna knows how to play doctor really good. And she has a baby boy at home named Mason." Lily turned back to her work.

Aaron met Jenna's gaze with a smile. So they were

sharing secrets.

"We've had a great time; she's really no trouble at all," Jenna added handing Lily a small sack. "Here are some things you can take home in case these sweet dolls need more bandages."

Lily took the bag, grinning and turning back to her play.

"Hey, what ya say?" Aaron scolded.

"Thank you." Lily never turned back around.

"So how is the ramp?" Jenna folded her arms walking closer.

He shrugged. "Good. They'll have it in place by afternoon, for a little beginning practice with Maxus."

"Why do I feel like this is a bigger deal than you are making it?" she asked sitting on the table, her legs dangling.

"All the stunts can be a big deal if we aren't careful." He walked closer, taking a peek to see that Lily was still playing, chattering with her dolls. He leaned in closer when Jenna smiled and placed his lips to hers, settling between her knees with a growl. Well, that wasn't going slow was it? "She says you are really good a playing doctor."

Jenna pushed him back and whispered, "Not the time or place. There were a lot of questions after you left us at breakfast about our kisses."

He nodded. "Guess the word's out."

To his surprise she grabbed the front of his jacket and tugged him in for another whisper. "I told her we were just friends."

"Good answer." He kissed her again but Jenna pulled back, clearing her throat with a glance behind them.

He turned, stepping away from her.

"Daddy, Jenna is the doctor; she needs to come to the hospital, right away." Lily turned back toward the cot, as if their kiss or at least close proximity had been nothing.

He took a deep breath and let it out thought a puff of cheeks.

"The doctor is needed." Jenna hopped up, pushing him out of the way with a grin. "Why don't you let her play in here for a while? She's fine. If I get a call I'll take her with me." Jenna walked toward the back of the tent.

Aaron gave a little growl, she could go play doctor, but he was in need of a cold shower. "I'll be back a little later. I've got my cell."

Jenna grabbed her phone out of her pocket. "Wait; call mine so I will have it in my phone."

Aaron snatched the phone from her hand as he got to her. "I'll put it in for you."

"Hey." Jenna tried to grab the phone back but he turned from her pushing buttons, keeping it higher than she could see, laughing.

After a minute he handed it back to her. "I'll text you."

"All right, then." She grabbed the phone and turned back to Lily.

He left the tent heading back toward the barn. He did have plenty to do, and it was always more challenging with Lily. He took a deep breath. Those two kisses had nowhere been enough, and if he had his way, there would be no going slow at all with getting to know Jenna Wilder up close and personal and soon.

Chapter Nine

Jenna sat on the cot listening to the chest of the doll Lily was holding. She smiled, having a great time, thinking it had been a long time since she'd played dolls—though she was good at playing with trucks and balls with Mason. She'd left her sleeping son with Ms. Lucy for the eight hours on the set, but there was no doubt he'd enjoy playing with Lily if they ever had that chance.

She studied Lily as she played. She had long curly brown hair and large green eyes like Aarons. She had chuckled softly when Lily referred to one of her dolls as *Munchkin* as her father called her. They'd been in the tent playing most of the day, leaving to grab sandwiches from the catering tent for lunch and she was surprised Lily hadn't asked once of her father.

It was on the walk back from the catering tent she had seen Aaron on Maxus in the distance, riding the horse up the ramp and back down a few times and then racing off on gallop away from the set. He was so handsome, as if he belonged on horses, his hair blowing in the wind like the horse's mane. She'd held that picture of him in her mind thinking she could use the description of him as one of her old west cowboys. She had wanted to stop and watch him, but Lily had been bouncing along toward the medical tent ahead of her, moving so like her father it was almost as breathtaking.

Lily handed her a doll. "She is here for her check up. Does your little boy like to play hospital?"

"He's only one so not yet but maybe when he is a little bigger." Jenna handed the doll back to Lily who laughed and scampered back to play. She had so many actions and mannerisms like Aaron, she stopped to watch. Her brown curling hair was much like Aaron and her expressions gave no doubts at her belonging to Aaron. She was just precious, smart, and feisty.

Jenna's phone vibrated, and she lifted it from her pocket, sliding her thumb across the screen and smiling. The text was from '*Stuntman*' and it read '*Tonight, dinner my place?*'

She began texting back, unable to hold back a grin.

'*Dolly hospital busy but will wind things down and join you.*'

She put the phone back in her pocket. "Nurse Decker, your father says it is time for dinner. Want me to help you get everything ready to head back to the camper?"

"Okay, but I have to put my bag of band-aids in my backpack." Lily began gathering all her dolls and the small sack of bandages and shoving them in her backpack, dolls crammed in between bandages.

"Let me help." Jenna assisted her tiny hand to zip the overstuffed bag, their hands touching. Lily was such a sweet child, and Aaron had done so well with her.

"I'm going home with Gabe. He's taking me for pie at the diner with Grandpa Amos," she explained as Jenna helped her with the backpack.

"That sounds like so much fun," Jenna answered, raising her voice an octave.

"We get chocolate pie from there, and Uncle Gabe

says it is better than sex." Lily said it as if it were nothing at all.

"Well, uh, that must be some kind of pie." It was evident Lily had been raised around single grown men and it was rubbing off, though her innocence made it hysterical. She stifled her giggle.

"Yep." Lily pulled her ahead toward the barn as Aaron emerged, the front of his shirt and jeans, wet and soapy.

"Hi Daddy, is Uncle Gabe back yet?" Lily handed her backpack to him.

"Yeah, he's taking a shower in the camper. Apparently, the Indians got chased through the mud. I finished washing Scout and Charger who were not too happy about it. They were a mess. Guess I am too." He shivered, walking to toss Lily's backpack into Gabe's truck.

"We had fun, Daddy." Lily danced around the small picnic table outside the camper.

"That's good, Munchkin." Aaron grabbed a towel and brushed his jeans off, looking at Jenna. "So, simple supper in my lovely camper?"

"Sounds nice." She wondered at being alone in his camper with him. She'd thought a lot about tossing her fears to the wind and letting what was happening between her and Aaron just happen. Wasn't that all right? Didn't she deserve to be happy? These days there didn't have to be promises for the future to simply enjoy each other's company, right?

Gabe exited the camper, walking to toss his bag into the truck. "Whew, hard playing an Indian on a horse all day. I'm beat."

"Uncle Gabe, did the cowboys get you muddy?"

Lily asked walking closer.

"Yep, are you ready to head for home?" Gabe hopped into the seat of his truck, turning over the engine.

"Yep, but I'll miss you, Daddy." Lily ran to hug Aaron who scooped her up in a bear hug, swinging her around.

"I'll be home tomorrow night to tuck you in, I promise." Aaron kissed her cheek and forehead multiple times.

"Okay." She wiggled out of her father's arms and ran for Gabe's truck. "We are getting pie at the diner."

"Yep, supper first and then pie." Gabe rubbed his belly.

"Best behavior, Lily." Aaron followed her to the passenger side of the truck.

"All right." She climbed in, and Aaron buckled her into her car seat. "I love you like roses."

"I love you like horses." Lily giggled. "Bye, Jenna."

"Bye Lily, I sure enjoyed our day together." Jenna walked closer, glad she hadn't been needed anywhere on the set, though she had items in the schedule for the next day.

Lily waved as his brother backed the truck up. "I love you, Daddy," she yelled again from the half rolled up window as Gabe drove them away from the set.

Aaron watched until the truck had disappeared and then turned back to Jenna. He stepped closer and shook his head looking at her.

"Good-night is hard I'm sure." She smiled.

"It is what it is, but I have to hang out here tonight." He looked back at the camper and turned to her. "Are you hungry?"

She shrugged. "A little."

"I need a shower first." He led the way inside the fifth-wheel camper.

She stepped inside, it having been years since she'd been in any kind of camper. It was fairly roomy inside and to her surprise organized and clean. A lot of the crew and even some of the cast had trailers and campers parked on the other end of the set. Aaron's camper was the one near the barn and she imagined others didn't want to be too close to the animals.

The camper was really like a home. The living area they had stepped into had push out walls making it a bit more spacious and to the left was a kitchen with all the modern conveniences. Thick dark brown carpet covered the floor except for the tan linoleum in the kitchen. It even smelled fresh inside.

"This is nice." She spoke as Aaron closed the door behind them.

"Yea, Gabe and I got this at a steal, and he, Jeremiah and I refurbished the whole thing ourselves." He walked ahead of her pointing. "Console with all the hook ups, compliments of Gabe who's an internet junkie. Kitchen with all the fixings, and television, music and books." He pointed to a nearby book shelf, loaded with a variety of novels.

So he read. She loved it when a man read books. Funny, Aaron surprised her in so many ways. On the outside some kind of longhaired biker man and on the inside, a keen mind and tender heart.

"I had no idea you men were living in such luxury out here." Jenna traced her thumb along the books on the shelf.

Aaron kicked out of his boots, leaving them at the door. "It's home away from home. I'm gonna get a shower. You can read or turn on the television. I won't be but a minute."

"I'll be fine." She turned back to him, having been eyeing the books, and nearly lost her breath. He was pulling his shirt off, and she caught herself admiring his physique once again. He carried a six pack of muscles to meet a fine scattering of dark hair across his chest. Seeing him as a nurse when he'd taken the water spill was one thing but seeing him now made it more personal. She turned back to the books and moments later the water in the shower was running, giving her racing heart a break.

She turned around and eyed the inside of the camper again. She'd never stayed in a camper except as a teenager when she went camping with some friends. It was still hard to believe that three single men kept the place so nice. There were no plates lying around, no clothing on the floor, a small basket of what were probably Lily's toys sat in the corner as the only thing that seemed out of place.

"You can help yourself to a beer or juice if you like." Aaron called from the shower. Jenna folded her arms, the image of him showering crossing her mind. She pushed her thoughts away, heat flowing to her center.

"Sure." She walked toward the refrigerator trying to let go of her bit of nerves. She'd kept telling herself she deserved a chance, and it was all right to let someone care for her again. And it was, wasn't it? She opened the door and took out two beers, struggling to twist the caps on both. She took a sip of hers and set them both on the small kitchen table.

Thinking of making herself useful, she opened the cabinets and found plates and began setting the table, unsure what he had in mind for dinner. The shower stopped, sending an image of Aaron naked to the forefront of her mind once more. She took a much needed deep breath and glanced out the small kitchen window, to free her mind of the mental picture that made her pulse race. Most of the set was winding down with dusk was setting in and a few of the crew were walking about with equipment.

"What's so interesting?" Aaron entered running a brush through his long, wet hair and wearing jeans—unbuttoned jeans. *Oh God he is so sexy, I have to be dreaming.*

He yanked a dark T-shirt from his shoulder and began pulling it over his head.

She found her voice with some effort. "Just looking. I set the table but wasn't sure how I could help with the meal."

"Won't take but a minute." He tossed the brush to the bedroom.

"I opened a beer for you. I hope that's all right." She nodded toward the table.

"It's kind of a staple around here for Gabe and me, at least some evenings after a hard day on the set, though Jeremiah doesn't drink." He lifted the light beer and took a sip.

"Because of his work? That's usually my issue." She took a sip of her own and let the bubbles ride her tongue and swallowed.

He shook his head. "No, his parents were alcoholics, and he remembers too much. You'll see him

112

sip on one all night but never really drink it. I guess it is easier not to answer the questions."

"Sorry, I didn't mean to—"

Aaron interrupted. "It's fine. Nothing's really a secret with any of us. I was always in foster care, don't know anything about my parents. Don't remember anything. Gabe remembers his mother from what he says and lots of parties and drugs. He was pretty young as well."

"That's such a hard life you all had until you found your parents." She added hoping that was the right way to say it. "I miss my parents most all the time. Mom died with cancer too young. And my dad died a few years ago. They had me at a much older age and sometimes I feel cheated, but I had a wonderful childhood."

"I'm sure that's hard." He turned to open the refrigerator to grab what he needed. "I sometimes wonder how we would've ended up without Amos and Sarah. Do you eat Sushi, smoked salmon?"

"That's fine." She sat at one of the chairs at the table and watched as her readied what he needed. She loved sushi, but she hadn't expected him to make it right before her. *Amazing. Now she was certainly dreaming.*

"So you call your parents by their first names?" She was curious if nothing else.

He placed the wooden plate and spread cold sticky rice across it, nodding. She looked on as he added the salmon and cucumber slices along with a bit of cream cheese and avocado to the roll. "When Amos and Sarah took us in, it was some time before I referred to them as my parents. I wasn't sure that it wasn't just another foster home for a while. Jeremiah was young, and it came natural for him to call them Mom and Dad right away, but Gabe and I were older. Amos and Sarah kind of stuck. I call Amos *Pop* and Sarah *Mom* sometimes."

She listened, surprised at his disclosure, respecting that he was telling her part of his life that might have been difficult. He didn't hesitate with his words at all but seemed to be thinking, not looking at her as he prepared yet another roll.

"I kept calling them Amos and Sarah, but it wasn't ever an issue. They're great. Really great, but until Lily came along I didn't realize the impact of being called *Daddy*." He sipped his beer and then sliced and put the sushi rolls on each of their plates.

"Well, she is a pretty amazing little girl," she added. "She is so much like you. I think I just kept staring."

"Thanks again for today. Sarah had to take Amos in for his check up, and it's easier without Lily along." He handed her chop sticks and poured soy sauce over slices of ginger into a small dish he sat between them.

"So how is your father doing?"

He picked up a slice of the sushi, dunked it in the mixture and leaned forward. "I need to call and check on him but he's not getting any better." He raised the chopsticks toward her, offering her the first bite along with a tender smile.

Jenna's heart raced, being fed by him. She leaned forward, and he placed it in her mouth.

He chuckled as she grabbed her napkin and closed her mouth chewing. She wasn't sure whether she should be embarrassed or ask for another, given his grin. The sushi was actually amazing the salmon rich and as fresh as the vegetables.

She sipped her beer to wash it down. "That's really good. Who knew cowboys ate sushi."

He took his own bite, chewing and swallowing hard. "Stuntman."

She gave into a small laugh. "Yes, I have that on my phone."

"Well, you see. There's lots of cowboys out there but few stuntmen, and it drives the ladies wild." He raised his eyebrows, and his green eyes sparkled with the lights of the camper.

"Is that right?" She met his gaze in match.

"Yep, makes them all but swoon, like those friends of yours at the hospital." He took another bite of Sushi and sipped his beer.

"My friend's think you are the hells angel type," she kidded.

He laughed. "I'd tell you I'm sorry, but not a chance. I like kissing. A lot."

She smiled though heat rushed her cheeks. That kiss had stolen all the breath her body had held. "No apologies needed, Stuntman."

He took another bite and pushed the plate away, leaning back in his chair to watch her.

Jenna swallowed. "Not hungry?"

"I'm six-one and a bit heavy for what Magnus needs to jump with, cutting back a little to help." He sipped his beer. "For every greasy burger I consume, I try to have a meal like this."

"So the pancakes this morning call for a healthier meal tonight." She nodded.

"Yea, that usually works. Then once we jump, it's steaks on the house." He smiled.

Jenna finished her sushi, leaving one piece which she used her chopsticks to lay on the plate with his leftovers. "I'll help you clean up." She took the plate of remaining sushi to the fridge.

He nodded and was up behind her tossing their plates in the sink and turning on the water to let everything soak. He grabbed their beers, holding them in one hand and took her by her other hand. "Come on, we'll clean up later. I've got a picnic table with a view." He handed her his coat and followed her outside.

She wrapped the coat around her shoulders and followed him to the table where he sat on top and pulled her to sit on the bench between his knees. There was something cozy about sitting there, the warmth of him around her.

"The sun's setting, and the colors are sometimes nice." He pulled her back against him, used both his hands to pull her hair free of his coat collar, making her shiver. Oh, God, but something in her wanted his touch so much.

"So have you had much time to work on the writing you do?" he whispered, massaging her shoulders now.

She had to focus to speak. "I work on it a little each day, some days more than others, but the current story is coming along."

"Tell me about it." His voice showed enthusiasm.

She turned to look at him, surprised as his interest. "Really?"

"Sure." He shrugged.

"Well," she began, "the current thing I'm writing is actually something I first wrote as a novel, but I'm redoing it into a script. You don't want to hear this do you?"

"Go on." He continued with the massage of her shoulders, and she leaned into him wanting to moan, "That feels nice. The story is more of a family saga. There are four brothers, and when I am done, I'll have a story for each I think."

"What time period?" he asked.

"Late eighteen-seventies." *Oh, God, his hands were amazing.*

He nodded, his fingers kneading deeper.

"I have some completed stories but I really like the characters in this one." She focused to take in a deep breath to keep talking. His touch was so much; so much of what she hadn't had in such a long time. Somehow, she wanted to let go, melt into him, and stay in his embrace.

"Oh, maybe I am just rambling but I do work on the stories each day." She stopped, unsure how much more to share and changed the subject. "The lights are nice. Big Sky they say. I suppose I never believed that until I got here. I describe this kind of sky in my stories."

He didn't say anything but continued with his massage, watching the sky with her. It was nice, being with him, so close. She rolled her shoulders and moaned in spite of herself, thinking he could likely do magic of all sorts with those fingers.

After a time she shivered, and she wasn't sure if it was from the cold or him.

"Are you cold, we can go inside?" he offered.

She nodded. Her current chills caused her to pull his jacket fully around her but the slight scent of him lingered on the jacket, and she'd caught herself inhaling deeper. Going inside was dangerous wasn't it especially after the sensations he'd created with the massage? Somehow, she knew it was and while she had at first run from him, overwhelmed by her own emotions, she wasn't going to run any longer. She was worth it and she did deserve to touch and be touched, to love and be loved, and she was going inside because she wanted to...

Chapter Ten

Aaron pulled Jenna closer once they were inside, taking his coat from her and tossing it aside. The closeness was comfortable, though his mind wanted to wander to the things he shouldn't be thinking with them alone. Ah, there would be time for that when she was ready, but he still didn't want to let her go.

"There. Warmer?" He turned up the tiny thermostat to warm to camper, concerned as the night had turned off colder than he'd expected, even if inside him a heavy furnace of passion had built with letting his fingers massage her shoulders and neck. And as much as he didn't need to delve further in caring for her…he was helpless in not wanting her fully.

"I'm fine. It was a very nice day with Lily and now…with you." Her amber eyes held his gaze for a length of time.

Was that an invite? He hesitated. The hell if he was good at reading the thoughts of a woman, but for the life of him he couldn't resist. He kissed her, drawing her closer nibbling her tender lips until she placed her hands against his chest, clinging to his shirt. He pulled her to fit his body and deepened the kiss. She was a great kisser, parting her lips and dancing her tongue along his. It'd probably kill him to have his way with her, but that might be worth dying for. There was no way she could deny the chemistry between them, and the physical attraction for him was evident, straining against his jeans.

He scolded himself as he didn't want to give her another reason to run from him. Time. He'd said he would go slowly but couldn't force himself to let go as their breath tangled. He pulled away. It was best, though difficult. "I'm sorry if I'm not going slow enough…" He took a deep breath, running one hand the length of her dark hair. "God, you are beautiful."

She glanced down and back to him, her cheeks a fine mist of pink. "Then don't…go slow, Aaron."

He tilted a glance at her for a moment and whispered. "This from the same woman who ran not so long ago."

"I needed a bit of time to think, but each moment I spend with you…" She leaned into him, wrapping her arms around the girth of his chest. "I know this is right."

In spite of himself, he took her mouth for his own and let his hands wander the curves of her body, memorizing every inch of her.

Jenna ran her fingers into his hair, and some part of him warned he should send her home without delay. But as their bodies tangled, she wrapped her legs around his hips and hung on as he consumed her neck and shoulders with urgent traces of his lips. He walked into the small bedroom, carrying her, and fell with her onto the top covers of the bed, planting himself between her thighs.

He shifted to his elbows, lifting himself above her gaining some of his sense back with the realness of the moment. He wanted her like he'd wanted no other woman but he had to make sure. "If you're not ready it's okay."

She was already shaking her head, speaking in an urgent whisper. "I want this, Aaron, with you."

He pulled his shirt over his head, looking at her on his bed. He might die this very night, but not before he'd found the ways to please her, the ways that would drive him damn insane once this night was over. He lay back against her. "Tell me what you like, Jenna?" He kissed her cheek, letting his hands roam her body, slowing to feel the curves of her hip and the flatness of her belly.

She whispered and brought her lips to his. "It's been so long."

He began with the buttons of her blouse, taking one at a time as she watched him. With each he kissed her lips, meeting her gaze and going to the next. The beating of his heart paced along with hers. With the last button, he opened each side of her blouse savoring the view of her black lace bra and full breasts.

"What about your son?" He tasted her lips again.

She was breathless as she answered, her chest rising and falling in rapid succession. "Brianna has him. I'm due on the set early tomorrow to help with make-up, and she's off tomorrow."

He kissed her chin. "You're sure?"

"He'll be fine…" She panted against his ear, tugging him closer.

He rested his hand along her ribs under her breast. How was it a woman could be so bold and then shiver when he touched her? It had been a long damn time since he'd had a woman, but tonight would be about her.

"Answer my question. Tell me what you like." He

traced his hand down her arm and brought her hand to his mouth and touched it to his lips, waiting. He wasn't going to rush a second of being with her if it did take all night.

"Only you." She sighed as he rocked his hips, the pressure in his jeans growing.

He rolled to his back and pulled her across him, letting his hands wander to the clasp of her bra and tugging it away from between them. He kissed her again, letting his tongue tease along hers, running both hands down her back and pressing her to his chest as he turned her, still wedged between her legs.

"I knew you were beautiful, but…it's still fine if you aren't sure…" Holy dang, if he had to stop now, he'd need an iceberg to calm things down.

She pulled away from the next kiss, tucking his hair behind his ear. "I want you, Aaron, only you."

He kissed her lips with a slight brush. "Mornings after nights like this are sometimes filled with regrets and as bad as I want this, I don't want you to wake tomorrow thinking it was a mistake, because I sure as hell won't."

"I don't expect anything more than tonight." She shook her head, her fingers sliding through his hair. "I certainly don't expect a trip to the alter because of tonight or other nights like this."

He rocked his hips again, enjoying the sigh that escaped her lips. She was having a hard time speaking when he moved and he damn well liked that. "Darn, I was kind of planning one of those quick Vegas weddings with Elvis doing the ceremony."

"You are impossible." She shuddered as he moved again and sucked in a stifled breath never taking her eyes from his, her mouth partially open as he pressed several more times. He ran a hand into her dark hair, the hardness in his jeans seeking relief. He bent his head to kiss her breasts and drew a nipple into his mouth, rasping his tongue across it.

She tossed her head back, giving him full access to both. She tasted of salt and sweetness all at the same time and she pressed her hips forward against him with each tug of his lips. He switched breasts, fluttering his tongue over the other nipple, enjoying that she moved to meet him. He continued for a long while, rocking back and forth, enjoying the little sounds she made in trying not to make any as he teased and played. And suddenly, her body bowed, as if resisting him and her thighs clamped around his rocking hips.

"That feels so…" She didn't finish speaking her breathless thoughts, but arched fully to meet him, a long sigh escaping her as her short nails dug into his back.

"So. Damn. Sweet." He rocked harder, grinding against her to draw out her pleasure, enjoying he was able to watch, but shocked it had taken so little. Hell, they both still had their jeans on and this was getting real.

She opened her eyes after a long pause, still trembling, and leaving him mystified for the most part. "Oh God, that…was…"

"Downright excellent." He smiled, still lying between her thighs rigid as hell. "There's plenty more where that came from."

He climbed out of bed, lifting her feet to toss her shoes aside and in one swift move he relieved her of her jeans, then returned to take his time with her panties, unwrapping her as if she were fragile. He sucked in a deep breath at the sight of her fully naked on the bed and bent to kiss her, lingering as he ran a hand from her breast to the dark mound of curls. He stood again and shucked his jeans, digging through the nightstand drawer for a condom, cursing under his breath until he landed one. He lay back down beside her thinking he'd have to thank one of his brothers later. "Are you sure?"

She ran a hand into his hair, drawing him to her lips again. "Touch me, Aaron, all of me."

He tore open the condom, fitting it to himself, surprised she reached to help. He groaned, lifting her leg over his hip. He held her gaze as he traced his fingers to her, finding her slick and warm.

She sighed, her body shuddering again.

"You are beautiful, Jenna Wilder." He traced the tiny swollen nub of her pleasure, then sank two fingers inside her, twisting them in her warmth.

Her hips moved in the rhythm he set and when she tightened around his fingers, he withdrew them. Not wanting to wait any longer he pinned her to the bed with one deep thrust, both of them moaning in unison.

"God, Jenna." He held onto her hip for leverage, taking the pace slow at first and sucking back in a breath he'd lost. He closed his eyes fighting for control as he propped on his elbows, sinking deeper.

She traced her hand into his hair and then down his shoulders and to his back, holding him against her as they moved together. Each thrust of his body against hers brought him closer and he upped his pace until she began to sigh with each stroke.

She traced her hands lower, pressing him to her and wrapping her legs around his hips, urging him. He rocked harder, fighting his own body until she shuddered, taking him with her. He slammed himself harder, the echoes of her cries consuming him as he shattered inside her, hanging on for all he was.

The quiet hum of the camper heater was the only sound as he lifted his gaze meeting her sweet amber eyes; no words leaving him. And she clung to him, burying her face in his neck, still breathless as he rolled beside her, tucking her close.

****

Aaron woke with the first hints of sunlight, peeking through the window on the far side of the camper. It only took a second for him to remember Jenna was sleeping beside him. He hesitated to move not wanting to wake her out of fear she would let go of his arm and move her leg from resting across his. Damn she was something to look at, beautiful beyond her physical attributes, given they'd exchanged parts of themselves in making love for the first time.

They were supposed to have taken things slow and there was the possibility he'd blown that even though she'd consented. Still, having her made him want her more and going slow wasn't even an option any longer. He'd known there was something about Jenna the moment he laid eyes on her but now he was all but sure he'd never be the same man again.

She stirred, rolling closer.

He ran his hand down her arm, pulling her to him as she opened her eyes. Meeting her sleepy gaze, he kissed the top her head. "Morning."

She groaned. "What time is it?"

"It's early, before five."

"I slept like a rock. You?" She yawned looking at

him with the hint of a smile, her hair a mess, but somehow still beautiful.

"I slept." And he had, but not all night like her. He's spent a few hours watching her as she'd slumbered. He brushed strands of her dark hair from her face and kissed her wondering if words of love were due. "So, no regrets this morning?"

She shook her head. "None whatsoever, except I'm due in make-up to help at six. Can I shower?"

He nodded toward the small camper bathroom. "It's small but the water's warm if you let it run for a second. You, uh, gonna need any help?"

She smiled and took the sheet with her, leaving him to scramble for the top covers as she smiled. "Later, Stuntman. But…there's an overnight bag in the back of my truck, if you could get it."

He narrowed his gaze. "Always prepared or anticipating a long night in my lovely camper?"

She grinned but didn't answer as she shut the bathroom's tiny door. He shook his head and after a moment of listening to the shower and thinking of her lathering her luscious body, he jumped out of bed with a groan. Maybe he should have told her he loved her, but it was hard to judge when words like that would come best. He was sure he loved her but speaking it would only cause him to fall harder if he hadn't fallen enough already. And too much too soon was bound to cause her to run again, something he couldn't take right now.

He made his way to the tiny kitchen. The least he could do was put on the coffee she loved and get them both something for breakfast. She had make-up, and he needed to check on the animals and look at the schedule as later in the day, all four horses were needed for the filming of a Cavalry scene.

He stepped into his sweatpants and went to the small kitchen, searching in the fridge and deciding on bagels and cream cheese. He set the container on the small table and turned back for the left-over sushi for himself. Grabbing paper plates, he placed two on the table and filled the coffee maker with water and ground coffee beans. He clicked the button and a surge dimmed the lights for a second in the camper. He glanced up, and the lights returned to full. He'd have to have Jeremiah check the camper hook-ups later.

Stepping into his heavy boots at the door, he pulled on his overcoat, grabbing Jenna's keys from the counter. It didn't take long to find her truck near the medical tent and grab her bag, returning to the camper.

Inside he paused back in the kitchen, Jenna talking on her phone. Her voice was soft and from what he could tell content. "Kiss him for me and because I was here early, I can leave by two this afternoon."

He listened as he kicked back out of his boots, a grin crossing his face. She was likely on the phone with Brianna, who had Mason, and her friend was pushing for details. He leaned closer, halting his efforts.

"Stop it! That is totally none of your business, even if you are my best friend. I will see you later." She hung up.

Aaron knocked, even though the small door was open to the bedroom. He shouldn't have eavesdropped but given the confinement of the camper it wasn't like he'd done it on purpose. He handed her bag to her, his jaw nearly hitting the floor at the sight of her.

"Thank you." She was wearing one of the dark

brown towels from the bathroom, and her damp hair was pulled back in a ponytail. His heart raced, and all he wanted was to touch her again.

"Hungry?" he asked, sucking in a narrowed breath.

She walked closer. "Coffee?"

"Gotcha covered." He turned leaving her to dress, thinking if he stayed a moment longer, they'd both be late and while that would be damn worth it…he shook his head.

"Uuuggghhh, sushi for breakfast?" Jenna entered the kitchen, fully dressed much to his disappointment.

He nodded at her plate. "I figured you for bagels and cream cheese."

She sipped the coffee. "I was talking to Brianna, and Mason slept all night. She's taking him with her shopping today. You've got film time this afternoon?"

He looked on as she added the cream cheese to the bottom half of a bagel. "Evidently the Cavalry have come to town so all four horses are needed."

Jenna chewed and then spoke. "I saw another bunch of horse trailers come in yesterday."

He nodded, smiling to himself that she hadn't gotten all weird about their night together. "Extras, just for numbers. Mine are most often for the stunts and jumps, but those are from a local ranch."

She took another bite and stood, sipping from the mug of coffee. "I need to run…some of the Cavalry need made up to have suffered an attack from the local Indians."

Aaron stood. "I'll catch up with you…" The moment held between them, and he struggled for words. "I don't take what happened lightly." He shook his head and tried again. "I'm just not casual

128

about…never brought a woman into the camper until now, and I've never shared Lily with…anyone."

She touched his lips with her finger. "It's the same for me, but I liked being with you, Aaron."

She stepped into his embrace, and he held her close, kissing her hair and speaking again. "I thought, it's coming up on the weekend. Maybe you could come by the ranch. Bring your son and hang out with Lily and me and meet Sarah and Amos. We could go fishing and I can show you my cabin if you want."

She leaned back and met his gaze. "That would be nice."

"The cabin's small and not fully furnished or finished but Lily and I go there some weekends partly to give Sarah a break from her and me. Pack an overnight bag, then…or am I pushing to fast?" He shook his head, thinking that might be a bit much, but he was surprised when she nodded and smiled.

"That sounds nice. Mason would enjoy being outside and playing with Lily." She hurried to sip her coffee and made her way toward the door.

"I can pick you guys up around ten?" he offered, helping her with her coat.

She lifted her bag and shook her head. "How about I find my way there. Text me the address. I'm late."

He stopped at the door with her and kissed her hard and wanting, lingering near her face. "You could, uh…come back here on your lunch break."

"We both have to work Mr. Stuntman, but it was very incredible." She embraced him, then opened the door and tugged away.

She trotted away into the makeshift town which was coming to life with activity. She bounced along but turned back once more to look at him and smiled. He held up a hand and let it fall as she slipped from his sights for the day.

Chapter Eleven

Jenna stepped outside her apartment carrying Mason on one hip and their bags on the other. Turning to check the lock on the door, a small vase of flowers at her feet caught her attention, nearly tripping her.

"What on earth?" she whispered and bent to lift the card, her first thought of Aaron. Would he have left flowers for her? And if so why had the delivery person not knocked at the door.

Struggling to keep the bags across her shoulder, she adjusted Mason on her hip and pulled the card from the envelope, turning it around to read.

"*Cowboy Up!*"

She flipped the card over, confused as it had nothing else written. Shaking her head, she glanced around them. Aaron hadn't done this; he only delivered flowers to her in person. It might have been that Drake Masters was sending one more thank you, but why would he think more was needed?

She glanced at the beautiful yellow buds, tiny roses and shrugged, lifting them and bobbling with the keys to unlock the door. Stepping inside her apartment she set them on the table, adjusted her bags and juggled her son once more and headed to her SUV after locking the door.

"Want to go see horses, baby?" Jenna asked as she tucked Mason into his car seat handing him his stuffed lion. His eyes lit up but not about the horses as much as his little best friend. The lion went where Mason went. She smiled as she gave him his sippy cup he'd just started using now that she'd weaned him from his bottle. He threw his head back to the car seat and chugged on the watered-down apple juice with a toothy grin. She shut the door and got into the driver's seat cranking the engine and heading toward Sun River, butterflies in her belly.

Meeting Aaron's parents made her a bit nervous, but even more, she figured the nerves were that she was anxious to see him. After their intimate night together, she wasn't sure what or how she felt. She hadn't planned on meeting anyone any time soon, but she could still feel his warm breath on her skin and heat of his passionate kisses. And afterward, he'd wrapped his arms around her thought neither of them had spoken words of love. Making love didn't necessarily mean they were obligated, but meeting his parents obviously gave way to the idea of things moving fast.

She'd headed toward Sun River but pushed the plug from the GPS into the lighter socket and waited on it to calculate the address she'd entered earlier. Glancing at the clock it seemed she'd arrive early and slowed her speed as it wasn't that far from Great Falls. It probably wasn't proper to show up ahead of time and with a child in tow.

The GPS instructed her on an upcoming turn and she veered off the main road and so did the vehicle behind her. She adjusted the rearview mirror, watching the black truck unable to see the driver due to the glare. When the truck finally took a right veering a different direction, she inhaled a deep breath. At some point in her life she had to stop looking over her shoulder with fear. *Get it together, Jenna, this is crazy.*

Little by little, the terrain of the small city faded behind her as a dense forest and rocky juts of cliffs filled her vision. It was a beautiful day though the morning news reported it would be into the twenties by dark. No matter, it would be fun having Mason meet Lily and spending time with Aaron.

As the ranch came into view, she glanced into the review mirror at Mason who had fallen asleep. She smiled, hoping she was doing the right thing for him as well. Turning into the long drive, she marveled as the stone and cedar house widened before her. It was beautiful and matched the nearby barn and several out-buildings.

Aaron was there. Waiting on her in the drive, easing her nerves though her pulse raced at the sight of him. He was wearing a flannel shirt, jeans and boots, and his hair was banded. He was so handsome wasn't he, something like those models she'd eyed in GQ Magazine? She rolled down the window and smiled, meeting his gaze.

"So you found us." He pointed for her to pull near the fence by the barn and followed.

She put the engine into park, unbuckled, and took a deep breath before stepping out of the SUV. "Is this okay?"

"That's fine, we kind of park anywhere." He took her hand and leaned closer kissing her cheek. "I've missed you."

"Me too." She nuzzled into him, inhaling the deep scent of Aaron and in spite of it all, she relaxed. "And I have someone you should meet though he fell asleep."

He stepped to the back door of her truck and glanced at her son as she lifted Mason from his seat and propped him across her shoulder. "He'll be excited to see the animals."

"He's a handsome guy." He touched the baby's dark hair, something inside her warming at the gesture.

"You think your parents are ready for us?" she asked, glancing at the house a little overwhelmed at the idea.

He grabbed Mason's diaper bag. "Take a deep breath, you'll be fine."

She remembered the flowers. "Aaron, did you…flowers were outside the apartment this morning…"

"Not me." He shrugged, seemingly unconcerned. "I only give those in person."

"Well, maybe they were from Drake Masters, letting me know he was better, as the card read *Cowboy Up*."

"You must have made quite an impression on him." He kidded with a smile, though knowing he hadn't been responsible for the roses left her a bit on edge.

"Jenna!" Lily flew out the front door and down the porch stairs, hugging her around the hips.

"Hi you!" Jenna tousled her bouncing curls, reminded how much she looked so like Aaron.

"That's your baby? You have to come and see my room. My dollies are all wrapped up in bandages, and they are sick and my teddy bear too." Lily's bright eyes were full of life as she chattered along.

"Lily, tell ya what, munchkin. Why don't we let Jenna meet Grandma and Grandpa first and then after dinner we're gonna head off to the cabin and you and Mason can play all afternoon." Aaron nodded toward the house. "I heard Grandma say she needed help making brownies just before I came out here."

"Jenna, you can help too, come on." Lily ran ahead, yelling for Sarah as she got inside the house.

"So easily distracted." Jenna adjusted Mason on her shoulder, following Aaron to the porch.

"It takes us all to keep her busy." He chuckled. "She's a handful sometimes."

"She's precious and the house is lovely and this land, really beautiful." She glanced around them as they made it to the porch.

"The house there in the distance is where we lived when we first got here." A tinge of pride rode his smile. "Amos started on this one, making us help. I don't think any of us were too keen on the idea, but when he let us help and really plan and build it, giving us a sense of purpose and discipline. A lot of growing pains went into this one."

"So who lives there now?" Jenna glanced at it again, hidden in the distance on the other side of a small stream, at least a mile away by what she could tell.

"Gabe's redoing the inside. Making a couple of offices and reconstructing the kitchen to make it bigger." He shrugged.

"For your boys' ranch?" she asked, curious about all his plans. "I'm sure it will be a wonderful place when you have it all done."

"I've managed the down payment on the first forty acres but there's a hundred or so in all." He pointed behind the old house and to the fencing past the barn and across a stream. "I've got everything plotted out but gotta get it paid for first. We've got about a hundred head of cattle, but I'd like to see that grow. I want the boys to learn the value of working with their hands, raising the animals and a garden. But mostly find it a place to call home. If I set it up right, the ranch can run itself and even pay for itself with the produce."

"And your family is supportive?" She loved the idea but supposed that much acreage was expensive.

He nodded for her to go inside and followed her. "They all help where they can. Do you want to lay him down?"

She glanced around with a nod. "He gets heavy these days, growing so fast."

"There's a bed in the guest room, low to the ground." He led her to the hallway and into a bedroom of rustic wooden furniture and watched as she lay Mason down in the middle of the bed. She covered him with a blanket, tucking his stuffed lion beside him. "He'll sleep a bit longer, always out like a light when we ride anywhere."

"Come on…when you meet Amos, he'll say about anything. Just go with it." He took her hand and led her further inside the house.

"This is beautiful." Jenna turned a full circle at the living area, though her pulse raced at his words. There were large frameless windows that allowed for taking in the woodlands to the north and the furniture was made of heavy cypress, giving it a welcoming warm feel. The smell of fresh baked bread wafted through the air, and the kitchen seemed to glow as they ambled that way.

Having no family, save, Brianna, it sounded nice to have a house full of people. It was good Aaron and his brothers were all still living home, but the house was spacious, probably making that comfortable. Sometimes her apartment was all too quiet when she lay awake at night with Mason sleeping in his crib nearby. She missed her parents at times enough to bring her to tears, but Mason had somehow been her saving grace on family.

She followed Aaron into the kitchen, taking a deep breath.

"Sarah, this is Jenna." Aaron gave her hand a squeeze and let go.

Sarah turned from the stove, wiping her hands on an apron tied to her waist. "Hi, Jenna, it's a true pleasure to meet you." She leaned to give Jenna a hug, ignoring her outstretched hand.

"Very nice to meet you Mrs. Decker." Jenna smiled, thinking she was much younger than she'd anticipated.

Lily was stirring a bowl of brownie mix, chocolate staining her top lip. "Daddy kissed Jenna."

Jenna stifled a grin biting her lips as she glanced at Aaron.

"Hey, go back to your brownies munchkin." He pointed to the bowl of batter and lifted his brows as he caught her gaze.

"It's very nice to be here. You have such a lovely home." Jenna made small talk, hoping to get past Lily's comment.

"Jenna's a real nurse but she doesn't have on her doctor suit today," Lily added, licking her chocolate stained fingers and plopping scoops of the batter into a baking dish.

"Yes, I know." Sarah's smile was genuine. "Amos is on the deck if the two of you would like to say hello.

I have an early lunch almost ready as I am sure you all would like to get to the cabin in time to do some fishing before the temperatures drop."

"We put her little guy in the spare room on the big bed. He's napping." Aaron grabbed Jenna's hand, leading her from the kitchen.

"I'll check on him, you two go ahead." Sarah turned back to help Lily with the brownie batter.

"Should I be concerned?" Jenna asked as Aaron led them into a long hallway.

He laughed, still tugging her along. "Nope. You should run and never look back."

She stopped in her tracks, noticing the candid pictures on the walls in the hallway. "Aaron, I'm not kidding."

"It'll be fine. He's a good man, but he'll push your buttons a bit." He led the way again squeezing her hand tighter.

"These are extraordinary." She touched the frame of a picture that showed Aaron and his brothers at a much younger age fishing alongside their father. The colors were magnificent, each boy captivated in his own thoughts and Amos watching intently. She turned to the opposite wall admiring the photographs of Lily as a baby and toddler, the progression of her growth caught picture to picture.

"Sarah is the master photographer around here. She's had a number of landscapes published over the years in magazines." He nodded to ones of the landscapes.

"She seems to find all the right colors," Jenna said as she admired the scene that looked much like outside the house.

"Always has a camera in her hand and only recently went digital." Aaron walked them through what was her studio. More pictures on every walls in various sizes. "I got her hooked up with a computer and scanner and a really good printer. Now there's no stopping her."

She smiled, still admiring the wall of photographs.

"Ready?" Aaron gave her hand a squeeze as they stepped out onto the deck. "Hey Pop. I want you to meet someone."

The elderly man turned in his chair, folding his book closed and laying it across his lap, where a blanket covered his knees. He glanced from Aaron to Jenna and nodded to the bench across from him. "Well, have a seat so I can take a look at ya."

Aaron gave her a wink and sat as she did. She held Amos Decker's gaze, the old man's deep brown eyes studying her.

"I'd stand in the presence of such a pretty lady, but I'm a bit winded today." Amos' oxygen tubing stretched across his face attached to a small tank on the deck. He was a handsome man, though much older than his wife by the looks of it. His gray hair was cut short and neat and he wore a full mustache as gray as his hair. Her first thought was that he could have passed for Sam Elliott, especially with the western cowboy hat that sat atop his head.

"It's a pleasure to meet you, Mr. Decker." Jenna took the man's outstretched hand and flushed as he leaned to kiss the back of it.

"My son didn't tell me you were such a pretty thing, a real hottie as he and his brothers might say." The old man chuckled as Jenna's mouth fell open.

"Come on, Pop." Aaron smiled as he shook his head catching her gaze.

"Well, I apologize, but I try to stay hip on the things that the young men say these days." The older man laughed again. "I was as smooth as that one in my day, minus that long mop of hair…thinks he's Sampson."

Jenna smiled, realizing she was somewhat safe with the teasing.

"So, Sampson here tells me you're a nurse." Amos asked.

"Yes, I work the emergency room at St. Anthony's and of course on the set," she explained.

He adjusted in his chair. "Well, that's admirable work. You must make pretty good these days, least I hear nurses do well."

"Come on Pop, you don't ask a lady what she makes." Aaron gave him a raised eyebrow in warning.

"Nope, I guess not." The old man's face lit up with a genuine smile and he continued. "So if I can't ask what you make, may I ask your intentions where my son is concerned?"

"Enough already, Pop." Aaron leaned back against the railing, stretching out both arms and giving his father's boot a nudge with his own.

"Oh, lighten up Sampson, she knows I'm kidding." Amos looked at her again. "Aaron here is a tough one, and what he doesn't want me to tell you is he's smart and handsome and would be a great catch."

Aaron shook his head and spoke to her. "I warned you."

"So you did." She gave into her own smile turning back to Amos, finding him intriguing.

"Did you bring that boy of yours?" Amos asked.

Jenna nodded. "He's sleeping in one of the bedrooms."

"So are you sleeping with Sampson here? He needs a good woman and has for some time." The old man grinned paying no attention to Aaron who growled, throwing his head back in defeat.

Jenna's mouth opened but nothing came out as she glanced at Aaron in disbelief.

"I finally bring a girl home, Pop, and you're gonna run her off." Aaron scolded but turned to her with a wink. "He's hopeless."

Jenna gulped a breath at the exchange with Aaron playing along. Well, she could play too. "Well, as a matter of fact I am sleeping with Sampson, and there must be a good bit of strength in that hair of his. Any more questions?"

Amos held her gaze for a long moment and then burst into a giant bought of laughter. "I like a woman with spark. Nope, no further questions at the moment. If he doesn't mind his manners, you let me know."

She smiled and gave him a nod, glancing at Aaron whose mouth finally closed.

Sarah came to the door, carrying Mason who was rubbing his eyes and whimpering. "Dinner's ready in five minutes, and this little fellow wants his mama."

Jenna hopped up and took Mason, who hid his face in her neck, but whimpered no more, cuddling his lion. "It's all right, sweetie."

Aaron helped his father up, chuckling. "Come on, Pop. If we feed him we sometimes don't have to cage him at night."

Jenna gave into a giggle and followed them back

inside the house. Mason glanced up from her shoulder as they entered the kitchen, eyeing Lily who scampered over with a grin.

She patted the chair beside her. "Jenna, you can sit by me. Can I hold the baby?"

"I bet after we eat he will be more than ready to play." Jenna glanced at Aaron and sat by Lily, placing Mason in her lap admiring the dish place settings. "I love your dishes."

"Thank you." Sarah turned from the counter. "I've collected Fiesta in a variety of color for years now."

"It's like eating on a rainbow. Hey Mason." Lily touched Mason's hand, and he giggled, leaning back against Jenna and tugging his hand free.

"Jenna, he's just beautiful," Sarah said with a glance at Mason.

Jenna kissed the top of Mason dark hair. "He's a handful, about to walk any day now and busy."

"She spends all her time at flea markets hunting those dishes and adding to her treasures," Amos said with sarcasm, making it into his seat. "And makes a mint selling her pictures of this dish and that."

Jenna glanced from him to Sarah again. "I saw your photos in the hallway. You do amazing work."

"It's really just a hobby." Sarah shook her head.

"Well, they are fabulous," Jenna added.

Aaron sat beside her and leaned closer to whisper. "Good comeback out there."

"I know." She lifted her brows at him and leaned back as Sarah placed a plate of spaghetti with meat sauce before her.

"Where are the boys?" Sarah looked toward the kitchen doorway. "Do you want a small plate for

Mason?"

"He can share with me," Jenna answered thinking that easiest with the mess Mason could make when feeding himself.

"Gabe, Jeremiah?" Sarah yelled toward the hallway as she placed a plate for Aaron and Lily, and then returned again with plates for herself and Amos.

"I told them Grandma, are they going to get time-out?" Lily danced in her seat as she lifted her fork.

"Well, they just might." Sarah played along.

Gabe strolled around the corner and into the kitchen. He made a heaping plate of the spaghetti and tossed himself into one of the chairs, speaking to his father. "Hey, Pop, that load of lumbers gonna be a few weeks…on back order. Got a call yesterday. Afternoon, Jenna. Who ya got there?"

She smiled in greeting. "This is Mason. My son."

"Well, get to it before full spring. Snow's predicted again, and I can almost feel it in my bones." Amos shrugged and removed his hat, setting it aside.

"Ah you stay cold, Pop," Gabe chided. "We'll get the fencing done."

Sarah passed the large basket of bread as she sat. "Jenna I wasn't sure of your likes, but I thought the noodles would be all right for Mason."

"Are you kidding? He won't let go to walk, but he will eat anything I let him have." Jenna couldn't see all the fuss as Aaron handed Lily the parmesan cheese.

Jenna gave Mason a bite of the spaghetti after she blew the heat away, and he gobbled it right up, not protesting at feeding himself which was a surprise.

Aaron held Mason's gaze and grabbed a noodle sucking it inside his mouth and making the boy laugh.

Mason waited as Aaron did it once more and Lily joined in, sucking in a long noodle noisily.

Mason and Lily both giggled then.

"Well, Sampson there is a health food nut, won't touch the fried stuff. And won't eat a full plate of anything." Amos nodded to Aaron.

"Gotta make it easy for Maxus and Thor to jump," Aaron defended, glaring at Gabe's snicker.

"Not me...fried chicken all the way." Jeremiah popped into the kitchen and plated his spaghetti and sat next to Sarah. "Good to see you, Jenna."

"He's Mason," Lily explained to her uncle. "We're gonna play."

"Hi," Jenna answered.

"Hey there, buddy." Jeremiah dug into his food, winking at Mason, who hid his head once more.

Amos spoke then. "I'll say grace."

As if rehearsed, the entire family held hands, Aaron taking one of hers and Lily grabbing Mason's tiny hand, though he struggled to free it. For a moment as Amos Decker prayed, Jenna fought the urge to allow tears, the scene reminding her of her own family. That was how a family should be. She leaned into Mason's dark curly hair, inhaling the sweet baby scent of him. He deserved a life like this and so did she.

"A-men," Amos spoke loudly, pulling Jenna from her thoughts.

"A-men!" Mason echoed in a shout, clapping his hands.

Everyone laughed, and Aaron glanced at her with a smile.

"So Jenna, working as a nurse on the set must be interesting." Sarah said as everyone began eating.

"I've enjoyed helping with makeup but besides Drake Masters' accident and a few splinters, things have been quiet. Oh and of course Aaron's fall into that cold water."

Gabe chuckled. "Maxus one. Aaron zero."

Aaron never missed a beat, but grinned. "Maxus and I have an agreement. We've worked things out for future takes like that."

Lily was quick to defend her father and the horse. "Daddy says Maxis is just ornerary."

Aaron corrected her. "Ornery."

"What about the big jump?" Sarah asked, a hint of worry edging her voice.

"The ramp evens things up from one side of the river to the level of the other. It's high but not so far," Gabe explained, digging into his meal.

"You still working with the boys making the ramp?" Amos glanced between his sons.

"Got it, Pop. The best wood and a solid base. Steady." Gabe stabbed a piece of bread with his fork, dropping it to his plate.

Aaron explained further. "Maxus is better when there's a challenge anyway."

While Aaron sounded confident, it was Sarah who dropped her gaze and went back to her food. Jenna hadn't thought to be worried herself, but maybe it was something she needed to discuss with Aaron.

"Well, you trained him from a colt so he's got your own determination." Amos sat back in his chair looking at Lily. "And who made the brownies for our picnic?"

Lily continued eating, as she explained to Jenna. "Papa and me have a picnic every night on his bed and watch the moon and sky. If it rains we have flashlights.

But, Papa, we are going to the cabin today."

Amos said, "We can picnic tomorrow night."

"Oh, well, that does sound like fun." Jenna had to smile.

Aaron answered after a sip of water. "We're gonna head to the cabin and get some fishing in."

"Uh-huh." Gabe smirked, and Jeremiah kicked him under the table.

Aaron glared at his brothers but said nothing, leaving Jenna to handle the bit of heat sweeping her cheeks. Well, these men were brothers and likely cut each other no slack.

"He's been working on that cabin since Moses was a boy and that's older than me." Amos chuckled. "But he's done it all by hand."

"And where would I get making it to perfection from?" Aaron questioned his father with a grin.

"Well, I'll have to go inspect and tell you what all you did wrong." Amos pointed a fork at his son.

Aaron shook his head.

"Seriously, he has a great cabin. The best wood, solar panels for heat and a water pump," Jeremiah added. "I'm gonna let him do all the hard work and then I'll buy it from him."

Aaron smiled. "It's gonna cost ya."

Jenna continued to feed Mason, who was taking in the home cooked meal as fast as she could feed him with bites for herself in between. Well, she didn't have to worry about what Amos thought about the overnight trip, but she did wonder what Sarah might be thinking.

"He's a good eater." Aaron glanced at Mason, who opened his mouth again.

"He loves getting real food these days. I haven't

found much he doesn't like." Jenna glanced around the table and back to her son. "Oh, Aaron I meant to stop for milk for tonight."

Mason picked up Lily's Barbie doll, done with the food.

"That's my doll. Her name is Barbie." Lily ran a hand gently across his hair, making Jenna smile.

Sarah answered. "You can take what's left of the milk in the fridge. I'm heading to the market later this afternoon anyway. You two go ahead, Aaron, so you can enjoy fishing while it's warm. I'll get the dishes."

"Thank you," Jenna said, enjoying Lily's entertaining Mason with her Barbie doll voice.

"Thanks, Sarah." Aaron got up. "Lily, go potty before we go."

Lily protested but took off out of the kitchen and down the hallway, Mason leaning to watch her as she disappeared.

"I think you finally filled him up." Aaron stood glancing at Mason and then her. "You ready?"

Jenna stood, lifting Mason to her hip with a nod. "It was a pleasure to meet you both, and I do thank you for the wonderful meal."

"Oh, you're so welcome." Sarah stood and placed her hands on Amos' shoulders.

"Make sure you come around more often, get that boy there used to horses and teach him to fish." Amos sipped his coffee, smiling at her with a nod.

"I'm sure he'd enjoy that." She glanced at Mason and back.

"He's a fine boy. *Samson* will have him riding in no time," Amos added. "Lily was riding a horse as soon as she could hold on."

Jenna smiled. "I've seen her."

"Lily, grab Mason's bag from the back bedroom." Aaron directed as she returned. She took off once more smiling and humming as she danced along.

"You two have a nice time." Sarah went about her work. "Gabe, I think the sink outside by the garden is stopped up."

"I'm on it, Ma." Gabe jumped up, placing his plate in the sink.

"We'll be home tomorrow afternoon." Aaron nodded for Jenna to follow, and she smiled once more at his parents. While it had been nice meeting them, she took a deep breath once they were outside on the porch. The family was incredible, so normal, reminding her of how she wanted to make Mason's life.

"You survived." Aaron turned to her as Lily bounced ahead.

"Yep, they're very nice," she answered, juggling Mason to her other hip.

"Amos is a tough one but I think you handled him well enough." He chuckled. "Actually, I think he likes you, and so do I." His gaze held hers and once more while her heart raced she melted into the idea of Aaron and now his family, though there were times she was so uncertain she should entertain any ideas more than the here and now.

Chapter Twelve

Aaron grabbed Jenna's bags from the SUV and turned. "This all you've got?"

"Yep, that and Mason's bag. How are we getting to the cabin?" Her face held a puzzled expression. "You said it's not far."

His green eyes narrowed though he grinned. "That depends. By the way of the eagle not far at all, by way of motorbike the terrain's too rough, but by way of horse, about twenty minutes if you hang on tightly."

"I thought your horses were on the set?" she questioned, glancing toward the barn.

"I brought Scout home yesterday. I'll take him back next week, but we have others. Gabe keeps a number of quarter horses, most good riders." He placed his fingers at his mouth and whistled twice, making Mason jump in her arms. "Think you can ride Scout and hang onto him?"

Her eyes widened. "I...yes, if you get us started."

Scout came from the other side of the pasture and stopped at the fencing along with several other horses. The large painted horse snorted about the time Mason squealed in Jenna's arms, kicking his feet and pointing.

"Horsey." Jenna spoke to him, smiling at his excitement.

"Wanna see the horses?" Aaron set the bags down and held his arms out.

Mason hesitated and when Jenna didn't move him closer, reached out his arms and let Aaron take him. He was light as a feather as Aaron sat him in the crook of his elbow, reminded of when Lily had been the same size. He stepped up to Scout as Gabe's horse Beau hung his head closer.

Mason shied, leaning into his chest, tucking his hands into his middle.

"It's fine." Jenna touched the horse to show him. "Horse, horsey."

Aaron took Mason's hand and tugged. "See."

Mason shook his head, but when Aaron let go of his hand he reached on his own, not necessarily intending to touch Beau, but the horse moved to nuzzle his small hand. Mason gave a shrill laugh and tried again, this time touching the animal on purpose with a giggle.

"Well, that works." Aaron tousled his dark hair, and Mason glanced up at him and then leaned for his mother.

"Want to ride the horse?" Aaron took a step away toward the barn with him, and Mason glanced over his shoulder content his mother was still close by. Well, that was a good sign he supposed. Both the horses followed waiting near the barn.

"I'll get these guys saddled." He handed Mason off to Jenna reluctantly. He was a cute kid with Jenna's eyes and facial features. He'd long forgotten what it was like to hold a baby.

He grabbed the first saddle and got Scout all saddled up, followed by Beau, and led them both outside the fence and closed the gate. Mason squealed again making him chuckle and Jenna smile. Damn, she was beautiful holding her son, though he'd wondered of inviting her on an overnight. Ah, it wasn't like much would happen with the children along, and that was probably best, though the night he'd held her had left him heated for days now.

"You're good then to ride?" he asked, making sure.

She hugged Mason to her. "It'll be fun."

"Lily, you and I'll ride Beau, and it would be best if Jenna and Mason rode Scout." Aaron figured Lily to balk at the idea.

"But Scout is my horse, and I want to ride with Jenna." She climbed up on the fencing.

"Well, Mason is a little guy, and he's never ridden a horse before. I think he'd want his mama, and Scout is our gentle horse. He won't buck or let Mason get hurt, and he knows Jenna is your friend," Aaron persuaded.

"You and your daddy can lead the way. And I know Scout will take good care of me and Mason." Jenna gave the horse a good rubbing of admiration.

Lily gave a nod, changing the subject. "Can I sleep in the loft in my room?"

Aaron nodded. "Yep."

"You've no bag?" Jenna asked him.

He shook his head. "We go up nearly every weekend I'm home, so it's fully stocked with food and clothes most of the time. I'll help you up."

Jenna gave Scout a pat to the side and touched his long mane, handing Mason back to Aaron once more. The little boy held out his hands whimpering for Jenna as she mounted up and sat in the saddle. She did well, as he'd taught her on the last ride and the quick glimpse of her backside as she did so made his breath catch.

"Stirrups good?" He pushed her knee down, and the fit was right, but Mason gave a shrill yodel, reaching for the horse. "Looks like he's ready."

"I'm surprised he's taking to it." Jenna's voice held an edge of nerves. "We have a cat, Bodi, that he adores but he's never seen a horse up close."

Lily stood nearby, twisting her ringlets of brown hair. "We have Kittyboy. He is old but he sleeps on my bed."

Aaron fidgeted with the stirrup again. "The main thing is not to get nervous. Put both your arms under Mason's and hang onto the reins with both hands. Scout doesn't startle easy at all and wait…" Aaron trotted back into the barn and returned with two helmets. He handed one off to Lily and the other smaller pink one to Jenna. "Think he'll wear it or mind that it's pink?"

Jenna spoke to Mason, who was tugging on Scout's mane oblivious. "Horsey hat." Mason sat still as she buckled the small helmet in place. "I don't think pink bothers him at all. This used to be for Lily?"

He nodded as Lily buckled her purple helmet, then he lifted her behind the saddle onto Beau. Grabbing the bags, he tied one to each horse. Then with a bit of effort he climbed up into the saddle, avoiding Lily and settling. "Hang on Munchkin. You let go and what happens?"

"You fall to the ground in a heap." Lily's laughter filled the air, and Mason copied her, glancing up at his mother. He was a cute little thing, having Jenna's dark hair and facial features.

Jenna laughed too and caught him watching, her cheeks glowing pink. What was it about her? The beauty was part of it, but she was a breath of fresh air like something new that held a comfort he wasn't sure he'd ever known.

He whistled and took Beau ahead, Scout following. Mason sat still in Jenna's arms, still playing with Scout's mane. Once they were out onto the other side of the pasture he allowed Jenna to catch up on Scout. "So you survived your first encounter with Amos."

She answered. "He was really kidding. I think."

"He's full of spitfire most of the time, but he's a good man. I think he worries over us all, wanting what's best." Aaron headed them past the fencing and across the stream. It wouldn't take long to get to the cabin and while it was cool, the sun was beginning to warm the afternoon a bit.

"I enjoyed meeting your parents, and the meal. The prayer was nice with holding hands. My family did that when I was growing up." She glanced down at Mason who held a big toothy grin grabbing the reins to help her.

"We've always done it that way." He shrugged and slowed Beau again to allow Scout to catch up. He nodded at Mason. "Seems he's taking to riding pretty well."

"I think so. He's taken the reins." She glanced down where Mason's tiny hands held to the reins above her own. "I was surprised he let you hold him, but I believe the horses win."

"Animals do it every time." He thought it true as Lily had loved animals from the time she could crawl.

She glanced forward, leaving him with the picture of her beauty once more. Holding her son as she rode Scout was a picture he could keep in his mind. Her dark hair blowing in the light wind was enough to make him want to touch her. Damn but if making love to Jenna hadn't stirred him somewhere deep inside. Holding her had been special but he hadn't expected how much he would want her again, all of her. The sweet cries she'd made had echoed in his mind since and he wanted to hear them again.

"Jenna, we are almost there. Hi, Mason." Lily glanced behind them as the edge of the cabin came into view across the rise.

Mason grinned at her but stayed more interested in holding onto the reins with one hand and the saddle horn with the other.

Aaron stopped Beau, waiting on Scout to catch up. "What 'ya think?"

Jenna scanned the cabin and all around. "It's so beautiful, like you must have carved it all by hand."

"I did." He smiled.

"I helped," Lily added as Aaron lifted her down off Beau and dismounted behind her.

She scampered off to the cabin porch.

Aaron tossed Beau's reins over the hitching post at the porch. He walked over to Scout and held out his hands to Mason.

The little boy leaned back against Jenna, reluctant to leave the horse.

"Come on Mason. Want to see the house?" Jenna pointed toward the cabin but Mason shook his head, not having any part of leaving the horse.

She lifted him from her anyway and Aaron took him as he burst into tears.

"It's all right, Mama's coming." Aaron tried as Jenna dismounted and took Mason back in her arms though he still cried, reaching for Scout as she walked away with him.

"We can ride again later," she coaxed.

"I'll get these guys out to pasture, you go on in with Lily." He looked on as she made her way to the porch where Lily waited. Turning he led both horses toward the fencing, turning them out inside the small pasture and stored the saddles in the tiny shed, grabbing the bags.

Glancing into the early afternoon sky, he made his way to the cabin and stepped inside. Lily sat on the floor with her basket of toys with Mason right beside her helping her empty the basket.

"Did you look around?" he asked.

Jenna watched the children play as she leaned against the counter that separated the kitchen and living area. She nodded. "It's really beautiful, every detail. In my writing, I often describe cabins in the woods like this, maybe not in Montana, but…I feel as if I have been here before. I know it's weird."

He set her bags aside. "Might be a bit modern compared to what you write. We have running water and plumbing."

She smiled, "well, the best of two worlds then. You don't have a barn here; will the horses be all right out there? I mean what with bears and mountain lions and…Bigfoot."

Aaron gave a hearty laugh. "They'll be fine; they'll warn me if they don't like what's hanging around. Not sure they know much about Bigfoot."

She laughed.

"Come on." He took her hand. "I've got more to do around here. Once I'm done I'll start on the furniture a piece at a time, all hand-made. For now, the old couch and chair have to do." He pointed to the loft above. "Lily has a small bedroom loft. She calls it her tree house and I have the room here, but I've got the plans to add on more as I have the time and funds. There's a stream down the way, thought we might try a bit of fishing."

"I haven't fished in years, but Mason will like the water I'm sure." She tucked a length of her dark hair behind her ear. Always a bit of blush when he looked at her too intently, yet he didn't drop his gaze. He liked that part.

"It's quiet here at night. I've got solar lighting, heating and air but most often use the fire pit." He hit the panel in the bedroom and the warmth of light filtered through the room. "Tucker, the guy that runs the business with Gabe, did the lighting and helped with the panels. The guy's a genius with electronics."

"It's perfect, really nice." She walked into the bedroom and glanced into the bathroom, turning back to him.

"I suppose I should have brought Mason a pack and play to sleep in." She glanced around the bedroom again.

"Uh…not to make things uncomfortable, but with the kids…you can sleep in here with Mason, the couch makes a bed and I can take that. Of course, Lily does sleep like a log once she's out."

Her smile spread as did her rosy cheeks. "I suppose we can play that part by ear, Stuntman."

That was a hint wasn't it? His groin tightened at the prospect, but he hadn't banked on much, given the children were along. Even if things did heat up, he'd still find his way to the couch due to all the little eyes.

"Oh, the milk Sarah gave us." She stepped out of the bedroom and headed for the bags. "I'll put it in the fridge."

Aaron followed and glanced at the children still playing. "Lily, don't let him have small things to put in his mouth."

"Okay, Daddy, he's got a ball right now." Lily didn't even look up but continued dressing her small doll with Mason watching, pacifier in his mouth.

Jenna returned from the kitchen. "Very attentive."

He grinned at her and stepped to the hearth adding wood to the fire pit. "Fatherhood changes a man."

"And you did most of this on your own?" she asked, walking around and looking again at all she had already seen.

"Ah, my brothers and Tuck helped." He stood upright again. "Oh, and for those of you who write and research, we have Wi-Fi."

"Out here?" she asked, surprised. "Well, I happen to have my laptop should a thought come along."

"I didn't plan much by the way of dinner for later, but we've got hotdogs and sandwich stuff, chips and some veggies," he offered, wishing he'd thought to plan for something more.

She laughed. "That sounds scrumptious."

"But first, we're going fishing, and if we're lucky it might just be trout for dinner." He shouted gaining the children's attention and dug into a bag on the counter.

"Yippee!" Lily stood, tossing her toys back in the basket, the chore seeming enticing enough that Mason tried to help, but missed with the ball he had. He crawled to pick it up, turning and grabbing the couch to stand so he could follow Lily.

Jenna sucked in a deep breath.

Across the room, Mason let go of the couch and took several steps, dropping the small green ball into the basket. He stood still a moment on his wobbling legs and then glanced at his mother with a toothy grin. Aaron grabbed the cell phone from his pocket and hit the camera, filming the moment as the toddler made several more steps. "There ya go, Buddy."

Jenna bent to her knees on the hardwood floors. "Come on; want to see the horse again?"

Mason, still holding his grin began taking steps toward her, his arms held high in the air as he gained his balance, the last few steps to his mother a bit of a scramble to fall into her arms.

"Oh, you silly boy, you could have been walking long before now." Jenna scooped him up and turned a circle, kissing his chubby cheeks.

"Yea, Mason." Lily clapped, running to Jenna's side and patting the toddler in praise.

"Aw, you filmed it?" Jenna's eyes twinkled with unshed tears when she turned to him.

"Can't let those moments slip away." He held her gaze, thinking there were a lot of other moments that shouldn't be taken for granted, like watching her with her son and with Lily. He wasn't sure what the future might hold where she was concerned, but for now he wasn't going to let a minute go by without keeping his sights and his hands on her.

Chapter Thirteen

"No Jenna, fish like this." Lily tossed her hook back in the small rushing creek, standing beside Aaron along the banks.

Jenna, on her opposite side, tried to do the same, tangling her line once again. "Oops, I guess I'm not the fisherman that both of you are." She'd fished a bit as a child and teen but it had been a while.

Aaron chuckled and grabbed her line to untangle it from the bush by his feet. This was the fourth or fifth time he'd had to help her, though he'd still managed to pull in a number of good sized trout in between.

They'd hiked through the woods a ways and stopped at the portion of the creek that held large rocks where the water fell into a small deeper pool of moving water. The sun was bright in the sky making for a nice afternoon.

"Sorry." Jenna glanced behind her where Mason sat playing with sticks and rocks Lily had gathered for him.

Aaron laughed. "We'll make a fisherman out of you yet."

"I think maybe I am a better writer than fisherwoman," she corrected him. "You and Lily keep going. I'm going to sit over here with Mason and do a bit of writing."

He nodded and tossed his line again as she sat on

the rocks behind him.

Lily had put her own line aside and sat down in the dusting of sand to play with Mason, chattering to him and handing him more sticks.

"I enjoyed meeting your family." Jenna tugged her laptop from her bag as Aaron snagged another trout. "Sarah invited me to go shopping with her and Lily some time. Mason and I would love that."

He talked as he dealt with getting a fish in and untangling it from the tiny hook. "Sarah's a bargain shopper, you might be out for hours."

"All the better." She lifted her cell phone and hit the app for her camera focusing on him in spite of the glare of the sun behind her. His hair was pulled back in a band and he wore sunglasses, the angle of the shot all but taking her breath. He was handsome, wearing baggy jeans and hunting boots and a dark t-shirt pulled over those tight muscles she'd clung to when he'd made love to her. It was a bit sneaky but she took the shot anyway.

She continued to watch him, calculated with specific precision as he fished. Like when they had been together. She shivered at the thought. He'd been so in tune with her as if he read her every move, so tender but full of strength. Heat flushed her cheeks at remembering.

He tossed his line a few more times, then reeled in and turned to walk back up the rocks to where she sat. He plopped down beside her, glancing at her screen.

"Giving up?" she asked, having written little.

"Never, but we've got enough for supper now. So what are you writing today?" He leaned against her as he glanced at the screen.

"Just editing my current story about the four

brothers." She was surprised as he really seemed interested.

He leaned back against the rocks. "May I?"

She hesitated but handed the laptop over with his coaxing.

"Come on. I've read a lot of scripts." He settled it on his knees.

"There's a brief explanation at the beginning." She turned to watch the children playing in the sand at the creek's edge. Lily handed Mason a small shovel and he went right to work putting sand in the small bucket she'd brought along.

"This is good, really good." He nodded as he continued to read, scrolling further.

"You think so?" She'd poured her heart and soul into this one script hoping that she would find a way to get it into the right hands.

"Yep, you've got talent going on here." He never glanced up.

"Daddy, look." Lily held Mason's hand leading him over the sand and small rocks. "He wants to see the fish. Come on Mason, that's a big boy."

Mason smiled ear to ear, hanging on to Lily as Jenna held her breath with him toddling along.

Aaron handed her the laptop speaking to Lily. "Careful, he's new at walking."

Jenna set it aside and lifted her phone to catch the moment. Both the children bent to look in the bucket and her son turned to grin at her pointing to the fish inside.

"Do you see the fish?" She snapped another picture.

"See, Mason, you can touch the fish and the first

one you ever catch you have to give a kiss for good luck so you will catch more." Mason shook his head, reluctant to touch the creatures moving in the bucket of water.

"I think he isn't too keen on the fish." Aaron chuckled.

"They are very sweet together." Jenna glanced at him. "So you think the script is good?"

"Sure." He leaned back, eyeing her. "Who taught you to put together a script?"

She shrugged. "I've studied for years, but it isn't until now I've thought I should pitch the idea. I've taken all four of the brothers' stories and will be done soon with mapping out a series."

"Then I think when you are ready you go for it." He glanced into the sky when she nodded with a smile. "I'll get us packed back up and we can head in, temperature's dropping a bit."

She put the laptop back into her bag as he took off to gather the fishing poles.

"You guys ready to go back? We can roast marshmallows?" Aaron spoke to the children as he lifted the bucket of trout, taking Mason by the hand.

Jenna couldn't stop her smile as Mason didn't hesitate to hang on with Lily bouncing along behind them. She tossed her bag over her shoulder and lifted her cell phone intending to snap a picture, but instead decided to watch. The picture of the children walking with Aaron tugged at her heart. Mason deserved a father, as life had cheated him out of a real one, and the sight of him walking alongside Aaron took her breath.

She brought up the rear of the little parade back through the woods, thick with large trees and bushy shrubs. The pebbled path they were taking was made by Aaron and Lily over the last few years. This was the kind of life she wanted for herself and Mason, the simple things that really mattered.

Aaron took it slow to let Mason walk at the pace he could manage. Mason glanced back every few moments to make sure she was there but remained content. By all rights, they might appear to be a family. Lily's brown curls were a shade lighter than Mason's darker locks that looked much like Aaron's. The children might have passed as siblings very easily. She smiled, following along and enjoying the walk. Maybe one day.

****

Aaron stoked the fire and turned back to Jenna scooping her up in his arms. "With the munchkins down for the count, we're going to sit and you can tell me one of your stories."

Jenna laughed. "What? I can't…"

He plopped in the recliner with her still in his arms. The old chair creaked as he kicked to push it back and settled her against him.

"Sure you can. Tell me more about the one I read this afternoon." He pulled her hair back kissing her shoulder and then putting his head back, closing his eyes. "I'm listening."

"How about a modern-day tale?" Jenna thought where to begin as she snuggled against him. He was warm and snuggly and his voice vibrated through her.

He didn't open his eyes but nodded.

"One of my stories is about a lady who lost her way and found herself hanging out on the set of a western television series, where a stuntman with a kind heart caught her attention." She shivered as he stroked his fingers through her hair.

"This story sounds like a real good one." His voice was soft and his lips tender along her shoulder.

She took his hand and raised it and kissed the back of it. "You are the sweetest man I've ever met. Thank you for sharing your family. Watching you and your brothers and your parents, even Amos... I miss so many things about having a family." Was she telling too much, was she not telling enough? "Oh, I have an aunt in Virginia, but I lost my mom when I was young and my father a few years ago."

The fire crackled. She did miss them and what little she could remember of her mother. Somehow, she had always felt cheated at losing them both, but life wasn't always fair, and that was something she'd learned the hard way. Regardless, she had enjoyed meeting Sarah and Amos. "Your parents are so nice."

He glanced at her. "They've had some good years. Amos has always treated Sarah very well and made sure we did the same. They have this unique bond and understanding of each other without so many expectations."

"I didn't realize Sarah was so much younger than Amos." She'd been curious.

He took a deep breath and let it out. "She's fifty-eight and Amos is seventy-four, but he smoked like a damn chimney most of his life. Still does."

"She's beautiful. They never had biological children though? I mean before you boys came along?" She shook her head. "I'm sorry, maybe I'm intruding." She didn't know what it was like to be adopted or to have been in foster care. Maybe some things were too personal for him to discuss.

"Jenna, there's nothing you can't say to me. I suppose Sarah could have had children, but it ended up Amos couldn't." He shrugged.

"She loved him, and sometimes that's all it takes," she added in full understanding.

"She had her photography, and honestly it was Amos who talked her into adopting, but I think neither one of them had thought of three half-grown boys." He smiled as he stared into the fire. "She'd been in contact with Clarice, the social worker I told you about, and she suggested us to Sarah, who called her back the next day to say yes." His voice was soft and she could imagine it was hard for him to share his past.

"You boys were all here in Montana?"

"Nope, we were in Boise Idaho at the time. I think there was a lot to getting us tagged together and across the state lines but Clarice got it done. She was young and new at her job and determined, never gave up on us or them." He chuckled stroking her hair.

"You think a lot of Clarice?"

He nodded. "She had my case since I was young. I don't remember anything but moving around a lot. She put me in the group home with Gabe when I was about eight. Though we were always trouble to the foster parents there. Jeremiah came to our group home when he was a little guy. Six or so. He cried at night and I use to sit on his bed until he went to sleep. No one thought he could talk but one day he did to me and finally Gabe. I guess he was in some kind of shock or something."

He stopped for a minute but then continued. "Then the group home had to close. We got split up again even though Clarice fought hard. That's when I took the beating. I don't remember much. He was a big guy, drank too much. I fought him at first but I was twelve, kind of scrawny then. What I remember most is curling into a ball and holding my head and not even crying…it just didn't hurt anymore. I woke up fighting in the hospital but Clarice was there. She comes at Christmas every year to visit. Says she'll come work for me when I open the boys' ranch."

"Your ranch will be a beautiful thing." She placed a hand on his cheek. "Taking care of boys needing a safe place to call home."

"And your story is no different." He offered the crackle of the fireplace the only sound around them.

It was probably time she confided her story, though her pulse raced at the thought. He had to know from what had happened between them there was a reason she'd first run from him, though he hadn't pressed the issue. "It isn't the physical part of what happened but getting over the mental aspects. He beat me one night, near to death. I never saw it coming. And now I've spent so much of the last two years looking over my shoulder."

Aaron's fingers traced hers and she went on. "I apparently asked one too many questions about the money filtering into his campaign. A politician. I realized too late who he really was and the price was heavy. Part of the reason I moved this far from…" It was too much to force the words, but she did so anyway in a whisper. "Atlanta."

Aaron squeezed her hand tighter, hugging his other arm around her. "It's all right, Jenna. You don't have to…"

She hadn't realized until then she was visibly shaking but telling him was important and she went on.

"I didn't know I was pregnant until the E.R. physician let me know the baby was fine. Imagine the shock. Vince's father had been with me, promised he wouldn't tell his son."

"He doesn't know about Mason then?" Aaron asked.

"No. I don't think so." She sucked in a needed deep breath, surprised she wasn't in tears. "His father allowed me my freedom, making sure I got all that belonged to me and seeing that the divorce went smoothly without my need of even being there. He knew his son…too well."

He touched her chin pulling her in for a tender kiss. "No wonder I frightened you at first. It's fine to be afraid, but not of me. You're shaking." He hugged her tighter.

"Aaron?"

He held her gaze as she turned to look at him again.

"I've needed something good in my life for a long time now. I've hidden from it all trying to protect me and Mason. You make me feel alive again." She smiled; it was true, so very true. "Today was so wonderful."

The edge of his lip turned to a slight smile as he toyed with the hair at her temple. "An angel flying a little too close to the ground. I'm sorry for what you've been through but no worries, no matter where we go from here you have no reason to fear me like that."

"I know." She touched his lips with her finger and then kissed him tenderly.

"I'm glad you told me, wasn't sure how long it might take you," he said so soft spoken she wanted to melt into him.

"I needed to tell you, so now I can move forward in everything." She smiled and swallowed the lump in her throat that she hadn't given into for tears. And then she kissed him again, this time lingering. "And if we didn't have the chance of little eyes…"

He growled. "Haven't been able to think anything but being with you like that."

She smiled, heat warming her cheeks and entire body. "Me too."

He smiled and closed his eyes again, pressing his forehead to hers. "We'll get to that again soon enough."

She snuggled closer and kissed his cheek. "I have a feeling it would be best if I go on and sleep with Mason for the night, otherwise it might be that I can't be trusted."

He lifted one eye lid and gave her a grin. "Careful…I'll already need a very cold shower by morning."

She kissed his cheek again and got up, heading into the small kitchen for a drink of water and to fix Mason a sippy cup of milk. "Maybe next weekend you could come visit me at my place. Brianna is off and wants to take Mason to see her aunt over night. She does that now and then. I think she likes pretending he is hers."

"Sounds like a plan," he answered. "How about you pick something nice for dinner and then I get to choose the dessert?"

She laughed. "How come I think dessert has nothing to do with food?"

He purred like a lion, making her laugh. She lifted the milk from the refrigerator and poured Mason's cup half full, knowing he'd wake for it soon enough. She placed the milk back in the fridge and turned from the kitchen.

"I suppose I can accept those terms." She giggled and turned but stopped in her tracks.

Aaron was lying on his back in the recliner with one arm over his head and the other across his belly, fast asleep. She watched him for a moment and lifted the afghan from the couch laying it across him and dimming the lights. Glancing around the cabin once more, it was peaceful, as peaceful as she'd known in a long time. She climbed the stairs and peeked at Lily who'd been asleep since before Mason. She slept curled around a big stuffed bear, a slight snore escaping her. She was so good with Mason and he seemed to adore her. She smiled and stepped back down and grabbed the sippy cup once more.

Strange how she'd been very protective of exposing Mason to anyone new in her life, but then there hadn't been anyone new except for Aaron. She inhaled a deep breath and turned for the bedroom, crawling in the king-size bed beside her sleeping son. Snuggling closer, she wasn't sure she could sleep given the hints of Aaron's scent that rode there. She closed her eyes and thought of the next day and that she'd relish in every minute she could spend with Aaron and Lily too. For the first time in a very long time, her future seemed promising and disclosing what she'd been through had been a relief. She closed her eyes and listened as Aaron's light snores drifted to her, content in simply being near.

Chapter Fourteen

Aaron pulled Jenna closer, inhaling the strawberry scent of her hair as he entered her apartment behind her. It had been a week since they'd found the time for much more than a quick kiss or embrace near the camper on the set. They'd sat in his camper earlier as he studied the upcoming script for the ramp jump. She'd curled up on his couch with her writing and he'd caught himself watching her as she was lost in the stories she wrote.

He could tell how important her writing was and felt a bit guilty for saving a copy of her script onto a jump drive. He planned on sending it to a good friend, Thomas Campbell, at Epic Productions. She was wasting her time with Horace and LeLand Films.

"You smell good." Jenna hugged him as they stepped inside her apartment. "Thank you for dinner, it was scrumptious."

"You're welcome." He smiled not able to take his eyes from her in the hot black dress and heels she'd been wearing when he arrived. He'd left Lily with Sarah and Brianna had taken Mason to her Aunt's house. "So this is Jenna and Mason."

Her apartment was nice. The living room cozy with an overstuffed brown couch, love seat and recliner. The pictures on the walls were diamond designs with brownish red and shades of purple. Everything neat with little clutter from what he could tell, well except for the random scattering of small toys.

"It's not much. I had every intention of purchasing a house, but Mrs. Lucy is right downstairs. It's so easy here and with Bri next to me, it's really perfect." She pulled her coat off, laying it across the recliner.

"Upkeep is a lot of my day with the ranch." He walked to the window, the view of the outskirts of the city below them. "Nice view."

"I have my desk in the bedroom where I can see the same view as I write," she added.

He turned back to her, still feeling guilty about the script. Well, if Thomas took it like he thought he might, she would have to be thrilled.

"Who's this?" He spotted the cat across the room, lazing on the back of the loveseat by the window.

"Wait, Bodi isn't always friendly, still has his claws," she warned. "Though he has been all right with Mason since he became mobile. He gets up higher somewhere if he wants to be left alone."

Aaron leaned down before the cat and held out his hand. The cat bristled for a moment, then sniffed his hand and got up with a big meow stretching and jumping down to lean against his leg. Aaron threw caution to the wind and picked the cat up, rubbing the large gray tabby behind the ears as he hummed.

"That's incredible, he hardly likes anyone. Brianna hisses at him to make things worse." She scratched the cat's head.

"Animals know who to trust. Hearing a voice is part of that. So you aren't the grouch she thinks you are." He put the cat back down. "And the other part is giving him a bit of space."

She tugged her long dark hair behind her ear, holding his gaze.

"You look rather…stunning tonight if I haven't already said that." He wasn't waiting much longer to consume her as planned.

She stepped from the black pumps, taking his hand. "Thank you."

He followed her lead as she took him to the couch and sat, tugging him down beside her. "Dinner was nice. So Lily won't miss you too much?"

Aaron nodded. "She's used to me being gone with nights I stay on the set."

"She has mannerisms like you. When she laughs, her eyes are so much like yours." She leaned back against him, glancing across the room.

He opted to change the subject, running his fingers into her hair. "So about your script. You'd really like to get it out there?"

Her eyes brightened and her voice carried an octave higher. "Of course, but there's so much I need to learn about the business."

He thought about what he'd done. He should tell her he'd used a jump drive to make a copy a few days before, but maybe it was best to wait and see. He imagined if Thomas took the script he could beg for forgiveness later. "What if your story was put on the big screen?"

It took a minute for her words. "I…don't know. I suppose I'd be shocked but happy. I believe in this story though. Big dreams in a small town."

"If anyone can do it, you can." He'd like to see it happen for her.

"Maybe it's a far-fetched dream." Her smile faded.

"But the writing, it's an escape, a place where I get to control what happens and it fills me up somehow."

He rubbed a hand down her arm. "Gotta have an outlet. I ride Maxus for hours at a time, alone, so I can think. Clear my head."

"About planning your boys' ranch?" she asked.

Aaron thought on things and nodded. "Some."

"Tell me about your ideas?" she asked.

She was stalling, but he could take a bit to answer her questions.

"It'll be a couple of years yet." He'd spent years planning what would be needed. "With *The Bounty Hunter* pay for this season, I'll have the down payment for part of it, and if the series continues for a while, I might even be able to pay for the whole thing."

"What do you do in between television contracts?" she asked.

He shrugged. "I buy and sell horses and cattle. Gabe runs a construction company, and I work for him. When he has a big job, Jeremiah and I both do. And Tuck of all things, is a P.I., so Gabe helps him out a good bit. They were special ops in the military for a few years. Iraq. Can't get it out of their system I suppose."

"I'm sure it was hard with him away. So you've never lived away from home?" She rubbed a hand along his arm.

"I never had a home 'til I was twelve, never felt the need to leave. I've always thought when I have the cabin done, I'd live there." He'd get there one day. "I went to college, got a business degree. Gabe chose the military."

"The cabin is so beautiful," she added, leaving him to think she had no idea what a beauty he held right this minute.

"I've got the ranch idea planned with bunk house style living, where the boys work to make the next bunk for more kids. I can teach them about the care of the animals and gardens, farming a bit." He lifted his brows. "But I think we have better things to discuss for now…you are stalling."

She smiled with that oh so fantastic blush. "I am?"

"Yep. What did you like about it last time?" He was making her uncomfortable, but there was something fun about it.

"Aaron," she scolded in a whisper, though she leaned in closer, turning to face him.

"Answer the question."

Her mouth fell open, speechless.

He waited, wanting to know what she liked so he could understand her better. She could be quiet, she could be talkative but most of all, in spite of wanting to plant himself inside her body again, he wanted inside her head.

"I've had orgasms, but never like that… I can't believe I am even talking about this. Yes, I liked it…all of it," she whispered, her cheeks bright red as he leaned to kiss her.

Hell, that wasn't helping the conversation. He adjusted his position. "So I'll ask again, what do you like?"

She laughed. "Aaron!"

"All right…" He held up his hands in defense, laughing at her.

"You're impossible." She gave him a little shove.

"No, I'm very, very probable." They'd known each other a short time, but he hadn't any doubts he wanted

Jenna Wilder for a lifetime but he also had to be patient for himself and for her. Sarah had always told him and his brothers when the right one came along they would know it. She'd said it wasn't about bells and whistles, but about a comfort that would bring them to their knees. He'd never fallen easily, not even for Pamela, but falling to his knees for Jenna was already done.

"Wait, you answer the question. What do you like about it?" She turned the conversation giving him her lips for a tender kiss.

He took the kiss and began. "I like it when I feel your body let go, knowing I brought you to that moment, when you twist because it's too much and not enough at the same time, when your legs shake and you lose your breath. When it feels good and you whisper my name or sigh."

"I had to ask." She laughed, her cheeks nice and rosy.

He touched her hand. "I also like the giggles you and Lily share and how confident you now ride Scout. I love how much you are in love with your son. How you handle emergencies on the set and how you sleep with your hair all around your face and even how you look in the morning."

She held his gaze her eyes glassy.

"I woke the other morning, with you still beside me, feeling your warmth and didn't move for a long time, because I didn't want to let you go." There, he'd poured out more feeling than he ever had to anyone.

To his surprise she picked up. "I enjoy watching you with Lily, like the two of you are this big magnet, pulling each other along with laughter. I like watching you on the set when you ride the horses and are so in control and focused, but I also like when you do that little chuckle under your breath when you make me all flustered talking about things."

"Talking about what things?" He grinned.

"The love making things…" Jenna nudged him like he should have known.

"See, I got you talking a little." He smiled hugging her against him.

"You are so what I never expected Aaron, but I'm still embarrassed about that first time. I hadn't known it was going to happen like it did." She shook her head and dropped her gaze.

"What?" He lifted her chin. "That was my all time favorite part. I'd like to try that again sometime." He brought her hand up, coupling their fingers close to his heart and leaning against her to kiss her. After a long moment, their breath exchanged and she sighed and pulled back from him.

"Let's…now," she said in a whisper her breath catching.

"Your wish is my command." He stood, tugging her with him. She was hot in that dress and he was going to enjoy peeling it right off her.

"I feel like I'm dreaming sometimes." She let him lead the way, though he hadn't any idea which room was hers.

"You aren't dreaming, babe and neither am I." He glanced right and bypassed the room with the crib and went into the next.

He stopped in her bedroom next to the bed. "I'm sorry for teasing you. I don't take this or you for granted, Jenna."

"It hasn't taken me long to realize you are special,

Aaron." She smiled and turned her back to him.

"Good, then let's not waste time." He began on the zipper of the dress with a chuckle.

"Should I be afraid?"

"Naaahhh, the cat even likes me," he encouraged.

"He's a very smart cat." She shivered as he drew her dress down over her shoulder, nibbling the bare skin of her neck. He let the dress fall, leaving her in her black lace bra and panties. He was sure he didn't take her for granted but he'd never stopped being surprised at how beautiful she was. His body deceived him in seconds, but he was damn well going to enjoy this.

He traced one hand to her breasts squeezing her nipple through the black satin of her bra and sucking along the tender skin of her neck, standing behind her.

He whispered in between light touches of his lips on her skin. "I want you talking to me tonight, telling me what you like." He ran the same hand lower touching her through her panties with a groan.

She sucked in a deep breath. "Yes…"

He pulled his sweater over his head tossing it aside, turning her to him, taking her lips. He pushed her until she lay back on the bed, taking him with her. She felt right under him, hanging onto him, running her hands across his chest, sighing as he kissed his way to her breasts. He tugged ever so slightly on her bra to expose her nipples, liking how the bra pushed her breasts higher for his access.

He licked one nipple and then the other, blowing on them and watching as they puckered. Jenna ran her hands into his hair and held him to her, her breath coming faster as he continued.

He rose up on his elbows above her, leaning to kiss

her lips once more, "Not yet. I want to taste you…would you like that?"

"Yes…" her breath hitched, her amber eyes dilating in the reflection of light from the hallway.

"Then tell me you want it." He went back to her breasts with a nip for each.

She didn't hesitate. "I want you to do that, what you said, to me."

"Say it." He tugged hard at her nipples, grazing his teeth across one and twisting the other between his fingers.

"Taste me Aaron, put your mouth on me." She had her hands in his hair and gave his head a push in the general direction.

He chuckled and worked his way down her body with kisses, falling to his knees on the floor at the side of her bed. He grabbed her legs and pulled her closer, tugging her panties off, letting them drop, tracing kisses along her inner thighs. "You are so damn sexy."

Nudging her legs apart, he traced his hands up her inner thighs. She shivered a sigh as he opened her and placed his mouth against her. He swirled his tongue around her, tasting all of her but not fully touching the part of her that sought him. He teased and played everywhere but not there.

"Aaron, please." She whimpered, gripping the sheets.

"Please what?"

She moaned as he returned to his task.

"Tell me what you want, Jenna?" He slipped two fingertips inside and her pelvis lifted as he curled them, a soft groan of pleasure leaving her.

"Say it." He was rigid with need but teasing her

would make it all the better. He licked across her several times and then stopped, taking his fingers away. "Say it."

"For God's sake, Aaron…" She was totally breathless.

Only then did he place his mouth on her, giving her no mercy from the rapid lashes of his tongue across the quivering, pert nub.

Her body arched. She moaned again trying to move, but he held her steady, giving her the fervent attention she craved, eliciting the first of multiple gasps from her. He'd thought it might take longer but her legs were tensing, her entire body shaking as he took her to the edge and finally sucked. Hard.

The last of her words were lost as she rocked against his mouth, gripping her hands in his hair as she convulsed time and again. He lightened the touch of his tongue as her body relaxed and her chest rose and fell as she tried to recover.

He kissed her thighs in turn. "That was damn sexy as hell."

"I'm not so sure." She shook her head but moved nothing more.

He stepped into the bathroom, washing up. Grabbing a towel from her shelf he dried his face and beard, returning to the side of the bed. She watched as he unbuttoned his jeans, pulling a small chain of condoms from one of the pockets, holding them up with a sly smile.

"I'll never survive it." She had moved up in bed pulling the covers across her.

"You haven't felt anything yet." He stepped out of his jeans and boxers, rolling on one of the condoms as she watched. He was about ready to explode but he'd please her again more than once this night.

He crawled back on the bed between her legs, watching as she slipped her bra away. "How about nice and slow this time?"

"After that I don't know if I have the energy."

"Oh, I think you got this." He kissed her and slid against her, filling her full and groaning at the heat. She wrapped her legs around him as her warmth tightened on him. Withdrawing, he nipped at her lips and pressed in again.

She ran her hands down his back, squeezing her legs tighter against his hips.

He could make love to her a thousand times and never be satisfied that it was enough. What amazed him was how perfect they seemed to fit together. Built for each other, comfortable. He closed his eyes, memorizing the feel of her as he pressed deep and withdrew fully to do it once more.

She met his gaze when he opened his eyes again. "You're smiling."

He raised himself up changing the angle of his stokes. "I'm admiring."

She ran her hands into his hair, her smile sure and sweet.

He whispered, "Look at me this time when it happens."

She nodded.

He didn't change his stroke, sliding himself deep, holding himself there and then withdrawing almost fully to do the same thing again and again. In a short time, Jenna was pushing her pelvis toward him. Her legs quivered gripping his hips tighter, her hands grasping his sides to urge him. He continued and she built, growing tense, opening more and reaching her body to meet him.

"Look at me…" He whispered and she shattered in a series of cries never taking her eyes from him as the climax took her.

Aaron fought to stave off his own release, wanting one more from her. It wasn't likely as it had taken all he was to hold off. He withdrew from her and turned her with a whisper and gentle nudge. "On your knees."

"Aaron?" She did as he asked, glancing back at him.

"Shhhhhh." He entered her from behind, pressing himself fully inside her, tossing his head back. Damn, he'd never last. He traced his fingers to find her again as he pumped rapidly. He pulled his thoughts away. It was mind over matter. Holding off would make it even better. He focused on her and in a short time her breath came short and she placed her hand with his own against her.

Aaron bent across her back, whispering close to her ear. "Too much, and not enough."

"Yes…" Her entire body shuddered and tightened around him, her sweet cries matching the thrust of his hips. That was it. He let go, hanging onto her as if she were life itself, holding her until he was spent and until they fell together in a heap on her bed. She turned and he gathered her into his arms and buried his face in her neck, content as never before.

Chapter Fifteen

Aaron urged Maxus up the ramp on the set. Since the first hints of daybreak, he'd been practicing the climb by walking up the ramp, pulling Maxus by the reins behind him. And now the horse seemed unconcerned with Aaron riding him up the ramp and backing him down. He'd done ramps before, but the animal didn't need much repetition before he tired of the training.

The ramp was sturdier with the extra supports and railroad ties, and so far Maxus had good traction climbing, though it wasn't as steep a grade as it was high off the ground toward the end of the ramp. He'd progress the horse to a gallop to make the actual jump, but that might take a week or more. And he'd do one or two practice jumps prior to filming. That was the usual.

He stopped Maxus at the top. The ramp had safety rails on each side which would be removed for later practices and on the actual take. The rails would hardly hold him, much less the horse if they went off the side, but for now they gave Maxus a border. To have the ramp appear like a bridge, the last ten feet of it had bridge looking side rails which would not be removed but hadn't startled the horse at all.

After a few warm weeks, it was downright cold, and even in his heavy coat, he'd about had enough. Glancing below him, the set was beginning to come to life. Production was setting up teepees outside the little town where the bounty hunter was to fight the Indians, but due to the cold, filming outside was delayed, though some inside takes were being done.

Funny, he hadn't seen Jenna all day but he missed her every second she wasn't within his reach. He'd called her last night and talked for more than an hour, needing to hear her voice. Damn, he had it bad, didn't he?

He'd done a lot of thinking the past few days about himself and Jenna. They'd both spoken words of love and for him those three words were a first to any woman and the surprise was they had come easily. It might have been that he would have said them first, but his fear of being too much for her too fast had held him back. She'd surprised him—brave he thought after what she had confided she had been through. The thought of her having been beaten made his insides cringe. No woman deserved any part of something like that no matter the situation. He shook his head and pushed away the mounting anger inside of him that came with thinking about what she'd endured.

"Hey, spotting lookout for Indians?" Gabe stood below.

He laughed. "We're playing tree house."

"Scout and Charger are set. How's he doing?"

"Good, a little shy at first. He's settled now that we are just standing here. I'm going to the other side of the river, make sure he knows it." Aaron began backing Maxus down the ramp, the horse resisting.

"Work with me here." Aaron tightened the reins. "If I fall, you fall and trust me, we won't like the landing."

Gabe walked closer to the lesser end of the ramp. "Smoother than last time."

"He's never liked going backward." Aaron dismounted once he had Maxus on the ground, the horse rocking his large head in agitation. That was enough for one day and he was about done with it too.

"He's never liked doing anything he didn't want to do." Gabe tilted his hat back. "Production's going to keep the ramp flooring covered to keep the ice off with snow coming in."

"That'll work. I'm gonna ride him to the other side while he's warm." Aaron took off on Maxus, avoiding a few frozen puddles on the ground. If the temperature didn't warm, he'd delay filming as Maxus didn't need to slip on the ramp. Snow and ice would delay filming anyway.

Once on the grassy area behind the set he galloped Maxus along for the exercise. The horse, tired of the small corral, took off. Aaron hunkered down letting Maxus have the reins. This was where he was best, the wind hitting his face, the ride hard and his thoughts his own, though all those thoughts went right to Jenna. He smiled and ducked closer allowing Maxus the full run, the horse not the only one that needed the hard ride.

****

Jenna left the make-up tent, thankful for the small heater the crew had brought in. She'd spent the entire morning assisting Sheila with making up some of the extras as burn victims from a hotel fire. They all looked real enough to roll right in the emergency room. They had made some of the ones that were to die, charred, while others sported deep red burns with blisters. Burn victims in the eighteen hundreds rarely survived, and if they did, they succumbed to infection, but this was television.

The weather man had predicted heavy snow and the producers had let everyone know the set was closing due to the weather, but she'd yet to see Aaron and she needed to get home to Mason.

She hopped on her cart and rolled forward, thinking if nothing else he'd have the heaters going in the barn and camper. Riding closer, it wasn't Aaron but Gabe who was leaning across the corral, with binoculars in his hand, watching in the distance.

She pulled closer.

"Hi." Gabe turned, pulling the binoculars from his face. He was very handsome with his jet-black hair and deep blue eyes and a bit taller than Aaron.

"Hi, what're you doing?" She stopped the engine and ambled over, pulling her coat tighter.

Gabe nodded toward the river and she followed his gaze. Aaron was on Maxus, running the horse to the river and turning him hard away once they got near the water. It seemed odd that he kept repeating it over and over.

Gabe handed her the binoculars.

She juggled until she found Aaron in the lenses and followed him as he kicked hard and got Maxus to a run, jerking to halt the horse at the river and then turning him to run him. "Why does running him toward the river do?"

Gabe turned back to her. "The way this jump is going to happen, Maxus will leave the ramp and land right in there on that shore. The idea is to get him acclimated to the landing area. It's also about control and Maxus knowing Aaron is the boss on this one."

"He won't throw Aaron back in the river, will he?" She couldn't fathom the number of injuries he must have taken over the years and if she had her way, she wouldn't watch anymore of the mishaps that left her stomach in knots. It scared the daylights out of her to anticipate Aaron getting hurt.

"You never know with Maxus, but he and Aaron have some strange kind of bond. Like that damn horse knows what he is thinking." Gabe shrugged and with a sarcastic tone continued, "Aaron's the best at training horses I've ever seen."

Jenna handed the binoculars back to him. "How long will he be?"

"I'm heading out, got some work on the other side of town and need to get back home before the storm." Gabe smiled. "If you want, wait in the camper, it's too cold out here."

"I'll head that way." She smiled. Gabe gave her a wink and trotted to his truck. She pulled her cart by the camper and went inside. It still amazed her that the camper stayed as warm as it did, like a regular home. She clicked on the television to see about the weather, scanning channels until she found the local report. As she flipped her mind strayed.

She'd hoped to speak to Drake Masters but the actor had been tied up with filming, not giving her an opportunity to catch him alone. Well, she supposed it could wait for a now, as there wasn't much else she could do.

Aaron slammed open the camper door, shaking large flakes of snow from his coat and hair and shut it behind him, shivering. He glanced up, "Hey. I saw your cart, pulled it inside the barn."

"I came inside to get warm and check the news about the weather." She got up anticipating she needed to get on the road and soon, but she hadn't wanted to do so without telling him good-bye.

"It's coming down now, and one of the heaters in the barn went out so I've gotta take a look at it." He bent to kiss her, wrapping his arms around her for a tight hug. "It's best you head out now before it hits."

She nodded. "I will, Mason's with Ms. Lucy."

He shook his head, "I'm doing the all-nighters with the weather and the horses here."

She tugged free of his embrace and walked to the window and looked out. It was snowing but lightly, though the wind was whipping. She'd never get used to the quickness of the weather changes in Montana.

Aaron walked toward the kitchen grabbing a coffee cup.

"Will the camper stay warm enough with the drop in temperatures?" she asked as she turned back to him.

"Yea, I've got plenty of gas and a butane heater if I need it, but I gotta get to that heater in the barn first." He sipped from the black mug and set it down.

"Will it be hard to fix?" she asked.

"Possibly, but I'd rather be fixing you." Aaron smiled and held her gaze.

"The heater, Stuntman." Heat rushed to her cheeks though she grinned. "As much as I would enjoy that I have to get back to pick up Mason."

He lifted her chin kissing her lips until she gave a sigh. "I've got plenty of fixes for you for later. Sarah took Lily to visit her sister for a few days and Gabe is gonna be home with Amos. I can't drive my bike through this anyway. Trapped."

"Gotcha, Mr. Stuntman." She kissed his lips with a slight peck. "I'd love to be trapped here with you but Mason would never forgive me."

He smiled, those green eyes capturing her. "You gotta get started home, then I won't worry."

"I'll call ya later." She smiled and hugged her arms around his middle. "I love you, Aaron."

His gaze narrowed. "You all right?"

He'd told her again last night on the phone that he loved her. She shook her head. "I guess I just still can't believe us. Have you ever been in love before, Aaron? I mean I know we've said the words, but really in love."

He looked at her for a long time before answering. "Yep. She was…special, my heart was taken, forever."

Jenna held his gaze, uncertain but then a dimple creased his face just above the edge of his beard. "She weighed seven pounds and she's had me wrapped ever since. I've loved, Jenna, but never been in love…until you. Remember, it's not the fall, it's the landing."

"And have you landed?" she asked, wanting to open her heart further.

He let her go, tracing a hand along her cheek. "Oh, yeah." He touched her lips with his finger. "I love you, Jenna, so damn much it hurts and I've never said that to any other woman, not even Lily's mother."

Jenna gathered herself to him, holding him as if her life depended on it, tighter than she'd ever held onto anyone in her own life. Aaron Decker was all she'd ever dreamed of, the knight in a little girl's dreams and the man of a woman's heart. Her heart.

Chapter Sixteen

Days later and a bit warmer, Aaron hesitated and then hit the send button on his laptop. He'd done it. Sent Jenna's screenplay to Thomas Campbell. He leaned back in the tiny kitchen chair folding his arms across his chest. He'd thought about telling her that he'd get it to Thomas, but he wanted it to be a surprise if Campbell took it like he thought he might.

He reached for the pile of bills before him finding a letter from Sun Realty. He hadn't realized it was there but he'd been waiting on a written statement that spelled out the costs of the one hundred acres he'd been planning on for such a long time. He opened the envelope and unfolded the triple folded print out. The description and pictures of the land reminded him how much he wanted this to happen, but the price tag was steep to say the least.

The land was available for a little over two thousand dollars an acre. Jim Barnes at Sun Realty was a family friend and had prepared the statement for him. The total costs for the acreage was around two-hundred thousand dollars. Looking at the break-down of what he'd need for a down payment and what his monthly payments would be, seemed right for the first forty acres. Getting a loan for the full acreage wasn't going to happen, at least right now, but he could start with pieces of the land for now.

Even if he was working steady enough for a piece of the land now, there was still the building of the boys' home that wouldn't come cheap. They would need more cattle and a few more horses, sleeping quarters which he envisioned like bunk houses. Barns, fencing and feed didn't come cheap. Of course once he had kids coming in, there would be the potential for state funding options and grants, but his plan was never to deny a boy a home.

He shook his head. As an angry young man in the foster care system, he'd never have thought he would have grown into such a dream, but he wanted this and had for a long time. He shut down the computer and got up, grabbing his coat and tossing it over his shoulder. He needed to practice with Maxus again and then take the animal out for a little exercise and he needed to make a run by Jenna's medical tent to see what she was up to.

He stepped outside the camper as Gabe ambled up with a mug of coffee in one hand and Maxus by the reins in the other.

"I thought you had construction work today? Didn't hear you drive up," he asked as he checked the saddle.

Gabe's hair was ruffled from the ride with the window down. "Got the boys on it, thought since it had warmed up you might want a practice jump."

Aaron glanced across the old west town and then into the sky. Funny how his brother could read his mind and Maxus was following commands well lately. Now was as good a time as any. "It feels right."

"I figured with it warming up a bit, you'd try it alone if I didn't come." Gabe pulled the ball cap from his back pocket and settled it on his dark locks.

Aaron winked, but glanced toward the medical tent. He would go there afterward; it was likely Jenna was helping with set up makeup somewhere else anyway.

"Let's do it." Gabe walked closer. "You gonna pad up?"

Aaron shook his head. "No, if we miss this one, pads will weigh me down in the water."

"I'll check the other side. I walked the ramp a bit ago, it's good and dry." Gabe headed toward Aaron's motorcycle.

Aaron cleared his throat loudly, folding his arms as he glared at his younger brother.

"Hey, it's quicker than the truck." Gabe shrugged, never stopping his pace.

"Treat her kind," Aaron scolded and mounted Maxus. Gabe cranked and revved the engine, throwing gravel on purpose as he rode toward the jump without a helmet as usual.

Aaron urged Maxus to a canter and then a light gallop. A practice jump was risky but he usually did one or two prior to something big. One mishap and he and the horse would be hurt, even if it wasn't that far of a jump. He waited talking to Maxus.

"All right boy, one practice jump and the real thing soon enough." He took Maxus to the ridge. He glanced below and some of the crew from the set were making their way over. Russell, from the film crew, had a camera on him and Trey, from construction, was watching, having crossed the bridge to wait with Gabe. Jenna would probably scold him later that he didn't let her know he'd be making a practice jump, but he needed to focus.

He turned Maxus and glanced toward his brother, who gave him thumbs up. That meant no ice on the ground and with the horse cooperating, a soft landing.

He took a deep breath and cleared his mind, hoping the horse did the same. "Okay, bud, here we go." He kicked to start Maxus on a run so the horse would know this was the real thing. As they hit the ramp, he lightened his grip and tightened his thighs. "Up."

Maxus made the climb with little effort and at the top stretched and jumped across the break, tossing him and Aaron into the air. It was as always, hanging in the wind, the world moved in slow motion as the ground on the other side came closer. Maxus had cleared the ramp in an effortless motion. Aaron titled forward as the bounce of landing jarred him, but the horse sailed smoother on past the landing, speeding away.

"Yeah!" Gabe cheered along with Trey and the others.

Aaron turned Maxus and took his first deep breath since the horse began the climb. The ornery horse had done it. Riding back over to Gabe he dismounted catching his breath.

"Damn good, brother." Gabe walked closer.

Aaron gave Maxus a pat. "Good boy." He rubbed the horse's face getting a nuzzle and then a snort as he lingered too long. The horse seemed to have handled it as if it was nothing, but his own knees were shaking. An adrenaline rush after a good stunt meant it had gone well.

"How'd the ramp feel?" Gabe asked.

Aaron glanced back at the monument. "Solid, no shaking on the lift off. Sturdy. Gotta lose those side rails."

"I'll get the rails down. You think anything needs tightened up?" Trey asked, shoving his hand in his pockets.

Aaron shook his head, "Nope, it's good."

"I'll check things daily to make sure, gotta head over to see about adding to the saloon." Trey grabbed the radio from his belt, trotting away.

"You want one more?" Gabe asked about a second practice jump.

"Nope. Don't want Maxus too confident." The jump had gone perfectly.

Gabe hopped back on the bike. "I'll park her gently."

"You do that," Aaron scolded, as his brother rode back across the bridge on the motorcycle.

He led Maxus on a slow walk back, watching his gate and checking each leg. It had been a wise decision to try, the sunlight good, the wind little and the ramp dry.

"Aaron," Russell called from across the river.

"Yeah." He stopped Maxus, straining to hear.

"Good one, we can use some of the footage," Russell yelled.

Aaron nodded in acknowledgement, tossing up a thumb.

"You did good boy, even though you are such an ornery cuss." He laughed and urged Maxus toward the bridge to head to the corral.

****

Jenna froze, unable to breathe, her legs nearly buckling. Across the tent, on the exam table sat a vase of white roses. She sucked a quick breath of dread, her pulse racing and her heart in her throat. Fighting off the impending sense of doom she moved closer, lifting the envelope. She pulled the card free and thought it was blank. Turning it over, she shook her head fighting tears. '*Cowboy Down.*'

Who was behind this and what did that mean? That was it, she needed to have a chat with Drake Masters, star or not. Enough was enough. This wasn't some kind of game, it was frightening. She turned and pushed through the flap running smack into Aaron and stifling a scream.

Aaron caught her by the arms to steady her. "Jenna?"

She gulped a breath and fell into his embrace. Safe, she needed to be safe. If this wasn't Drake's doing, then there was only Vince… Oh, God. She'd been avoiding that thought for some time, but what if he'd found her?

Aaron tugged her back from him. "What is it?"

"I…got more…flowers, Aaron." She pushed the words free of her tightened throat, the struggle difficult.

He shook his head. "Flowers, what?"

She backed up then, trying to gain her composure, shaking her head.

"Jenna? You're pale as a ghost, what happened?" He grabbed her by both arms. "What?"

She lifted her gaze and met his wide green eyes. "He knows I'm not interested. Why does he keep on if it is him?"

"Jenna, you're shaking." Aaron bent to see her better. "What about the flowers. Who?"

She shook her head. "Flowers came to my apartment and now there are more in the tent, he has to stop this. They keep coming with notes about 'Cowboy up' and 'Cowboy Down.' I don't know why he's doing this."

"Wait, Drake is sending you flowers? Why?" Aaron bristled, still holding her by both arms.

"I…I don't know, but he sent flowers to the hospital and then I got them at home and in the tent before—now here again." Jenna handed him the card in her hand. "There was also a vase of flowers at the hospital with no card…but…"

"But what?" Aaron questioned. "Jenna, talk to me."

"I don't know, it's just…" She couldn't fathom her thoughts. It couldn't be Vince, could it? Not after so long.

"I'll take care of this and right damn now." Aaron stormed from the tent.

"Aaron, wait!" She raced to catch up with him, fighting the bile in her throat. His anger could get him in a lot of trouble and if it was Drake Masters sending the flowers then a simple conversation should be enough.

"I'm putting an end to it right now." Aaron never turned, marching with purpose passed the roped off area mark with a small sign 'celebrities only.'

Jenna grabbed his arm and pulled him to a stop. "You can't lose this job on my account, please, Aaron…please. It isn't worth a fight."

"You're shaking Jenna. Scared. This is out of hand." He shook his head.

"Let's just make sure, please…" She could hardly make her legs do what she wanted them to do, but it wasn't Drake she feared.

"Aaron, please." She touched his arm, but he only

glanced at her as he pounded on the door of Drake's trailer.

Drake appeared at the door, pushing it open further, smiling ear to ear. "Hey, there."

Jenna stepped in front of Aaron, her pulse racing. "I…Drake, I am really flattered and all, but the flowers are becoming too much and they are just not necessary. Really."

Drake stepped outside the trailer, glancing from her to Aaron and back. "Flowers? I sent flowers to the hospital right after my fall, but…"

"Yes, and a number of others." Aaron raised his voice. "Here, her work and her home. It stops now."

Jenna put a hand to his chest and pushed lightly. Drake backed up, holding his hands up in innocence. "Jenna, I sent flowers to the hospital after I was injured, but I've sent no more. Something's not right here?"

Aaron ran a hand through his long dark locks, narrowing his gaze on the actor. "Cut the crap, Masters."

"Aaron, you got the wrong guy. I knew she was smitten with you that night I went to the hospital. I had flowers and pizza sent for everyone there…no more than that. Come on man, I know when a woman's heart is taken. I told her so." Drake glanced at her and back holding his hands up as if innocent.

Jenna's heart dropped to the ground, her next breath coming short. A deep burning dread began in her chest and her vision wanted to blur. She was going to pass out. If it wasn't Drake then the one other answer was—Oh, God, she had to go, she had to get Mason and leave. She backed up, holding Aaron's gaze until she turned to run.

"Jenna?" Aaron called after her.

Urgency traced his voice as he called again and finally caught her outside the barn, spinning her around. "What is it, what, Jenna?"

She shook her head and tried to pull from him, but he held her all the tighter. She couldn't find her voice, her breath was short, and her mind scrambled. "It can't be…he can't—this isn't right…"

"Jenna, if you don't tell me what the hell is going on." He was losing his temper with her but she couldn't focus. She couldn't think. Mason, she had to get him and leave town, run somewhere, anywhere.

"I can't." She pulled away. This was never going to end. Never. With it not being Drake Masters sending the flowers, then it was—Vince. Why now after all this time? The money, it had to be the money. Or, worse than the money, Mason. Maybe he'd found out about his son.

He grabbed her again. "Wait, it's him isn't it…your ex? You think he did this? We'll call the police."

"No, you can't. He's evil, Aaron, capable of anything," she spouted, near hysterics, losing it without a doubt.

"Let's go back to the camper. We'll figure it out. We will." He took her by the arm, but the world seemed to fade. She was conscious that he lifted her and she fought to hold on tightly as he took her into the warmth of the camper. She was in shock. As a nurse, the symptoms couldn't be mistaken, fast heart rate and rapid breathing. She had to calm down or she would do herself and her son no good. So if this was Vince, why the scare tactic? Why didn't he come right out and say what he wanted, though she'd never part with her son.

"Lie back." Aaron tucked a blanket around her and lifted her legs onto the couch. "I'm gonna make some calls and get to the bottom if this. I can promise you that."

"Mason, Oh God, I have to leave, Aaron." She tried to sit up but he held her still as he manned his phone.

"Hang on; we need to figure some things out first." He slid a thumb across his cell phone and put it to his ear.

She nodded and did as he said; wanting to close her eyes and withdraw from the world all except for the part where she wanted her son in her arms. She needed to call Ms. Lucy and make sure Mason was all right. She lifted her phone and texted to older woman who cared for him while she worked. The happy response was quick. All was well.

Aaron explained it all to Gabe, but she couldn't focus. His words blurred as she ran everything through her mind once more. Tears formed again and he sat on the couch with her as he talked taking her hand to reassure her. He would protect her and Mason, she had no doubts there, but if Vince had returned, they were all at risk.

****

"All deliveries have been legit and I check everyone coming through by the master list." Doug Forest, the security guard from the set, sat at the table inside Drake Masters' camper. It was Drake who'd called in Doug, Horace Leland, and Aaron to discuss what was going on.

"You've seen who delivers all the flowers?" Aaron

studied the man with a hard gaze. He'd gotten Jenna back to the camper and left her on the sofa, covering her with a blanket and making her swear she would stay put. She'd said little but had promised. That she was so upset, the others probably knew there was more to the story, but it wasn't his to tell, with Jenna not wanting the police involved and until he knew who they could trust on the set.

"Yes, sir. I don't let anyone through that gate without the proper credentials. I stopped the florist and delivered the flowers myself. I didn't know there was a problem in taking the flowers to Jenna's tent. They were for her, but the delivery boy is a kid maybe sixteen or so. I don't let him on the set. Drake gets flowers too, like a lot of the actors and actresses. Do the deliveries myself." Doug glanced around at them all and rested his gaze on Aaron.

"Of course he does. I'll make sure we beef up security around here, but like you, I'd prefer to keep to local police on the sidelines or this might end up all over the tabloids." Horace was more than annoyed. "Gentleman, I have a series to film. If I can be of further assistance, please let me know."

"It might be best to halt flowers on the set for a while and see what happens." Drake eyed Horace and shrugged.

Aaron nodded in agreement, unsure he trusted any one of them.

"Fine. And please let Jenna know new measures are in place." Horace exited the trailer.

Doug was quick to follow. "I'll stop flowers at the gate, but Drake, you get flowers every day and sometimes more than once."

"You are welcome to have them donated to a local nursing home or something like that." Drake followed Aaron outside his trailer.

Doug nodded and after a quick glance at them both, lifted his radio and headed back to the gate.

Aaron turned back to Drake. "Sorry for jumping to conclusions, but I've never seen her so frightened." He'd studied the man, finding no hints of someone who was lying. Doug, on the other hand, was jittery, forcing himself to hold eye contact his voice wavering. Either he was scared of losing his job or knew more than he was telling.

"No worries." Drake nodded toward the medical tent. "If I had a woman like Jenna I wouldn't take this so lightly either."

Aaron nodded. It was the best he could do for the moment. He wanted answers and if it wasn't Drake, then Jenna thought it to be her ex-husband and he wasn't sure at all what that might mean.

"I saw your jump earlier. Looked really good." The actor lifted his brows as if amazed.

"Timing was right and it went off smooth." He had to agree, though it seemed now the jump was the least of his worries.

"Better you than me." Drake offered a hand and he took it briefly. "Let Jenna know we'll pay attention to things and if I can help in any way. Anything at all."

"Thanks."

"See you on the set." Drake headed off that direction on a trot.

Aaron glanced around the set as he went back toward the camper. People came and went everyday from the minimally guarded set, but it wasn't that things were just happening at the set. Jenna had gotten flowers at the hospital and her home. If it was her ex-husband then he already knew too much. She'd been fine with confronting Drake Masters, but then he'd watched her wither like a desert rose when she realized all the flowers weren't from him. He needed to pay attention to who was hanging around, besides the security guard; he was on the set more than anyone else due to the horses.

He entered the camper, finding Jenna still on the couch where he'd left her. She looked a little better as she sat to face him.

"Are you all right?" He sat on the couch at her feet, pulling her legs across his lap.

"I don't know." Her eyes were swollen from tears but at least the color had returned to her face.

"I know it's hard but you have to tell me everything, Jenna. All of it. We won't call the police, but Gabe's friend, Tucker's a P.I. and a good one." He spoke soft but sure, thinking his brother and Tucker could just about figure out most anything.

"It has to be Vince, I'm sure of it." She shook her head, "but why he would jeopardize his career now? He even has a new wife and her children."

He shook his head. "He'll have to get through me to get to you or Mason, best he doesn't try it. Either way, Gabe and Tuck can give us a hand. But you aren't staying alone anymore. I'm taking you and Mason to the ranch." If her ex-husband had found out where she lived and worked, it was likely he was well aware of her visit to the ranch, but he wouldn't know anything much at all about the cabin if it came to that.

"You can't put your own family in danger," she

protested, shaking her head.

"You are not free to choose this one, babe." He pushed a strand of hair back from her face and wrapped an arm around her. "What's Vince's last name?"

"Hanson." She held onto him and sniffled. "Vince Hanson."

He studied her for a moment. Jenna Wilder, the woman he loved. "You didn't take his last name?"

She shook her head, "I did but changed my name back after the divorce was final."

He nodded, having thought so.

"Afterward, I could hardly breathe, my ribs were broken. My mind was so foggy. I was bleeding from my nose and mouth and my eyes were so puffy I could hardly see. The police wanted me to press charges but I couldn't out of fear I suppose."

He took her hand in his, tracing her nails with his thumb. While he needed to know more, seeing her in this kind of pain was his undoing.

She sat back and brushed away tears. "But it was his father who came to the hospital. He said if I wouldn't press charges he'd see to it that Vince left me alone and that he would send my personal things, allow the divorce. At the time it seemed best. I was so confused and shocked it had even happened and that I was pregnant. I hadn't known." She shook her head. "I made the great mistake of questioning where all the money was coming from. Large amounts were being dropped into our accounts out of nowhere and I knew it wasn't from his father. Strange calls were coming to the house from those that seemed to have a vested interest in those funds. And one day I asked a little too much about where it was all coming from." She sniffled and rested her elbows on her knees, drawing her hand away from his.

"Afterward, I was afraid, so afraid. So I left Atlanta for Virginia and stayed with Brianna, but I didn't know about the money. I mean Vince's father told me he'd send all my personal things and the money that belonged to me."

"What money?" Aaron questioned. If she had serious money then this would explain a lot of things.

"Like money could ever…" She burst into tears.

"Jenna, what money?" He raised his tone an octave.

She lifted her head to look at him. "Brianna found the statement in the mail and brought it to me. My daddy left me a great deal of money when he died, and Vince's father made sure I got it back. He'd opened an account in my name and put it there. But I was so afraid; I cashed it out and put it in a number of new accounts so it couldn't be traced."

He pulled her against him, hugging her tight, letting her sob. There was nothing worse than a woman in tears, but Jenna in tears crushed his heart right into the dirt.

"I haven't seen him since. So I don't understand, why now? It's been nearly two years. What if he knows about Mason? Oh my God." She tried to get up, but then leaned forward to cover her face with her hands for a brief second.

"Jenna, how much money are you talking about?" He had to ask to understand the full impact of the situation.

She held up two fingers as she turned to him with tears streaming her face.

"Two-hundred-thousand?" He narrowed a gaze on her.

She shook her head and whispered. "Million. Two Million—a good bit more by now."

Aaron lifted his brows. Well, that made things quite complicated either way. "Where's the money now?"

"In various accounts, CD's, money market, IRAs. I was so confused and shocked. Oh my God, I have to get Mason out of here." She stood and glanced down where his hand still held to her forearm.

"Jenna, don't do anything in haste. I'm gonna put Tucker and Gabe on this and right now we just have to act normal, finish out the day." He tugged her back down beside him. "I'll get you and Mason to the ranch. If it is Vince and you run, he'll just find you again."

"Aaron you can't let everything go to protect me. You have the ranch, your job here with the jump in a few days and Lily. I've got to be at the shoot out at the saloon in a bit." She wiped her face. "I texted and Ms. Lucy and Mason are fine, but I need to get to him right after."

"When you are off, we'll go get Mason and pack a few things and get you to both to the ranch." He kissed her forehead, hugging her close for a moment more. "We're not taking any chances here and running isn't the answer."

If he could get her settled at the ranch, then he could protect her there. Meanwhile, he'd have Gabe and Tuck look at things, starting first with the whereabouts of Vince Hanson.

Chapter Seventeen

Jenna lay awake in Aaron's bed, unable to sleep. It had been late when he had gotten her settled in, with Sarah more than kind to make sure she had all she needed for herself and Mason. She was a very kind woman but the worry on her face told the story. She shivered in spite of being warm, inhaling the scent of Aaron that rode the heavy covers and content that Mason slept soundly in his pack and play in Lily's room.

Vince had to be the one behind the flowers and it had to be he'd returned for the money or, her worst of fears, Mason. Money made people crazy and it was why she'd relished in her simple paycheck, having never touched the money she hidden away. It was long after midnight and she was certain sleep wouldn't come. Aaron had been downstairs for a few hours now discussing the issue with his brothers and Gabe's friend, Tucker.

That alone was alarming, as she'd brought possible harm to this beautiful family and she was sure of nothing. The last she'd even read related to Vince was that he was assured a seat in the senate, victories were coming for him left and right and his new wife and her children had been in the one picture. All she could remember about that was the sorrow she felt for what the new wife likely didn't know—yet. So if he was so successful in meeting his father's dreams for his career, why did she or Mason even matter at this point?

Vince's father had known of her pregnancy, but he'd sworn to keep her secret. And after he'd wired her the money that belonged to her, she'd changed her name, her accounts and anything that linked her to the past. She was now and had been for some time, Jenna Wilder. The pen name she'd planned to use one day had become her 'real' name and Mason's last name as well. She'd never shared with Vince the name she was using, so how could he have found her? At times she'd been plagued with guilt of not letting Vince know he had a son, but she wouldn't subject a child to the beating she had taken and a full escape had been the only way.

But what now—

"I didn't figure you'd be sleeping." Aaron stood in the doorway, his tall body leaning against the frame, his dark hair banded away from his face.

"I dozed a little," she lied.

He smirked a bit of a laugh. "No, you didn't."

She sat up in bed, leaning against the carved wooden headboard. "Well, I tried."

He set a plate of apples and cheese on the nightstand and pulled his dark t-shirt over his head. "Here, eat. Done some talking with the boys. Tucker found out Vince Hanson's in Mexico, raising funds for some relief effort. He isn't expected back to the states for a few weeks at least according to his office."

She nodded. "His office always covered for him. There were times I didn't know where he was, like a lot of unexplained things." There had been days at a time she never saw him only to get a phone call about how much he loved and missed her. Funny, she'd never believed him, but neither had she pushed, until she understood the illegal things going on where money was concerned.

He shook his head. "He's not in Mexico Nothing tracks him there unless he is traveling under an alias. Tuck found several names he must've used from time to time."

"I found an I.D. once that had him listed as Vincent Gallagher, but questioning him, he lied as usual. That was when I knew I'd been living a lie." All of it came back now, all the little things like Vince's white lies, missing dinner dates with her, not coming home. She'd been an ornament, the perfect wife he needed for the purpose of the seat he was fighting to gain. The same role the new woman and her children were playing in his life now. Poor lady probably had no idea.

"That was one of the names, but there are several. Ahh, we think it's best to keep things normal for now, all but a few things." He stood to kick out of his boots, setting them across the room and slipping from his jeans leaving him in his boxers. "You and I need to go to the set as planned, do our work. You'll need to drive on your own, by way of back by your apartment and pretending to leave Mason with Ms. Lucy."

"Pretending?"

He nodded, moving closer. "I'd like to leave him here with Sarah. She keeps Lily daily and he'd be safer. If things turn, I can have Sarah pack them both up and meet her sister so they can take off somewhere none of us know."

"Aaron, I can't... Oh, my God, I have no idea how to do this..." She shook her head, terror blazing through her chest as if she might suffer a panic attack. This was a living nightmare.

"This is where you gotta trust me, babe. He's going nowhere right now, but if these flowers and notes are the precursor to what's coming, we need an escape plan for the children. And...maybe even you." He hesitated, "And you can't tell Bri or Ms. Lucy anything for now."

"Oh, God, Aaron, yes, but this isn't fair to you...I want Mason and Lily safe. Your whole family doesn't deserve this." She ran a hand through her disheveled hair. Nope, she wouldn't cry. It was time to stand up and figure out what she had to do to make her world safe once more. "You know Brianna knows we are here and she knows about the cabin. Ms. Lucy knows a bit of my past but not like Bri does, and I worry about them both."

"I'll have Tuck or Gabe keep an eye on them." He held her gaze then. "You can trust Tuck and my brothers. You know that, right?"

In the darkness, he was her guardian angel, telling her all would be well. And she leaned into him. "Yes. But I have the money to pay Tucker and Gabe."

"No worries about the money. Tuck won't take money anyway." He kissed her, taking her mouth gently with just the press of his full lips then spoke. "I waited a long time for you. You are worth it, all of it. Now rest. I suppose it would be best that I sack out in Lily's room."

He stood and she grabbed him by the hand. "Stay."

He shook his head. "Jenna?"

"Hold me; lie here with me...to be close. You can slip out before Lily wakes." She'd never sleep if she couldn't feel the warmth of him nearby and while they hadn't wanted to share a bed in front of the children, it seemed the least of evils at the moment.

He took a deep breath, turned, and closed the door, making his way to lie beside her. The warmth of him enveloped her as he spooned closer, his large arm covering her. "Rest. It's all right. I'm here."

She snuggled into him, his warmth the first she thought maybe she'd felt in a long time and though she didn't allow the tears she sniffled.

He pulled her closer, kissing her hair and then her shoulder.

And she closed her eyes, listening as Aaron deep breaths, letting the comfort of him lull her to move past her fear and into a much-needed slumber.

****

Jenna startled awake, bolting upright in bed. Aaron's bed. "Mason?"

Aaron tugged her back down with a whisper. "He's fine. Sleeping still, he and Lily both."

She tried to clear her mind, glancing at the clock. She must've slept hard. Almost four in the morning. "Sorry, I was dreaming."

He touched his lips to her shoulder, spooning behind her. "Been laying here, watching you for the last hour or so, wishing I could fix this whole damn thing for you."

She lifted his hand and kissed his knuckles. "I'll be fine, Aaron. I have to be in order to protect Mason. I actually feel much better now that I've slept, thanks to you."

"It's gonna be all right." He mumbled into her back, kissing the skin of her shoulder again. "God, you smell so good."

She turned in bed to face him. He was so sexy with

his sleepy green eyes, dark hair tied away from his face, his beard nuzzling her cheek. The warmth of him was all she needed and in spite of her worries she kissed him.

His gaze held her, and while there was desire there, he held back. That was on her account with all that had happened. Her body tingled with his touch, her own need to escape her thoughts drawing a hint of pleasure at the idea of making love with him again. She needed him, to be held, to know he was her protector, and to yield to something good in her world.

"Make love to me, Aaron." She was shocked at her own request. He probably thought her too fragile, but she needed to forget, and his touch would do that for a time.

"You should rest, there's time for that." He shook his head, though he didn't let her go.

She pulled him to her, stopping him from saying anything more as she touched her lips to his and spoke as she kissed him. "Now Stuntman."

He pushed her back to the bed with his body, holding her there and looking at her, the early morning light leaving the room a light gray.

She was suddenly aware of the boldness of her words and her entire body flushed warm. Good Lord, she *had* been writing for too long, and giggled at her thoughts.

"What?" He nuzzled into her neck.

She laughed. "I am running words through my head about us that…never mind, I've been writing way too long."

His face held puzzlement for a moment, but then he grinned. "I'll take your word for it. Keep thinking like that."

She smiled. Even if it felt her world was sitting on the edge of falling apart, he was the one thing holding her together and she wanted…no she needed his touch, his hands on her…

Aaron found her mouth again, wrestling her from her clothing and laughing at the efforts at which he made swift. Somewhere along the way he'd become as naked as her, his furry legs letting her know that as he rolled aside, digging in the night stand drawer for a condom, she suspected. Heat took her center as he turned back to her, fighting the foil wrap in the morning darkness.

"Wait." She grabbed his hand and pushed it to the bed, the packet still there unopened.

He froze, watching her as she kissed his chest, touching her tongue to each of his nipples sliding her hand lower. She wasn't sure what had come over her, but as much as her body burned for him, she wanted to please him, to take over the lovemaking, love him…and take him to where their bodies collided as one in sweet relief.

Aaron sucked in a breath as she gripped him, lifting his head to watch her as she slipped even lower with her kisses. "Jenna. Jenna, you don't have to…"

She stopped him short by taking him into her mouth, swirling her tongue around him. Once, then twice again.

He groaned, tossing his head back to the pillow and playing his fingers through her hair. His hips bucked and she repeated the effort without mercy. This time his hands guided her pace with another groan and pulled her away from him.

"Uh huh…I won't last two seconds to see to you." He fumbled with the condom, the strain evident in his voice, her own urgency leaving her breathless.

She lay back as he put his hand between her legs, tracing until he'd found her, rubbing hard and taking a nipple into his mouth. She bowed, breathless. "I need you, Aaron, now. Oh, God."

He said nothing but drew on the other nipple, working her with his fingers, sinking them deep, his thumb on the core of her. She was going to…easy as that, his warm tongue on her breasts, his thick fingers inside her…but he withdrew, leaving her on the very edge. He tossed the blankets from them and leaned back against the headboard, urging her on top of him. His hands rested on her hips as she straddled him, both of them moaning as she took him inside her fully.

She shivered as he urged her to move, her pelvis tilting forward with him deep inside.

"Oh, God, Aaron…" it was the slightest whisper, the thickness of him quenching her aching need, so full her body quivered around him. He lifted her and tugged her back down several times and she moved with him, hanging onto his shoulders as his hips pumped into her once, twice, three times…

"Let go, Jenna." His sweet whisper filled her ears and she shattered, her breath lost in a half cry of his name. And she clung to him as he continued the slow pump into the depths of her, bolts of fiery pleasure rippling through her until she fell limp against him. She gasped as he pulled her down on him over and over, his lips along her neck and his heavy breath in her ear.

Somewhere as she came back to herself, she heard him say her name as his own body shuddered against her his hands trembling along her hips and his lips along her neck.

After a time, he spoke in the slightest whisper, rolling her beneath him as his body shuddered again. "I'll never have enough of you, Jenna. It's gonna be all right."

"I know it will be…" The dread tried to return but she pushed it away as he moved from her and fumbled in the nightstand. What was he doing? He opened her hand and placed a black velvet box there, holding her hand closed around it. Oh, Good Lord was this…

His voiced shook as he spoke. "I was saving this for a more appropriate time and place. I've never been really good at timing, but I think, given what is happening, I need you to know how much I love you and Mason now. I mean right now and always. Open it?"

He sat up in bed as she did, pulling the sheet across them as they leaned against the headboard. Oh, God was he proposing…giving her forever?

She glanced at the small velvet covered box. Was this what she wanted from Aaron? Forever? Yes, without any doubt in her mind.

She looked at him again aware she trembled as she lifted the top open. She gasped. Inside was an engagement ring as beautiful as she'd ever seen. The thick band of gold was etched with feathers in the design with a solitaire diamond in the center in a brilliant cut. Tears rimmed her eyes of their own will and she didn't try to stop them as they fell. "Aaron?"

"Marry me, Jenna." He held her gaze, his green eyes focusing on hers.

She glanced at him and down at the ring once

more. And all she'd ever wanted was love, real love, the kind that didn't hurt, the kind that was forever, and the kind that she wrote about in her stories. "Yes."

He took the box, and lifted the ring, putting it on her finger. "No one will ever love you like I do."

Tears continued to spill from her eyes as he tugged her into him, embracing her. "Shhhhh…"

Moments passed before she had the composure to speak. "I love you, Aaron. You make me so happy."

"We don't have to rush anything." He seemed a bit nervous now. "I needed you to know how much you mean to me and how far I will go to protect you and Mason. You're special and I knew that the first moment I saw you, standing in that tent, unsure about the new job and more beautiful than any actress who'd shown up to film."

"You're so sweet, Aaron." She glanced at the ring on her finger tracing the tiny feathers, quills actually.

"Because you write." He grinned. "Had it special made, but when we have time, I want to take you to the cabin, just me and you and propose the right way."

"No, this was perfect; though if our children ask one day, guess I will have to tell them you proposed naked in bed." She chuckled.

"Leave it to me to do the unique and different." He smiled, touching her cheek.

"It was perfect." She kissed him and hugged him close against her. "You are all I never expected, Aaron. Thank you for loving me and my son."

"I told you that you were worth it, and I will spend every day of my life showing you how much so," he whispered and snuggled her closer.

Jenna clung to him and studied the ring on her

finger. She really wanted to slam on the lights and take a good look, but he'd worked hard on the words he'd spoken to her and she wouldn't ruin this moment, even if they were naked. She glanced at him, but he had closed his eyes a slight smile of satisfaction across his lips. She leaned against his chest, closing her own eyes.

The passion between them was something more than she'd ever experienced, but the love was something as real as she'd ever known. And even in her worst moments he was of sorts her hero, the man in her story that would always hold her up when she couldn't stand on her own, and she would be the warmth he needed in his heart always.

Chapter Eighteen

Aaron sat atop Maxus, dressed in jeans and walking the horse along the path he'd take later in the afternoon for the jump. He'd met with the camera and lighting crew, Drake Masters and Horace Leland for the last-minute details. While he'd do the real jump, there would be footage of Masters riding Maxus up the ramp and riding away, once the jump was done. Now it was up to him and Maxus.

Horace Leland had explained again what he'd like to see with the jump and landing, like he knew anything about being on a horse. But Maxus had done well with the practice jump, almost effortless for the ornery cuss of a horse and he could make another.

He'd spent the morning with Gabe, going over the ramp once more, figuring the glare of the sun and working with the cameramen who agreed, five-thirty would be the best time to make the jump. The sun would be in the western sky falling lower and would give a mirrored look of oranges and yellows, shadowing him and the horse in slow motion footage.

He smiled with a thought of Jenna. She was amazing, wasn't she? Her gentle spirit and strength alone reminded him of his reasons for loving her. While she'd been a victim, she didn't play one even if at times she was terrified. There was reason for caution, but more than that, there was reason to make sure she felt safe and so she'd remained at the ranch with her son. There had been no more flowers, but quiet didn't mean things were still and it wasn't often he slept through the night as he held her.

Jenna had seemed better, often admiring her ring and him; though he was well aware she worried every second. And Mason had slipped right into his heart as well. A spry little guy with her same spirit and a giggle that made him chuckle to himself any time he heard it. The night before, he'd carried on a wrestling match where Lily and Mason had him pinned to the floor in a winning round. It had been a quick glimpse of what life with Jenna and Mason would be like for him and Lily.

"You all set for the jump?" Gabe walked closer giving Maxus a pat as he arrived back at the barn.

"He's in a good mood, the wind's low." He glanced into the sky again and back at his brother.

Gabe folded up a sandwich wrapper, tossing it in the barrel of trash that sat nearby. "Jeremiah called, he'll be here in a few minutes. He's off and Amos is downtown sitting at the diner, insisting he could drive and have a day out on his own."

"Shit. He shouldn't be driving and he knows that." Amos had eaten lunch at the diner for years, but with his failing health didn't get to go as often as he'd like.

"Nope, but can't stop him. Tuck called too. Not much more on Hanson's location but it looks like a good bit of money filtering, large amounts of cash with no trail. Word has it he is one bad dude to mess with." Gabe scratched a hand through his dark unkempt hair and added a baseball cap.

He studied his brother, not surprised at what they might be up against. "There's a lot she didn't know about him. She knew money was coming from somewhere and asking too much got her the beating."

"I'm not sure we can be convinced it's him. With her job, what about angry patients, staff? Hell, we have to think about people here on the set as well, but we have to make some kind of positive connection." Gabe shook his head. "Why's she so convinced it's him?"

Aaron thought about what he had and hadn't told Gabe. "The man beat her nearly half to death, she's afraid. I guess he'd the first person she could think of because of the money and her son."

"Drake's good. Never even been arrested. Just a bit of Hollywood crap." His brother shrugged. "But security is pretty tight around here, now. Got Doug moving his ass a bit more. Did a search on him too, but he's got nothing going."

He nodded in agreement. "At least it seems to have calmed down a little and she's sleeping better the last few days."

Gabe laughed raising his eyebrows in question. "You lettin' her sleep?"

Aaron tossed the gloves he'd removed from his hand at his brother, but grinned. "Sleep's overrated."

His brother shook his head, picking up the gloves from the ground and handing them back to his brother. "Well, come up for air now and then. Can't believe you are gonna really do it."

"Had no choice. Can't get her out of my head." He still couldn't believe he'd asked Jenna to marry him. "We've no set plans."

"You got it bad, bro." Gabe laughed, shaking his head.

He glared at his brother. "Enough already."

Gabe waited. "Well, congratulations then, but best we figure this bullshit out with Hanson first."

His brother's gaze held more than he was saying.

"What?" He grabbed Maxus by the reins and followed.

Gabe scratched his jaw, turning to face him, his deep blue eyes serious. "Look, uhh…we ran a check on Jenna too and I don't want you blindsided. She's clean all except the part where her name used to be Jennifer Amiker. Looks like she changed it about that time she took the beating, I get that. But the trail is still there. Be careful, Aaron. There's a couple of political figures who have kinda bought the dust somewhere in relation to Vince Hanson. He's lethal and you really don't know what political crap she just might be involved in as well because of him."

Aaron narrowed his gaze. "Whatever his issues, they aren't Jenna's. She was scared half to death, changing her name was a good start. You and Tucker find him, so we can put an end to this."

Gabe held his gaze, his eyes going dark. "That's just it, Aaron. It might be he finds us first."

****

Aaron nodded, turning Maxus to the barn. His brother was right. If Tucker and Gabe thought Vince Hanson was bad news, then he was without a doubt some kind of dangerous. All the more reason to make sure Jenna was free of the situation. He let Maxus go in the corral, hanging onto his bridle.

Looking toward the medical tent, he headed that direction. He hadn't seen Jenna since morning as she had been needed with make-up to help dress up the injuries for an Indian massacre.

Reaching the tent, he looked inside and she was sitting across at her table writing again. Watching her for a long moment, he could tell she was lost again in one of her stories. It occurred to him he might need to read her full script when he had the chance. And there was still that bit of guilt at having sent the script off without her permission.

"Hey." He walked inside, capturing her gaze.

She set her laptop aside on the table. "Hi."

"I saw a few cowboys sporting arrows and blood." He smiled.

"The people who took arrows back then didn't die right away. They died slowly of the bleeding or infection weeks later, but apparently television needs to move a bit faster." She giggled, warming him inside.

"Most likely Horace needs to move faster," he agreed.

She leaned back on the table looking at him. "So Maxus is ready and you are too?"

He nodded. "The wind and lighting will be right. Maxus is being himself but a good day for him. You coming?"

She shuddered. "Apparently, I'm getting paid to watch."

"It'll be fine. Besides it's not the fall, it's the landing and we've got that covered now don't we." He pulled her against him in a tight hug. "Isn't that right Mrs. Decker?"

"Well, you seemed to have landed pretty well last night. But I still have to pinch myself about the Ms. Decker part." She glanced at the ring on her finger

"Are you happy?"

"Yes." The hint of a smile traced her lips. "I called

Brianna. I've shared with your mother and Sally here on the set. A girl has a right you know."

"I've got Tuck watching out for Brianna and Ms. Lucy but calling too often isn't safe for now." He wasn't sure just how long he might keep saying the same thing. They were all waiting like sitting ducks and he hadn't liked any of it.

She shook her head. "Apparently, Gabe gave her a new phone to use."

"Jenna, look at me." He spoke softly, trying to convince her. "It's going to be all right. It is."

"I know." She tried for a smile.

"Hey, I'm going to do some last-minute planning with the film crew, get into make-up, jump the horse and kiss my girl at the bottom of that landing." Aaron winked at her. "I thought later I could take you out, let Sarah keep the children."

Jenna hopped from the table. "I'll be waiting for that kiss and dinner. I love you, Aaron."

He glanced at her once more, smiling and made his way out of the tent, leaving her to her work and thinking he'd make his jump, kiss her, take her to dinner and then make love to her until he had her writhing beneath him in his bed once again. That would be his reward for a hard day's work. He chuckled as he took off on a trot for the set.

****

The view was right, the lighting and sunlight hitting the ramp with no glare. Horace gave Aaron a thumbs up, standing with the crew closer to the jump. He glanced around from the top of the ridge. Actors and extras were below to watch him and Maxus jump. He took a deep breath, his chest pounding, now in costume, dark jeans, light shirt, vest, and hat. A complete cowboy package. He chuckled to himself. *Hardly.*

He eyed the ramp, tracing the path along the wooden incline and then peered across to the other side. There wasn't any real challenge for Maxus; the length of the jump was about ten feet, nothing for the horse. The end of the ramp was level with the ground on the opposite side, though there was about a fifteen-foot drop to the river.

He turned Maxus away from the set, taking him on a short gallop and turned the animal back. Below, Jeremiah sat on the medical cart with Jenna, but it was Gabe's warning that still echoed in his mind where Jenna was concerned. The fact she had changed her name wasn't surprising. Women did that all the time after a divorce, especially one such as she'd been through. Most likely she'd done it to protect her son and he understood that one well enough. He took another deep breath trying to clear his mind.

He rode Maxus for another quick gallop returning and looking into the sun. It was about time and he'd gotten the thumbs up. There would be no call for action, but he'd jump when he and the horse were ready.

"All right boy, let's get it done." He spoke to the horse, Maxus urging ahead, ready.

Taking a deep breath and pressing the cowboy hat to his head tighter, he waited a second before hitting the reins. "Up boy…up!" He kicked and Maxus took off down the ridge toward the ramp on a gallop picking speed.

Aaron focused, blocking out all below except the mouth of the ramp. Adrenaline surged through him and the animal beneath him took the reins, unrestricted. He was on his mark and Aaron gripped his thighs tighter to hang on as Maxus took the footing to the ramp, the shoes on the horse's hooves clapping hard across the thick wooden boards. The world slowed in motion. He and the horse moved as one, as easy as before. Maxus pulled up the steeper part of the ramp, the take off several feet away.

"Up!" Aaron shouted as a reminder to the horse, but then the crack of thunder lifted him and the horse, tossing them forward and sending him from the saddle, dust exploding around him taking his breath and the blast muffling his hearing. All of a sudden, he was falling, fighting the air trying to right himself.

Bend your knees, land on your feet, grab something to break the fall, anything to slow the impact of the ground.

He reached out, bending his knees, not knowing his position as he fell backward, trying to turn. His body hit the ramp mid-way, jolting pain ripping through his side and he curled to the pain, falling further. He'd lost his bearings, trying to suck in a breath he couldn't take. What in the hell, some kind of explosion? He braced himself, as the hard earth took him, the air he did have pushed from his lungs, the world closing him off around him. *Maxus?*

Chapter Nineteen

"Aaron!" Gabe ran toward Aaron who lay unmoving on the ground below the broken ramp, white smoke filling the air. "Call Nine, One, One!"

Jenna stood up on the cart, her heart in her throat, not believing what had happened. There had been an explosion of some kind and Aaron had fallen. "Oh my God!"

She put her hand to her mouth, bile rising in her throat. He had been thrown from the horse and fell to the ground, while the horse remained on the ramp rearing in the confusion. The explosion had been deafening across the set, startling all those watching. Now panic crossed the set with people running and screaming. She had to get to Aaron, but couldn't think to make her body move, frozen for the briefest of seconds.

Jeremiah jumped back to the cart with her, yelling. "Go, Jenna!"

She nodded, slamming down in the seat and turning the key to crank the engine. She couldn't breathe and her heart pounded inside her chest as bolts of sheer terror rode through her. Would Aaron have survived the fall?

She pulled the cart as close to Aaron as she could get, his body unmoving. The camera and lighting crew hovered around him, shouting and pointing. She fought the tears that threatened. *Oh please God!*

She wasn't sure what she would find with Aaron, but falls like that… She wanted to panic and run, but there was no choice. She was the nurse. She was the professional and she was going to be his wife. Everything was up to her. Aaron's survival was in her hands, if he was alive. And the horse, Maxus was still on the ramp, saliva hanging in streams from his mouth as crew struggled to get him off the twisted smoking ramp.

She gripped a fist to feel the ring on her finger. She couldn't lose Aaron like this, not now, not after thinking she would never find love or her life again. She slammed the cart into park and grabbed her bag, working through the small crowd.

Aaron lay motionless on his back, surrounded by crew and Horace Leland who was on his radio calling for rescue.

"Aaron, Aaron…breathe, brother. He's not breathing." Gabe looked up at her as she hit her knees on the ground beside them, opening her bag and grabbing her stethoscope. *Oh God, I can't do this.*

"Aaron?" She touched Aaron's neck, feeling for a pulse, wiping tears from her eyes with her sleeve. *Remember your training girl, you can do this.*

Aaron's eyes flickering open and closed again, his mouth seeking a breath he wasn't taking. *He was alive.*

She reached to hold his chin, keeping his neck aligned. "Aaron, take a breath, go ahead. It's all right, I'm here." Her voice cracked as she turned to Jeremiah beside her. The look of shock on his face, told the story.

"I'll get a C-Collar." Jeremiah jumped up heading to the cart.

"And oxygen. Breathe, Aaron!" She tried again as his body jerked several times, and he gave in to a gasping breath, letting out a crying growl, shuddering in pain.

"That's it Aaron. Come on another." Gabe was encouraging him, hanging on tightly to his shoulder.

Aaron sucked in another breath, grabbing the left side of his chest with his right hand, groaning as he took another struggled breath.

"No, Aaron, don't move. Please don't move." Jenna held his head and neck still. The chance of spinal or head injury was no doubt the biggest issue, that and internal bleeding from such a fall. Her body shook with adrenaline and the picture of the explosion replayed in her mind. How had this happened? But then—she knew.

Jeremiah arrived with the C-collar and a back board from the cart, an oxygen tank and two medical bags over his shoulder. He helped get the collar around Aaron's neck, while Jenna held his head steady.

Aaron continued with gasping breaths, grunting with each, fighting and trying to move himself, grabbing at the air as if he were still falling. He was moving arms and legs and that was a great relief, but there could still be neck or spinal injury but the next thing was assessing him and making sure he continued to breathe as they stabilized him from moving.

"Aaron, lie still." Jeremiah fought to hold him down, along with Gabe.

Blood ran from Aaron's nose, his eyes glazed in fear. Scratches and scrapes covered his arms, face, and neck. He was pale and his body shook hard in spasms. Shock.

"Start the oxygen and get an I.V. line in. Push normal saline wide open," Jenna shouted as she probed his body wither hand searching for further injury.

Jeremiah prepped the I.V. tubing, though his hands were shaking. She grabbed her stethoscope again, listening to Aaron's chest. He was clear on the right side and diminished on the left. He probably had broken ribs and a collapsed lung, but what scared her more was that falling that far could mean damage to his heart or aorta. She listened to his heart, the beat rapid and strong.

She pulled the stethoscope away from her ears and let it hang from her neck, placing the mask over Aaron's mouth and nose and then grabbing the scissors to cut his shirt away from his chest. The bruising there was already evident though he continued to breathe.

She ran her hand around Aaron's cheeks and to the back of his head, finding a large lump behind his left ear. Head injury no doubt, but there was no bleeding. She used her penlight to check his pupils, finding them both reactive and equal, which was a good sign, though his confusion wasn't.

"Aaron, do you know where you are?" She spoke getting close to his face.

He blinked his eyes, trying to focus from what she could tell. He finally growled through the mask, "...the ground. Jenna?"

"It's me Aaron, can you squeeze my hands?" She gripped both his hands eliciting a yelp from him.

His left hand was swollen with a small protrusion on the back of his hand, probably broken. She felt along the bones from his shoulder to his elbow and then his wrist. Aaron groaned and tried to pull his hand away.

"Hold still brother." Gabe leaned near Aaron to speak. "I know ya hurt."

"I.V.'s in." Jeremiah handed off the bag of fluids to someone behind him, who held it in place.

"His hand is broken along with his ribs and the lung is collapsed," Jenna spoke to Jeremiah.

"I got it." Jeremiah sprinted away and returned with a brace, taking care to put Aaron's left arm and hand into it.

Jenna traced along each of Aaron's legs, feeling for fractures, finding none. He'd been moving both his legs in trying to fight. He'd hit the ramp on the way down most likely saving fractures to his legs, but it would be hard to tell at this point about his back or neck.

"No!" Aaron let out a stern whisper, his face grimacing in pain as he tried to stop her when she touched his chest where the ribs had been hit.

"That was an explosion, fucking...damn. Gotta get the horse." Gabe glanced behind him where men on the ramp were having trouble controlling Maxus from what Jenna could tell in her quick glance.

Jeremiah scooted down Aaron's body and pulled Aaron's boot carefully from him one at a time. "Aaron, move your toes brother, wiggle your feet."

Aaron was still growling to breathe but a moment later, both socked feet moved.

Jenna grabbed a blood pressure cuff and pumped, shoving the stethoscope into her ears. Listening carefully, she watched the dial fall lower than she had expected. One-hundred over sixty. Grabbing his right wrist, she counted his pulse at one-hundred forty and his breathing was rapid at forty-six. With his low blood pressure, he could be losing blood but it was most likely shock.

Aaron tried to talk, pulling at the mask. "Maxus?"

Jeremiah shook his head. "They're getting him off the ramp, he didn't fall, Aaron."

Aaron grabbed his side, tears streaming from his face as he cried out in pain, gulping for air in rasping breaths.

Jenna continued with Aaron, applying a dressing to his bleeding elbows and counting his pulse again. He fought for a moment to glance toward Maxus, grimacing with the effort.

"Lay still, Aaron. Gabe's got 'em." Jeremiah tried to calm his brother, who gave up and lay unmoving, his body shaking and tears streaming the sides of his cheeks.

"Son…of a…bitch," he whispered with a struggle and closed his eyes.

"Get the blankets across his legs and raise them." Jenna palpated Aaron's abdomen, finding no tenderness or rigidity. The oxygen had helped his breathing little and he'd begun to shake harder.

"Let's get him on the back board." Jeremiah slid the board in place.

Jenna picked up Aaron's splinted arm. "We need several men helping, we're going to roll him slightly toward me and get the board under him. We need to move him all as one, keeping his back and legs straight."

She held Aaron's arms across him and leaned down to look in his eyes, getting his attention. "Aaron, we have to roll you to get you on the back board, don't try to help, let us move you."

He blinked hard and gave her a slight nod of the

chin against the cervical collar.

"The chopper's five minutes out, get a landing area cleared." Horace's voice rang out. "Clear this area if you are not involved. Is anyone else hurt?"

"All right, on three all together," Jeremiah directed. "One, two, three."

Aaron's body began to roll toward Jenna, the men holding him and others sliding the back board under him.

He growled and went rigid trying to fight them, pushing at Jenna.

"Don't fight, Aaron." She held him tightly as the board was lowered back down. He cried out again, closing his eyes, gasping to breathe, trying to pull the mask away from his face.

Jenna leaned over him, holding the mask in place. "Look at me, Aaron. It's fine now, a helicopter is coming to get you to the hospital, they're almost here." Her voice cracked. "Breathe Aaron, breathe sweetie."

Aaron grimaced and took a breath.

"That's good, try again," she coaxed and Aaron followed her command, taking another breath and grunting with the effort.

In the distance, the batting of the chopper closed in. "They're here, Aaron. I probably can't go with you. I'll be there as soon as I can. I love you." She had to yell in his ear, letting tears roll down her cheeks, pulling his mask back to kiss his lips softly. Oh, God what if she never saw him again…

He touched her hair, but his hand dropped. "Lily…tell her…I love her."

Jenna shook her head. "You tell her…you are going to be fine, Aaron Decker. Don't you dare try to say good-bye."

He closed his eyes for another long moment. Jenna touched his face praying with her own eyes closed that he would be all right.

"Maxus?" he asked about the horse again, opening his eyes and trying to move.

"Gabe is taking care of him," Jenna answered him, smoothing his hair.

"I fell? Tell Lily." His voice was barely heard above the noise of the chopper which had settled nearby.

"Yes, you fell, but you are doing really good. Aaron? Aaron?" Jenna called to him as his eyes rolled back and his body went into spasms.

"Seizures." Jeremiah lifted one of Aaron's eyelids.

Jenna nodded. A seizure was due to head injury, but even a mild concussion could cause that.

"You men, help me lift him and we'll meet the chopper, now. It'll save some time," Jeremiah shouted above the noise.

Jenna held tightly to Aaron's hand as Jeremiah and the other men lifted the backboard and made their way along toward the chopper. His limp hand in hers was almost more than she could handle. She held tightly anyway, thinking there was so much more she should have said to him. *Please, Aaron be all right. Oh God please.*

A paramedic jumped free of the chopper and spoke to Jeremiah who called Jenna over.

"This is Jenna Wilder; she's the RN on the set," Jeremiah introduced her.

"What ya got?" The paramedic had his pad to take notes, but the sound of the chopper was so loud she found herself yelling to relay the report.

"Fall of maybe twenty feet, he hit on the way down. Confused, broken ribs and collapsed lung on the left, diminished. Left radial fracture. Vitals. One-hundred over sixty, one-hundred and forty and forty-six. Moving well, pupils equal and reactive. Follows commands but confused and seizing, a good hematoma behind his left ear. Abdomen soft, no rigidity. Heart sounds good."

The paramedic made his notes. "What's his age?"

"Thirty. No history of surgeries, he got a head injury as a kid when he got beat up once. No other history." Jeremiah followed talking to the paramedic. "I'm his brother."

Jenna watched as last-minute notes were made and the paramedic jumped inside to begin working on Aaron, who had been loaded through the underside of the life flight rescue chopper.

Jeremiah shut the hatch under the chopper and trotted out of the way, glancing back as the aircraft lifted from the ground and flew into the rose-colored evening sky.

Jenna pulled her hand to her mouth and burst into tears, crumbling to her knees. "Oh, God."

Out of nowhere, Sally wrapped her arms around her. "He will be fine."

Jenna wiped her eyes, "How did this happen?" She looked down at her hand to the ring. How had things gone from the happiest moment of her life to this? And explosion, but then—Vince had done this and it was all her fault it had come to this.

"Come on, we're going in the ambulance, so they can cut the lights on and travel fast." Jeremiah spoke to her and Sally, racing toward Gabe who was fast approaching.

Sally tugged her along and soon enough she was running behind the men with Sally on her heels. Jeremiah opened the back of the parked ambulance and she and Gabe climbed in behind him.

"Sally?" Jeremiah held to the door.

"I'll bring your Jeep, you go, but please call me." Sally stepped back her eyes resting on him as he tugged the keys from his pocket and tossed them to her.

The ambulance pulled away, sirens blaring. Jenna held on as the rough ride off the set jolted the vehicle back and forth.

"That was a damn explosion." Gabe leaned hard against the wall of one side as the truck shifted on the dirt roads leading out of base camp. "Rusty took Maxus, looks like the blast got his eyes, but he was too worked up to tell."

"Son of a bitch!" Jeremiah rubbed a hand across his face and shook his head. "Think he'll have to put him down?"

"I'll let Aaron decide that, but I don't need him kicking my ass for it." Gabe growled, looking out the window.

Jenna's breath caught. This wasn't a freak accident. Vince's notes on the flowers had read *Cowboy up. Cowboy Down.*

She pulled her cell phone from her pocket, searching for Brianna's text box in the rocking vehicle that was pulling onto the interstate. She began texting and then slammed off the box and dialed instead, not able to concentrate to type the text. She was losing it.

The phone rang and Brianna picked up on the other

end. "Hey, girl."

"Bri, are you on?"

"Yes, what is it, Jenna?" Brianna voice was urgent.

"Bri, they're bringing Aaron in…who's on?" Her voice cracked and tears welled in her eyes.

"Doc Gates. Jen, what happened?" Bri shouted.

"The ramp jump, he fell, there was some kind of explosion. He's coming in on life flight. Bri, you have to take him." Jenna held tightly as the truck picked up speed, the lights flashing and the sirens blaring.

"Wait, the call's coming in." Brianna stopped her and Jenna held on. "All right, what are his vitals? Level of consciousness?"

"Got that…trauma two, Shay." Brianna came back to the phone. "He's two minutes out Jen; his vitals are stable, in pain and confused."

"Take care of him Bri, we're on the way," Jenna whispered and cut her phone off, glancing at his brothers. "He'll be there in two minutes. He's in pain and confused, but vitals are good."

Gabe shook his head. "He made that jump, who's been in camp the last few days near the ramp? Or for that matter this morning?"

Jenna shook her head and whispered. "It had to be Vince."

"You don't know that for sure." Jeremiah shrugged.

"Yes, she does, but I went over that ramp this early this morning, if he put explosives he did a damn good job," Gabe cursed and glanced back out the window.

"He worked with explosives in the military." It dawned on Jenna to remember that Vince had done so as a younger man in the Navy. The impact of terror hit the pit of her stomach once more. Perhaps the flowers and the one note had been a warning she hadn't heeded. She pulled her arms around her body again and fought the tears. This was her fault, all of it and now Aaron had been hurt and it was all because of her.

Chapter Twenty

The chopper landed with a jolt. Aaron stirred, his mind groggy, though the morphine the paramedic had given him helped less with the pain than confusing him even more. Every breath hurt to the point he wasn't sure he wanted to take the next one. His back and neck ached and the pounding in his head was excruciating. He'd startled a few times on waking thinking he was falling again, only to have the paramedic try and calm him. He was confused and things weren't making sense as he tried to clear his vision which distorted with each blink of his eyes.

"Mr. Decker, we're here. You're doing well. The pain better?" The young paramedic yelled to be heard over the roar of the spinning chopper blades or was that his head?

Aaron blinked, nausea making him gag. No sense talking over the noise of the engine. He'd fallen, the ramp giving way. Jenna? Jenna had been there with his brothers. Maxus? Someone needed to get the horse. He had to get up, but he was strapped to the stretcher. He fought the restraints until it hurt, forcing him to stop.

"Relax, Mr. Decker, you're at the hospital," the paramedic yelled over the noise.

He opened his eyes again. Had he slept? The lights above on the building reminding him he was at the hospital and it was dusk. Or was it morning? He was off the helicopter and being rolled inside. Oh, he'd fallen. What the hell with that ramp? Maxus!

"Gabe?" he called, but no one responded as they rolled him inside the building. Each bump along the way drove pain right through his back and side. He closed his eyes, shaking with every effort to breathe. He tried to get up but couldn't move. He needed air. His chest was tight. No one was listening. He couldn't breathe.

The outside sky turned into the ceiling of the hospital, white tiles, some with brown areas of water leaks, but a smoother ride relaxed him. The lights rolled right past him with the paramedic spouting out all kinds of medical information about him. Yea, he was sure he had broken ribs too, he'd done that before, but he'd never hurt like this. Head injury, is that why he had such a damn headache? A concussion too. But Maxus? *Son of a bitch!*

The stretcher stopped and Brianna was there.

"Aaron, it's Bri. Tell me where you are?" She flashed a light in his eyes, his head pounding all the more.

He blinked, closing his eyes and talking through the mask. "Hos…pital. I can't…breathe. Jenna?"

"Jenna called me and she and your brothers are on the way…we're gonna get you taken care of. Tell me where you hurt? Remember Dr. Gates?"

Aaron grimaced as the doctor touched his chest.

"Tell me what you remember?" The doctor had a damn light too, making his head pound. He closed his eyes blinking hard and gagging with the nausea that rode through him.

"I fell, the horse… Gabe?" Maxus was hurting, he

could feel it. Where was Gabe?

"How did you fall?"

"The ramp blew somehow…Gabe needs to get the horse." Aaron tried to tell them, removing his oxygen mask. They weren't listening. Where the hell was he anyway? Oh, the hospital. He was at the hospital.

The doctor spoke to Brianna and the others in the room. "Get a CT of the head, chest and abdomen stat. CBC, BCP, heart echo, keep the fluids going. X-ray the arm, spine, and skull. Give him some Zofran for the nausea and let's get some Decadron on board."

The doctor placed his stethoscope to various places along his chest listening.

"Can't breathe." Aaron fought them, they didn't understand. Maxus?

"You've got a number of broken ribs and a collapsed lung Mr. Decker. Set up for a chest-tube. You've a good concussion from the looks of it so we can give you a bit more morphine but the chest tube is no fun." The physician took the kit Brianna handed him, with several other staff around him, cutting away his clothing.

He tried to sit, pulling hard. "Maxus needs help."

"No Aaron, lay still, you're in the hospital." Brianna got in his face and continued, "Jenna will be here soon. Lie still. Gabe will take care of Maxus. He will."

Jenna. He'd fallen and her eyes had told him the story. It was bad. Where was she now? Maxus? "Maxus. Gabe?"

"Let's get the tube in and he'll breathe easier." Dr. Gates turned back to him. "Mr. Decker, I'm going to put a tube in your chest, here on your side, to drain the blood from your lungs. It's likely your ribs have pushed into the lung area and you have bleeding inside. This will help you breathe easier."

Aaron was aware the ribs were broken, but no wonder he couldn't breathe. "Sounds…like…loads of…fun."

Brianna took his hand and lifted his arm above him, where someone else held him. Cold liquid hit his side, taking what breath he'd managed.

"Jack's going to hang onto you so I can work. I'll get you a good dose of something for the pain once we know that your head's in good shape." The physician traced along Aaron's ribs, pressing to find the right area.

"Ahhhh, can't take… that." He was out of breath but fighting hurt worse than lying still.

"I'm going to numb you up a bit. Just a sting, but I won't lie to you, the tube is going to hurt." The physician pushed.

Aaron tried not to flinch, the stinging of the needle bad, but not as bad as when the doctor applied pressure to push the tube through.

He went rigid, unable to fight, being held by Jack. "Damn it…ahhhh." He lost his breath, the pain unbearable.

"Hang on buddy, he's almost done." Jack kept talking to him, the elderly tech built like a truck.

"CT's here. One minute, we're getting a chest tube placed." Brianna glanced back at him. "All done, Aaron."

They lied. The damn tube hurt like hell going in but it relented little in staying in place. He groaned trying to touch his side but Jack pushed his hand back.

"Blood, hemopneumothorax, keep him to gravity."
Dr. Gates glanced back up, his blood covered gloves
held high. "Go ahead with the scan."

Aaron lay still and Brianna took his hand. "It's fine
Aaron, you're at the hospital, you've slept for a few
minutes. How is your breathing?" Brianna leaned over
him, wiping blood from his face and cheek, and then
listening to him with her stethoscope. Had he slept?

Had he slept again? "Jenna?"

"Jenna should be here shortly. The CT scan is good
on that hard head of yours. You just need to rest. A
pretty good concussion, but you'll be fine. I gave you
something for the nausea and you can have something
for the pain every hour or so," Brianna coaxed brushing
the hair back from his face.

Aaron winced, but he was now free of the collar, a
softer one in place. "My head…damn it."

"Do you remember what happened, where you
are?" Brianna asked.

"I fell, the hospital. Jenna's here?"

"Not yet…" Brianna smiled.

"She was…scared. Could see it…in her eyes."
Things were fuzzy like he was dreaming or was that the
medicine?

"Well, that Jenna is a tough one and she'll be here
in no time." Brianna pulled the blankets higher on him.
The medications seemed to take over his mind, dulling
the pain but making him feel as if he was fading. Sleep,
sleep would be good. Maxus? Damn.

He closed his eyes, unable to keep them open,
unable to fight the effects of the medication numbing
his thoughts. Thinking of Jenna, he let go to a
medicated slumber, wanting to be free of the pain,

wanting to hold her. The pain would leave him if she were with him, wouldn't it?

****

Jenna exited the back of the ambulance, having said nothing further on the ride to the hospital. Gabe and even Jeremiah had agreed to the idea of Vince being behind the explosion and both had remained quiet on the ride, unnerving her all the more. What must his brothers think now?

Shay met them, coming around the desk. "He's in the back. Dr. Gates and Bri are with him. Come on, you can all wait in the family room." Shay hugged her and ushered them inside the private room.

"Can I go back?" Jenna pleaded knowing the answer.

"Jenna, you aren't a nurse right now. Doc and Bri are in there and he was doing very well. Bri will let you back when she can." Shay shook her head. "Staff rules."

"How long before we know something?" Gabe asked.

"I'm sure it will only be a short time. All his tests are back and the doc is reviewing them," Shay explained.

"I'm sorry, Shay this is Gabe, Aaron's brother and you know Jeremiah," Jenna introduced them to the clerk.

"I know you are all concerned, but he was awake when he came in and I know they will let you know something very soon." Shay motioned to the coffee. "Please help yourself to coffee or water. I'll be back in a short time, let me know if you need anything. Jenna, anything." Shay waited until she got a nod from Jenna and then headed back off to the ringing phones at the desk.

Jenna turned back around meeting Gabe's intense stare and then looking at Jeremiah for reassurance. "Dr. Gates...is very good. Brianna too."

Jeremiah sat down in one of the chairs, putting his head in his hands, "He is the best there is."

Gabe simply paced at the door, watching who he could see behind the small window of the double doors leading to the back where Aaron was being cared for.

Jenna sat in a chair opposite Jeremiah, gulping to keep more tears at bay. She still couldn't believe what had transpired. This was her fault. It was. There was no other explanation. There couldn't be. She had to make sure Aaron was all right and then she had to find somewhere for her and Mason to go—somewhere safe.

"Decker family?" Dr. Gates appeared at the door.

Jenna stood, meeting glances with the doctor she knew well, unable to read his face.

"We're his brothers. Gabe Decker and you know Jeremiah," Gabe answered, as Jeremiah stood.

"He's doing very well. He's got a severe concussion, some periods of being confused, which I think will pass. The seizures haven't returned. He has four broken ribs, and I put a chest tube in for a collapsed lung. His left wrist has a fracture. With, falls like this, it's hard to say. I expected to find more broken bones or even spinal injuries, but everything looks good. We have to watch him for heart issues, aortic dissection or bleeding, but so far so good."

"He'll be all right then?" Gabe was shaking his head as if he couldn't take it all in.

"He needs heart and vascular monitoring, bed rest.

Pain medications. He kept asking about the horse," Dr. Gates added.

"The horse has eye injuries, but we don't know." Gabe shrugged.

Dr. Gates held his gaze and nodded. "We'll move him to ICU once we have a bed. For now, I'll have Brianna let you back to see him, but he's got a hell of a headache…let him rest."

"Thanks, Doc." Gabe shook Dr. Gates' hand.

Jenna took a deep breath and stared at her ring, taking the first deep breath she'd taken since Aaron had fallen and then she cried, weeping silent tears. Dr. Gates didn't sugar coat things and the report while concerning was still better than she had thought it might be.

"I should call Sarah and Amos." Gabe turned to Jeremiah.

"Let's wait. I'll call them once we see him." Jeremiah shook his head and took a deep breath, leaning back in his chair banging his head several times on the wall behind him.

It was then Gabe turned to her. "You, were…amazing back there."

She didn't want the praise. It was her fault that Aaron was hurt, and she knew that without a doubt.

"Hey, none of that." Gabe walked closer and, of all things, hugged his arm around her shoulder. "It's fine now. He'll be all right."

How was it he did this when he'd seemed so hard to her at times. She'd needed his words but quickly wiped her eyes. "Thank you."

"Hey, folks. Bri says I can bring you back. We're supposed to let two visitors back at a time, but I think we can make an exception." Shay led the way, giving Jenna a slight hug as she led them to the door of Aaron's room.

He lay on the stretcher, eyes closed with a soft collar and the head of the stretcher up. The heart monitor blipped with each beat of his heart, matching her own racing pulse.

Brianna turned to them. "He's resting but wakes every few minutes." She motioned Gabe and Jeremiah over, pushing them closer toward Aaron's side.

"Thanks, Bri." Jenna fell into her embrace, fighting more tears.

"He was in a lot of pain, but much better controlled now. What in the hell happened out there?" Bri waited, holding her gaze and shaking her head.

"Part of the ramp exploded." Jenna glanced toward Aaron and back.

"Jenna it's him isn't it?" Brianna needed no explanation. Maybe they had both known this day would come.

"He's supposed to be in Mexico, but..." How could she answer? Brianna had to know how bad it was now with this happening.

Her friend nodded, her eyes wide. "Jenna, he's crazy, we have to get you out of here, somewhere."

She whispered then. "I know he's behind it all, the flowers and this. Gabe and a friend named Tucker are working on things to keep the police and tabloids out of it, but with an explosion..."

"Jenna. This isn't a game." Bri's voice rose to a harsh whisper.

Jenna shook her head. "I know."

"Well, you take care of him right now. I'm here but

I won't let you be next in this nasty play from Vince. We've got him a bed in the Intensive Care Unit. I'll move him once you have a few minutes with him," she added, walking to wash her hands and turning back to Jenna. "He was asking for you."

Jenna held her friend's terrified gaze. Brianna knew way too much, actually she knew all of it but the latest happenings. She dropped her gaze and turned to Aaron, touching his shoulder and leaning to kiss his cheek.

"Aaron, it's Jenna, we're here with you." She spoke close to his ear.

He stirred and struggled to open his eyes, though he closed them once more.

"Doc said you'll be good as new in no time," Gabe added, touching Aaron's good arm.

He opened his eyes again. "Maxus?"

"Rusty got him off the ramp, he was pretty spooked, and the blast affected his eyes we think." Gabe glanced at Jeremiah and then Jenna, shaking her head.

Aaron focused on his brother and closed his eyes again.

"You're doing good, Aaron. We'll call Sarah and Amos in a bit," Jeremiah added.

Aaron nodded. "They don't…need to worry, and Lily…don't tell her until I am better." He reached for Jenna's hand, but she made it easier by placing her hand in his.

"Aaron, do you remember what happened?" Gabe asked.

Aaron closed his eyes, rubbing Jenna's fingers in his own. "Something blew." He opened his eyes again, blinking several times in the light dimmed room.

Gabe waited. "That ramp was secure. You were set up brother."

Aaron winced in pain, letting go of her hand to hold his forehead, the heart monitor beating faster. "You…watch the videos, look…at the take on the…ramp. Find out who was on that set."

"Aaron you have to rest, not get upset. Please." Jenna held a hand against his upper chest.

Aaron kept his eyes closed but spoke to Gabe. "Gabe, get Tuck on this."

"I got it brother. You do your part to heal." Gabe left the room and Jenna couldn't be sure he hadn't been fighting his own tears of relief.

"He'll be all right." Jeremiah glanced at her. "You rest, Aaron, or I'll tell them to tie you a good one. I'm gonna call Sarah and see about getting everyone a sandwich, coffee or something."

Jeremiah touched Aaron's shoulder. "Rest, Aaron."

Jenna turned back to Aaron. His face was bruised, the hematoma behind his ear solid purple. She wanted to tell him she was sorry, that it was all her fault.

Aaron jumped, waking again and squeezing her hand.

"Aaron, you can have something else for pain?" she offered.

"Hurts like hell." He tossed the blankets back and tried to touch where the tube entered his chest, the bloody dressing around it taped in place.

"Don't touch; it's helping you breathe by getting the fluid off your lung." She pulled the covers higher on him where his chest wasn't exposed. Nursing habits hard to break.

Brianna slipped back into the room and checked Aaron's I.V. and documented his vital signs from the monitor. She then turned to hold Jenna's gaze. "Where's Mason?"

"He's with Aaron's mom still." Jenna held tightly to Aaron's hand. She sniffled and quickly wiped her tears, not wanting anyone to see, but Brianna hugged her again on the way out.

"Hey." Aaron was looking at her when she opened her eyes again. "It's…all right."

"This is my fault, Aaron." Her voiced cracked.

"No, this…isn't your…fault." He shook his head and grimaced, closing his eyes. "I won't have you thinking that."

"Aaron, it has to be him." She fought to keep more tears at bay.

"This isn't your fault." He opened his eyes again, forcing the words and holding his side.

"Aaron, if this is Vince, he almost killed you and I…couldn't survive that." Jenna tried to scold to convince him. "And Mason…"

"Let Gabe…take you home to Mason at the ranch." Aaron tried to raise up and growled through his pain.

"Aaron, I can't endanger your family, Sarah, Amos and, God forbid, Lily…Aaron, I can't." She shook her head. "I can't stay here and bring more harm to you…"

Aaron grabbed her arm hard, his words slurred. "Jenna, you can't run, not anymore. Not like…this…you go home with Gabe, and you stay there." Aaron fell back to the stretcher. "Shit, I can't even damn talk…right with the medicine making me crazy… Jenna, please don't leave here, not even one…minute alone. Promise."

She shook her head at a loss for words.

He touched the ring on her finger. "Jenna…stay at the ranch and we'll fix things…together. Promise."

Brianna came running in the room. "Jenna?"

She turned, glancing at the monitor. "Aaron you have to relax…your heart rate is going up…please Aaron."

"Don't leave here, Jenna…"

"I'll go to the ranch," she promised wondering if she could keep her end of the bargain but hoping her response calmed him. She rested her head against Aaron's hand as he finally relaxed. How could she not be there for him now through his recovery? He'd be months healing from this. Filming would go on but the season would be over in a few more weeks. Aaron was right, she couldn't keep running, but then maybe she had no choice when it really came down to it and she should have known that two years ago.

Chapter Twenty-One

Aaron startled awake, confused until the pain in his side reminded him. He was in his hospital room and Maxus was being cared for by a veterinarian specialist from Helena. He touched his side, gazing around the darkened room. Was it dawn or dusk? He hadn't any idea which, nor did he have any inkling how long he'd been in and out of the drug induced haze. Blinking hard he turned to find Jenna sleeping in the chair beside him, a white hospital blanket covering her.

He squinted to focus on her. She must have gone home with Gabe at some point and returned. He shook his head, trying for a deep breath, but the bigger mistake was moving. *Son of a bitch!*

"Aaron?" Jenna jumped out of her slumber.

"You should have stayed at the ranch." He scolded not liking the idea he couldn't protect her with his injuries.

She smiled and tugged the hair across his brow back from his face. "I was worried so Gabe brought me back."

"How…long has it been?" He held his chest, still concentrating on breathing, and thinking it hard to get the right words out. Damn the medication.

"It's evening. You've been sleeping since last night." Jenna tugged his blanket higher.

He grimaced and closed his eyes.

"You have a concussion, but you can have something for the pain," Jenna offered.

He grabbed her hand. "I've had…enough drugs. I can't even…think. Please…go to the ranch."

"I'm not leaving you, Aaron. I can't. And Mason seems fine with Sarah and Lily." She couldn't hide the tears that filled her amber eyes.

He brought her hand to his cheek. He wouldn't have left her, either. "Where are the boys?" He'd been aware his brothers were with him, on and off, but the medication confused him, making him lose time with strange dreams.

"Gabe went to the set for he and Tucker to have a look around and Jeremiah had to work," she said.

He let go of her hand touching her cheek. "You look…tired."

"I'm fine as long as I'm with you."

"No…you're not…but you will be." He adjusted his position and tried to stifle a cough that pounded through him anyway. "Damn it."

"Don't try to do too much right now." She straightened the pillow behind him.

He concentrated on breathing again. "We'll see what…Tuck and Gabe find out."

"Aaron, this isn't some kind of thing to be fixed. I know it's Vince, and he's dangerous. Look what he's already done." She stood, walking to look out the window, folding her arms.

"Tuck is good, Gabe too… I need you to go to the ranch and stay there." He tried to sit up, but the idea was too much. "Did Gabe tell…Sarah and Amos?"

"Yes, but Aaron this is dangerous for your family and my friends here. Vince…he has men anywhere he

250

wants them, doing whatever he needs them to do. I never really understood that about him until it was too late. He's taken so much from me, I'm not even sure…who I am anymore, but I can't let him hurt all of you."

Aaron pulled himself up in bed, in spite of the pain, biting his bottom lip and focusing on taking in air. "Jenna, damn it, I can't get up…come here."

She turned and looked at him for a long moment and finally walked toward him and sat on the side of his bed again, tears streaking her cheeks.

He wrapped his good arm around her, wanting to comfort her, but shaking in the effort. He hurt like hell and moving simply doubled that, but he couldn't let her suffer with all uncertainties alone.

"This is going to end, but you…have to believe that," he tried. "It's going to be all right."

"You are in no condition right now. You'll be weeks healing. How are things going to be all right? And oh, God, poor Maxus, Aaron…" She shook her head.

He touched the ring on her hand. "I made you a promise. Jenna, I would…walk to the ends of this earth…to make sure you took one more breath. You have to trust me." And he would do as he said, even if Maxus would never be the same horse.

She wiped her eyes. "When you fell…I thought…"

He stopped her. "It's not the fall, it's…the landing…and I've landed right here with you again." His head was splitting but tried for a smile. He groaned and she helped him lie back once more.

"Aaron?"

He grunted through several breaths, closing his

eyes. "Just…tired."

"I love you, Aaron and I'll be right here. Rest."

He opened his eyes again, shaking his head. "What did Horace do…about the take?" With him out of commission and Maxus likely blind…

"Sally said there was enough footage to finish the take." Her voice was little more than a whisper.

"It's all right. I know how it works. They made it look like Maxus went over." He nodded. They'd had enough footage with his practice jump to fill in any gaps, in spite of the fall that had been an accident.

She touched his brow, hesitating. "Evidently and the episode and season will be dedicated to you and Maxus. That was at Drake Masters insistence."

He looked away. It was a nice gesture, but it hardly did an animal like Maxus justice and he didn't need pity from anyone over what had happened.

"You know Horace and Drake came by and stayed here for hours until we knew you were going to be all right," Jenna added, pushing a cup of water his way. "Drink."

He sipped as she held the cup. When he'd taken enough he nodded and she lifted the cup from his lips setting it aside.

"I suppose it made…the evening news?" He figured it without a doubt.

"It's been on the news, but no footage shown, though the FBI have been nosing around according to what Gabe found out." She shook her head. "I fear they might make Vince even more vengeful."

"We don't need the feds in this. Where's my phone." He looked toward the bedside table, forgetting and reaching with his casted wrist. "Shit." He jerked his arm back, cradling his hand with the other, throwing his head back.

Jenna picked up the phone from the small bag of Aaron's personal items Gabe had brought by.

"Call Jeremiah…and tell him to sit on top of Amos as he'll probably try to drive down here eventually." Aaron shook his head and studied the cast on his arm.

The door to the room popped open, and Amos Decker ambled into the room, lugging his oxygen canister over his shoulder.

"Amos is driving in the city, take cover." He mocked Aaron's words with a chuckle.

"Tell me…you didn't." Aaron adjusted in bed again with a growl.

"What I want to know, is why I have to hear about this on the news, my own wife not even telling me. You're my son and I have a right to know you've been hurt. You're damn lucky to be alive. Now what in the hell happened out there?" Amos continued in the room, taking the chair beside the bed.

"Amos, you should…be home resting. I'm fine, or…I will be." Aaron looked from him to Jenna, who came to sit back on the side of his bed at his feet, facing Amos.

"Fine? You fell forty feet they said on T.V. and Maxus caught the bad end of the deal too. Gabe said the ramp was blown, Tucker thinks so too." Amos looked hard at his son.

"It was." Aaron had no better answer and his father had most likely figured a thing or two.

"I taught you boys to check and check again," Amos scolded. "Though I guess we all know what's happened. How did he get that done on the set with you boys checking that ramp?"

"I looked at the ramp about an hour before the jump and Gabe too, but Tuck found evidence of hidden wires we never would have seen, should've damn known like you said." Aaron dropped his gaze.

Amos' face softened. "Least wise you are alive. How bad ya hurt?"

"Broken ribs, a collapsed lung, broken wrist and a pretty bad concussion." Jenna took over to answer, pressing a hand to this thigh. "And I can't help but feel responsible."

"Hold up right there, missy. You didn't do this. I think we all know that and you be sure to stick around. The show's not over yet." Amos held her gaze as Jenna brushed away oncoming tears.

"He's right, but first you need some rest and I do too." Aaron took Jenna's hand, but turned to his father. "Let Jenna drive you home, Pop."

"He thinks I am a hazard on wheels." Amos chuckled.

She smiled. "I think he worries about your safety and mine."

"I'm safe enough, who do you think taught him how to drive?" Amos smiled at her.

"Amos, let her drive you home. I don't want…her alone." Aaron shook his head. "Come on, Pop."

To his surprise Jenna agreed, though her reluctance was evident. "It really would be no trouble Mr. Decker. I know Gabe is coming here tonight to stay with Aaron and I need to give Sarah a hand with the children."

Amos smiled, "Well then, I suppose I wouldn't mind being escorted by a lovely young lady once more. I'll be back tomorrow, if I can…find my way or this lovely lady brings me back," Amos said it sarcastically, leaning to kiss his son on the forehead. "I'll wait outside so my future daughter in law here can kiss you proper." Amos made his way back out into the hallway, leaving Jenna still sitting on the foot of Aaron's bed.

She bit her bottom lip a hint of pink rushing her cheeks. "He's really endearing, but it's so dangerous for all of you."

"Endearing? He's hard-headed." Aaron looked toward the door and back. "But you heed my words, sooner or later Vince will screw this up. If nothing else the ramp explosion put him in the headlines. My guess is his world just got a little more complicated."

"I just keep thinking what if you had…" She leaned against him and held on. "Aaron, it keeps getting worse."

He held her as best her could. "I'll be all right, but you have to trust Gabe and Tuck to helps us get this done. Put Vince right out of his misery."

"I trust, but things could get worse. You didn't ask for this and neither did poor Maxus."

Aaron touched his thumb to her lip. "It's going to be all right, it is."

She kissed his cheek again. "I know."

"Go to the ranch and sleep, don't worry. Spend some time with the kids." He pressed the issue. Even though she looked tired and worried, she was still the most beautiful creature he'd ever seen, her amber eyes sparkling in spite of her broken spirit.

Jenna squeezed his hand, and he placed his lips to hers for a brief kiss. She made her way outside, looking back once and offering him what little smile she could. He shook his head and lay back further trying to adjust to a comfortable position, thinking of Vince Hanson. He wasn't sure how or when, but the man would pay for all he'd done to Jenna and her son, to him and to one damn good horse.

****

"Girl, where are you?" Brianna was on the other end of Jenna's cell phone. "I figured you not to leave Aaron until he was heading home. I worry, Jenna. You know this scares the hell right out of me. I went by his room and you weren't there."

Jenna pulled the damp towel from her hair, renewed after her shower. Now in Aaron's bedroom on the ranch, she'd had a moment to think about what had happened, but Brianna could read her like a book.

"I'm fine, you know where I am if I am not with Aaron. Bri, it's complicated but…you have to just act like nothing is going on and we can't talk much for now." She stopped, wondering how much was too much to tell her friend. "I can't risk something happening to you too."

"If this is him, Vince. Jen…you have to get Mason and yourself away from all of us, now," Brianna whispered loudly. "Not for our safety but your own."

"I know, but Aaron made me promise." Jenna sat on Aaron's bed, tossing the towel aside and glancing at Mason who slept nearby in the portable crib. "I can't fight Vince alone and if I leave, then I will spend my life running. What kind of life is that for Mason? I am so tired of this whole thing, Bri, even you disrupted your own life to come out here and…it's time to end it." Brianna waited. "Jen, you have to call the police, the F.B.I or even the national guard for God's sake."

"You know I can't and now the Police are all over

the set. Tuck and Gabe know things about Vince even we didn't. Mason and I are safe here for now, but if things get worse…" Jenna pulled her knees up wrapping Aaron's robe tighter around her, inhaling the light scent of him.

Brianna's whisper jumped an octave. "It has turned worse now."

Jenna's voice broke. "Aaron thinks with the explosives on the ramp and the police onto things, that Vince won't be able to hide as well."

"Jenna, I'm scared for you." Panic laced her best friend's voice.

"I know. Please Bri, I'll be here and then I'll be in touch." Jenna tried to control her emotions and it was all she could do.

"You text me something each day several times. And how do we know for sure these phones are safe anyway." Bri's voice was tense with worry.

"Gabe and Tucker were special ops military for a while from what Aaron says. Tucker is a P.I. They know what they are doing." Jenna wasn't sure is she was trying to convince Bri or herself.

"This Tucker seems nice enough, but Gabe…" Brianna cleared her voice. "He is rather pushy and you know how I don't care at all for that."

"He's a good guy, Bri. Just go with it, Okay. I'll be in touch." She hung up before giving Brianna a chance to say anything more. Pulling up the edge of the robe's collar, she inhaled deeply and then looked down at the ring on her finger. She'd waited her whole life to find the fairy tale she had dreamt about. Now it was threatened to be ruined by the past that she now figured to haunt her forever. She traced her fingers on the robe, thinking of Aaron. She should have stayed with him, but Mason had been overjoyed at her being back at the ranch. She needed to call the hospital and dialed, now that he was asleep.

"Hi." Gabe's voice sounded tired and horse.

"How is he?" She waited.

"Finally talked him into the pain medicine earlier. He's sleeping for now."

"I'll be back in the morning." Jenna glanced at Mason who rolled over in the pack and play.

Gabe cleared his voice. "Let me ask you something?"

"All right." She sat up in Aaron's bed again, a bit unnerved as Gabe began speaking with a hint of caution.

"When's the last contact you had with Hanson himself?"

Jenna's heart drop as she remembered. "Not since the night he beat me. Nearly two years ago."

"And you took the pay off and changed your name?" Gabe lifted his brows in challenge his tone very clear.

"While it is none of your business, the money was mine, inherited from my father about a year before we married. My fair share from the divorce if it comes down to it." She stood, narrowing her gaze at this interrogation. "And I changed my name as I could no longer be that woman he beat near to death. I had to protect myself and my son, Gabe. But that's not what this is about, is it?"

"I get your reasons, but…what do you think he is really after? The money, you or your son?" His voice softened, but his implications hit hard and an implosion of true fear rolled through her chest, taking her breath.

"Vince is here, isn't he? Tell me the truth." Fear rode through her so profound she gulped an empty breath in already knowing the answer to the question she'd asked.

Gabe didn't hesitate. "He's here."

"I'm not sure he even knows about Mason, but he never wanted me, just the money he didn't get to keep," Jenna whispered, glancing at Mason. "But I've never touched any of it myself. I put it in various accounts to hide it after my name change. You're thinking a pay off, well I would pay it all in full to keep Mason safe. And Aaron and Lily, your family."

Gabe inhaled a deep breath and let it out. "No payoff's gonna do much for this guy. He's a bit psycho. Guys like that aren't happy until they've won it all, no matter the price. Care to tell me different about him?"

She shook her head. "No, but I am concerned for you and Tucker just as much as Aaron and the children."

"Tuck and I got this, but I need you following orders," he warned

"Yes, but please call me if he wakes and wants to talk to me," she said.

"Got it." Gabe hung up.

Jenna lay down on the bed, pulling the covers over her, deciding to sleep in Aaron's robe. She dimmed the lamp and pulled the blankets higher, the cold emptiness of being alone riding through her. It was clear that Gabe was covering all the bases and seemed to trust her little, but she couldn't blame him. Tears rimmed her eyes and rolled down her cheeks as she forced her eyes closed, willing sleep.

Vince could only be back for the money, right? Two million dollars was a great deal of money, but it was rightfully hers, and besides that, his father was worth ten times more than that. She could only pray he knew nothing of Mason. And she did figure it best like Gabe, that she go nowhere alone, though filming had been halted for a few weeks due to the police investigations on the set, that Horace had been none too happy about.

Two weeks would hardly get Aaron back on the set but Gabe had said he and Jeremiah would handle the last few stunts for the few episodes left to film the first season. He'd also let her know that the networks had picked up *The Bounty Hunter* for a second season, but now she wasn't certain if there would be a second season where she was concerned.

Chapter Twenty-Two

Aaron sat up in bed, adjusting his position as he growled out his curses. "I knew it. Son of a bitch!"

Gabe folded his arms and nodded. "He's been here for a month. I tracked him on a flight through Chicago to Helena. Got a couple of names of men with him, three so far all arriving at different locations."

"He had someone on the inside, FBI's all over it that now, given the explosives. Gonna be hard to protect Jenna's story much longer." Tucker ran a hand through his light hair. "They'll question you and Jenna next."

"I figured as much." Aaron shook his head. "What's the footage show?"

Gabe nodded. "There were explosives in the joint on the high parts of the ramp, all of them out of sight, even checking as we did each day we would never have seen them."

"We can cooperate with the FBI, but that may just complicate things further. Might be best if I get Sarah and the children out of here." He'd been thinking the time for that would come, but he suspected Jenna would never be agreeable to letting Sarah disappear with the children.

"He's onto all of us by now, might be a bit late for that." Gabe shrugged, with an edge to his voice.

"I'll get him tracked down, but you need to keep

Jenna nailed to the ranch. She's agreed but let a woman get antsy and she'll bolt every time." Tucker spouted the last few words in a hurry as his cell phone buzzed and he grabbed it trotting from the room.

"I'll talk to her." Aaron clutched his side at the added effort and watched as Tuck waved in understanding and disappeared out the door.

Gabe shook his head. "You don't date a single woman for years and then you pick one that nearly gets you killed."

Aaron held his brother's gaze.

"What do you really know about her, Aaron?" Gabe walked closer shoving his hands in his pockets.

"You know all I do. What?" He was damn tired of Gabe continued comments. He still hurt like hell, even though he no longer sported the chest tube and had little patience.

"She's living under an alias, as you know and there's probably more than that if I'm guessing right." Gabe's voice hit a higher octave.

"Cut the bullshit!" He snagged the envelope, glaring at his brother.

He opened it reading through the report, reading the names, Jenna Wilder and Jennifer Amiker. Her script had mentioned her pen name was Jenna Wilder, but he knew nothing of the other name. He hadn't asked her about it even when she had confided the truth.

When he said nothing more, Gabe continued. "I asked her point blank how long since she'd seen Hanson and if she had changed her name. She was truthful on both as I'm sure she knew Tucker dug that up on her."

Aaron shook his head. "Jenna Wilder's her pen

name she's been using since he beat her, but she made it legal and all."

Gabe shrugged. "Looks like it."

"She ran scared, obviously changed her name for protection," he spat the words at his brother. At least with the chest tube gone he could deal with the pain, but he wasn't dealing well with his brother's accusations.

"So you're playing with fire brother, and we might not know how damn hot things will get." His brother narrowed his gaze and stepped closer "This guy Hanson is bad news—fraud, embezzlement, and a line of death along the way from what Tucker suspects. Seems Hanson's father died recently and that's about the time he showed up here. I'm saying you'd better make sure you know her and what she's up to. If he's come back after all this time, he wants something more than money and he obviously doesn't care who gets in the way."

Aaron said nothing more His brother was on a mission, and given his background in special ops, he was more than intense and most likely right.

"So he's after the money, her son, or her. Why the ramp, what would be the point in me or Maxus for that matter?" Aaron tried to understand the connection.

Gabe shook his head, having no answers. "Maybe it isn't about the money or her son, maybe it's about who gets the girl."

"He beat her and threw her away." Aaron cussed under his breath. "The son of a bitch doesn't want her."

"Nope, but my guess is he don't want you to have her either." Gabe turned, stopping at the door, "Look, I'm happy for you, Aaron. Really, I am. But you gotta check things out, bro. I like her, a lot. But do you really know who she is?"

Aaron growled, pulling himself to the side of the bed as his brother left the room. Lifting his shirt, he struggled to get the cast on his left arm through the sleeve. He could dress and bathe for the most part, but that was more than fatiguing at best. How the hell was he to do anything to help Jenna at this point? He just had to hope she stayed put and would agree to send Sarah off with the children when and if the time came.

He stood up and wiggled his socked feet into his sneakers. He could see himself in the mirror at the sink across the room. He looked like hell and felt worse. His face still had bruising, and opening his shirt, even with the chest tube gone, his left side held deep purple bruises that would take weeks to heal.

"So you're anxious to get home." Jenna entered his room, pushing a wheelchair and wearing a smile.

He smiled. "As long as I am leaving with you."

"Well, I happen to have your discharge paperwork and your prescriptions have been called in. I saw Gabe's truck pulling out as I drove in and Tucker was with him, wasn't he?" She pushed the wheelchair closer with a smile.

"Busted," he answered and tried to explain, "Tucker's checking on things at your apartment. Bodi's good and Brianna's fine as is Ms. Lucy. Gabe said he gave you a panic button."

Jenna took a deep breath and shivered as she touched the dragonfly pin on her collar. "I suppose it's necessary at this point."

"I want you safe." Aaron nodded to the wheelchair. "Can't I walk?"

"House rules." She raised an eyebrow and grabbed

his bag, already packed on the foot of the bed.

She hugged him gently. "Everyone's at the ranch, waiting for you." She leaned up to kiss his cheek and ran a hand through his damp hair. "You already showered."

"Yea, wasn't easy, maybe next time you get to help me out." He grinned, enjoying her slight blush. God she was beautiful but the edge of fear that lingered on her face crushed him, as usual.

"I miss you too, Aaron Decker, but I hardly think you'd enjoy it right now." She moved the chair closer.

"We'll give it a few days." He nodded in agreement. "Are you all right?"

She shook her head. "It's hard sitting and waiting. Aaron, I don't care about the money but he won't stop until…and now the FBI wants to talk to me and you."

"Then we'll talk to them. They already know about Vince, from what Gabe says and the whole scene has made the news, but Horace is sticking to filming as usual to finish the season."

"But even the FBI can't find him." Her words were almost a whisper.

"Nope, but his career is trashed now regardless." He touched her cheek and sat in the chair with a groan.

"Lily can hardly wait to see you." Jenna continued pushing him down the long hallway.

"I've missed the munchkin. Mason too." His chest had nearly crushed in with the pain of it.

"Here we go." Jenna rolled him into the hallway and onto the elevator. In no time she'd gotten him gingerly into the front seat of her SUV and was headed back toward Sun River.

Riding wasn't as easy as he thought it might have

been and each bump in the road jarred him until he sat forward holding the dash.

"Aaron?" Jenna slowed the truck.

"I'm good, it's easier like this." He held onto the dash and his side, easing back into the seat.

"I'll slow down." She glanced in the rearview mirror. "I know you'll be glad to be home."

He nodded, watching her as she drove toward the ranch. "Yep, but listen, I need you to stay put on the ranch unless you are out with me or one of the boys."

"I've listened to Gabe, haven't been far at all. I did go by the apartment to check on Bodi, but Tucker was right there to meet me," she explained.

He shook his head. "Tuck seems to think he'll slip up somewhere. Might even be the Feds will get lucky before we do. I just want you to trust we'll put a stop to this."

She nodded, but she glanced back to the mirror. When she said nothing, he wondered if she believed him or if she were contemplating further escape. There was nothing he could say to calm her fears or even his own for that matter. Hell, he could hardly do anything in the shape he was in. It would be weeks before he was fully healed, but as they approached the ranch it was Maxus who crossed his mind. Gabe and Jeremiah had the horse stalled in the barn and he was healing but the veterinarian said the horse's eyes were too damaged and that is was very unlikely anything could be done.

"Do you want me to stop?" Jenna slowed the SUV at the barn.

He shook his head. It was too raw now for that. "Keep going. I'll go out once I see the children."

He'd visit the horse when he was alone and when

he could promise the animal he'd see Vince Hanson placed in the hard ground where he belonged.

****

Aaron glanced down and adjusted his position as best her could, Lily lying asleep in the recliner beside him. He'd missed her so much; he'd had Jeremiah sit her in the recliner with him, making her understand she had to sit still. They had watched a cartoon ballerina movie with Jenna. She was upstairs now, rocking Mason to sleep.

He touched Lily's hair and put his hand on the tiny one that rested across his thigh. He couldn't figure it, but she seemed to have grown a few inches in the short time they were apart. He'd also walked to the barn alone and spent an hour brushing Maxus and talking to the animal who shuffled a bit inside the stall at any touch. He'd never be able to jump the animal again, but there was hope he could still ride the horse from time to time. The animal's broken spirit mimicked his own for the time being, but they would both recover eventually.

Jenna came from the kitchen with two cups of fresh brew. Drawing him from his saddened mood over the horse. "I thought you might be asleep by now."

Aaron nodded. He hadn't had much appetite but coffee sounded good.

"She's out like a light," Jenna whispered with a glance at Lily.

Aaron looked down at Lily's quiet face once more. "I probably need to get you guys to put her to bed."

"Could I?" Jenna continued to whisper and set the coffee cups on the end table beside him.

He nodded and watched as she carefully pulled Lily up to her and laid his daughters head on her shoulder, turning to head to the stairs. She looked so natural, the picture of all he'd ever wanted for himself and Lily.

Moments later she returned and sat, handing him his cup of coffee.

"She went right down."

"All the excitement of me getting back home." He shook his head. "Thought I'd be moving better by now."

She sat on the couch next to the recliner, sipping her coffee.

He hated to break the conversation away from where they were. "How're you feeling after the chat with the Feds?"

She set her cup of coffee aside, her hands trembling visibly. "They were already after him for murder, Aaron. I never knew he'd…killed someone. How didn't I know something like that?"

"It's not your fault, Jenna, a man like him, there's probably more here than even the Feds know. I think that's why they are worried little about the explosion, they want him for more than what he is causing here, which is why his trashed career matters little now and why we still have to be careful."

She shook her head, folding her hands. "Aaron, no one is safe with him here. Look what's already happened."

"We are gonna get him." Aaron grabbed her hand.

"How?" She shook her head.

"I don't know, but for starters wait him out." He held her gaze as seconds passed.

"Aaron, he did this to you. I know he did, because of me. I can't stay here…endanger you and your family further." Her voice cracked. "God, it's never going to end."

"If you run, you will run the rest of your life, Jenna. We've talked about that. Let's end this now, here, where you have help." Aaron leaned to squeeze her hand. "If running was the answer, I'd let it all go, take you and the kids somewhere safe and never look back, but running isn't the answer, babe."

She brushed back the tears and shook her head. "I try to stay sane each day, not think about it..."

He needed something profound, something to get through to her. "Jenna, you didn't let it make you a victim when he beat you. You continued forward with your life, even when it was hard, but you have to hang in here for now. We can't prove much, but Gabe and Tuck will get to the bottom of it."

"Aaron, I'm so afraid." She whispered and blinked hard.

He scooted forward, wanting to hold her but could hardly get out of the chair. "Help me get the recliner down."

Jenna got up and pushed the foot board down slowly as Aaron adjusted his position from the chair to standing.

"Come on, let's go upstairs." He wrapped his good arm around her, holding her close.

Inside his room, he shut the door and watched as she walked aimlessly to the bed and sat down. He hated this, seeing her so worried and broken, much like Maxus and him if he had to compare.

"Aaron, you can't put your life on hold for me, for this." She shrugged and walked away from him but turned back, holding his gaze.

"My life is nothing without you in it. You have to trust me." He tried; anything to keep her from running and thinking that would stop Vince Hanson.

She shook her head putting her hands to her face and dropping them. "He almost killed you Aaron and I wouldn't have survived it and to think he could hurt your family or God forbid Lily or Mason. I can't let that happen."

"I can watch you here, but I don't need you out on your own alone at all." Aaron ducked to make her look at him again.

"Trust me for now," he tried again.

She nodded. "I've warned Bri, but I at least need to get a few things at my apartment and check on Bodi. I saw him once a few days ago, and even if Tucker is checking, he probably thinks I've left him for good."

Aaron shook his head. "Give me a couple of days to rest and I'll take you. Maybe he can bring him back here at some point to get him used to things."

"Aaron, I'll be fine. I'll go during the day and be quick, watching closely. Besides, your friend Tucker is always nearby and you can't be riding all over in your condition," she chided.

Aaron could tell she was trying to make it all sound good but he wasn't falling for it. "Regardless, I'll get Gabe or Jeremiah to take you then."

"All right." Jenna pushed him toward the bed. "But only if you rest like the doctor said for now."

Aaron sat easily on the bed. "Where is everyone? The house seems quiet or I guess I got acclimated to all the bells and whistles at the hospital."

"Sarah went on to bed earlier with Amos. I'm not sure about Jeremiah. He was outside and Gabe still isn't home. You look so tired." Jenna stood beside him. "I know I am adding to your stress, but please don't worry about me. Please rest." Jenna tried for a smile. "Nurses orders."

He gave into a nod and she helped him remove his shirt and sweat pants, leaving him in his boxer before her. He grinned. "Damn lucky for you I'm injured."

"You are in no condition, which is why I will lay here with you tonight." She turned, walking into his small bathroom and pulling off her clothing to put on one of his t-shirts.

Aaron settled back against the pillows to a comfortable position and watched with keen interest as she readied for bed, washing her face and brushing her teeth. He thought to curse at his body's reaction but there wasn't much he could do about it at this point.

She walked back to the bed and dimmed the lamp, crawling into the bed carefully. "Are you comfortable?"

"I was." Aaron teased her, moving to adjust his position.

"Oh, you are bad even when you can't be bad. Rest Aaron," she scolded.

"I'm better every day. And soon enough you will be too." Aaron slid his hand over until he found hers and gripped it tight.

"Aaron?" She spoke in a whisper.

"Huh?" Aaron closed his eyes.

"I love you, no matter what happens." Her voice was as sweet as he'd ever heard, but the fear in her words was evident.

He turned and held her gaze. "Babe, a lot of things have happened and there's most likely more to come, but he crossed the line in hurting you and my horse.

Nothing's gonna happen to you or your son as long as I can draw a breath. I can promise you that."

She snuggled closer as he continued.

"Spent my whole childhood wanting a family and then fought like hell not to let them love me when I got one. When Lily came along…" His voice cracked and he took a breath. "I held her for the first few hours, thinking I finally had a family of my own, but it always felt like something was missing. And since you and Mason, that gap has closed and no force on this earth is gonna take that from either of us. I can promise you that."

She nodded and he was aware because of her own tears she couldn't speak. So he hugged her as best he could, ignoring his physical pain in wanting to comfort her. He was in no shape now to be of much help, but he would be soon and if his brother and Tuck didn't find Hanson first, then there would be nothing to stop him from taking the man down one way or the other.

Chapter Twenty-Three

"Hey, Daddy. Did you have a spend-the-night party with Jenna?" Lily waltzed into Aaron's bedroom, dragging a large teddy bear behind her, rubbing her eyes.

Jenna bolted awake, sitting up, still in Aaron's bed, grabbing for the blankets. She glanced at Aaron saying nothing and then back to Lily. Aaron moaned opening his eyes, holding his side. Mornings were harder, but how on earth would he answer this one?

Lily ambled over to Mason's portable crib peeking inside as Mason stirred to life with a whine, standing up. With Jenna on edge, he'd moved Mason into their room to give her peace of mind, much to Lily's dismay.

"Uh, Jenna was taking care of me since I'm hurt." Aaron struggled to adjust his position and sit up.

"You slept like a mommy and daddy in a family. Hi Mason. Hi." Lily rubbed the top of Mason's head. He held his arms out to her and Lily tugged him from the portable crib and handed him his small stuffed lion.

"Careful, baby." Aaron grabbed his side again, focusing on his daughter but taking Jenna's hand. "What would you think about us being a family? Me and you and Jenna and Mason."

Jenna gulped, but waited as the scene played out. While Aaron was all her dreams come true and Lily the added bonus, things were still uncertain in her mind.

She had to wonder if telling Lily was a good idea for now. She'd woken nearly every hour with vivid dreams of Vince chasing her and her running into nowhere.

"Jenna could be the mommy?" Lily asked looking at Jenna and back to Aaron.

Jenna lifted Mason to the bed and into her covered lap. He giggled, waiting on Lily who plopped up on the bed causing Aaron to groan.

"Easy, no bouncing," Aaron scolded but then lifted Jenna's hand, the one wearing the ring he'd given her. "Daddy gave Jenna this ring, so we're gonna be a family real soon if it's all right with you and Mason."

Jenna glanced at the ring on her finger, the constant reminder that she'd found herself again, through this incredible man beside her. Her fairy tale. Her knight in shining armor. Oh God, Vince couldn't ruin even this, could he?

"Can we all have a spend-the-night party?" Lily handed off her bear to Mason, who dove forward on the large stuffed softness with a giggle.

"Yep, once we are a family," Aaron answered.

"That sounds like great fun," Jenna added, wishing she could cut the intense dread inside her.

"Can Sammy and Lion come too?" Lily picked up the bear once more, but Aaron grabbed it from her with a pretend growl making both children squeal.

"I…don't know, he's kind of furry and big and takes up a lot of room." He juggled the bear in his good hand, tossing it back to them.

"He likes spend-the-night parties." Lily hugged the animal close.

"Well, what do you think?" Aaron asked Jenna.

This was a beautiful moment, even if she was still

afraid that Vince wasn't done. "I think, he's furry and big and right for the party."

"Then, it's settled. And Lion too!" Aaron touched the lion in Mason's grasp.

Lily looked at them both and in a very serious tone asked. "And I can call Jenna mommy?"

Jenna nearly choked on her on saliva. While she wouldn't mind it at all, she hadn't expected it to come so quickly.

Aaron squeezed her hand. "I suppose that would be up to Jenna."

Jenna took what little breath she could, fighting off the tears that wanted to gather. There was nothing she'd want more than to love this little girl as her own. "I think I would like that a lot."

"I'm going to see if Uncle Jeremiah is awake. He's going to make French toast and watch cartoons with me and Mason." Lily sprang up as if the new situation were all normal. She jumped from the bed and waited as Jenna lifted Mason off the bed.

"Hey, hold Mason's hand on the stairs and tell Uncle Jeremiah he needs a diaper change," Aaron said as they watched Lily lead the way into the hall.

"All right, Daddy." And with that she and Mason were on their way.

"Aaron?" Jenna looked down at the ring and back to him. "Of course I adore her, but she has a mother..."

"Who has never cared two cents about her. It's fine..." Aaron looked at her in question. "If it's fine with you."

"It's perfect." Jenna's voice cracked, "I adore her and she's so good with Mason. But are we rushing with all that is going on... Aaron, I'm so afraid of your getting hurt and…"

He didn't let her finish. "It will end soon. Tuck and Gabe have a few more leads, but we have to be careful."

She wiped her eyes and gently wrapped her arms around him, hanging on as tightly as she could without hurting him. She didn't want to let go of him ever, not ever.

Aaron held her. "Shhhh. You're safe here."

She'd spent hours last night watching Aaron sleep and she'd come to a few more conclusions. When she could manage to slip away, she'd take some of the money she'd put away and purchase the land Aaron wanted in full for him. He would never take the money, so she would have to put the motions for purchasing the real estate into play without his knowing and that wouldn't be easy, given she was never on her own. "Aaron, promise me, no matter how life goes, you will build your ranch."

He studied her for a moment. "I know what you are thinking, but this will end soon and then we'll do that together, you, me and the children."

She nodded, wishing she didn't feel like the world was caving in. That was the problem. It would all end soon, but it wasn't likely it would end well, given how things were going. She'd thought of running, but then…Aaron was right, she would be running for the rest of her life. But if things got much worse maybe her only choice would be to run, in order to keep Aaron and his family safe. And if it did come to that, leaving would break Aaron's heart and somehow it would shatter her own into a million tiny pieces.

****

Aaron walked from Gabe's truck to the corral on the set, meeting Thor. Somehow the horse seemed rather lonesome without Maxus, or maybe it was Aaron that was lost without that damn stubborn horse. And while he felt much better, being on the set brought it all back quick.

"Good-boy, how ya been?" He patted the horse, fighting emotions that wanted to erupt.

It had been weeks now since his fall, though he still wore the half-cast to his arm. His ribs and back were better but he was far from being fully recovered and it was most likely Maxus never would be. He'd spent the earlier part of the morning taking Maxus for a small walk outside the barn, wondering if it had been a blessing or a curse the animal had survived. It seemed all the spirit was gone from the animal, who now startled easily as was expected with the limited vision he had retained.

He looked toward the fallen part of the ramp that still lay on the ground, roped off and unmoved. Gabe had discovered where the joints of connectors were blown and suspected just like the Feds, that Hanson had placed someone on the inside of the set, but they weren't as interested in Jenna's part of the story as they were at simply locating Hanson.

He thought of Jenna and the fact that she'd seemed a bit better, as weeks had gone by with nothing more out of Hanson. The presence of the FBI had probably kept the man quiet for now. He'd left Jenna at the ranch, sleeping alongside Lily, with Mason nearby in his play pen. She hadn't needed to come with him as all he wanted to do was check on the horses.

"Want to take a look at the ramp?" Gabe had

parked the truck and joined him.

He nodded, his pulse racing at the idea, since the first glimpse of the heap. He could remember the fall, hitting on the way down and then nothing.

"I talked to the film boys again and they've slowed down the pictures, nothing shows but the ramp giving way," Gabe explained.

"Let's look at the ramp first." Nausea hit him like a brick at the idea of watching his fall and seeing Maxus panic on film. He hadn't expected his physical reaction but followed his brother ahead. A large portion of the ramp lay crumbled below the remaining supports, charred edges easy enough to spot where things blew.

"So Horace let it all stay for now?" Aaron took a step closer, touching the charred wood where the ramp had broken apart his mind drifting over the last moments before he fell.

"You know Horace; he's hoping to avoid a lawsuit. But Hanson did a damn good job of hiding the placement of several explosives on timers. Small and expensive, a professional job. The night guard says no one came thru the set for several nights before it happened. My guess is he made his way inside through the woods. We found a few tracks; two different sets of boots passed the saloon. The FBI hasn't looked further here, but they are still hanging around." Gabe bent and pointed to the areas of damage.

Aaron stepped back. All he could see was Maxus. He held his side and sucked in several forced breaths.

"You all right?" Gabe stood again, touching his shoulder.

"Yeah, I just want the bastard." Aaron tugged free of his brother. It was one thing that he and the horse had been injured but it was completely something else to see Jenna live in fear.

"He knows the Feds are onto him. He's been too quiet." Gabe looked at him, pushing his ball cap further back. "He's just timing things, but he isn't done."

"Yeah, well this playing games is getting old." Aaron shook his head. He'd had time to think hard while mending and it wasn't over. Not even a little, but when it was time, he'd find a way to free Jenna of it all. One way or another, if it came down to it.

"You know if we don't end this, Jenna, Jennifer, whoever she is, is only gonna live on the run and…"

"Don't you think I know that? But that's not what this is about, is it?" Aaron cut him off. There was something that Gabe didn't like about Jenna and there was no need for his brother to beat around the bush any longer.

Gabe looked at him for a moment and then answered him, his tone stern. "What the hell are you doing, Aaron? You fall for this chick, knowing nothing about her, and still don't. She almost gets your ass killed and then you move her right into the house. Who gives a shit if you don't care about yourself, but did you ever stop to think about Amos and Sarah, or how about Lily, for God's sake?"

So that was it. That's how it must've looked from the outside. Yes, he'd thought of the dangers, but to leave Jenna out in the cold was something he couldn't do. "Yes! I have thought of that but just because you can't trust anyone—" He stopped mid-sentence.

Gabe's face reddened. "This isn't about my *trust issues*. We've grown up, Aaron. This is about you risking it all. Putting the bait right smack dab in the middle of our home. She'd better be damn worth it."

Aaron looked at him hard, having no words. How could he even ask that?

"This isn't a game Aaron, you almost died. Scared the fucking hell out of me too, bro." His brother softened his tone. "Look, I get you care for her, but I'm telling you to be sure, because this is one hell of a mess and this dude don't play fair."

"I know full well what's at stake, but I can't help her without you and Tuck," Aaron defended, grabbing his side.

Gabe leaned on the nearby fencing. "You need to be prepared…this is going to get ugly and we need to find him before he finds her."

"Look, just fill Jeremiah in, we're gonna need his help too before this is over." He asked because Jeremiah wasn't a P.I., and due to the work he did with the local fire department, they hadn't wanted to risk his being involved.

"I told him this morning but he's pissed as hell we didn't come clean before now," Gabe answered.

"And Amos?" Aaron kicked the dirt disgusted. Because things had been quiet, didn't mean Hanson and those working with him weren't watching. And as much as he hated it, there might come a time to send Sarah off with the children.

"Pop's been cleaning every gun in the house." Gabe shrugged. "He knows what's going on too, though I'm not certain as to how much."

"Sarah knows too." Aaron had told her everything all along, so she would know to protect the children if it came to that.

Gabe nodded the direction of the film shack.

"Come on let's look at the video. We're not accomplishing shit out here."

Nausea hit him in a strong wave once more, his knees weak. Watching himself fall was one thing but watching Maxus' struggle wasn't going to be easy.

Gabe entered the wooden shack where quick film edits were done. "Boys."

Jack stood and stuck out his hand when Aaron entered behind Gabe, "Aaron, how ya doin' man?"

"I'm good." He tried to sound convincing.

"Well, I think you look like shit." Eric chuckled.

Aaron gave him a shove into his chair and moved in behind him appreciating the razzing to remove a bit of his nerves. He swallowed hard.

"Aaron, I thought that was you. So, how are you?" Drake Masters trotted in behind them with a big toothy grin.

"Better every day," Aaron answered, still unnerved at what he was about to see, but surprised at Drake's arrival.

"I was at the hospital when you were pretty out of it, but I didn't want you to think I wasn't concerned," Drake added.

Aaron shook his head. "I appreciate that. I don't remember much the first few days."

"Slow-motion that footage." Gabe sat down in front of the monitors, twisting a few dials beside Jack.

Aaron walked to stand behind his brother, the air in the small outbuilding a bit thin. He focused to suck in a deep breath. *It's just a film. Let it go, Aaron.*

Gabe leaned forward, waiting on Jack to get the footage started.

Aaron studied the screens where the ramp

remained empty and then as the first glimpses of Maxus' front legs appeared moving onto the screen frame by frame. The picture was blurry from the slow speed. Seconds later he and Maxus were in full view, climbing the ramp. His gut clenched and he held his side, his heart racing.

"Here's the ride up…and here, the ramp is good, but here!" Gabe touched one of the large screens and the footage stopped.

Aaron struggled for a breath, the first implosion below him and the horse. *Son of a bitch.*

"There's the fist spark there then the other six or so most within the three seconds," Gabe escalated, pointing again.

Bile rose in Aaron's throat as the footage continued. He watched as he pushed himself to fall away from Maxus, hitting the ramp and then falling vertical to the ground. Maxus remained on the ramp, startled and rearing, then stamping his front paws in panic. Aaron looked away. He'd kill Vince Hanson if given the chance.

It was then Drake Master spoke up. "FBI's all over the place, but there's reason to take a look at the flower deliveries again."

"What about the flowers?" Gabe turned, fixing his gaze on the actor, folding his arms, and tilting his head in question.

Aaron held his side trying to hold it together after seeing Maxus' struggle.

Drake glanced from Gabe to the other men and back. "I was getting ready to watch the jump and Doug Forrester, the security guard, was walking back toward the set. It made me wonder, even though he's security, why he'd be walking away from the jump, with everyone else wanting to watch. He's in your footage." Drake twisted one of the dials and reversed the film. "There."

Gabe ran the footage back again reaching for the controls from Jack.

"And he had a large bag. I'm not placing blame here but wondering the story." Drake pointed out Forrester in the corner of one of the screens walking opposite a few extras.

"I hadn't given him a second thought. He checked out clear on background." Gabe ran the video back.

"He's carrying a bag and it kind of made me wonder why he was even near the ramp," the actor explained further.

Aaron couldn't breathe. The confinement of the small wooden room and seeing Maxus had nearly done him in. His chest felt tight. There was pain. He was going to pass out cold. *Breathe Aaron, breathe.*

He made his way toward the door to get outside in the cold air. If that bastard of a security guard had done this—helped Hanson somehow…

"Aaron?" Gabe called to him, but he pushed his way out the door past the other men, holding his side, thinking he might lose what little breakfast he'd eaten. He stopped and concentrated on taking in air, bending to put his good hand on a knee for long enough to steady himself. Then he stood and headed toward the security shack.

Gabe followed. "Aaron, wait, you're in no condition."

"He did this right under our noses, the son of a bitch!" Aaron held his side, nausea making his head spin. Gravel crunched under his boots as he made his way to the security guard hut, Gabe on his heels.

Aaron fumed, fighting off the nausea taking him. If Doug Forrester was behind it, he'd have some answers and he'd have them today. He banged on the locked doors with his good fist.

Doug Forrester jerked the door open, a smile across his face. "Good morning gentlemen…"

Aaron didn't wait a second but smashed his fist into the man's jaw sending him backward to the floor and taking his own breath with the score of pain through his ribs.

"Aaron, no." Gabe pulled him off the man.

"What the hell?" Doug held his bleeding mouth, jumping up, struggling to gain his balance.

Aaron shrugged free of Gabe. "What do you know about the ramp blowing?"

Doug wiped blood from his lower lip with the back of his hand. "What are you talking about?"

Drake entered the guard shack, followed by Jack and Eric.

"You were seen shortly before the jump and had some bag over your shoulder. I want some answers and I want them right damn now," Aaron spat, shaking hard from the adrenaline coursing through him.

Doug backed up, shaking his head. "I was there to make sure it was clear when you jumped. I had nothing to do with anything else. You guys have the wrong guy here. I haven't done anything wrong here."

"Well, let's see about that." Drake held up the blue canvas bag from the corner of the room, unzipping it.

Forrester defended, "Wait, that's not mine."

Drake lifted pliers, and a cordless screw driver and

explosive putty.

The security guard held his hand up in protest, glancing at Aaron and back to the actor. "You have to believe me; I don't even know where that came from. I've been set up, man. I found it near the ramp wondering what the hell it was and removed it because I thought it might be in the way of the jump."

Aaron burst across the room again, Gabe shoving him aside to grab Doug himself. He slung the man in the office chair and slammed it against the desk. "And you couldn't bother telling us what you found? My brother nearly lost his life!" He grabbed Doug's hand and slammed it on the desk, pulling his knife from his belt.

Doug swallowed hard. "You can't do this. Look I am not even a real cop, I'm just a guard and I didn't even know what that stuff was. I found the bag when I made rounds on the ramp before the jump like I told you."

Gabe put the knife across the joint of Doug's thumb and pressed. "You know it's our thumbs that separate us from the other animals."

Doug tried to pull away. "I know nothing more, I swear. Please, I need this job and I was just trying to keep debris clear of the jump area."

Aaron gripped his right hand into a fist again, stepping closer. "You found a bag with explosives and didn't bother to tell us or the FBI?"

Doug dropped his gaze. "I…I thought I would be in trouble because the FBI would think it was mine and I didn't even know it was explosives, like I said I've…not had any formal cop training. Look, I will testify or whatever, I just don't want to be in trouble here."

Gabe lifted the knife away. "He's telling the truth."

Doug jerked his hand free eyeing his thumb and shook his head. "I was just trying to do my job."

Aaron held his gaze for a long moment. "You owe me a horse."

Chapter Twenty-Four

Jenna ran her hand across Maxus' jaw. He rocked his large head and settled to her attention. She'd seen Aaron off to the set in Gabe's truck, as he hadn't ridden his bike, given his injuries. He'd needed to get to the set to check on the Thor, who remained for the last few days of filming, but she hadn't been able to shake that he'd been more than distant for the last week or so. He'd blamed it on watching the footage of the fall, but she hadn't been so sure.

"He's a good man, isn't he?" She scratched her nails across the velvet fur of Maxus' snout, surprised the horse allowed it. She glanced at the ring on her finger. Maybe she was doing better too since things had been quiet. It seemed Vince had disappeared back to his hole somewhere and even the FBI couldn't find him and now he was national news. The hopeful for a senate seat, now a wanted fugitive.

She shivered. Vince was here. She could feel it. Maybe he'd been here all along, but if so what was he waiting for? Why hadn't he come and found her and did what he had to do?

"I'm so sorry this happened to you." She was as responsible for this animal's injuries as she was for Aaron's.

"A penny for your thoughts."

Jenna turned as Sarah walked up.

"I'm afraid my thoughts are a bit tangled these days." She tried for a smile, quickly turning to brush away the tears.

Sarah glanced at Maxus and back to her. "I'm sure living here and looking over your shoulder makes each day difficult."

"Aaron wants us here to keep us safe, but I fear I am bringing danger to everyone." She'd been at the ranch for a time now, but all the reasons why were a common topic of conversation when the family was together. "I feel so responsible for everything. I never wanted any of this to happen, not to Maxus either."

Sarah nodded. "Aaron is healing and Maxus will come around, the Vet said he has some peripheral vision so he can still be ridden, once Aaron has some time to work with him. And this is what Gabe and Tucker do. I won't say it doesn't frighten me for all of us, but let's give them a bit of time. I've seen them work. They're very good."

She nodded. "I knew one day this would all come back to haunt me, but I was so afraid and there was Mason to think about. I suppose I thought I could disappear out here and Vince would go on about his career."

"Aaron confided to tell me all of the details." Sarah turned back to face her. "Amos knows as well, and we are here to support you Jenna. You and Mason in any way we can. You are family now and we Deckers stick together through thick and thin."

"That's the problem. Aaron…he almost died and I couldn't face another day if he had." Her voice cracked and Sarah wrapped an arm around her.

"It's gonna be fine, Jenna, in time." Sarah sounded

so certain.

She nodded and quickly wiped her eyes.

"Come on, let's get some breakfast and wake those two beautiful sleepyheads inside." Sarah tugged her along. "Aaron will be back from the set in a while and we're going to grill out this afternoon. Gabe and Jeremiah are supposed to be home later today too. You can help me put together steak and chicken shish-kabobs."

Jenna smiled. It did sound like fun and it would get her mind off things. She followed Sarah inside where Lily was coming down the steps, towing Mason by the hand.

"Good morning, Sunshine. Hold onto him careful. He's still little, remember." Sarah went to assist.

"And he is smelly and needs his diaper changed." Lily helped him to the floor at the bottom step and held her nose, grinning at them both.

Jenna scooped up Mason who giggled and fought the playful kisses she covered his cheek with. "Come on, we'll get you a diaper change and then some breakfast."

"I'll start on things. How do chocolate chip pancakes sound?" Sarah turned to Lily who cheered as Jenna took Mason back up the stairs.

In no time, she had Mason re-diapered and dressed for the day and was helping Sarah in the kitchen. "I hope it's okay, I tossed in a bit of wash for Mason and myself."

"Oh, of course." Sarah flipped the pancake in the skillet. "Lily, find the syrup and butter and put them on the table."

"Okay." Lily scampered over to open the

refrigerator, singing along, and of course Mason followed her every step as she found the syrup and handed him the small tub of butter. "Come on, we have to put it on the table."

"She is quite the little mother, these days." Sarah turned to look at the children with a wise smile.

"They are adorable together," Jenna agreed and turned with the ringing of the doorbell.

Sarah wiped her hands and headed out of the kitchen to the living room toward the door, her voice lifting an octave. "I don't know that we are expecting anyone."

Jenna glanced at the children who were off to the toys in the corner of the kitchen and peered into the living room where Sarah peeked out the curtain and then back to her.

Sarah opened the door with caution. "Yes?"

"Flowers, ma'am, for a Jenna Wilder." A young voice came through the door.

Jenna froze her heart in her throat. Oh, God, he knew she was here and Mason. Her pulse raced as Sarah took the flowers and set them aside, bolting the door and double checking.

Jenna held her gaze as Sarah glanced down to lift the card reading it.

"Oh, God…no," Jenna whispered, terror scoring through her. They were alone; Aaron and his brothers off to their work and even Amos had been dropped at the local diner for the day. They were alone with the children.

"We'll call Aaron." Sarah turned for her purse, lifting her cell phone.

"What did it say?" Jenna could hardly force the air

from her lungs to create words and she wasn't sure she wouldn't pass out.

Sarah shook her head and read the card in a whisper. "Peek-a-boo."

Jenna's knees went weak. "He knows about Mason. Oh my God. I have to go and now. Sarah...I can't... Oh, God." She turned a full circle glancing at all the windows. He was probably watching right now. Mason. That was it, she had to leave and without any delay.

Sarah grabbed her by both arms "You are going to sit right here until I get Aaron on the line. Then we'll decide what to do. I'm here, Jenna, it's all right." Sarah scampered over to the stove and turned it off, sliding the skillet away from the heat. She then went to the alarm system setting it with them inside.

Jenna glanced at Mason, panic scoring through her enough to take her breath. He and Lily were oblivious to what was going on. She needed to gather their things. She needed to see what Aaron said. She needed to...

"Aaron, Oh, thank God." Sarah's voice held a hint of relief. "Flowers came... Yes, she's here and the children. Amos is still at the diner. Yes, everything is locked tightly, yes. Be careful, Aaron." Sarah hung up the phone and turned back to her speaking just above a whisper. "Aaron parked Gabe's truck on the set and when he got back to it, there were more flowers. He's about ten minutes from here. He wants us to pack for me and the children."

Jenna's heart sank along with her body and her next breath wouldn't come. She couldn't stand and sat nearly falling onto the bottom step. She couldn't stop shaking her head. Pack to go where? It wouldn't take her long as she and Mason were still living out of suit cases. But more flowers at Gabe's truck. "What did those flowers say?"

Sarah scuttled back to the kitchen, ignoring her question and began cutting up pancakes, making quick plates for Lily and Mason. "Lily, you and Mason eat right here at your doll table. Here's a sippy cup for both of you."

"Sarah?" Jenna quickly wiped her eyes, sucking in a gasping breath.

Sarah turned, glanced at the children who were now sitting at the small table with tiny chairs. "Lily, eat slow so that Mason will take his time. Show him how to dip the pieces in syrup. Jenna and I will be right back."

Sarah turned to her then and led the way into the living room once more. "Jenna, Aaron's on the way. He'll know what to do."

"What did the card say, Sarah?" Jenna shook visibly in meeting Aaron's mother's gaze.

Sarah took a deep breath and let it out. "Little Boy Blue."

Jenna blinked the pain so profound through her chest that she couldn't force herself to breathe. She collapsed to her knees with Sarah by her side.

"Jenna, Aaron will be here. We have to get things together." Sarah patted her face. "Look at me. We have to protect you and your precious son. Now, wipe your face and let's get to it."

Sarah's stern words brought her back to the surface. She nodded and let Sarah pull her to her feet. "I'll get the children fed. You go and pack up for yourself and Mason. I'll put together some food and milk for the children. You can watch them while I get

Lily and me packed."

Jenna could hardly remember touching the stairs. She glanced at her suitcase in the corner. In seconds she had tossed in her clothing and toiletries and began working on Mason's clothing, tears streaking her face. What did this mean? Maybe Vince was even watching right now. Maybe he was in the house. Oh, God, she should have left weeks ago as she'd thought to, but Aaron had been so sure she would be fine at the ranch.

Jenna finished packing their bags, her heart in her throat, unsure she could let Mason go. She grabbed the packed suitcases and headed down the stairs as Aaron came through the front door. He bolted it tightly behind him and set the alarm. He turned and she dropped both bags on the floor, diving for him and bursting into silent tears.

"It's all right." He held her as tightly as he ever had and spoke to Sarah who came from the kitchen. "I think it's time for plan 'B'."

Sarah nodded saying nothing.

Jenna lifted her head and sniffled, brushing her face free of tears once more. She couldn't panic worse— she had to see what was next as she couldn't think clear. "Plan 'B'?"

Aaron held her by both arms, his green eyes clear and sure. "Sarah's gonna take the children and go to her sister's and from there they are going someplace we have no idea about. We have to get the children out of here."

Jenna was already shaking her head. "I can't…let Mason…"

Aaron's voice went up an octave. "Look at me. We have to get the kids to safety. This is the only way.

Sarah will have her sister's help and move every few days and even we won't know where. Gabe and Tuck were on Vince's men this morning."

"Oh, God, Aaron. How can we…" Jenna wanted to scream. She couldn't part with her son, and at the moment she couldn't even breathe.

"Jenna, think about it. If we don't even know where they are then neither will Hanson," Aaron tried to convince her, his green eyes so intense it reminded her of when he'd first been injured.

"He's looking for me, so I stay here." It wasn't a question but a statement and he was right. If she parted with Mason he was safer even if she thought she might implode with pain. "All right, but what do we do?" She was all Mason had except for Brianna and—Aaron.

"You and I are gonna stay right here until we hear from Tuck." Aaron walked across the room and lifted a tan box high on a shelf and pulled a nine millimeter pistol from it, shoving it in the back of his jeans.

He held Jenna's gaze. "Tuck will be here any minute. I need to know what you're thinking, babe."

Jenna held his gaze a moment longer and went into the kitchen past Sarah. She held her tears, not wanting to scare Mason or Lily and sat on the floor by their small table.

"Jenna, we are going on a trip and Mason gets to go with us to play." Lily was all smiles.

Jenna gave the best smile she could. "I know, and it will be so much fun." She touched Mason's dark curls and leaned to kiss him, inhaling deeply the sweet baby scent of him.

Her son grinned and dipped his pancake in syrup and licked the syrup off. Moments from now he would no longer be where she could touch him and rock him to sleep at night and play with him during bath time. Maybe she would never see him again but if that were the case it was much more the reason to allow Sarah to take him.

Behind her, Aaron and Sarah scrambled up and down the stairs, getting last minute things together and adding them to the pile where she'd left Mason's suitcase. She studied her son with his bright eyes and dark curly hair, his sweet face, her best friend since the day she'd given birth. There was no love like that of a mother she supposed and in keeping him safe; she would pay any price, even her own life if that is what it took. She tugged him into her lap, him being oblivious of anything save his yummy breakfast. She placed her cheek to his dark hair and wept silent tears, memorizing the feel of his pudgy body and the weight of him in her lap. She wasn't sure how much time had passed but Aaron's words broke her thoughts.

"Tuck's here." He touched her shoulder.

She stood then, with Mason in her arms as Lily scampered off, excited about the trip.

"Grandma, we are gonna fly in the plane right now?" Lily lifted her Teddy bear and walked over to hand Mason his ruddy little lion.

"Yep." Sarah set Jenna's bag aside as Tuck came inside and began carrying bags out.

Jenna nodded to him and while she'd seen him on the set a couple of times, his eyes held the same worry as Aaron's. She hugged Mason tighter and closed her eyes. With Sarah, Aaron, and Tuck busy loading bags, she had this last moment.

"Baby. Mason." He looked up at her with a grin,

hugging the lion close. He had no clue what was going on and he was so young. How would he understand she wasn't there and for how long? "Mama loves you so much, you are such a big boy, be good, Mason. Always be good." With that she hugged him to her to the point he tried to wiggle away but offered her his lion for a kiss.

She laughed then and kissed the stuffed animal with animation and then kissed him. That was how she would do it. Let Aaron take him to Sarah while he was happy and laughing. She kissed him again as Aaron came back inside.

He shook his head, the pain clear on his face. It was as hard for him to send Lily away. "This is the right thing, Jenna."

"I know." She held Mason tighter as he chewed on the lion's tail, drooling. It was only a whisper as she handed her son off to him and followed to the door.

Mason went without issue, glancing outside and giggling as Aaron handed him off to Sarah, who sat in the back of Tucks work truck with both children. Somehow, she'd thought she might simply collapse and fall to the floor in tears, but in handing off her son for his safety, she found strength inside herself she hadn't been sure she owned.

Her heart raced so hard in her chest. If this had gotten so bad she had to send Mason off to somewhere safe, then it was time for it to end one way or the other. She would run no more and she would take charge of what she could to make sure her son didn't live a life on the run. When Tucker's truck had disappeared from sight, she turned to hold Aaron's gaze. "This ends now."

Chapter Twenty-Five

Aaron sat on the front porch, using a small saw he'd taken from the barn to cut away the plaster cast to his wrist and hand. It was early, the sun peeking across the horizon and he'd slept little, holding Jenna close most all night. White dust flew as he angled the cast to where he could saw through at his thumb. It had been almost six weeks and it was time to get the darn thing off.

He coughed and clutched his ribs, still tender, but better for the most part. He glanced out across the ranch for a second. Gabe had called earlier to say Tuck had run across two men near the set but hadn't been able to tail them close enough to get an I.D., though they were the same men from the day before.

The plan was for Jenna and him to continue life as usual, going to the set during the day and returning to the ranch at night after work. He wasn't sure anything was safe, though Tuck had sent Sarah, her sister, and the children off at the airport with no trouble.

Not knowing where Lily was crushed him, but he suspected it was far worse for Jenna, worrying over Mason. The seriousness of the situation was out of control and he'd resorted to carrying pistols and hiding weapons around the ranch, as well as in the camper and barn on the set. He'd offered Jenna a small gun for her purse, but she'd opened her bag, showing him the one she already carried. The fact she carried a gun wasn't a surprise to him. They were in a great deal of danger with Hanson knowing where the ranch was located, and while he'd planned on hiding out at the cabin, it seems not having transportation other than horses left them at possible risk.

"Doctors hate it when you do that." Jenna appeared on the porch, fully dressed and sipping a cup of coffee. She'd probably not slept any better than had he, but she looked as pretty as he'd ever seen her.

He smiled. "Docs charge another fifty bucks to do what I can do for free."

She walked closer and set her cup on one of the tables, taking the saw. "Let me, I do this all the time, though a cast cutter makes it much less dangerous."

He held his casted arm out. "Did you sleep?"

"Some." She began at the wedge of plaster between his thumb and first finger. "I should have pressed full charges back then and ended this." She focused on the sawing, wiggling the piece of plaster until it gave as she tugged it away.

"He's got a few murders behind him. Likely it would have been you if you had fought him then. Tuck and Gabe said to go about our day so they can track us and see about finding Hanson and the men with him. Won't seem as anything is different or out of the ordinary," he answered. "I suppose that means we both go on to the set, even though you've not been, you're staying with me. Filming for this season is winding up and you can pack up your clinic."

He dug in his pocket, lifting the dragonfly pendant Tucker had given to him. "You need this all the time so we can know if you are in trouble and where you are.

Just push the button here if you need us, but it's best you aren't alone."

Jenna took the pin. It looked as simple as any other piece of cosmetic jewelry. "I hope I never need it, but…"

"Listen, it's best. Tuck waited at the airport and made sure Sarah and the children boarded with no problem. She'll meet her sister somewhere, best we have no idea. I'd thought the cabin might be best, but if he knows the ranch, then it wouldn't take long to figure out the cabin." He waited as she sawed with effort down the length of his arm and then lay the saw aside.

"I'll do what you think best, Aaron." She used both thumbs to pry the cast apart and he lifted his arm from it.

Damn, he remembered this, the soreness that went with being cast free and the limited movement. His wrist hurt like hell in trying to bend it. He let out an exasperated sigh at the effort.

She rubbed his arm and hand gently. "It takes a bit when you come out of a cast, maybe a wrap or brace for a time."

He shook his head. "It'll get there. And soon enough this whole thing will be over."

She nodded and smiled, still sitting beside him. "If we ever see the other side of this, Aaron, I'm going to be a stay at home mom and love Lily and Mason every day as they grow up. I won't miss one breath of loving you all the while."

He wanted to chuckle but drew her closer. "I swear to you on my last breath, we'll have that, like you want it."

"I feel like my chest will cave in without Mason.

And Lily for that matter." She glanced at the horses who had ambled up to the fencing by the barn, surprised that Maxus was there too. "Maxus is in the corral."

"He seemed interested in following the others so I turned him out. It's hard missing Lily too, but Sarah's good with them and this is the right thing." He gripped her hand tighter. "Come on, we'll head to the set, have breakfast with Sally. One step at a time. Tuck and Gabe are tracking us in Amos' old truck. I gotta check on Thor, pack up the barn and you the clinic. Horace wants to close the set by the week's end. It'll keep us busy."

With that, he led her inside. Neither of them would likely be of much use, but he needed to check on the horse and wait for anything from his brother or Tuck. Going to the set was dangerous but so was sitting idle on the ranch. He'd thought about sending Jenna somewhere like he had Sarah and the children, but she was the lure to get Hanson to crawl out of the hole where he was hiding and this time he'd be ready.

****

Jenna glanced into the early afternoon sun coming across the set. Her nerves had eased little during the day but going through a bit of routine gave her moments where she was distracted, though missing Mason caused her moments of physical pain and panic. Her only solace was knowing this was the only way she could keep him safe. And that was all that mattered if it came down to it, even if moments of panic took her. She supposed it would be this way, pretending and trying to survive one day at a time. Aaron had barely let her go to the bathroom alone, much less spend this few minutes packing up her clinic, which was in the middle of the busy hustle to close up the set for season's end.

There had been a bit of jubilation from all those working the set, given *The Bounty Hunter Series* had been picked up for the next season. Aaron was as happy with that as was she was, since Horace had made time to run by the tent and speak to her. He'd let her know that she was indeed welcomed back to the second and future seasons if she still wanted the position. She nodded and accepted her last payment of which he'd paid her in full. She hadn't expected that with the time she'd missed, but she would love to see her life back to normal and she had enjoyed working on the set.

She bagged up the linen dressings and tossed the bag in the box of items she needed to lock away in the cabinet for the season's end. It was hard to imagine that her life might be normal again by the time filming started again next year. She went to the metal cabinet and hesitated. She'd once opened it to find flowers from Vince. Well, she wasn't afraid anymore, she couldn't be if she wanted her son and her life back. She slammed open the cabinet doors, finding what she expected, the other supplies she'd put there a while back.

She glanced around, having boxed up most of the items she used. Those closing off the campus would be around to rope off and tidy up each of the tents and buildings before the day was out.

"Well, that does it." She turned to go, walking back toward the camper, wondering if Aaron had returned from where he'd gone to meet with the breakdown crew about needs for next season. She'd been surprised he had let her pack up her clinic alone; though he had walked her there to make sure she was safe.

She entered the camper and locked the door behind

her. The camper was warm and inviting against the chill and she took a deep breath thinking of Mason and Lily. Thank God they had Sarah to help, and while not having Mason with her, she wasn't worried of his care with Sarah. Having him safe was enough. She walked into the tiny bedroom and tugged off her jacket glancing at the clock. It was after one and it would be a while until they headed back to the ranch.

She grabbed a towel from the floor and lifted one of Aaron's shirts off the back of the chair, folding it. She set the shirt on the dresser and stepped into the tiny bathroom and froze.

Flowers. Again.

Her body shook as she forced herself not to make a sound, tears welling in her eyes. The tiny flowers were in a ceramic blue elephant vase as if for a newborn. Her knees wanted to buckle and her heart skipped a beat but she took a breath and snatched the card open.

'When the bough breaks'

She crumbled to the floor, holding her mouth to keep her cries quiet. What if Vince had Mason, had discovered Sarah and the children.

"Oh, God, Mason…" She shook her head hard. It wasn't likely Vince had found Mason but this was proof enough Vince was still here. She turned a full circle and thought hard. There was little possibility Vince would know anything about where the children had been taken as they didn't even know. But there was something she needed to do without Aaron's knowledge. She had one task to complete and she had to do it without Aaron.

She stuffed the flowers, card and all into the kitchen trash and grabbed her purse and jacket, thinking she could beg forgiveness later. Searching at a frantic pace she located Aaron's keys and opened the camper door, glancing all around. She had to slip away for a few hours without Aaron knowing, even if he would be angry she hadn't followed orders.

Frightened for Mason, she brushed the tears away and stepped outside, trying to act as if nothing were out of the ordinary. Tossing her purse into the front seat of Amos' beat up truck she cranked it and, looking behind her, backed it away from the camper and off to the road behind the set buildings. She had to get to the bank and glanced at her watch. Plenty of time, though she needed to hurry.

Amazed she made it out of the set without much notice; she hit the pavement and made her way onto the highway back toward her apartment. Tears rimmed her eyes, but she wiped them with the sleeve of her jacket and increased the speed of the old truck. She had put her son in protection and now she would make sure of one last thing, in case things didn't go the way they needed to.

"Oh, Aaron will be so angry, but this won't take long and I need it done." But he would have never allowed what she was about to do and once it was done there wouldn't be anything he could do to change things.

That Vince had gotten flowers all the way into Aaron's camper meant he could get anywhere and as they had all suspected, the showdown was coming. She slammed the old truck into fourth gear and squeezed tighter to the steering wheel glancing in the review mirror as she put on Aaron's sun glasses.

"This one thing, please God." She spoke to herself

as she pulled off the exit and into town, the ride giving her too much time to think. She rode past her apartment building twice making sure no one was around, before pulling the truck in and parking it behind the row of buildings where she, Brianna and Ms. Lucy lived. She waited inside the truck, gathering her shredded nerves and then stepped outside, putting on one of Amos' baseball caps to cover her face. Climbing the stairs on the back side of the building she skirted to the front and used her key to enter her apartment, her heart pounding.

She glanced around, the toys all over the floor reminding her of Mason. The longing for her old life was so profound she lifted one of Mason's shirts and smelled it. No, she didn't have time to cry now. Running to her bedroom she opened the small jeweled case in her sock drawer and lifted the key to the safety deposit box.

She raced to the kitchen and opened several cans of cat food for Bodi who was tangling his way around her legs, meowing in rapid succession. She bent, setting the large bowl of canned food on the floor, the old cat raising his back as she rubbed a hand down to his tail. "Oh, Bodi…Tuck will look after you. I hope you are being nice when he feeds you."

She stood again, lifted the key, and stuck it in the pocket of her jeans. She grabbed Mason's shirt from the table where she'd tossed it and folded it into the pocket of her jacket. Trotting to the refrigerator she opened the freezer and dug for a packet of tin foil and shoved it inside her purse. There was five-thousand dollars along with a new identity hidden there, should she need it. She wasn't planning on changing who she was anymore, but she wanted to give Aaron the money, as he'd sent Sarah off with all the cash he had.

She turned once more to survey her home. For a moment she thought to crumble, fall apart over the idea that Vince was aware of Mason. She'd known she should have told him about his son, but with how things were, she had full proof that would have been a terrible idea. Mason deserved a father, not a mentally deranged stalker who was now in trouble with the law.

She slipped back into the old truck without being noticed, still wearing Aaron's sunglasses and Amos' hat. She cranked the old engine and, shifting into drive, pulled the sputtering vehicle out onto the main road headed for the bank at the end of Great Falls.

Looking back on all that had and was happening; she wanted to scream to have her son in her arms again. She still wasn't sure the she shouldn't have just taken Mason and disappeared once more into another life. She forced a deep breath to clear her head. And running…again. It wouldn't have changed much, would it? And Mason might have… She wouldn't think about that. Mason was safe and she had to keep telling herself that.

In no time at all, she turned in to the bank parking lot and stopped the truck, digging in her pocket for the safety deposit box key. Her hands shook as she held it trying to steady her nerves to no avail. She glanced around. Nothing but those wishing to bank and busy cars on the road speeding past them. The bank was bustling busy and that might make things easier, but she still needed to hurry. Exiting the truck, she tossed her purse over her shoulder and made her way inside. Opening the inner doors of the bank she was visibly shaking, and even though it was cold, she was perspiring. She had little control over anything much in this whole situation but what she was about to do meant one thing good would happen. She scanned the offices and one of the agents there smiled, motioning her inside.

"Good morning." Jenna's gut clenched.

"How may I help you?" the clerk with a badge showing her name was Anna Briggs asked.

"Yes, I have a safety deposit box and need access, please." She gave a slight smile, slowing her breathing.

"Your name?" She exited from around her desk leading the way.

Jenna followed her into the vault. "Jenna Wilder."

Anna made small talk as she opened the card box. "Yes, here you are. If I can check your I.D."

Jenna fumbled into her purse, pulling out her wallet and handing over her driver's license.

"Sign here." She handed Jenna a pen.

Jenna managed a deep breath and signed. "I wondered if I could also have a check cut for two-hundred and fifty thousand dollars today."

"I think that would be fine, though it does take five business days to clear." Anna placed the key into one slot, nodding for Jenna to use her key.

"Thank you." Jenna nodded. "I'm sure that would be just fine."

"I do appreciate this, and I know its last minute." Jenna reached inside her purse, pulling out a piece of folded paper.

"Oh, well, it should be fine, given you have the cash." The teller went to work on her computer.

"And who are we making the check out to?" Anna asked her.

She'd managed to swipe the page from Aaron's pile of papers at his small computer desk in his bedroom. It was the ad for the land he wanted to purchase, complete with the Sun River Realtor logo. "You can make the full amount to Sun River Realty. I'm headed out of town and I need to make the payment before I go."

The teller took the money and spoke as she stood and headed to the door. "I'll go ahead and have the check processed and post dated for the five days. Oh, and approved by our president; he's right upstairs."

"Thank you." Jenna waited as she stepped away, the moments until she returned nearly unnerving her. She had to hurry before the realtor closed or before Aaron figured out she had left the set, though he probably already had. But she needed to do this one thing—purchase Aaron's land in full for him so that if nothing else good came of the whole situation she would do right by him in seeing that his dreams did come true.

"And here you are, Ms. Wilder." Anna returned startling her from her thoughts.

She stood, accepting the envelope and taking a quick glance at the check and stuffing it in her purse. "Oh, I thank you so much. Is there anything else I need to do?"

"I don't think so; it is post dated and signed by the bank president." She smiled. "It's been a pleasure to serve you."

"No, and thank you again." Jenna tugged her purse over her shoulder, shook the teller's hand and slipped from the bank, never looking back.

Entering the old truck once more her heart

pounding so hard, her chest thumped with each beat. She'd done nothing illegal, so why did she feel so like a thief of some kind? The money was rightfully hers to do with as she wanted and what she was about to do would make sure Aaron's dream came true, no matter what the future brought.

She glanced at her hand, at the ring Aaron gave to her. He'd loved her enough to place it there and it had been the happiest moment of her life, but now if this craziness with Vince didn't end and well, she would lose everything.

"Time for something good to come out of all this." She cranked the old truck once more, heading toward Sun River, glancing into the review mirror. If Vince was onto her, she hadn't noticed anyone following her, but since this had begun there was always the feeling of being watched.

It seemed a short drive as she turned into the parking lot of Sun River Realty. She looked around, having never been inside.

She parked Amos' old truck and pulled the check from her purse, making her way inside. She'd made a phone call earlier in the week to check about the pricing, though the gentleman she'd talked to had said he had another potential buyer of the land, and that the first forty acres had already been purchased by him, but he'd let her know the price of the remaining ninety acres. The cashier's check would cover it all in full for Aaron, if she could convince the realtor it was for him.

"Good afternoon, may I help you?" The petite lady looked to be in her late sixties but had a giant size smile.

"Hi." Jenna shook off the cold and her nerves.

"It's cold out there today. They say it won't warm up for another month." The woman shivered too.

"Yes…I spoke to a gentleman about purchasing a large piece of property about a week ago. I believe his name was Jim." Jenna waited.

"My husband. Jim, Dear," the woman shouted toward the office across the hall. "I'm Essie."

"Coming." The elderly man walked from the room dressed in a golf shirt and khaki pants, already reaching out to take Jenna's hand. "I'm Jim Barnes, very pleased to meet you. What can we do you for today?"

Jenna let go of his hand. "I'm Jenna Wilder, I spoke to you about the land that is connected to the Decker ranch, a week ago."

"Yes, ma'am, I remember." Mr. Barnes took a step back rubbing his forehead and dropping his gaze.

"Well, I've gotten a cashier's check to purchase that last ninety acres and complete the payment for the first forty acres in full." She waited but he frowned, as he glanced at his wife.

"Well, this is kind of unusual. Someone else owns that forty and is making payments and he's also inquiring about those last ninety acres too." He shook his head.

"I am actually wanting to purchase this anonymously for him. For Mr. Decker." Jenna was interrupted by Mrs. Barnes.

"Do you know Aaron Decker?" She smiled.

Jenna's heart all but stopped as the woman continued.

"I thought so, I saw you having lunch with Aaron, downtown in Great Falls recently. Remember Jim, when you took me shopping?" The old woman smiled, batting her eyes at Jenna.

"Yes, Aaron is a very good friend. He would never accept me purchasing this for him, but I want to pay for it, in full, in his name. I have the money though it will take five days to clear but I want it to be a surprise. Once it clears, then Aaron can handle the closing and sign all the papers to make sure it is all in his name. He has plans for a foster care ranch, so look at me like an investor in his plans." Jenna's heart fluttered worse than at the bank. This had to work.

"Of course, but paying in full…" Mr. Barnes scratched his head.

"Unfortunately, I do have to leave town this afternoon but I have this note, a card that goes with the surprise if that can be given to Aaron at closing." She waited.

Mr. Barnes accepted the check and envelope. "Well, I can draw up the paperwork. This is kind of unusual. It'll take me several days, working with the land owners."

"Please if there is any way you can let me do this for Aaron. I come from money and Aaron would never let me purchase this land for him." Jenna tried for a smile. "You know how men are."

It was Mrs. Barnes that nodded with a smile. "Well, Jim, don't you think that is romantic… I thought I saw a little romance going on at that lunch table." Essie reached out to pat Jenna's hand. "That Aaron is so sweet. At one time I sure did think he was one of those Hell's Angels but seeing him on that motor cycle and that cute little Lily on the back. He is such a good father, though he could use a haircut and a shave." She began typing on her computer as she continued to talk.

"Actually, all three of those Decker sons are good boys, from what I hear. Amos and Sarah are incredible people to have raised such fine sons."

"Yes, they have. I would like to keep this quiet for a time, until the check clears and all the papers are ready for closing. I had it made to Sun Realty, so you can disperse the funds as needed to the owners." Jenna played along as best she could. Frankly, she'd almost like to kiss Mrs. Barnes as her husband simply shrugged and nodded for her to follow him into his office.

In less than an hour, Jenna pulled from the parking lot of Sun River Realty. In a few days Aaron would own his land in full. She thought of the words written inside the card, which would explain to Aaron her reasons about the land.

'Dear Aaron,

I can't begin to explain more than simply saying I want you to have your land. If anything good can come from all this it would be to know that you have the land to make the boys' ranch what you want it to be. Remember, you taught me it isn't about the fall, but about the landing and once all this if over, my prayers are we both land on our feet. Not every woman has the chance to love a hero, and you are mine. Please accept this gift and build your dream. I will love you always,

Jenna

She wasn't saying good-bye by any means, but should things get worse, these last words from her would go to him. Her hands shook as she held tightly to the steering wheel of Amos' old clunker of a truck. The words sounded silly, and for a writer, she'd stressed over it too long and finally went with it. She bit her bottom lip to try and stop the tears that flowed anyway. She'd done it. No matter what happened now, Aaron's dreams would be realized; if only she could be assured she might still have her own.

Chapter Twenty-Six

Aaron cranked Gabe's truck and jerked it into gear as Gabe scrambled into the passenger side of the truck, almost losing his balance in the effort.

"What the hell are you doing? Son of a bitch!" Gabe grabbed the dashboard, swearing as the truck peeled out of the set throwing gravel. "At least let me go with you, damn hard headed."

"I have to find her before they do. Damn it, I told her to stay put." Aaron cursed along with his brother. He'd gone back to the camper, expecting to find Jenna, but she'd not been there and Amos' old truck was gone. And then he'd found more flowers from Vince in the trash. Either Jenna had made her run or Vince had taken her and he didn't know which.

"She's the one who put the flowers in the trash. Where would she go?" Gabe asked as the truck threw more gravel and fishtailed onto the highway, outside the set.

Aaron didn't answer but struggled to pull his cell phone from his front jeans pocket with his right hand, while he gripped the steering wheel as best he could with his still tender left hand. He slid his finger across the screen.

Gabe shook his head in obvious frustration. "Dude, you told her not to answer you. I'll get Tuck to trace her."

"We'll check out her apartment, but she's kept the panic button on her." Aaron glanced at his brother and back to the road.

"She'd be crazy to go there alone," Gabe responded texting on his cell.

"And that's why we're going there first…" Aaron blurted. Jenna was headstrong. She wouldn't hesitate to run by her place during the day, if for nothing else to check on Bodi, but he'd made her promise not to go anywhere without him. He tried to get her to bring the cat the ranch, but she'd been certain he wouldn't do well with the change.

"Women are damn strange creatures. That's why I don't need one," his brother scoffed.

Aaron ignored him and raced the truck in and out of highway traffic. How long she'd been gone he had no idea. She had at least a couple of hours on them and he wasn't sure he understood since she'd been so frightened. He listened to the endless ringing of her cell phone.

"Damn it." He slung the phone onto the console, as it had gone to her voice mail yet again.

"If she's running, bro, she isn't going to answer," Gabe said, hanging onto the dash.

"Got it Sherlock." He spat. "She didn't run. Something's wrong."

Gabe's phone rang, and he slid his thumb across the screen. "Yea? Okay. Got it. We're on the way. She bailed from the set in Amos' truck, you seen it? Yep. No."

"What?" Aaron glanced at his brother.

"Tucker tailed Hanson to Jenna's apartment. The bastard trashed the place but parked a van there that hasn't been moved, but there's no sign of him. Tuck said he must've had another vehicle there. No sign of Jenna or Amos' truck. He's trying to trace her now," Gabe explained.

"Son of a…" He didn't finish, cursing himself for her letting her out of his sight. But she wouldn't run without her son, so the only thing might that she was trying to protect him.

"Tuck's still there, waiting on us." Gabe lifted the Glock from his belt, checking it and returning it. "He may have her, Aaron."

Aaron picked up speed, his gut clenching at the idea. If she had gone to her apartment and Hanson caught her there, then things were worse than he thought. But why didn't she push the button? "She hasn't kicked the panic button, maybe not."

"Tuck's been watching for a few hours. The only person who's been around is her nurse friend. What's her name?" His brother shrugged.

"Brianna," he answered staring ahead at the road, trying to think what Jenna might have done.

"She's pretty hot." Gabe raised his eyebrows. "Maybe she knows something."

Aaron scowled at him. Leave it to Gabe in a crisis to think about women. "She's likely too much for you to handle."

"Can't blame a man for looking." His arrogant brother chuckled. "Busy all the time from what I gather, and never off her cell."

Aaron's cell phone rang and he bobbled to grab it, letting the truck swerve.

"Shit." Gabe grabbed the dash yet again.

"Yeah," he answered.

It was Amos. "Aaron, Jim from the realty office called. Said a woman came in, made a purchase in full for your land and left a note there. She was in my truck, son. I won't ask what the hell is going on, but what the hell is going on?"

Aaron took a deep breath and let it out. "Call Jeremiah to go right now and pick up the note." Why would Jenna leave a package with Jim? Nothing was making sense. "Call him, Pop. Do it."

"She's on the run then?" Amos continued.

"Tell Jeremiah to call me, Pop. I'm hanging up." He tried to sound convincing, but he wasn't about to answer the questions he wasn't sure of. Maybe Jenna did run, but he didn't think so, without Mason. But the land, why would she do that?

The click of the phone sent dread through him. What the hell did the note say? It seemed to take forever to get to the outskirts of Great Falls and then to Jenna's apartment. As he pulled the truck into the apartment complex, his pulse raced.

"She took off, didn't she? Ran?" Gabe waited for an answer already nodding his head.

"She left a note with Jim Barnes at the reality office, paid for the land in full." It was him who shook his head this time.

"Where would she go?" Gabe pointed. "There's Tuck."

"She wouldn't leave without Mason. Something's not adding up." Aaron pulled Gabe's truck closer and cut the engine slamming it into park. Gabe jumped from the truck, shoving another pistol from under the seat in the back of his pants. He trotted over to Tucker's truck.

"Boys," Tuck greeted with a nod.

"What've you got?" Aaron wanted answers.

"He came in that van over there and trashed the place. I tailed him here but his cronies were on me and I had to run around until I lost them. I got back in maybe ten minutes and he had to have taken another vehicle he'd planted here. I can't get a trace on Jenna, the pins not picking up." Tucker shook his head.

"Wait, you finally saw him?" Aaron asked touching the pistol resting in his own belt.

"Yep, things are coming down, Aaron. We need to find her. Where else would she go?" Tuck turned down one of the radios in his truck and scanned the laptop shaking his head.

Aaron's gut clenched in dread. What if Hanson had Jenna? "Jeremiah's headed to the Realty office in Sun River. She was there earlier this morning, left a package. I'm going inside."

"No one's inside except that cat from hell. Even though I feed him that is one bad ass critter. Might be he scared Hanson out of there." Tucker chuckled. "Not sure why I can't get a trace on her. I had her this morning on the set, but nothing now. Even if she dumped the button it should pick up."

"She wouldn't dump the button. I'm looking around inside." Aaron trotted toward the building and climbed the stairs two at a time, ignoring his ribs. He turned the corner to face Jenna's apartment door, his brother and Tucker on his heels. Touching the knob, he pushed and waited. She'd been here without a doubt, but that wasn't something his brother or Tuck would understand. He could feel her and walked inside.

Jenna's usually neat apartment was in shambles, her bookshelves overturned, drawers pulled out and the contents spilled. Nothing seemed to be in its place and nothing was left untouched. The couch cushions were shredded, and the curtains had been torn down.

"He did a number on the place." Gabe put his hands on his hips and stopped inside.

"Did you see the cat?" Aaron turned to Tuck, who was snapping pictures of the damage with his cell phone.

"Yep. Took me twenty minutes with a broom to shut him in the bathroom off the bedroom." Tuck shivered from head to toe.

"Would've liked to see that one." Gabe laughed as he glanced around the shambles of the living room.

Aaron headed straight for Jenna's bedroom. With the place being ransacked and given what Tuck said, it was no doubt Bodi was fit to be tied. Aaron talked at the door, waving off Gabe and Tucker who'd followed. "Hey, Bodi, I'm coming in."

Aaron went inside slow and sure and knelt down. Bodi was under the vanity hissing and squalling. He held out his hand, steady, but didn't offer to touch the frightened animal.

Bodi hissed again and backed up but then touched his nose to Aaron's hand sniffing up and down and then walking out from under the vanity with a slight meow. Aaron picked him up.

"What are you, the damn cat whisperer?" Tucker took a few steps back, pushing Gabe with him.

Aaron walked from the bathroom, carrying the cat. "If he's still here then Jenna didn't run. She wouldn't leave for good without her son or the cat."

Tucker lifted his brows. "It looks like his father died a few months ago, his career's in the shitter, the

Feds are on his tail and if he has Jenna, he has nothing left to lose except…"

"Except the money and his son." Aaron spoke in anger. "What about the van outside?"

"I was about to break in but you got here." Tuck led the way back to the living area.

Gabe looked hard at Aaron, "You bringing the cat?"

"Can't leave him here. Why, you scared?" Aaron challenged.

"Hell, yeah." Gabe backed up.

"See if you can find a pet carrier." Aaron wasn't about to leave the cat to be in the house with all the shattered glass if nothing else. Gabe nodded and headed off to look.

Aaron followed Tucker back into the living room and glanced in the small kitchen. Things were uprooted there, including the food from the refrigerator and freezer dumped. Every carton of food was open or spilled. He shook his head.

Tuck stepped into the kitchen. "She fed the cat."

Aaron glanced at the bowls on the floor and back.

"I fed the cat out of those over there." Tuck pointed to another set of bowls in the corner.

Aaron turned back to the living room. If Jenna had come by and fed the cat, getting what she needed at the apartment, she'd narrowly missed Hanson's visit for slashing the place. And if she had made it to the bank and the reality office, he couldn't have gotten to her until after that. "Did he come here more than once?"

"Nope." Tucker followed.

Gabe held up a cat carrier. "Criminals don't return to the crime scene unless there's a reason, and he's been here more than once before today if we've guessed right. He either found the money or her."

"Time's wasting." Aaron grabbed the carrier from Gabe and gently shoved Bodi inside.

Tuck scratched his head, "It's hard to outthink this guy, Aaron. He's twisted, man, and if he has her."

"Then it's time we get her back." Aaron hissed.

"Let's check the van." Gabe turned.

"What in the hell!" A female shriek caused all three men to turn, drawing their weapons. "Oh my God, don't shoot!" Brianna screamed, holding her hands up in defense.

Aaron took a deep breath and let his hand drop, putting the gun back into his belt.

"Sorry, you sneak up people and you'll get that pretty rear of yours shot." Gabe shoved his gun in the back of his jeans, walking closer to her. "You seen Jenna today?"

"No, I haven't. Aaron?" Brianna glared at Gabe but turned to Aaron. "Where is she?"

Aaron moved closer. "We don't know? What?"

Brianna placed a hand to her chest, still catching her breath. "She called me, earlier, but wouldn't tell me what was going on. Wait…that bastard has her, doesn't he? That's why you all are here. Oh, my God."

"We think so," Gabe answered.

"I knew it." Tears spilled from Brianna's eyes.

Aaron picked up Bodi's carrier. "Did she give you any idea where she was going?" He headed toward the door, the others following.

"She was so upset on the phone, but said she had some errands and was letting me know she was all right. She called from the phone here." Brianna followed Aaron down the stairs to the parking lot.

"Let's take it one step at a time." Aaron made his way to Gabe's truck and shoved the carrier with Bodi in the short back seat, walking to the abandoned blue van.

"Wait." Gabe pulled a baseball bat from the back of the truck and without any hesitation knocked out the driver's window with the butt of the bat, glass shattering with a loud crack.

"Oh my God, we're all going to jail." Brianna took a step back.

"Shhhhh." Gabe raised an eyebrow at her.

Aaron reached inside and opened the van door. Besides the two front seats there was very little inside. Empty boxes in the back and rusted tools of some kind in a small toolbox. Likely stolen. He climbed inside looking around the dash at papers and trash, including various food wrappers. Someone had been sitting here and watching her for a time.

Gabe walked to the other side of the van and tapped the window with the bat.

Aaron leaned to open the passenger door and went back to searching, tossing aside papers as he looked through them, nothing giving any hints.

"Aaron." Gabe had opened the glove box.

Aaron leaned closer. Inside was a single black rose with a small picture of Jenna and a large card. He grabbed the picture and then the card, letting the black rose fall to the floor of the van.

"What is it?" Tucker asked.

"Another flower." Brianna put her hands to her mouth.

Aaron looked at the picture of Jenna. It wasn't current as her hair was shorter. He opened the large folded card.

'Up for an old-fashioned gunfight? Come alone, Cowboy, and bring my son or there's gonna be a hanging'

It was scrolled in tidy red ink penmanship. Aaron turned the card over. On the back was an inked handprint. He touched it, comparing his hand to the size of the print. Jenna. So the son of a bitch did have her. He bolted from the van, tossing the card aside.

"Aaron, wait." Gabe took off after him.

Aaron pulled the gun from his belt as he arrived back at Gabe's truck. Removing the cartridge, he checked the bullets and shoved the cartridge back inside the gun. Laying it on the console he climbed in.

Gabe wedged his boot in the door, stopping him. "You aren't going alone, bro."

Aaron glared hard at his brother.

Tuck walked over having bagged up the evidence of the note, picture, and black rose. "Old-fashioned hanging…what the heck does that mean?"

"He's gonna kill her, isn't he? Isn't he?" Brianna screamed, her body shaking as tears began.

Gabe took a deep breath. "We don't know…hold off for a minute until we figure this all out, then you can cry all you want."

Brianna wiped her eyes, her mascara smearing as she gave Gabe a scowl.

"He's at the set." Tucker understood. "Old fashioned hanging."

"No!" Aaron shouted. "I'm going alone. The set was closed this afternoon."

"That's plain suicide, brother. You aren't in any condition to put up a fight." Gabe ran his hands through his short dark hair. "Not happening."

"He's setting you up, man," Tuck added shaking his head. "We go together."

Aaron growled. "So be it, but I'm going to get her back."

"How, by getting your ass shot?" His brother walked away but turned back around. "He'll think you are alone, but we'll be there with you. We can come in the back way, the loop road to the canyon. No one knows much about that but us."

"The set's deserted by now; he waited us out, doing it right under our noses." Aaron shook his head. They were wasting time and he had to get to Jenna. If she had only stayed put, but then she would have already been on the set making Vince's job easier.

Gabe looked at Tucker. "I'll have Aaron drop me a mile up the road before the set. When you make the turn for the loop road, I'll meet you in the woods."

"Got it. I'll wire us all with mics." Tuck jogged toward his truck, already on his cell phone.

Aaron cranked the truck as Gabe walked around to the other side and climbed in. Looking at Brianna who still stood beside the truck, Aaron nodded to the back seat. "Can you take the cat for now? I'll call you as soon as I can."

Brianna opened the back door where Bodi's crate sat. Instead of taking it, she pushed it to the other side of the truck, across the seat. Without asking, she climbed in the back seat, slammed the door shut and tugged on her seat belt. She folded her hands in her lap, looking straight ahead.

Both men turned to eye her in confusion.

"She's my best friend." Brianna set her jaw. "I'm

coming along."

"No way," Gabe spat.

"Uh huh." Aaron shook his head. "This might get ugly."

"I am not getting out of this truck unless you boys think you can remove me physically, but I have to warn you, I bite, kick and scratch worse than the cat in this crate." She gave them both a set of raised brows.

"Sounds like a damn challenge. Drive on brother." Gabe chuckled looking at her for a second and then turning back around.

"Hang on." Aaron ripped the truck into forward, peeling out and sending black smoke across the pavement. If he knew anything about Brianna, she was rather feisty and he didn't have time to deal with a hysterical, fighting woman.

It was early afternoon and by now the set would be a ghost town.

Gabe laid a large gun on the seat and reached underneath Aaron, pulling out an automatic pistol. Dropping the cartridge, he double checked and put it back, clicking the safety, nodding to Aaron, and setting it on the console beside the other.

"Maybe we should call the police." Brianna's eyes widened.

Both men turned in unison, "No!"

Brianna shifted left as Gabe leaned over the seat back, reaching above her to grab a rifle from the gun rack. She ducked as he brought the weapon to the front. "My God, you men have more weapons than The Army National Guard."

Gabe smiled at her and pulled a large knife case from the seat back behind Aaron. "The one with the most toys wins."

Brianna shivered.

"A little insanity helps in times like this." Gabe turned back around, leaning to shove a smaller knife into Aaron's boot.

"There's another pistol in the door," Gabe said as he loaded up his own arsenal of weapons.

Aaron's phone buzzed and he struggled to slide a thumb across the glass. "Jer."

"Aaron?" Jeremiah was on the other end. "Look, I went to the realty office and got the card from Jim. It's from Jenna; you're not going to believe this one brother. She's purchased the back one hundred acres in full for you, deeds in your name. All legal, according to Jim."

Aaron remained quiet. He sucked in a breath still shocked but worried more about what he needed to anticipate in getting to Jenna, "Read the note." The truck swerved and he fought to gain control.

Gabe grabbed the dash. "Easy with my truck man, should've let me drive."

"Oh my, God," Brianna shouted from the back hanging onto the seat back as the old cat squalled his meows.

Aaron righted the truck and made himself take a breath. It was all he could do to speak again. "Read it."

On the other end of the line Jeremiah spoke. "Uuuhhh. *Dear Aaron, I can't begin to explain more than simply saying I want you to have your land. If anything good can come from all this it would be to know that you have the land to make the boys' ranch what you want it to be. Remember, you taught me it isn't about the fall, but about the landing and once all this if over, my prayers are we both land on our feet. Not every woman has the chance to love a hero and you are mine. Please accept this gift and build your dream. I will love you always, Jenna."*

Numbness plowed through Aaron. Gut punched to the point he had to focus hard to drive. Had Jenna been going to leave? She couldn't have. Even if she left him she would never leave Mason. He knew that for a fact.

"What the hell's going on, Aaron? You told me enough for me to know it's gone bad," Jeremiah shouted into the phone.

Aaron handed the cell phone to Gabe. "Tell him."

"Jer?"

Aaron listened as Gabe talked to Jeremiah explaining the details. He let his mind wander. So if Hanson had Jenna and he wanted a fight, he was about to get one. If the bastard so much as touched a hair on her head, he'd kill the man without a second thought.

He still hurt like hell, but this was Jenna, and he could worry about the pain later. This was insane and now Jeremiah was on the way. Hanson was dangerous and he'd have men helping him no doubt. Putting his brothers and Tucker at risk wasn't to his liking, but what choice did he have? No matter how things went down, he'd get Jenna back—and of that he was certain.

Chapter Twenty-Seven

Jenna shifted gears, glancing at the road ahead. Amos' old truck sputtered through a stall and then forged ahead. She'd accomplished what she set out to do, making sure no matter how things went, Aaron would have his land. She gripped the steering wheel tightly as the engine stalled again but picked up. She'd been gone longer from the set than she had intended and Aaron would be terribly worried, though she wondered how she would explain other than to say there was something she'd had to do.

"Oh, he will be so angry, but it can't be helped." She talked to herself as she thought of Mason. She missed him so, the pain was almost physical but with the last flowers, the ones Aaron had probably found by now, she gulped a deep breath, knowing he was safe.

She glanced into the review mirror at the maroon car following idly a few lengths behind, always a bit unnerved that she might be followed, but the car turned off onto another road. She lifted her gaze again just in time to slam on her breaks at a large black SUV pulled out in front of her. She screamed as the old truck collided with the front end, sending her against the dash.

Trying to regain her wits, she blinked hard. And then the laughter found her and every part of the terror she'd been living the last few years bolted through her.

Vince. She glanced to the driver's side of the SUV and there he was, his evil gaze holding her hostage as he revved the truck pushing her further in the old truck. She hung onto the steering wheel, unsure what to do and contemplating her escape.

The old truck was edged to the ditch little by little, the tires and metal squeaking and scarping along the pavement until it hit dirt and rolled hard to its side, tossing her forward again. Her head bounced off the windshield as the old truck settled. Stunned, Jenna rubbed her head and her side, fading in and out from the impact and confused at first.

Vince pulled her from the passenger door of the old truck, jerking her to her feet where she swayed before she could do anything. She shrieked and tried for escape but he slammed her against the SUV, pinning her there.

"Hello, Jennifer, what's your hurry?" He shoved a gun in her face causing her head to hit the truck again.

She sucked in a needed breath, fighting the severe pain scorching through her head and trying to contemplate her situation. Funny she had been in such fear of Vince finding her but now, she shivered but more so from the cold. She fought to hold his evil gaze.

He wiped a sleeve across his brow and smiled. "What did you think, sweetheart, you could scheme against me with my old man?"

Jenna said nothing.

"He's dead you know, but he got the last laugh until now." His eyes narrowed and then he screamed. "Where's my son?"

Shock flew through Jenna, and anger welled to the surface. She spoke in loud even tones. "He will never be your son." Mason would only ever be her child, never his, never this monster's. And now she knew for sure that Mason remained safe and sound.

He grabbed her face and pressed her head back into the truck. "You knew right what you were doing playing dear old daddy for all his money, didn't you?"

Jenna met his gaze, gaining a bit of her composure. "That money was rightfully mine from my father."

He laughed then. "Sweet little Jennifer, you don't know do you?"

She looked at him trying to force her mind to hear his words, her head ached and she was sure she had a concussion if not worse.

"It seems my father wasn't so interested in my campaign after all. But he always saw the good in you, didn't he sweetheart?" He laughed again. "And he left all my inheritance to my son, so you will produce him or you will suffer. He's what, about a year old now? Cute I'll bet, just like me."

So his father had left his full inheritance to Mason? Mr. Hanson had been worth millions and Vince had long planned on what he would inherit when his father died. "That is not my doing, but no matter, you will never know any part of your son in this lifetime."

He laughed sadistically. "Well, let us just see about that. Think that cowboy biker might just be up to an old-fashioned gunfight to win the girl. Well, he won't win until I have my son, you bitch." With that he slammed her against the SUV, her head hitting hard and her world going dark.

****

Jenna sat in the back seat of a large black SUV, hands tied behind her back, belted in. She was groggy, her head pounding and the coppery taste of blood in her mouth lingered where she'd been hit—more than once. In front of her Vince drove the vehicle along back roads heading them outside of Great Falls, from what she could tell.

She'd been unwise; to say the least, in thinking no one was following her when she left the small realtor's office. But he'd come out of nowhere and pushed the old vehicle off the road, trapping her. She'd slammed hard against the steering wheel, bumping her head. He'd then grabbed her before she could regain her composure to run and he'd slammed her more than once against the large SUV. Her head ached to the point the sunlight hurt and she closed her eyes briefly.

She thought of Mason, reassuring herself that he was safe, and that he would continue to be so, no matter what was coming. And she had no doubts that Aaron would find her, somehow and some way.

"We'll be there shortly, in case you are wondering." Vince glared with an evil smile from the review mirror.

She said nothing but held his gaze. Sheer terror engulfed her even with her confusion, and she fought not to give him the satisfaction of her tears. He'd no doubt kill her, but at least she'd done what she set out to do. Aaron would have his land and Mason was safe.

"How did you like the flowers?" He adjusted the mirror for a better view of her.

"Where are you taking me?" Her voice was weak, surprising her.

"Well for starters, sweetheart, where's my money and my son?" he spat turning to look hard at her and then turning back to the road.

"I inherited that money from my father, it was never yours. As for the other, I knew nothing of it," she whispered and looked out the window, trying to figure out where they were.

"And my son?" He snarled running his hand through his short brown hair.

"He isn't your son and he never will be." Jenna leaned her head back, wanting so bad to have her hands free to hold her aching head.

"Oh, he's mine or at least he will be." He gripped the steering wheel until his knuckles turned white.

"I walked away so you didn't go to jail for beating me, so you could have your precious seat in the house. What happened? Not enough campaign funds? How's that working with your new family? Do you beat them too? You will never have *my* son." Jenna stopped, angry at herself for even speaking.

"Save your pity party. The old man paid you off and you took it. Don't talk to me about crooked deals." He hissed. "You know, I never could understand his fascination with you, the *'daughter he never had'*."

"That was money you took from my accounts." Tears streamed her cheek, not from her fear but from the pain inside her head.

He stopped abruptly and screamed. "Where's my son?"

It was so loud her ears rang and she cringed, closing her eyes. All she could see was Mason's face and pain scored through her chest at the idea she might never see him again. She opened her eyes again and looked ahead at the road. They were on the way to the set, from what she could tell. Why would he go there?

"I—want—my—money so you need to be thinking

about how that is going to happen. And then you know what?" he yelled again. "I will have my son, take him right out of your arms, sweetheart."

Jenna shook her head. "You can kill me but you will never have him. Ever!"

"What did you think, I'd let you have the money? I've been watching you all along sweetheart, waiting for the old man to kick the bucket." He hissed. "Oh, but what a surprise it was to find out I had a son who had inherited my rightful birthright! So I'll have him and the money, sweetheart. It's just a matter of time."

How had she ever let herself believe she was free of him? She glanced back out the window, trying as she could to press the lapel pin against her shoulder, acting as if her movements were about her headache.

"He can't save you, ya know, that biker riding cowboy." He laughed loudly. "Really, such a step down for you, hope he enjoyed his recent fall from the scaffolding."

"You almost killed him and he has nothing to do with this," Jenna spat.

He gave an evil roar of laughter, "Well, that makes things a little interesting."

Her cell phone rang. Jenna jerked a glance toward the console, where she recognized the ring as Aaron. *Oh God! Please Aaron.*

Vince looked at her in the review. "Well, if it isn't biker boy now. You'd be wise to remain silent." He grabbed it and slammed his thumb across the screen.

Aaron's voice came across loud and clear. "I know you have her and I'm meeting you on the set alone. What do you want?"

Jenna's eyes filled with tears.

"I see you got my message." Vince's sarcastic tone was evident. "I want my son."

"Put her on the phone," Aaron demanded.

"You aren't at liberty to call the shots here, cowboy, but I'll give you a little chat." Vince leaned to put the phone against Jenna's ear, straining to drive and reach her at the same time.

She leaned to keep her ear to the phone. "Aaron?"

"Jenna, do what he says and I'll be there." Aaron's voice was certain.

"Aaron!" Jenna called to him again as Vince pulled the phone away from her ear.

"See ya soon, cowboy." He pushed the button to hang up and tossed the phone into the seat. They were not all the way to the set, but somewhere off the road before arriving. Jenna waited as he got out of the truck and grabbed a large bag from the back. He tossed it over his shoulder and walked to get her out of the back of the SUV.

"Out!" He yelled. "We walk from here."

She struggled to get out of the truck with her hands tied behind her back. Vince lost patience with her and jerked her out by the sleeve of her jacket. She bobbled to gain her footing, as he nudged her along. She was dizzy and nausea plagued her. She shivered in the cold, thankful she'd had the good sense to wear boots.

"Jennifer Amiker, Jenna Wilder...which one has my money sweetheart?" Vince shoved her ahead.

Jenna struggled again to keep her footing, the ropes burning her wrists.

"It's awful cold and lonely in a deserted town. Should make for an interesting gunfight at the OK Corral and a really nice day for a hanging." He grabbed her, dragging her along by the elbow as the rooftops of the set began to appear.

Her head still hurt and she had a hard time focusing on the trail. Concussed probably. She jerked from Vince's grasp and fell to her knees retching in dry heaves and spitting to the ground. The nausea had become worse and at this point she could panic little over the thought of hanging.

He stopped but talked as she fought to catch her breath. "You could have had a good life not wanting for anything with me, if you'd kept your nose out of my business."

She looked at him. "Why now? You've lost your seat in the senate, the FBI is after you, take the money and run to Mexico. Why this?"

Vince jerked her to her feet again and shoved her ahead to walk along the poured gravel that made the main road to the set. The makeshift town was deserted as she had suspected. She scanned across the town looking for any sign of Aaron. He'd said he was coming. She'd watched Vince stuff his boot with a gun as they had driven along and the bag he carried clanked with metal.

"Let's hang inside the saloon, shall we?" He shoved her that direction, being cautious to look around them. When they arrived at the saloon, he pushed Jenna through the doors, following her inside.

The saloon was dark without all the set lighting in place. Vince opened the large bag he'd carried over his shoulder. Inside were a number of guns and rope. He removed a short rope and walked toward her, grabbing her and pulling her to one of the posts in the middle of the saloon.

Leaning her against it, he moved in behind her rubbing his body along her as he began to untie her hands. "Still as hot as ever, you haven't changed a bit sweetheart."

Jenna tried to resist, pushing back to push him away.

"Jennifer, you of all people should know how turned on I get at a woman's resistance, but right now, I've got a few cowboys to take out and then you're going to tell me where you hid my son." He shoved her harder, pulling her hands free of the ropes and jerking them in place to tie them in front of her, arms around the pole.

Her wrists burned as he tightened the ties. "I will die before I tell you where *my* son is."

"Oh, but I think you will talk real soon because death is on the way, sweetheart." He laughed.

The saloon was as cold as outside and her small jacket served little purpose. She was shivering and leaned her head against the pole watching as Vince went through his bag of tricks. He lifted radios and what looked to be remotes.

"That's right, darlin', got a few things up my sleeve here." He chuckled an evil laugh as he put an earpiece in his ear and a transmitter in his pocket. "I'm not sure that cowboy stuntman knew what hit him with me blowing that ramp, but he's gonna know what hits him this time."

She glanced toward the door as a vehicle pulled onto the set in the distance.

"We have company. Best he came alone, and brought the boy." Vince walked to her and spoke again, "Open your mouth, now." He slapped her hard across the cheek.

She screamed, stunned, her mouth opening and Vince pulling the gag tight. She gagged, but bit down to stop him from tightening it further.

"If you so much as make a sound I will kill him." Vince smiled and leaned against her whispering, "but right now we're setting up things for an old-fashioned hanging right here in Dodge City and Wyatt Earp has just arrived."

Jenna shook her head to free herself of him. She had to warn Aaron but couldn't yell. She twisted her hands trying to pull them free of the ropes and stifled a yelp at the attempt.

"Stay put, sweetheart." Vince turned back to the window, shoving another pistol in his belt.

Jenna still couldn't believe how it was happening, her worst fears in view. If Aaron was here, why had he driven right up to park at the set? And she knew he hadn't brought Mason. And what would Vince do when he figured that out? Why had she ever fallen for Aaron so that this moment seemed to be the hardest of all? Was she waiting for her own death, Aaron's, or both?

Chapter Twenty-Eight

Aaron pulled Gabe's truck to a halt outside of the set. He sat for a minute looking around, seeing no one. He had a knife in his boot and several guns on him as he reached for the automatic on the dashboard. He'd left Gabe and Brianna a mile back, with Tucker and Jeremiah. While none of them were sure of the plan, he needed to see what was going on and it had to look as if he were alone.

"Aaron?" Gabe came across the tiny wireless earphone in his left ear.

"Yeah?" Aaron answered in a slight whisper, not moving his lips.

"We got you in sight. Let the games begin."

He didn't answer.

He, his brothers, and Tuck were all on tiny wireless microphones with each other. Jeremiah was waiting on the rise in the distance with his power rifle. If at some point an outside shot was needed, he had it. Gabe and Tucker would enter town if needed but would remain on the outskirts unless things got rowdy.

"Careful, brother. I got you in sight." Jeremiah came through.

Aaron opened the truck door and stepped outside, not having to fight his nerves as he thought he might. Nothing mattered but getting Jenna back—alive.

He walked to the beginning of town and stood.

Waiting.

"Cowboy up." Vince's voice rang out across town on the set speakers.

Aaron couldn't make out where it originated as it echoed. So Hanson had his own bag of tricks as he'd expected.

Laughter came across the intercom, "Well, well, well, you did come, but then, 'let the games begin, careful brother' you didn't come alone as requested, nor do I see my son. Drop the wire, now!"

"Shit." Gabe's voice echoed on Aaron's microphone.

Aaron shook his head and pulled the earphone from his ear and made a point of tossing it aside. They should have thought Hanson was a professional if it came down to it. That's how he'd remained so elusive all this time.

"We'll play this how you want, me and you." Aaron stepped forward, holding his arms up, shrugging as he had no more connections.

"Better, but since you haven't followed the rules, I'm changing the game of play." Vince's voice rang out. "Jennifer's waiting. Finder keepers, *Stuntman*."

Aaron stepped forward to walk toward town. Without his brothers he was a sitting duck, regardless that he wore a bullet proof vest as did the others. Now he couldn't even predict what his brothers might do, but he hoped they would sit still for now.

"I think I have the unfair advantage. How do I even know you have her here?" Aaron yelled in challenge.

"That's for me to know and you to find out. And here I thought cowboys were some kind of tough." Vince kept going, "but then I thought I had rid myself of you with the ramp ordeal. Maybe you are tougher than I thought, but of course my condolences on the blind horse." The man's evil laughter rang out across the town echoing.

Aaron gritted his teeth and every muscle he had tensed. Maxus. Jenna next. Hanson was a dead man.

"Touched a nerve, did I? Come on, Cowboy, you want her, find her, but you won't get her back until I have my son."

Aaron walked further ahead, this disadvantage of no communication with the others was a problem, but what choice did he have?

As he stepped near the post office, a shot rang out, the bullet whizzing past his head causing him to duck for cover, behind a nearby empty watering trough. He'd pulled his pistol without even thinking of it, pain scoring through his ribs. Gabe was right; he was in no condition for this shit.

While the shot had been close, it was a warning. Waiting, he caught movement in the shadows of the bank across from the post office. Another shot rang and hit the water trough causing him to duck again.

"Son of a bitch." He waited, gun poised. No sense wasting rounds until he had a clear shot. There was the chance he could hit Jenna, if he wasn't careful.

Lifting his gaze, he watched the bank about the time a small explosion happened there. He ducked again as white smoke filled the air. He might have expected this too.

He needed a location on Jenna, but of course Hanson wouldn't make that easy. The shot hadn't come from him and neither had the explosion. There was movement in the bank. He could storm inside and take out the man in there but that was probably what Hanson wanted. Whoever was firing was doing so for distraction, and he'd guess the entire place was wired with explosives.

Ahead of him were several more buildings attached to the post office. He could make a run for the end of the buildings and with the angle of the sun to his advantage.

Taking a deep breath, still feeling the burn in his ribs, he pulled the gun to the edge of the trough. Firing a shot to the roof of the bank, he made a run for the vantage point he wanted. Shots rang out behind him, hitting the post office and shattering glass in the window. Aaron rolled into position, grabbing his side as he righted himself. He struggled for breath as he leaned against the outside of the building, grateful the bullet proof vest offered his paining side support. Closing his eyes, he could see Jenna in his mind. She had to be scared senseless and all he wanted was her safe in his arms.

"Well, full of surprises aren't we. Come on biker boy, you got better moves than—" Vince's voice stopped abruptly, with a loud hiss of static that deafened the set.

Aaron held his ears and shook his head with a grin. Tucker. The man was a genius when it came to wiring and electronics. If Tuck had made it to the other end of town, he'd probably shut down the power or whatever power that Hanson had put into place for the sound system.

Shots rang out again from various areas, the ricochet hissing past him and another small explosion happened so close his ears rang. He ducked his head and waited on the smoke to clear. A severe warning for loss of the ability to speak he supposed. Well, at least the odds on that were evened. Waiting, he eyed the bank again, where smoke hung in the air. The same guy was still shooting. It was then, that Tucker, on the far side of the bank made his way along to enter from the rear. If Tuck could get to that guy, they'd know where the next one was. Process of elimination would begin to narrow things down.

He leaned out past the building and made a move to the next set of buildings, a general store, barber shop and sheriff's office. Two of the three buildings were fake fronts for the set, with pretend porches. He made a run for the sheriff's office. Shots rang out from several areas as he ducked inside. He leaned against the wall and bent over to rest his elbows against his knees. He sucked in several breaths and jerked around, weapon poised when he heard commotion behind him.

"Aaron?" It was Gabe.

"Yeah." He couldn't see Gabe but heard him.

"Over here."

Aaron looked outside once more and walked to the far-left wall of the sheriff's office.

Gabe tapped at the wood from outside. "Right here, can you hear me, go to the back?"

"Okay." He checked the front again and moved to the back, where there was a small door. He heard Gabe scramble to hit the ground by the door, breathing heavy. He pushed to crack the door enough to make eye contact with his brother.

"Tuck scrambled the intercom system. I think he's on the guy in the bank."

Lucky for him, his brother thrived on episodes of

war games like this. "So now what? I'm getting tired of this shit. What did you do with Bri?" Aaron asked, leaning hard against the inside wall catching his breath.

"I locked her in the camper and threatened brute force." His brother chuckled but continued, "I figure he's got Jenna in the saloon. It's the only place big enough. He's probably there too. Our best shot is to take them one by one. These guys are good, and the sun's setting soon."

Two shots popped in the distance.

Gabe listened for a minute. "Tuck probably got one."

"What if they got Tuck?" Aaron wasn't so sure.

"Two rapids, he's got one." Gabe sounded sure. "Evens the odds. Let's move on down, ready?"

Aaron took a deep breath, or as deep of one as he could, preparing. It was time to get Jenna. He went to the door of the sheriff's office and listened, as Gabe scampered away. If Jenna was in the saloon, then he'd see what he could do to get there first. He made a run for the next set of buildings and dove to the ground as more rounds tore up the ground around him.

"Shit." He fired back in rapid succession as a man ducked back inside the painted props building. He crouched lower holding his side and looking toward the saloon. In spite of his racing heart and his aching side, he had to get to Jenna and time was going fast.

****

Jenna pulled hard, trying to free her tied wrists, her skin on fire and raw. Every time gunfire sounded she cringed, praying Aaron was safe. She'd never forgive herself if this took Aaron from Lily, Sarah, and Amos. *Oh, God, Aaron...please.* She pulled harder at the ropes, not sure what she'd do if she were to free herself, but she had to try.

Vince was still inside with her, firing shots, laughing as he did. "Bastard has no idea how things are about to go."

More gunshots sounded closer and Jenna looked up pulling her head away from the post, still shivering at the cold, her teeth chattering.

Vince pulled a remote from his belt, looking at it and waiting at the window, where he'd remained the entire time. At first Jenna thought it was a radio or cell phone, but then she noticed he was programming something into the device. He had explosives, as he'd said. He cursed, shaking the remote, and going back to the bag to dig inside. Just as he bent down, the back door of the saloon flung open. Vince dropped the remote, firing his pistol as a man hit him, both of them rolling to the wooden floor.

Jenna screamed her ears ringing, her head pounding.

Vince kicked hard and sent the man backward, following him and jumping on top of him, hitting him with the butt of his pistol. It was then Jenna caught sight of Tucker.

"Ahh." Tucker grabbed his head and rolled ramming his forearm across Vince's shoulder, the gun in Vince's hand sliding across the floor close to her.

She watched the two men continued to wrestle and stretched to try to reach her foot to the gun, but it was too far. She continued trying. If she could get it to her foot, then she could squat down and maybe get it in her hands and if she could, she'd shoot Vince herself. She pulled harder against her tender wrists to the point she had to grit her teeth, but it was no use. Tears filled her eyes as she watched the men continue to struggle, but in seconds of her leaning to wipe her eyes, Vince had gotten the advantage, gaining on Tucker and slamming his head to the floor multiple times.

Tucker groaned, trying to fight.

Vince pulled a small pistol from his pants and stuck it to Tucker's head. "Now, what a surprise, ex-marine."

Tucker struggled to stand, off balance. Vince grabbed him by the hair, dragging him forward and shoved him to his knees, handcuffing him to the pole opposite Jenna.

"You cowboys are all the same, trying to be a hero, but you aren't the one I'm looking for." Vince smacked him again with the butt of the gun.

Blood trickled from Tucker's mouth. He met glances with Jenna as Vince tied his hands behind his back. "You all right?"

Jenna nodded, still gagged.

"Keep it quiet." Vince kicked Tucker in the belly, doubling him over. "I'll be back for you, wise guy, and you're not going to like it."

Vince turned aiming the gun as one of his men raced inside, his own weapon held high.

"We're in trouble boss; they got the others, all but me." The man was out of breath.

"No matter, we've got a hanging." Vince scrambled to untied Jenna's hands making her yelp at the raw burn.

"Keep an eye on him." Vince sneered toward the other man. "Toss some ammo to keep the cowboys hopping out there. If I don't get my son, she takes a dive."

Jenna resisted as best she could, but it was no use as Vince drug her across the rough wooden boards of the saloon. "You have a short time to tell me where my son is, but either way it's done sweet, Jennifer. You've little time sweetheart." Vince pulled her toward the ramp where Aaron had fallen.

"No." Jenna tried to speak through the gag, dragging her feet to resist.

Vince laughed and jerked her to the ramp. He stopped at the base, picking up a noose and putting it over her head and pulling it tight.

"No." Jenna panicked, fighting as best she could and not caring about the pain. He was going to hang her. She had thought he would shoot her to a quick death, but this wasn't her idea of fast and easy.

"Where's my son?" He tightened the rope further. "One fall from this ramp and your neck will snap like a twig, sweet Jennifer."

He untied her gag and threw it to the ground. "Tell me, bitch, right damn now." He slapped her face hard enough to make her head pop back and nausea plague her. She heaved.

Her voice cracked as the last of what she said faded to a whisper. "You can't do this, Vince."

"Wrong answer." He shoved her ahead, holding the edge of the rope as they climbed the ramp. Jenna looked toward the top and realized the ramp had been moved, closer to the river, not the angle it had sat for Aaron's stunt. The crumpled part of the ramp was further back. Well, she might go down too but not before fighting harder. She dug in her heels, grabbing the wood with her tied hands.

"All right, if you won't walk, I'll drag you. Terror takes hold doesn't it sweet Jennifer when death is near," he growled.

Jenna went to her knees, trying to curl into a ball. If he wanted her to go to the top, he'd have to work for it. She dug her heels in. Vince grabbed her and dragged her by her wrists and she screamed in pain. Realizing Vince had gotten her to the top, she stopped struggling, for fear of falling. He tossed the rope down fidgeting with his gun. This was it. He would probably tie her and then shove off to her death. Strange, she'd had a moment of sheer panic, but now that it was time, she had no fear, numbness taking her. If she were to die then her son would live and right now that was all that mattered.

Chapter Twenty-Nine

Aaron scrambled behind the buildings, looking across in the saloon for a better vantage point. With the gunfire coming from several areas, he didn't have an exact head count, but things had been quiet for a few minutes. What he worried about was Hanson taking Jenna and running if things got even more intense. If that happened he might never see her again—alive.

He turned on a dime pointing his gun to the noise behind him. Gabe again.

"Aaron." Gabe slid in place beside him. "They got Tuck tied in the saloon." He was out of breath and reloading.

"What the hell happened, son of a—" Aaron shook his head. Hanson would kill Tucker without a doubt. This needed to end now.

"Damn it," Gabe cursed, kicking the dirt with his heel.

"Jeremiah still in place?" Aaron asked, not wanting his younger brother anywhere in the mix, not that he didn't worry about Gabe too.

"He's still on post, waiting." Gabe shook his head. "It's me and you, bro."

"Yep." Aaron took a deep breath. Trying to get to Jenna was one thing, but trying to get to her and Tucker was going to be tedious and he wasn't going to lose either one of them if he could help it.

"Storm the saloon?" Gabe shrugged in suggestion.

Aaron looked at him. "It's dangerous, but I didn't come here to play. Let's do it."

"Sun's fading fast, dark fall would be worse; he could leave with her. I'll make my way around and come in from the left, bust through the front. You hear me, you come in the back. All or nothing." Gabe smiled.

It *was* all or nothing for him, and he was about to get all of her back if it was the last thing he did. "Let's go."

He was up and waited on Gabe to disappear further away so he could back track and make his way behind the saloon. Gabe would give him a few minutes and track the other way to come in the front. Taking a deep breath against the feel of his burning ribs he made his way back the way he'd come. At this point anything was possible and a lot could be lost. He'd never had the military training Gabe and Tucker carried, but he'd been a hunter for a long time and he'd lived in the woods a lot of his life, fading into the scenery and paying attention.

Aaron ducked for cover and made his way to the second to last building on the set and waited. Gabe was probably close to being where he needed to be. It was time to cross the street, the one time he might be vulnerable. Taking a good look, his shortest run would be to the water trough on the other side, in front of the last buildings. He waited and made a quick run for it. To his surprise no one had fired on him or Gabe which meant things were a bit too quiet.

Reaching the building beside the saloon he waited behind it. No one seemed to be at the back, but there was no doubt that Hanson and his man had the place covered. He'd have to bust in with his weapon ready to fire, but at the same time make sure he didn't over react and hit Jenna, Gabe, or Tucker.

He took another deep breath. With no windows in the back, he could make it to the door, but there might be the chance he'd been seen. He crept along, making sure his boots made no noise across the gravel and crouched down to wait.

His heart in his throat, he held outside until he heard Gabe. That was it, his signal and he barged through from the rear, bracing as he knocked the door from its hinges with his body, ignoring the pain. He dove to the left and came up with his gun poised, trying to make sense of the chaos that followed. Gabe had bolted through the front door at the same time and positioned himself opposite where he landed.

On the floor of the saloon was Tucker, pelting Hanson's man in the face. It was then Aaron noticed the gun in the man's hand drifting toward Tucker's face. He gathered the strength to run and push into the wrestling men, sending the gun across the room to Gabe with one swift kick. As Tucker bolted forward, Aaron placed his gun right in the face of the man Tuck was pinning.

Tucker wobbled to his feet and kicked Hanson's man leaving him unconscious. "It's about…damn time. Hanson took Jenna…out back. Let's go!"

Aaron's heart sank as Gabe handcuffed the man to one of the poles and he ran outside. "Where'd he go?" Gabe yelled, following.

"I don't know. He grabbed her and ran once he had me tied." Tucker said, still out of breath, holding the side of his head and wincing.

"Where in the hell is he?" Aaron still held his gun in the air, looking back at Tucker and his brother.

"I don't know." Tucker bent, holding his head with one hand, blood still trickling from his nose and mouth.

Gabe ran to him, pulled his head up looking into his eyes. "You're toast, man."

"No, just got the headache from hell." Tucker forced himself back up, walking closer to Aaron, Gabe following.

"Aaron!" A female voice shrieked from the distance.

Aaron glanced toward the river and Jenna was at the top of the broken scaffolding. Beside her was Vince Hanson, gun poised to her head. Aaron's whole world seemed to spin out of control and he ran to the other side of the buildings, his brother and Tucker on his heels. As he rounded the corner closer to the ramp, he met her gaze, the fear in her eyes profound enough to stop his heart.

"That's far enough, all of you." Hanson yelled, taking Jenna to the edge. She resisted, the bruises to her face evident.

Gabe grabbed Aaron by the arm. "Careful, let's see what he's gonna do. Jeremiah's on him."

Aaron jerked free, never taking his eyes from Jenna, "No he isn't, the saloon's blocking him or he'd already have taken the shot." It was true. Jeremiah had been placed where he would have a good view of the town, but not behind the buildings.

"He's right." Tucker scanned the saloon behind him, still holding his head.

"I see you all came in for today's hanging. It's a

pleasure to have your viewing of this historical event." Sarcasm laced Hanson's voice as it echoed in the distance.

Aaron moved closer, in spite of Hanson's warning. A few steps more and he could see Jenna better.

"Hold off cowboy, she'll topple right over. Wouldn't that be a shame? Of course, we could have avoided all this if you had just brought my son, but since you didn't follow the rules, I'll win my son when his mother is dead. He will fall to my custody then," Hanson warned grabbing Jenna's arm and dropping the unsecured coiled rope to the wood at his feet. The rope that was around Jenna's neck.

Aaron continued slow and sure, not heeding his warning but whispering. "Truth or dare, you bastard."

Gabe jerked his phone from his pocket and hit the button. "Jer…where are you? Yes, go."

Aaron listened to the exchange never taking his eyes from Jenna. It might be their one hope to save Jenna, if Jeremiah could take out Hanson. But there wasn't time for him to find a new location.

"I said far enough." Hanson grabbed Jenna and held her at bay at the edge of the ramp, her body leaning in resistance.

Aaron stopped. "You don't have to do this."

Jenna was shivering and her eyes said it all as she struggled to keep her footing, her hands tied in front of her. God, he wanted to make a run for it, but he'd never make it and she'd fall.

Vince laughed. "Try again."

"Let's settle this man to man. Let her go." Aaron was grasping at straws, buying time. "Isn't it another chance at me you want?"

"This? This what you want, Cowboy?" He put the gun back to Jenna's head as he talked, pulling her back from the edge. "This right here, she owes me a great deal of money and I need my son to get it."

Aaron shook his head. "You already lost all rights to the boy, he's my son now. Surely it's me you want. Well, let's settle it."

"Nice try, but we're gathered here for an old-fashioned hanging. And you didn't follow the rules, Wyatt Earp. You brought the posse with you." Hanson eyed him hard and gave Jenna a slight nudge.

"You and I both know you had men here too, but let's settle this...right now, just me and you." Aaron motioned for Gabe and Tucker to back off. He turned, taking his eyes from Jenna for the moment. "Go! I mean it, go!"

"Aaron?" Gabe hesitated.

"Now, Gabe." Aaron raised his voice.

"Aaron, he'll kill her and then you," Tucker tried.

He nodded, "then so be it."

Gabe and Tucker backed off walking toward the barn, where they would still be in view.

"Uh, posse over there, better drop your weapons. Mr. Earp, you too." Hanson, laughed and waited, keeping the gun on Jenna.

Tucker shook his head dropping his gun. Gabe followed along making a point to lean forward and lay down his gun, but before he turned back around, Bri came running from the camper toward them.

"Oh my God, Jeennnnnnna!" Bri screamed, distracting them all including Hanson, as she came running around the corner.

"No, Bri." Gabe ran, grabbing her to stop her from

going further, wrestling to keep a hold on her.

"Jenna! No, you let her go," Brianna screamed at Hanson, fighting Gabe.

"Stop, he'll kill her." Gabe held her tighter.

"I'll kill him, let me go." She succumbed to tears, crying into Gabe's shirt, beating a fist against his chest. "Oh my God, how can he do this? Do something. Do something right now!"

"Jeremiah's on him. We've got nothing else," Tucker whispered not taking his eyes from Hanson, who still held the gun to Jenna.

Gabe shook his head. "Aaron?"

"All right." Aaron tossed his own gun aside, his gaze on Hanson. What the hell he would do now, he didn't know, but he still had a pistol in his belt and a knife in his boot. Neither would serve him, with Hanson having the gun to Jenna's head.

"Sorry Wyatt Earp, but unless you produce my son, this isn't going to end well." Hanson scratched his chin with the gun and put it back to Jenna's head.

"I'll trade places with her. Let her go and you got me." Aaron held his arms up as if he had nothing to hold him back.

Hanson laughed shoving Jenna closer to the edge again. "One wrong move from any of you and she goes over. Where's my son?" Hanson yelled and bent to grab the end of the coiled rope, the gun lifted away from Jenna with his actions.

Aaron stepped closer. *Son of a bitch!* He caught Jenna's gaze. She had to jump, it would save her life but there were seconds "Jenna, jump!"

Aaron's world slowed as recognition hit her face, and without any hesitation she let go, free-falling toward the water.

Hanson raised his gun toward, Aaron. It was then an explosion sounded from the top of the canyon and Hanson's body jolted backward sending him to the back of the scaffolding railing. He caught himself, the pistol firing and the ricochet piercing through the town.

Brianna screamed, running toward the river. "Jenna!"

Aaron met Hanson's gaze. Jeremiah had made the hit but not a good one and the bastard raised his gun again, but this time he began shooting into the water, though Jenna had yet to surface after her splash down.

Before Aaron could run for the river, a rifle blast came from behind him, deafening. Hanson's body flipped from the scaffolding and fell to the ground. Aaron turned, catching his father's gaze as Amos Decker lowered the rifle and leaned against the barn.

"Unbelievable," Tucker spouted.

"Brianna, call nine-one-one!" Gabe yelled running to follow Aaron to the river.

Aaron dove in the murky freezing water in the general direction where Jenna had gone in. He had to find her, but this part of the river was deep. The water was numbing and he couldn't make his body move as he wanted. He touched the bottom, rough rocks, and sand. It was black and he could see nothing, so he surfaced for air.

He surfaced, sucking in several breaths, looking toward the shore for his bearings. Gabe was there, pointing and kicking out of his boots as he entered the water.

"Which way? I can't find her." He heaved in deep breaths ignoring the pain in his side.

"To your right, Aaron!" Gabe shouted, diving into the water to help.

Aaron sunk deep again. That Jenna hadn't surfaced was a bad sign. Jumping had saved her life but now…what if he couldn't find her? The water was cold, she could survive, couldn't she? He hit the floor of the river again, fighting the current and swimming the direction Gabe had pointed. Searching in the darkness he found the rope. He grabbed it, swimming to the surface and sucking in a breath long overdue. He sputtered and swam drawing the rope slowly to him, not wanting it to tighten on her neck.

What was about twenty feet of rope felt like an eternity away from her and he was losing the ability to use his hands. He fought past the need for air and found her limp body at the end.

For the first time in a lot of years he prayed, calling on God to help her. *Please, God.* He tugged Jenna's body along with him not having much strength to do so. It was so dark he couldn't tell where the surface was and for a moment thought he might not be going up. Suddenly, he lifted from the water, coughing, and gagging and trying to take in air. He gulped and vomited water, kicking to stay above the surface and not let go of Jenna.

He held her head out of the water but she wasn't breathing, her eyes closed. Kicking hard he struggled until Gabe grabbed her, bringing her to the surface, the rope still around her neck.

Her eyes were closed, and she was pale and unmoving. He fought to stay above the water, watching Gabe swim back toward shore with her. He had to fight to swim, but it felt like a losing battle. It was Tucker who grabbed and dragged him through the water to the shore where he collapsed as he tried to stand. He had to get to Jenna. Hold her, make sure…and he began to crawl but collapsed, raising only his head to look at her.

Gabe laid Jenna down. Brianna met them, going to her knees checking if Jenna was breathing as Aaron made his way to her on his hands and knees, unsure he could get there. His body shook and he threw up more water, coughing through.

"Come on Jenna, you can do this, girl. You have to." Brianna was pressing hard on Jenna's chest, water spilling from Jenna's mouth with each stroke.

"Jenna." Aaron tried to stand but lacked the strength. "Amos?"

"Hang on and we'll get you to her." Amos tugged hard and Aaron hung onto him as his father helped him closer to Jenna. He dropped to his knees beside her.

"I got it." Tucker placed himself at Jenna's chest, finding his hand placement between her breasts, allowing Brianna to breathe for her.

"Start compressions." Brianna was out of breath, but stayed at Jenna's head, holding her in position as Tucker began compressing her chest rapidly. "Come on, Jenna."

Aaron shook so hard he could barely keep himself upright. This couldn't happen. He couldn't survive without her, not like this. He touched his right hand to her head and waited for Brianna to give her two more breaths. He watched as her chest rose and fell twice. He lowered his head to speak in her ear.

"Jenna, come on babe…Jenna…fight! Damn it, fight!" He had a hard time talking in between all the shivering. He coughed hard, water dripping from his long hair onto her face. He gently wiped it away. "Fight, Jenna…"

As Tucker completed the next set of compressions, Bri leaned to breathe into Jenna again.

"Jenna?" he whispered as Tucker went back to compressions.

Suddenly, Jenna gulped, her mouth moving in her attempts to take in air. She coughed harder and water escaped from her mouth and nose, rolling down the sides of her jaws to her neck.

"That's it, Jenna. Come on. Again." Brianna pressed on her chest again and more water poured from her mouth and Jenna coughed as her body pulled air into her lungs in spasms.

"Jenna?" Aaron called to her as sirens wailed in the distance.

"She's got a pulse. Take another breath, Jenna, you're safe." Brianna continued talking to her, turning her to her side, where she expelled more water with coughing and gagging.

Aaron held her against his knees as Jeremiah dropped beside them tossing his rifle to the ground. "Is she all right?"

"She's breathing and has a pulse, but she isn't responding." Brianna looked up at him and then back at Jenna.

"I couldn't get a clear shot. She jumped, didn't she? When he reached for the rope, I couldn't tell what he was doing but I saw her fall. Who got him?" Jeremiah shook his head. "I didn't have a clear view for a shot."

Gabe nodded to Amos. "Pop got him."

"Pop?" Jeremiah questioned, meeting his father's

gaze.

"You boys think I'm down and out, but I've been in a shoot-out a time or two in my day. Glad I didn't miss this one." Amos used his rifle for support, winded without his oxygen.

Tucker got up, holding his head. "Might need you on my team sometime."

The sound of a chopper echoed loudly as the aircraft topped the ridge of the canyon and found a spot to land as ambulances arrived at the gate of the set. Seconds later police and FBI agents were on the scene in several cars, holding guns on everyone until Amos explained to them the story.

Aaron kept his hand on Jenna's head as she continued to breathe on her own. That was good, wasn't it, but in truth she'd been under that cold water for a long time.

In moments, paramedics were there assisting with Jenna, Brianna giving them a full report. As the men scooted in to care for her, Aaron backed up to give them room but not wanting to let her go.

Jeremiah grabbed him. "Aaron?"

He had to lay down or he'd pass out. "Gotta rest."

"You're hypothermic." Jeremiah dug in the paramedic's box and drew out a silver foiled thermal blanket covering Aaron. "This'll warm you up quick."

Aaron shook his head. "Take care of her…"

Jeremiah grabbed a stethoscope and listened to his chest. "How about we give you a little oxygen?"

Aaron sat up as Jenna was lifted to a gurney and strapped in, a tube in her throat helping her breathe. He leaned to watch as the men carried her toward the chopper, Brianna running alongside them.

"Hey, hold still, Aaron, they got her." Jeremiah tried to hold him.

Aaron shook his head and got to his knees and then to his feet, jerking the oxygen off his face and tossing it aside so he could watch Jenna's motionless body being loaded into the chopper. It occurred to him that she'd probably felt the same way when he'd taken the fall. The chopper lifted into the sky, taking all he'd ever loved with it and the pain in his chest consumed him. He fell to his knees unable to stand any longer.

"Aaron?" Amos touched his shoulder. "You gotta let Jeremiah help you."

Aaron nodded, unable to speak, tears filling his eyes. "She has to be all right."

"She's a strong woman, son." Amos tugged him back up and helped him to lie down on the gurney that was waiting. He settled back and closed his eyes, Jeremiah placing an oxygen mask over his face once more. He still shivered as he was carried and then lifted into the back of the ambulance.

"Jer's bringing Amos and Tuck. Tucker took a good knock to the head, probably needs to get checked out." Gabe shook his head and jumped in the ambulance after Brianna.

Aaron closed his eyes. He was fatigued, not hurt. All this wasn't necessary.

"I thought I was going to lose you under that water too." Gabe sat, wrapped in a thermal blanket, water dripping from his dark hair.

"I couldn't find her." The weight of her limp body haunted him and he could still feel her in his arms. "She was under for so long, but it's good she was breathing on her own." Brianna burst into tears. "Oh, my God, he's dead, isn't he?"

Aaron nodded and closed his eyes again.

"Hey, hey, don't cry." Gabe glanced at her. "She'll be all right."

Brianna snapped to attention. "You said I could cry all I wanted to when this was over." She slapped his thigh with her open hand, "and I know good and damn well you locked me in that camper."

"Hey, it was for your own safety," Gabe defended, shivering.

"Well, I happen to know a thing or two about breaking and entering," she hissed and wiped her tears. "I'm a nurse, remember, we are just as clever as you military cop guys."

Gabe smiled, sizing her up. "Well, you did good then."

"She was under…for a long…time." Aaron looked at Brianna who sniffled.

"It's hard to tell, Aaron. The cold will help. She's so strong." Bri's voice faded as more tears streaked her face.

Aaron held her gaze. They had all done what they could do. The fact that Vince Hanson was dead did little to take away the pain plaguing him. All he could see was Jenna falling and the splash into the deep water, maybe one of the bravest things he'd ever seen. Now he had to hope that in doing so she'd saved her life. He couldn't lose her though, not like this. They had a wedding to plan and a life to build together with the children and he wouldn't let her go, not ever.

Chapter Thirty

Aaron sat at Jenna's bedside in the intensive care unit. He'd been sitting beside her bed for the last nineteen hours. Dr. Gates had called in a specialist who'd let them know that Jenna would recover, but it would take some time. He'd removed her tube and said when her brain was ready she would wake, that all the signs were positive, as she was breathing on her own and her vital signs were stable as was her EEG.

He and Gabe had been treated for mild hypothermia, and Tucker was being kept overnight for a mild concussion. Brianna had gone downstairs for coffee and now that he sat alone with Jenna, he touched her cheek. The last hours felt like a blur, but Gabe had let him know that Sarah and her sister had made it home with the children.

Fatigue had long since taken him, but he wouldn't rest until she woke.

"Aaron?" Sarah entered with a light knock, walking closer and touching Jenna's brow. "How is she?"

He shook his head. "The doc says she'll wake up when she's ready."

Sarah set a duffle bag on the floor and a small brown bag on the table beside him. "I brought you a change of clothes and some dinner. Did you eat?"

He shrugged. Had he eaten? "No."

"Well, you need to eat, Aaron, if you want to care for her. I have the children settled home. They're fine." Sarah reached inside the bag and pulled out a small thermos, opening the lid. "Homemade vegetable soup, thought it might warm you up."

"Disneyland?" He glanced at Sarah, who had met her sister with the children and then moved right into a Disney hotel.

"I figured it would be a lot of trouble to find us there inside the park. Lily is dying to show you the pictures and tell you all about it." Sarah smiled. "And Mason was all giggles the entire time. He is such a good baby."

He nodded. "I missed them both so much it hurt."

"Eat." She waited. "They really are fine."

Aaron dipped a heaping spoon and took a bite. The soup was still hot as it hit his empty gut. In spite of his mood, slight warmth spread through him.

"Good?"

He nodded taking another bite.

Sarah smiled, "Jeremiah's home with the children and Amos. I understand your father saved the day. Did him good I suppose."

"He's always been the best. Figured it all out, never blinked an eye." Aaron beamed. "Some heroes never know they are one."

Sarah touched his hair pulling back a strand and kissing the top of his head, hugging him. "I was so frightened, Aaron."

"I love you, mom." Aaron needed her to know and set the soup aside, standing to embrace her.

"You know I can never hear that enough." She wiped her tears. "You stay here and rest when you can.

I'll be with the children, please call us."

He sat again, glancing at Jenna. He needed some kind of reassurance. Something to give him hope. "I can't lose her."

Sarah bent down before him. "Then don't. You sit with her, hold her hand and talk to her. She needs rest and you."

Sarah made it sound all right, but it was hard to see. He fought the tears filling his eyes, swallowing the lump in his throat. Taking a deep breath, he nodded. "Jumping saved her life and she doesn't even know it but she saved us all. The damn bravest thing I've ever seen."

"She's a strong woman and she's been through a lot. She's going to need you when she wakes, but you must eat and rest so you can be what she needs." Sarah hugged him again, handing him the soup. "I'm going to head back home. Gabe said he'd be back in a while to sit with you. Oh, and in your bag is an envelope for Jenna from a Thomas Campbell. I wasn't sure if you might need to see what it was about, given all that happened."

He nodded. "I'll look. Let me walk you out first."

"No, you stay with Jenna. I'm fine." Sarah kissed his cheek and touched Jenna's hand once more before turning to go.

Aaron turned back to Jenna, grabbing his soup. He took another bite, letting the warm liquid hit bottom, closing his eyes for a moment. Everything still played through his mind. The terror in Jenna's eyes, her fall and then the feel of her cold body in the frigid deep water. If Amos hadn't snuffed out Vince Hanson, things could have gone much worse. As it stood now, Hanson was dead and the others working for Hanson were being detained and an FBI agent had been by to question him twice on what he knew about all that had taken place.

He glanced at his bag and lifted the envelope addressed to Jenna. This had to be Thomas' answer about her script. He took a deep breath and opened it, pulling out the documents bound by a clip. Glancing quickly at the opening letter he smiled. Epic Films was making an offer. He knew it and shoved the papers back inside, setting it nearby.

He took another bite of his soup and set it aside and touched Jenna's hand and spoke. "I'll be here, as long as it takes."

"Aa…ron." Jenna's hand gripped his.

Aaron sprang up beside her, startled. "I'm here." He searched and hit the nurse call button.

Her eyes fluttered at the light as she tried to focus. "I was so…afraid."

"Shhhh. It's over." Aaron pushed her hair back behind her ear.

"My head." She closed her eyes for a second and then looked at him again. "Mason…and Lily?"

"Had a nice trip to Disneyland. They're home safe." Aaron pulled the blankets tighter around her and brought her hand to his lips. "I thought I'd lost you."

She struggled to speak, holding her head. "Vince?"

He held her gaze for a moment and shook his head.

She nodded as Melinda, the nurse on duty came in.

"Jenna, you're awake." She came closer. "Do you know where you are?"

"The hospital," Jenna answered.

"Good." Melinda grabbed both of Jenna's hands,

"Squeeze."

Jenna grimaced, but gripped the woman's fingers.

"That's good, now wiggle your toes?" Melinda pulled the covers back from her feet watching.

Jenna wiggled her toes, her eyes closing again.

Melinda pulled a penlight from her scrub pocket and spoke, "Let's take a look at your pupils." She shined the light in each of Jenna's eyes more than once. "Your pupils look great and so do your vitals. You've had Decadron to help with your head."

Jenna nodded, and looked at Aaron. "What…happened?"

"You landed in the water and it was all I could do to find you…you were under for a long time," Aaron whispered, scooting to sit on the bed beside her.

"Explains…my head." She squeezed her eyes closed.

"I'll get you something for pain, but I need to let Dr. Conner know you're awake." Melinda pulled her blankets higher and entered her assessment into the Electronic medical record. "Everything looks good Jenna. I'll be back in a few minutes with something for pain. On a scale of one to ten?"

"Twenty…" Jenna closed her eyes and squeezed tightly to Aaron's hand as she left.

"I'm so sorry, Aaron. It's my fault… I thought he'd kill you or your brothers. I'm sorry I left, but I had only a short time to pay for the land." She broke into tears, her body trembling as she let go of her emotions, clinging to Aaron's shirt, raising up with all the strength she could find to bury her face in his neck.

"Let it go, babe. It's over." Aaron lay her back against the pillow wishing he could dry her tears, but maybe she needed those and had for a long time. "No more running."

"Oh, God. Aaron, there are so many things." She closed her eyes.

"Jen, you don't have to. Rest for now." Aaron pulled the blankets back up on her again.

"No, I…need to tell you. I was so scared for you and I saw Gabe and then Bri…Brianna. She's all right?"

He smiled. "She's been here the whole time. She went down for coffee."

"You've been here too?"

Aaron nodded. "Oh, yeah."

"When you yelled 'jump' I thought the rope would catch." Jenna shook her head, her voice cracking. "It was so dark in the water and I couldn't get my hands loose."

"It's the bravest thing…I've ever seen." He touched her cheek.

"It's not the fall…" She tried for a smile but winced.

"It's the landing." Aaron finished for her.

"It's still hard to believe." Her eyes filled with tears.

"I think you need to rest to find yourself again and you will," Aaron whispered, stroking her hair.

"Jenna, Jennifer, Jenny…I'm not sure I know anymore." She chuckled through her tears.

"One day at a time," Aaron assured her with a soft kiss to the forehead.

"I should have asked you about the land, but I knew you wouldn't let me…" She tried, her amber eyes more clear.

"You didn't have to do that. I told you to stay put." He still didn't believe it himself and he wasn't at all sure how he felt about it.

She shook her head. "My father left me that money as he used to say 'to build dreams.' I want this for you. And you wouldn't let me out of your sights."

He nodded. If that was how she wanted it. He still couldn't believe she'd paid it all in full. "We'll need a good nurse."

She smiled, "I'd like that."

"And I have a little something else Sarah brought by." He lifted the envelope from Thomas Campbell and handed it to her.

Jenna slowly opened the clasp and lifted the folded top, peering inside. She pulled out a thick packet of papers, laying them across her lap and setting the envelope beside her on the bed. She began reading but rubbed her eyes. "I can't focus, what is it?"

Aaron hesitated to explain. "I have to beg a bit of forgiveness here. I took your script and sent it off to Thomas Campbell with Epic Films. He's made you an offer on your script for a mini-series."

"But how did you…" She glanced at the letter and back to him, shaking her head.

"Theft, right off your laptop." He kissed her hoping for quick forgiveness. "I told you I'm not good at following the rules."

"Thank you." She brushed back tears with a slight smile and letting go of the packet of papers. "I knew you would come for me."

He chuckled. "To the ends of the damn earth, until my last breath."

She lifted the letter again. "Something's wrong

here. It should say Jenna Decker."

He smiled. "Well, I'll just have to speak to Thomas about that."

"Yes," Jenna said sniffling. "I want to do all the things we did again. I want to watch the sunrise and make love with you at the cabin. Take long rides on the horses with Lily and Mason along with us. Spend time getting to know your parents and brothers better and the only place I ever want to fall again is into you," she whispered, "and maybe…"

"Something else?" he questioned and waited.

Jenna smiled. "I know we have Mason and Lily, but I've always dreamed of having a big family."

Aaron smiled, wiping her tears. "Well, now, you've got some healing to do, but we can get right to that soon enough."

She raised herself up to hug him again and he held her tighter, remembering the first day he ever laid eyes on her. He had known all along she was made for him and he would spend the rest of his life making sure of her happiness. For himself… He had his land, her, and a new son he already adored right along with Lily. There wasn't much more he'd wish for, save giving her a child, if that is what she wanted. He chuckled and pulled her even closer. He hadn't another need in the world except to love her all he could.

Epilogue:

Aaron stopped the backhoe, brushing a sleeve across his sweaty brow. The quiet after using the heavy engine for the last two hours was almost deafening, except for where his brothers hammered away on the roof of the last bunkhouse. There were three now, each a ready home for four boys who needed one. He glanced behind him at the main office, which held a small clinic for Jenna and a rather large kitchen and dining room.

He shook his head. It was all coming together. Now it seemed the real work would begin, and donations had been arriving daily. Everything was in place and in about three weeks the first six boys would arrive. Ranging in age from seven to seventeen, it seemed his long-time dream was now a reality.

He glanced at the roof where Jeremiah slammed another nail in place and then turned. "Looks like we're done up here."

Both his brothers scaled down the ladder, Gabe tossing his shirt over his shoulder, sweat covering his brother's body. "It's done, now gotta get Tuck up here to do the last of the wiring for solar heat, the panels are up."

Aaron nodded as he climbed from the backhoe. "That's the last of the landscaping too. At least until we add on more."

Jeremiah tilted his cowboy hat back. "Hell, I've

gotta go back to the station to get some rest. A lot of hard work here, brother."

Aaron smiled and glanced around. "Gonna need myself a vacation, but I have a feeling the work's just beginning."

"Well, it is if you get any boys in here like that one." Gabe shoved Jeremiah aside, glancing toward the gravel drive as the roar of engines approached.

Sarah was driving the golf cart with Mason on her lap helping and Jenna sitting beside her with Brianna on the back. Amos was in tow driving the second with Lily supervising and to Aaron's surprise, Clarissa in the back. Aaron smiled. She'd promised to sign on to work for him when he got his ranch up and running and she'd made true on it by moving to Sun River.

Lily scampered over running to grab Brianna's hand. "We brought you a surprise, Daddy."

"You did?" He touched her curly mop of brown hair and lifted Mason into his arms when he ran over. "How's my boy?" He kissed Mason's cheek and walked to Jenna who was adjusting the strap on the baby carrier she wore strapped across her chest.

"Having trouble?" He sat Mason to his feet and untwisted the strap, kissing her forehead. He brushed a hand across the light hair of his son, three-month-old Lucas, named for Jenna's father.

"Thank you; I don't even know how I got it twisted." She held the baby's head as he slept against her body.

"So you made it?" Aaron turned as Clarissa stepped closer.

"Wouldn't have missed it for the world." Clarissa moved into his embrace and Aaron gave her a bear hug lifting her from the ground. "Aaron, put me down."

Aaron put her back to her feet as Gabe and Jeremiah hugged her next.

"You boys have done wonders here." She glanced around at the buildings in the middle of the forest, much like a camp. "I knew all those years ago there was something special up here on this ranch and now I get to be a part of it.

"I hope you know you already are." Aaron held her gaze. "This would never have happened if you hadn't brought us all here all those years ago."

Clarissa gave him a lift of her brows. "I think retirement is over rated and I can't think of a better way to spend mine, right here doing what I do best."

Sarah laughed, "I think I am right along with you. The vegetable garden and pictures are my new job to help out."

"Come on, Daddy, you have to see." Lily grabbed Aaron's hand.

Mason tugged on his jeans. "Daddy, see."

"What's the fuss all about?" Aaron exchanged glances with Sarah, giving her a wink. "Hey, Pop, guess you needed to come up today to make sure we'd done a good job of it?"

"Oh, I expect I will have to make you redo a few things here and there." Amos chuckled, lifting his oxygen to his shoulder. "You need to smooth that gravel more this way."

"Pop, we can't do it all in one day." Gabe jousted his father and turned his ball cap backward, but it didn't get past Aaron that he couldn't keep his eyes from Bri.

"You need to get up here and help us." Jeremiah sucked down a cup of lemonade Sarah handed to him.

"Here, Gabe." Brianna handed Gabe a cup, stepping closer to him.

Aaron chugged the cup full quickly and set the cup aside as did his speechless brother. "So what's the big surprise?"

It was Jenna who answered. "Well, you said you'd be done today but we all have one more thing to add before you can say you are finished." She smiled, taking his had as the children already waited at the back of the golf cart where Amos lifted a large brown package.

Jeremiah trotted to help Amos. "I got it, Pop."

Aaron glanced from the package to Jenna with a skeptical glare.

"You told me that the one thing you needed was a name for your place here so we could start putting it on all the legal forms. And we've gotta get moving on those, with the boys coming in a few weeks, so…" She took his hand and led him to the package. "Open it."

Aaron glanced at her and then all of them. None of this would have happened without each one of them believing in him, one way or the other. All of them helping.

"Open, Daddy," Mason chanted. "Open, me help."

"Lily, will you help us?" Aaron asked and waited as both children began tearing away the brown wrapping to reveal what was beneath.

Aaron sucked in a deep breath as the sign came into view. He was surprised but not, when the children had cleared all the paper. For a moment words wouldn't come. He'd left the task of naming the boys ranch to Jenna, who had been helping with all the legal papers for a while now.

"It's for Maxus, Daddy." Lily's excitement mimicked his.

"I can see that." It was the best he could force from his voice as he touched the large bronze etching of the horse. "Maxus House."

Jenna rubbed a hand across his back as he fought to gulp away the lump in his throat. "I hope you like it. The name, I mean."

"It's perfect. Maxus has come a long way just like these boys will as we help them have something good." He glanced at his family and all around him at what had been created with all their help.

"It's fitting for a place like this." Amos sat on the golf cart. "Gabe, you and Jer get this up right there on the main office."

"Yes, sir." Gabe grabbed a cordless drill and followed Jeremiah, who went for the ladder.

Aaron turned to watch his brothers hang the sign with a bit of bickering in order to get it done.

"Hold it higher," Gabe shouted as he measured for the bolts.

"Your end's too low." Jeremiah adjusted the whole frame. "It goes here."

Aaron rolled his eyes, glancing at Jenna. "Some things never change."

Jenna smiled and hugged him. "I knew you'd like it."

"It really is beautiful, and I am glad Maxus is doing a bit better." Brianna folded her arms, glancing where Gabe and Jeremiah continued.

"No, get that end lifted, it's crooked." Amos scowled, standing back up to direct the process as he walked over.

"Well, I for one love the name." Sarah handed Aaron more lemonade.

He sipped and studied the sign as Gabe and Jeremiah finished. It was perfect, and sooner than he was ready, Maxus House would open.

"Ride horse, Daddy." Mason jumped up and down before him.

"Yep, I promised, didn't I?" He tickled the boy, who giggled and patted Lucas' tiny back. "And I think it's about time we introduced this little guy to his first ride."

Jenna stepped back shaking her head. "Nope, he's too young."

Aaron laughed. "He's three months, it's past time."

"Jenna, get on the golf cart with the baby and we'll make a quick escape." Sarah grabbed Jenna by the shoulders in an effort to protect her.

Aaron chuckled as Jenna lifted the baby from the carrier and handed him off. "I am sure I will turn around one day and you'll have him on some pony before he can walk."

He took his son, placing the infant over his shoulder. "Everyone want to take a look inside, it's all done."

Both the children cheered. He wrapped an arm around Jenna and kissed the baby's head as they all walked toward the main building. "We'll let him wait a few more months before riding."

He glanced around at all they'd accomplished together as a family. He'd added another twenty head of cattle and Sarah had taken charge of tilling up an area for a large garden. His brothers had helped him with the building and his father had supervised all along the way. Clarissa had returned to help and Maxus had healed well enough to take small jaunts out for him to check the cattle. The filming of Jenna's miniseries would begin within the month and the second season of *The Bounty Hunter* had been completed with him and Jenna working side by side until the baby had arrived. Life was as sweet as it should be and holding Jenna in his arms each night was something he'd never take for granted.

A word about the author…

Kim Turner writes western historical romance and discovered her passion of writing at the age of eight by writing poems, short stories, and journals.

Kim graduated from Clayton State University with a Bachelor's of Science in Nursing and holds a Master's Degree in Adult Education from Central Michigan University. Working as a registered nurse educator for over twenty-eight years, she enjoys studying the medical treatments of the old west as well as keeping up with the latest western movies and television series. While she loves reading anything from highlanders to pirates, she claims to have an unquenchable thirst for the American cowboy when choosing her reads.

Kim lives south of Atlanta with her husband and calls her greatest accomplishment the birth of one daughter and the adoption of another from China-neither of which came easy.

Kim is a member of Romance Writers of American and Georgia Romance Writers. Kim's Motto: It's All About A Cowboy and the Woman He Loves. kimturnerwrites.com

www.ingramcontent.com/pod-product-compliance
Lightning Source LLC
Chambersburg PA
CBHW050026030726
47506CB00001B/141